Brandon Jones

EMET STUDIOS - LOS ANGELES

This is a work of fiction. Names, characters, places, and incidents either are the product of the author's imagination or are used fictitiously, and any resemblance to an actual person, living or dead, business, companies, events, or locales is entirely coincidental.

Copy Editor: Eve Porinchak
Story Editor: Amanda Troop
Cover and Map Designer: Jeff Delgado
Title Designer: Mitch Baker

Emet Studios
Los Angeles, CA

Library of Congress Control Number: 2023917411

Printed in the United States of America

To Mom & Dad,

for taking me to the park,

and then back home.

Contents

If you want to view paradise,
simply look around and view it.
Anything you want to, do it.
Want to change the world?
There's nothing to it.

Willy Wonka

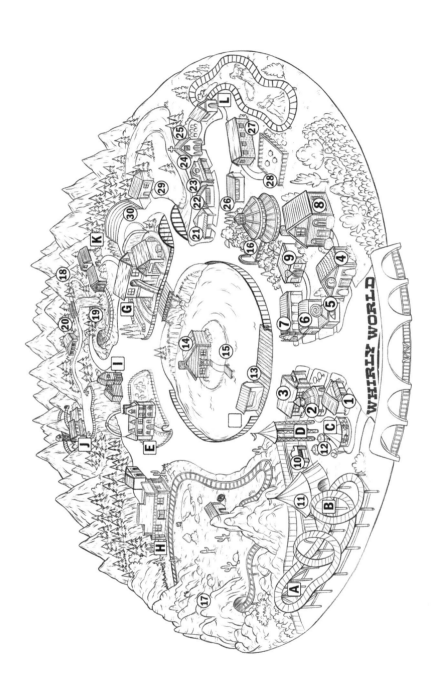

WHIRLY WORLD - PARK MAP - 2023
www.whirlyworldpark.com

MARKET STREET
1 - Five and Dime
2 - Palace Theater
3 - Mud Cup Coffee
4 - Visitor Center
5 - Treats & Sweets
6 - Maple Mart
7 - Calliope Arcade
8 - Worley House
9 - Silver Exchange

KINGSTON'S CIRCUS
A - Hooper Looper
B - Big Top Twist
C - Iron Jaw
D - Liberty Horse Carousel
10 - Kingston's Carnival
11 - Kingston's Theater
12 - Food Vendors

GIZZARD LAKE
E - Hollow House
F - Gizzard Rafts
G - Sawmill Splash
13 - Port Juniper
14 - Worley Lodge
15 - Stope Island
16 - Sunburst Gardens

SHALEY FLATS
H - Gangway Grotto
17 - Gabbro Caverns

CATLIN PEAK
I - Lucky Spelunker
J - Timber Tracks
18 - Linden Forest
19 - Florence Falls
20 - Ranger Station

BUCKTHORN
K - Skid Greaser
L - West Express
21 - General Store
22 - Hipshot Canyon
23 - Nellie's Saloon
24 - St. Charles Church
25 - Harriet's Rest
26 - Rootin' BBQ
27 - Marshal's Jail
28 - Dally Ranch

SCARLET FOREST
29 - Murray's Post
30 - Sterling Amphitheater

Chapter 1

Port Juniper

It is my firmly held belief that everyone should know their absolute favorite thing, otherwise life is just a waste of time. A ride on a track that goes nowhere, or worse, an endless queue where you wait and waste your days away. Not only that, your favorite thing should be your number one priority; the platform to which all tracks lead. Of course, I know what my favorite thing is: it surrounds me. I'm in it.

The only place I want to be: Whirly World.

I love standing at the edge of the harbor, looking out at Worley Lodge. The tiniest of waves are rolling against the dock beneath my feet. Golden light pierces the misty wall that weaves through the forests and faraway buildings. I've seen hundreds of sunrises here whether I attended an all-nighter event or saved up for an early riser pass, and this one is perfectly composed. This early in the morning, the cold air cuts right through my skin and perks me up better than caffeine. The chill in my bones reminds me that I'm alive. I hold each sensation in place as long as I can.

The view is so pleasant, it's hard to believe it's fake. Most of the mountains are real, too large to be manufactured, but the tunnels of Catlin Peak are manmade. After inheriting the silver mine (forever entombed after it collapsed in the late 1800s), Worley had the genius idea to turn tragedy into tranquility. The Worleys built a switchback railway over a century ago, shuffling people up and down the mountain, letting them appreciate the miles of open forests as long as they held on tight. Then, when ticket sales plummeted, they brought in a team from the UK who forged a truly awesome coaster. It cuts through the mountain at a cheek-flapping seventy miles an hour, careening through chasms that feel like they go on forever. But every wall is an illusion. The darkness feels like it never stops, but it's just paint and lights.

Before me is Gizzard Lake. Thirty-five million gallons of water pumped through a system regulating volume and purity. The water is artificially darkened so it looks much deeper, disguising the layers of copper intestines beneath. The original lake used to be much larger. The founders filled in the northeast corner to make it a near perfect circle. Whirly World looks like a big eye. Worley Lodge on Stope Island is the pupil, Gizzard Lake is the iris, and the roads are the vessels, shooting outward. The island in the center is just a pile of dirt resting on a column of concrete. But from where I'm standing, you have to really focus if you're eager to destroy the illusion. From these long cedar planks it all looks as it should: "Natural."

Understanding this gap between what's real and unreal is my passion. Or at least writing about it. Blogs don't pay the bills, but I'd much rather be here, dreaming up the history behind my next think piece, instead of filing paperwork at my uncle's law office. I wanted to be an engineer, designing attractions and building the impossible, but once I understood how much math was involved I gave it up. I prefer words and sentences to numbers and equations. My blog lets me explain how all these things came to be, and why I think theme parks are the highest form of art. I could write a whole book on why *this* location, the east corner of Port Juniper, is so impressive. Five-year-old Jason Green raced past this seemingly dull spot, pushing through the early crowds to be first in line at Gangway Grotto or Timber Tracks. Thirty-three-year-old Jason takes pleasure in watching Whirly World exist, marveling at its inspired design and the back-breaking work that went into its construction. There aren't many places like it.

Taking a stroll around Gizzard Lake gives you a snapshot of the park's mood at any given time, and this spot is the epicenter. 10 AM, with its frantic sprinting and promise of the unknown, feels much different than the somber yawns at 10 PM, as departing kids add up everything they didn't get to do. I get a kick out of feeling forty thousand people zigzag across this map, evolving their plans to maximize their ticket value. To most, other park patrons are speed bumps, adversaries to outwit and overcome. To me, they're an integral part of the experience.

But it's surprisingly quiet now. Even before the crowds have yet to roll in you can usually hear employees emerging from hidden entrances and exits, sipping coffee and shuffling toward their stations. But now there isn't even a whisper. If you get here early enough, on the right day, you might get lucky and sneak in before the masses take over. It's then that the park feels like it was built and operated just for you. The mood now is uncanny, but instead of being alarmed, my senses tingle at the prospect of something unexpected. Hardly anything really surprises me here anymore. It's the cost of experiencing your favorite thing too much. You understand it better, but its potential to move you delivers diminishing returns.

Behind me, there doesn't appear to be a soul along Market Street. The signs are lit. Each set of double doors is open. This feels like I'm watching a musical and someone's forgotten their lines. There's an expectant quality that needs to be filled with sound and life. The streets are spotless from the night crew blasting the ground with pressurized water. It's clear the staff has been here to set things up, but maybe they're gathered for a meeting. It wouldn't be the first time I've wound up somewhere I wasn't supposed to be yet, which isn't always a bad thing. Any park nerd like me understands the thrill of creeping past the veil. If you stay here long enough, or inside any theme park with understaffed security, you'll get to see how the sausage is made, so to speak. Perhaps I've stumbled upon such an opportunity, and my stomach does a little flip of anticipation.

April wouldn't see it that way. If she found herself in a scene like this, she'd assume something was wrong and say we should leave. She wouldn't seize the moment and experience something she may never forget. I love her, but she's never really "understood" Whirly World. Or at least how much it means to me. I wonder what she's doing right now. It's been a while since she's been to my happy place. It's not easy convincing her to cross two state lines, even if the drive is just under two hours. Since I met her, this place has gone from something I could add to any day without much thought, to a luxury I have to calculate and spend only if necessary. I get that she wants to spend time with me and do other things, but it's been a sacrifice on my part that I don't think she totally appreciates. To be honest, I prefer being here alone. I don't have to follow anyone's agenda. If I want to spend an hour eavesdropping, watching the sun pass over me, I can.

I try to get here at least once a week, preferably twice. I tell myself it's for my second job as a park blogger, but I know better. I'm hooked, like a shovelnose sturgeon, line and sinker. It's been a long time since I've brought my parents because it's not worth the effort. My dad wouldn't shut up about all the historical inaccuracies, even if they're often humorous and intentional. Mom would point out every building's second story that should be much taller, not appreciating architectural tricks like forced perspective.

So I'm used to being here by myself, which probably sounds pathetic to those uninspired by amusement, but it's not nearly as sad as it sounds. I'm lucky that the law offices of Mortimer and Wolowicz gives me Mondays off. A lot of my friends have kids, a temptation I'll never let get in the way of my hobbies. If I had a nickel for every time I saw a four-year-old bawl after not being given a giant stuffed animal, or a grumbling, ungrateful teenager moaning when their smartphone died during a long line, I'd be a wealthy man. Sure, I enjoy camping on family retreats, or visiting other parts of the country, but no matter how far I travel, nothing beats this place. Getting past the exit on the freeway, pulling into the giant parking lot, scanning the barcode on my pass - all pure, irreplaceable glee.

It's not unusual for me to get recognized by a ticket taker as I saunter through the front entrance. I've been here enough times and written enough articles about park life to make a name for myself. Not that it's a contest. It's impossible to weigh one person's fandom against another, but the truth is I am on a first name basis with dozens of employees and gained access to areas few have visited. I've never worked here, although I've met hundreds who have. I'm a boots-on-the-ground fan. I walk the walk and ride the ride.

Speaking of, I should probably get moving, but I don't feel rushed. No one is in line yet for Sawmill Splash, or Hollow House. The train for Gangway Grotto is parked at the station. There's no rattling rumble coming from the Hooper Looper. Even the boats docked at Port Juniper are barely bouncing along with the rippling surface of the lake. The park before me is locked in an unprecedented stillness that is too rare to ignore.

I bet medical personnel are gathered somewhere in the employee area to the southeast, tending to an injured tourist. It could be a fire, or a bomb threat. I've heard crazier stories. People can get so excited this early in the day that it can be hard for security to keep up. It's an art to coordinate and address an urgent matter without creating a panic. Still, an operation shouldn't require the attention of *every* employee. Unless it's a fire drill and everyone is outside. Still, workers have to keep up appearances regardless of what's going on behind closed doors. These rides don't operate themselves.

Just as a surge of anxiety pushes against my chest, I see someone. Not just someone, but good old Clarence Wilson, pushing his ice cream cart around a building to my right. I let out an audible sigh of relief. I was starting to wonder if I was dreaming. Seeing Clarence's colorful cart, with its assortment of balloons and shiny, silver edges, is always a welcome sight. Whenever kids spot Clarence and drag their parents over to grab a reward it always warms my heart. In the eerie silence of the park, I can hear the cart's wheels squeak as their loose, metal hinges quiver on the uneven pavement. Clarence seems unfazed by the emptiness around us, which also allays my building, chilly sense of unease.

It doesn't matter what's going on, Clarence always greets ticket holders of any age with an honest smile. He shares the same joyous disposition with every child, tipping his red and white cap, exposing the short head of wispy gray hair underneath. He was on the original employee roster when Whirly World opened on May 7, 1965. My guess is he's in his eighties by now, but I can never bring myself to ask. Clarence looks especially chipper today, and that's saying something, especially since there are no children around anywhere. Even with his hunched shoulders and the snail's pace of his cart, he's approaching me with an extra skip in his step and I can't tell why. I've searched online for details about his personal life, but it's as if nothing exists for Clarence outside this park.

"What a morning," Clarence exclaims as he nears me. "The sun is as shiny as a candied apple." He waves his right hand in the air, and just that motion seems to test his balance. His other hand remains secured to the cart, keeping him from falling over. I'm not sure where Clarence's barber-shop-quartet meets speakeasy vibe came from. He dresses just like the other merchants selling salty or sugary treats, but he has a classy way of going about it that feels carefully executed. Did he invent this character, or did management create it and he just played ball? Or is this actually him?

"Morning!" I reply, trying in vain to match Clarence's cheerfulness. He parks his cart near the edge of the dock and gazes at the rising sun. I realize I haven't seen Clarence in a while and I return his smile with a goofy grin. Every time he says "Hello!" I remind myself it might be the last time I hear from him. At his age, he has to be considering retirement, no matter how much he loves his job. In the three decades I've been steadfast in visiting this "world," I bump into Clarence during almost every visit. I'd ask him directly but I doubt I'd get an honest answer.

"A little early for ice cream, isn't it?" I say with a smile.

Clarence looks offended by this, in his playful way.

"Early!?" Clarence gasps. Without hesitation he opens the top part of his cart, removes a fudge pop, and snaps the top off with his brittle teeth. His eyes burst open with pleasure as a sugary drop falls out of the corner of his mouth. He grabs a handkerchief from his shirt pocket to wipe it off and lets out a "Whoo" to suggest the bite is colder than he was expecting. I honestly can't tell if he's exaggerating for my benefit, like I'm five years old again, hanging on every beat of his effortless physical comedy, or if it really is that satisfying to him.

I chuckle as a reward for the silly gesture. "Maybe after breakfast, then." Eating something seems like the thing to do, but my stomach doesn't feel the least bit empty. You can usually pick up the scent of candied nuts floating from the concession stand at the Palace Theater, but I don't smell a thing. A popcorn cart across the boardwalk remains unattended. Goosebumps rise on my arms as an icy sensation takes hold, but I don't feel the slightest gust of wind.

"Where is everybody?" I ask Clarence.

He closes the top of the cart and looks around. He must have noticed this as well. "Hmpf," Clarence says with a shrug. "Who are you looking for, exactly?"

"Well," I answer, gesturing around us. "Someone other than us. I mean, who else besides me is going to eat your ice cream today? The ducks?" I point to the lake, expecting to see at least one pair of ducks wading past. There are none. Not seeing people on Market Street is weird enough. Having zero ducks in Gizzard Lake swimming close to shore for a free breakfast is downright impossible. I look up. There are no birds in the sky. There is no life anywhere.

Clarence adjusts his hat as he looks south toward Market Street one more time. He frowns, which feels dreadful. He's chipper as a rule, and I'd hate to deprive him of that. I expect him to ignore the terrible things happening on this planet, clinging to the belief that any problem can be solved with enough sugar. But now I need him to be serious. I need answers. Shaking off my plea, Clarence rediscovers his inner child and a smile pushes back the wrinkles in his cheeks.

"The way I see it," he begins, dispensing wisdom with ease, "the more time you spend looking for people, the less time you have to appreciate the people you've found."

"Clarence, come on. Drop the act, just for a second. It's me. No one's around to accuse you of breaking character. You won't get in trouble with management if you just tell me there's been an emergency or the park's opening late today. Is the park open yet?"

"Well of course we're open. Why else would I be pushing this cart around?"

Maybe I shouldn't be asking him these questions. I consider Clarence as much of a friend a person can be in these circumstances, but on the other hand I'm a customer and he's an employee. He's on the clock and trying to make a living. Security isn't his responsibility, and neither is reassuring me. I plaster on a smile and try to shake off my worries.

"Well, if the park's empty then I'm going to enjoy it," I tell Clarence. "Take care of yourself." I nod politely and head south across the boardwalk. There's a bubble growing in the top of my stomach. I take a deep breath, hoping it'll pop. *In through my nose, out through my mouth.* I visualize pushing the bubble downward, but it seems to be expanding. I groan in frustration. This theme park is where I go to *escape* anxiety.

"Have a swell time, Jason!" Clarence calls from behind me. I'm flattered he remembers my name. Whenever I've told him something personal about my life, he's replied from a script. For as much warmth as he brings to the park, it's always under the guise of keeping the turnstiles spinning. I know he takes delight in each and every child because I've watched him do it countless times. But he still has ice cream to sell.

I turn to wave one last time but Clarence is gone. He's not shuffling away. The man has completely vanished. His cart is still there, but Clarence is missing from the picture. I'm alone again. Maybe he ducked behind the cart? No, I'd see his feet in the gap below, and that man's bones couldn't move that fast. In alarm I check the water. Did he fall in the lake? No, the surface is undisturbed. There was no splash. Panicked, I scan the perimeter of Gizzard Lake. Then a second, and a third time. He's gone. Impossible. My breaths are coming in short gasps and panic is about to overwhelm me when I finally get it.

I'm dreaming.

They're unpleasant, but we all get these unconscious trials every once in a while. Moments when our brain proves just how much dominion it has over the body. I'll wake up in a cold sweat and need the rest of the night just to wrestle with how messed up my mind can get. It's times like these that I lament being a creative type. When you aim to conjure more beautiful dreams, the more terrifying and inescapable they may become in retaliation. I let out a shaky laugh and scrub my hands over my face.

Let's get this over with. What pulls you out of your dreams? A jolt? Some kind of fright? I calculate how to slap myself awake as I step away from the boardwalk onto firm concrete. I can see clearly that all of the shops are open but completely vacant. The curtains are pulled to the side, and the doors are ajar, but there isn't a single person inside any of them. It's like I've stepped into a model, or frozen time before anyone had a chance to arrive.

"Hello?" I howl, nervously. No response. I scream at the absolute top of my lungs. "*Is anyone there?*" I keep the last word going so long I'm surprised how little it scratches my throat. My shout passes into nothingness. I've never heard my voice by itself in this place. It's novel but I'm so unsettled, I can't enjoy it. I'd rather have it drowned out by the din of a hundred happy conversations, by musicians in a parade, or bells and beeps from the arcade. There isn't a single plane in the sky. I feel like I've been loaded into a wonky simulation and someone forgot to put the rest of the world in it too.

The main gate is directly ahead of me. Looking at it gives me an idea how to end this madness. I can just leave. My therapist is going to have a field day with this dream. She'll say that I've become so attached to this park, that now I picture it without anyone here at all. The perfect construct of my amusement addiction. Then relief floods through me. Someone's at the gate. A lone security guard paces back and forth past the middle of the grand entrance. He's got to know what's going on in the park. I'm so excited I jump up in the air and wave my arms.

"Hey," I shout, like a lost child who has just been reunited with their parents at the Baby Care Center. "Good morning." I can't think of what else to say. I'm so thrilled to see another person. I skip like a fool. I can't help it. This place just does something to me. Outside Whirly World I'm normally so self-conscious about my behavior, trying to look cooler than I am, but in the park I don't care what I look like.

The guard puts up his hand in the air like he's stopping a speeding car at a chaotic intersection. I must have spooked him. All my energy, this early in the morning, probably came across as manic or dangerous. Especially if there's been an emergency. I stop jumping. The guard has a funky retro vibe going on. A close-cropped afro. Thick sideburns. His giant silver belt buckle blasts the sun into my eyes like a laser. Even his uniform fits his retro style.

"Stay where you are!" the guard yells. He's way more upset than I realized.

I thought I just startled him, but his eyes are boring into me with a burning intensity. I'm not eager to upset someone who's armed and here for my protection. Then I remember: it's a dream. He must represent some slice of my subconscious. I should apologize. "Sorry. I just got excited for a second."

"No one in or out!" he yells, getting louder.

I put one hand up and stop moving. "Okay, okay," I say, submissively. "I got it. I'm cool." What a curious situation I've created in my mind. My own brain is inventing all of this, yet I'm hungry for more details.

"We have a report of a missing kid," he says, with authority. So that's what's going on. That's obviously a red flag but it still doesn't explain where everyone went. I must look terribly suspicious, a man alone, rushing towards the exit. The guard's right hand stays at his side and slowly inches toward his belt. I raise my other hand into the air. Am I in trouble?

"Where did you come from? I don't recognize you," he shouts. "How'd you get in here? What are you up to?" He has a small baton and what might be a taser, maybe mace.

My insides are swimming so fast I don't know whether to grab my chest or keep my hands raised. "Whoa, easy," I plead. "I'm not doing anything. I'm a passholder!" I motion toward the gate, eager to point out that no one is manning the turnstiles. No crowd has gathered outside. He's not guarding anything. He's just something my imagination produced to give me a good scare. But telling him this will likely upset him further. I point past him. "I'm just trying—"

"I told you." He's fit to burst. "No one in or out." He lowers his ear to his shoulder and reaches for a radio velcroed there. I wish I could piece together his strange uniform. He's wearing a thick, dark blue jacket, which makes no sense in the summer. The western-styled flaps on his shirt pockets are an eye-catching dark brown. Park guards don't look like this. At least they haven't for years.

"This is Grier. We've got a smart one out front," the guard says into the radio. "I'm going to need some backup." He clicks the radio off and starts walking toward me.

Grier? Wait. "Eddie Grier?" I say, instinctively.

"What?" It has to be. Eddie's eyes flare with angry suspicion. "How do you know my name?" A rise in his voice suggests he's already convinced I've committed some crime.

I can't think what to say. He won't believe it anyway. I hardly believe this.

Why am I dreaming of Eddie Grier? He died, what, four decades ago? Right here, in this spot. He got stabbed trying to stop someone *fleeing the park.* Some degenerate whose accomplice had kidnapped a child only seconds earlier. Grier was the first person to die inside Whirly World. The original. An unfortunate distinction, and one I've been obsessed with ever since I learned the gruesome tale. Grier was dragged inside the gatehouse after the attacker cracked through his ribcage with a switchblade. The second guard to arrive on the scene tackled the armed thug. Grier passed away in the arms of a friend, barred from the prying eyes of park attendees. And yet here he is, standing before me. Hand at his hip. Eyebrows furrowed. What a crazy dream: I'm reliving park history.

Another security guard emerges from the side door of the gatehouse. Then another, and another. These men don't share Eddie's outdated uniform. They don't have holsters, or hats, or for that matter, faces. They don't move like human beings. They wobble like they're still learning to walk. They stumble toward me like they're drunk, arms raised, hands waving back and forth. They grasp at the open air between us. I back up, realizing how guilty it makes me look.

"Stop. Freeze," Eddie yells at me.

I wish I could. How many bad movies have I watched and screamed at the screen when someone won't do as they're told? When some idiot doesn't realize they'll just make things worse by not giving up. But sometimes your nerves won't let you make the right decision.

I run.

Chapter 2

WW

Market Street

My feet are moving as fast as they can, but the chilly air is keeping me from sweating. My muscles don't cramp so I don't slow down. I'm running so fast that I nearly plow into a wiry boy standing right at the crossroads. I skid to a stop and the kid turns, noticing me slam on the brakes. He looks to be nine or ten years old. Is he the one that's missing? His slate blue eyes are stern and focused. His black hair is short and ruffled. He's wearing blue jeans with the knees frayed open, and bright red running shoes.

I look behind me. Eddie and his friends are gone. This has to be a dream, because none of this makes sense. I guess dreams don't have to. If my brain is clever enough to recreate this park in my imagination it seems like a small leap to station Eddie at the gate. Something to keep me in line. You can go this far, but no farther.

I've dreamt of Whirly World plenty of times before. In one I was naked and all the clothes I bought at the store were too big. In another, I forgot my wallet and couldn't get past the main gate. Once I hung out with Worley himself, the park's founder. We rode the Skid Greaser and shot rifles at Murray's Post. That was a great dream. I've had nightmares here that horrified me beyond comprehension. I've been chased through the woods by Phuzzy, our beloved sasquatch and mascot. I've seen the place burn to the ground while crowds begged me to extinguish the flames, with no firehose in sight. I'm no stranger to weird Whirly World dreams. I've just never analyzed one this much while I was still in it.

What is this kid supposed to represent? Is this me when I was younger? Some sort of amalgamation of my childhood obsessions? Only one way to find out.

"Looking for something?" I ask, politely. I keep my distance.

The kid scans me up and down the way kids are trained to do. Don't take candy or answer random questions from strangers. Aside from his eyes, which are wide with surprise, he's not visibly shaken by the fact that we're currently the only two people on Market Street.

"Hi," he says, with a tiny, reluctant wave.

"Hi," I reply, with a much bigger wave. I keep my feet rooted to the spot. I don't want to freak this kid out any more than I currently am. I'll ask an easier question. "What's up?"

"Um." He looks in opposite directions. Probably looking for his parents. "Should I go to the train first or the water ride?" He points west to Gangway Grotto, then north to Sawmill Splash.

Ah, the ultimate question. What to do first? So many options, so little time. Maybe Eddie is my fear of authority and this little guy is my indecisiveness. The more work I do on this now the less time I'll waste in therapy. Maybe a trip through the desert with my inner demons is just what I need to get a deeper perspective on my emotions. I'll bite.

"It's still kinda cold, huh," I posit.

The boy sniffs at the air.

"Maybe Sawmill Splash is a bad idea. We'll get soaking wet." I play up the last few words by pretending I've just been doused. I walk in a circle shaking off the pretend water. The boy is not amused. For a kid with a theme park all to himself he's pretty reserved. Then again, he's not real.

"What's your name?" I ask, and instantly regret doing so. I've crossed some sort of "stranger danger" line. He backs away from me. I should let him go but I feel bad. I raise my hands and put on a nice-guy voice. "Oh, sorry. I didn't mean to…"

He turns and runs along the circle road surrounding the lake. Following him feels insensitive at this point, and I doubt he's the kid that went missing. I just watch his fast little legs carry him across the pavement. I guess it's a Sawmill Splash morning after all.

Somewhere past Sunburst Gardens, he vanishes. Poof. Just like Clarence and Eddie. It looked like he was passing through an invisible archway. His existence wiped clean. I guess my sleeping mind couldn't fathom him at this distance. It was like he dematerialized out of a video game. Another one of this strange dream's curiously specific rules.

Maybe my imagination, however powerful, can't handle the processing power of a thousand park patrons milling about. If it tried they might end up wobbly and faceless like those eerie security guards. I look back at the entrance gate but they're still thankfully gone. What if visiting different areas of the park makes different "people" appear? If I try to buy something, will someone come along like Clarence did to make the sale? It's worth a shot. How long is this wacky dream going to go on?

Closest to where I'm standing is the Five-and-Dime, an establishment specializing in selling knick-knacks and souvenirs. To the right is the superior Maple Mart, my personal choice for t-shirts and hats. Maybe they'll finally have that gray and black hoodie that's been out of stock for years. In spite of myself, I'm excited to find out. I pass through the entrance and see it's as devoid of people as everything else. Not only that, the floors, walls, and even ceilings are polished to a glorious shine. The maintenance staff has always worked hard to keep the joint looking spiffy, but this is some next level cleaning at work. My brain likes to keep this place nicer looking than my apartment.

I scan the racks. No gray and black hoodie. Not even in my dreams. I grab the nearest shirt for the sake of this experiment. It's pink and says *See Ya At Whirly!* in puffy black lettering with a cartoonish illustration of someone being pulled behind the words by one of the park's coasters, hands waving in a level of rapture no human could ever achieve. I carry it up to the register and place it on the counter. No one appears. I lean over the counter, something I've never done in real life, to see if someone's ready to pop up. Perhaps another kid that's as lost as I am. Nobody.

"Man, am I in the mood to spend some money," I shout, jokingly. I do a spin to catch whoever might suddenly appear, but I'm still alone. If I take this shirt to the street outside, will it disappear as well? Or maybe shoplifting will trigger someone to come out of hiding at last. If this dream is going to keep going, let's have fun.

I walk out to the street and wait. No one comes running. Not even, I note with relief, Eddie Grier and his bizarre security team. I drop the pilfered shirt to the ground. It looks so strange, sprawled out on the otherwise spotless street. My inner perfectionist gets the better of me and I pick it back up. After it's folded and placed on a shelf, I step out to the street and face the ultimate question: What's next?

Commercials claim it's impossible to see everything Whirly World has to offer in one day, a challenge I have conquered on multiple occasions. Not to brag, but a person just has to go on the right day and know what rides to do back-to-back. I've heard all sorts of theories on the "best day" of the week, month, or year to visit theme parks. In my opinion, they don't exist. Sure, some holidays are busier than normal days, and you can count on smaller crowds a few weeks out of the year, but it's always a roll of the dice. You just get lucky sometimes.

The crowds don't get smaller than this. Outside, the rows of shops are still uncharacteristically barren. The sun has risen higher in the sky, making the scene exceedingly unusual. Not even in pictures or amateur documentaries have I witnessed this street, in broad daylight, entirely devoid of people. I should be impressed that whatever is inside my head can conceive of such a thing, but this dream train is starting to creep me out and I'm ready to get off. After a few rides at least. Gotta take advantage of a low attendance day, after all.

So what's first? Kingston's Circus is closest to me but I can comfortably scratch that area off my list for now. The garishness of the Hooper Looper, and the whole circus vibe sits in jarring contrast to the rest of the Gold Rush themed park. How that clown factory ever got approved is still beyond me. It slices through the quaint normality of Market Street like a rusty, old-fashioned car horn blasting through a classical symphony.

Gangway Grotto sounds like a peaceful option to kick off this weird day. I'll take a cool trip through the caverns, admire the faux limestone, and wave at the hanging bats and herds of animal statues.

Newly determined, I take one step to the north and suddenly there's someone new. A woman is standing just outside the entrance to the bathrooms. Whenever I make up my mind to go somewhere, a person materializes to slow me down. Like Eddie, she's dressed in an outdated uniform. Janitorial, not security this time. She's also not a dead person from what I can recall. No wait, she absolutely is.

"Oh, a new one," Beverly Thompson says to me. It's a pleasant greeting, but I detect a somber tone underneath that I don't enjoy. Eleven years ago Beverly had an epileptic seizure in the men's bathroom in the middle of the night. The seventh person to die in the park. For as much as I know about the people who've croaked here I'm surprised I haven't dreamt about her or Eddie before. I always say "Hello" whenever I stop in that particular men's room, but Beverly's spirit never answers. And now *she's* starting a conversation with *me*.

She's just as endearing as I always pictured her to be. She's short, rosy-cheeked, and her gray hair is set in perfect curls. Despite the dirty job she did every night, her light blue uniform is spotless. Her hands are clasped at her waist. Beverly exclusively worked nights, after the park was closed, so she wasn't an employee I got a chance to know personally. But her sweet disposition made it into her obituary, which I eagerly added to my morbid "Deaths at Whirly World" collection.

"Beverly," I say. I sound like someone shouting at their favorite member of a boy band after spotting them at the airport. What can I say? Beverly's a legend. As are all of the people who have died here. I never tire of telling their stories to those who haven't heard them or have the details all mixed up.

Beverly's eyes light up at the mention of her name. "Oh. You know me?"

"Know you? I wrote a paper about you in college. I was so sorry to hear of your passing. We never got to meet. I'm Jason." In a moment like this I would usually raise my arm to shake someone's hand, but I keep my distance in case she decides to call in armed specters to haul me away. It seems out of character, but who knows?

"Welcome." She bows. "Did you arrive today?"

"Well, yes." What a strange question. Believe me, Beverly, if I could sleep inside the park overnight, I would. "Why do you ask?"

"Oh, first days can be so hard," she says with a sigh. Beverly walks to a nearby bench and sits down, giving the seat next to her a welcoming pat. She doesn't seem to be in any hurry. An opportunity to chat with Beverly Thompson is too good to pass up so I join her. Well, technically not a real "chat," I remind myself. My brain is making all this up, regardless of how spectacular and scary this dream has been. Am I going to meet all the ghosts of the park before I wake up? I mentally craft an article about this for my blog as I sit next to her.

"What's so hard about spending a day at Whirly World?" I ask. Beverly looks up at the sun and breathes calmly. I wonder if she heard me. Maybe she'll vanish soon like the others. I try to think of something interesting to ask her while she's still in view. She looks back to me, filled with some sort of inner light. She seems so peaceful, I can't help but join her in a shared, relaxed breath. It's a nice release from the tension that's been building up in my chest.

"The Lord," Beverly begins, but then pauses for additional reflection. *Oh, right.* I remember reading that she and her devoted husband attended church regularly. In an interview with

ParkFansUnited, her bereaved spouse of several decades sounded oddly accepting of her sudden departure. The silver cross necklace around her neck should have tipped me off. I've never practiced a religion, but I suppose that sort of comfort in closure is one of the benefits of an unshakeable faith. This park is my "church," I guess. These rides are my temples. Theme park fandom is my religion.

"The Lord prepares us for these things. These eventualities. But whether we accept him into our hearts or not, we can never be ready to say goodbye."

"Okay 'dream Beverly,' tell me this: What does the Bible have to say about empty theme parks?" I immediately regret my tone. I hope I haven't offended her.

Apparently I haven't, because she chuckles. A warm, bird-like, grandmotherly laugh, like I just said "boobie."

"Nothing specifically," she replies.

"Well, I'm pretty darn excited about the prospect of an empty Whirly World."

"This park brings you that much joy?" She gives me another warm and calming smile, and I feel more of the bubbles in my stomach pop. "That's fortunate. It will make it easier for you to accept things. You may *want* to stay. Some don't."

"Oh, sorry," I say, and the illusion of her being a person slips away. Back to reality. This is a fun anecdote for my next article, nothing more. "I'm not staying, Beverly. This is just my dream. You're a construct built of memories and my obsession with the secrets most people don't know about Whirly World. You're probably brought on by stress, or my need to connect with things that are forever out of reach. My therapist will tell me that you're a tool for me to use when I find myself getting too close to my work."

Beverly's face crumples as a small frown tugs the corners of her mouth downward, and she pulls away from me a bit. I start to feel guilty for being so blunt with her, or it. The dream, whatever. This whole thing has been poignant and reflective but I am ready to wake up. Someone, anyone, get me outta here. Beverly looks up at me, sorrowfully.

"Dear," she says with quiet conviction, "you're dead."

Chapter 3

Parking

I stare at Beverly with my mouth open wide. She places her hand on my knee like she knows I think she's full of it. I give my head a shake. Her faith is getting the best of her. Of course she believes in spirits, she worships one. But if that's true, if she is delusional and I'm the clear-headed one, why does her hand feel like ice? Why is the air getting colder? Why do the walls of this park feel like they just doubled in size? Beverly keeps her eyes locked on mine like I'm seated at my own intervention, avoiding the realness of the situation because I'm addicted to the alternative. I've participated in an intervention, talking with my uncle, telling him that there were no more options. There's only one way to get out of that room. You have to admit you're an alcoholic. You have to go straight to the hospital. I have to admit I'm…

Oh, god. Oh, no. I died. I'm dead.

It feels like a bolt of lightning struck my body. My legs shake. My mind goes numb. Beverly reaches out her hand to stabilize me. I nearly fall off the bench as I try to back away from her. I'm having an episode; a panic attack. I'm freaking out. *Wake up. You idiot, wake up.*

"Take a moment, Jason," Beverly says. "Oh, honey. Dear, take some time."

How can she be so calm about something like death? Her death? My death? What could be more personal and horrifying? Dead. Does that mean I'm lying in the park somewhere, staring up with milky eyes at traumatized children? Is Clarence dead? Is that *kid* dead? What is happening? What is this?

I've stumbled several steps up the street toward the lake without knowing it. I turn to see if Beverly is still there, expecting her to have vanished. But she's sitting there, pitying me. Then she fades away like the others. The other *ghosts*. They were ghosts. They *are* ghosts. So am I. A ghost. I'm a goddamn ghost and I am trapped in Whirly World.

Oh no. I'm going to be *infamous*. If this had happened to *anyone* else, I would have been positively obsessed with it, soaking up every last morbid detail. It's been seven years since a death was publicly reported at this park. Somehow Clarence's passing slipped my radar, but if my death happened out in the open, there goes my reputation. I'll no longer be a "park expert," I'll just be "that guy that died in Whirly World." All that hard work I did to grow an audience for my writing is going to be burned to ashes. Before I can stop my brain, I find myself hoping that someone will add my death to my online list, to keep things up to date.

I can't be dead. At least, I very much don't want to be. I feel fine. Cold, yes, but otherwise fine. Beverly's words are sinking deeper than I can dig them out. I know it now, like I know my name is Jason and the year is 2023 and the sun is in the sky right now. I'm dead. That is a fact. I can run from it forever but all I'd be doing is running. I dash to the lake and look into the water. I see my reflection for the first time since I got here. I'm wearing my purple polo shirt, braided brown belt, and baggy blue jeans. No visible injuries. No patches of blood on my shirt or dents in my head. How did I die? It's disconcerting that I don't know; that the last moment of my life was stolen from my memory.

Do the other ghosts know they're dead too? Clarence spoke to me like it was just another day in the park. Now that I think about it more, it had been a while since I'd last seen him. I must have lost track of a year or two. I presumed we missed each other on opposite days or he had taken time for a vacation, or due to illness. But he was *dead*. And I missed it. Beverly knew she'd died, but she's had eleven years to sort that out. Maybe it just takes time to come to terms with something that's impossible to accept. If I hadn't bumped into Beverly, who knows how long I'd be roaming this park, searching for an end to a dream that has no exit?

No, they don't all know. Eddie was clearly confused and defensive. He acted like not only was the park still in full operation, but there was an imminent threat. He summoned other - what were those things - spirits? Guards without faces because they were never really people to begin with, just "backup" phantasms.

I look up. The sun has risen even higher, blending with the few wispy clouds I can see on this movie backdrop painting of a sky. It's a near perfect day. How does weather work in the afterlife? Do I see the same sky as not-dead people? Ugh. I have so many questions and clearly no one to answer them. And I feel like I'm wasting time standing here, but I suppose that's all I can do now. I always felt that, regardless of what year was my last, there was no way it would feel like enough. That everything would end and there'd be *nothing* and I wouldn't have enough to show for it.

But this at least feels like *something*. I could be snoozing in the dirt right now but I'm not. I'm in Whirly World. Alive Jason would have killed for an opportunity like this. No lines. No crowds. No price tags, or distractions, or responsibilities. Maybe this is my reward for a life of faithful devotion to this theme park. Exactly where I've wanted to be all along. There were so many times in my life where I thought, *I wish I could be at Whirly World right now,* and now there's nothing else. Whirly World has become my entire world.

Or not. Maybe I'm not actually stuck here. Sure, Eddie got tripped up when I headed for the exit, but he's just a boogeyman, like me. What's he going to do, kill another ghost? If he can spawn a bunch of freaky guards, then I can charge out of here in a suit of armor if I want to. I think it's worth taking a few ghost bullets to test this theory. I'm going to head for the parking lot and believe in my heart, or whatever I've still got, that I can make it there.

I turn on my heel and walk steadily past the row of open yet vacant shops. As I get closer to the front gate, I'm thankful to see Eddie is nowhere in sight. Maybe he's doing rounds or trying to find where I've run off to. I can see the trees past the exit, but not much else. It all looks the same so far. I've just never seen it so empty. It's like I'm walking toward a concept painting, or I've been shrunken down and I'm scampering through a diorama of the park, like an ant.

Then, as if we're pulled together by my desire to escape, Eddie appears. One of the employee exits bangs open, and I'm not sure if I saw his hand on the doorknob when it did. The borders of this park seem to contort themselves around Eddie's intent. Luckily, I'm next to a row of tall ferns that provide a decent hiding spot, and I throw myself behind them. Smooth. I'll probably only get one shot at this now that Eddie thinks I've wandered off. I'm one radio call away from getting dragged down into the basement jail I've heard so much about but never had the dubious luxury of seeing for myself. Eddie hasn't noticed me, thank goodness. I have to plan this moment carefully.

I laugh in spite of myself. I've never tried to break out of Whirly World before. I have tried to break *in*: twice. First, when I was young and impressionable and stupid. In other words, fifteen. A couple of my less scrupulous, erstwhile friends were dead set on getting in after hours, and even though I was the tireless rule-keeper, I never had the courage to say no to them.

The tall, metal fences that line the property were and still are insurmountable, their slick steel sides topped by curved and pointed hooks. But, I grudgingly shared with my friends, the backside of several buildings also comprise part of Whirly World's border. And it so happens that the employee locker room lines up perfectly with the northeast edge of the eastern parking lot. So me and my idiot friends, Tom and Mike, pulled up in Mike's dad's '81 Chieftain RV, and then scaled the back of the building thanks to the six-wheeler's vertical boost. None of us had the balls to break open any doors to the obviously locked interiors, so we just ambled through the streets until we were spotted by a guard who chased us back to the RV.

The second time was a maneuver I'm still unironically proud of. I was twenty-two and my annual pass had expired because my credit card on file had hit its limit. Whoops. I was home over spring break during my senior year in college and hadn't visited the park in quite a while. When the long drive over state lines ended in failure, I refused to head back empty handed. Instead I scanned the front gate and saw Paul, a ticket taker I knew, and surmised that after seeing me come and go so many times over the years, he wouldn't raise a fuss when my card "mysteriously" didn't work.

The major flaw in this plan was the metal-clanging alert that sounds if the card doesn't go through, instead of the affirmative ding of a cowbell. Paul's manager, a woman I was much less familiar with, heard the telltale clang and stopped to investigate. My heart sank as she approached, realizing that, not only might I not get to enter the park, I could get into trouble and possibly have my membership revoked. But Paul saved the day, laughing off the error as he scanned his employee badge and I got in scot-free. I'm just realizing now that I never properly thanked him for that. I never paid him or the park back for that "good deed."

Now I'm about to try to dodge a hyper-vigilant ghost with the goal of seeing how far I can sprint into the unknown boundaries of the afterlife. Yep, there's no experience I can draw on for this scenario. At this moment there's just Eddie between me and the parking lot. Maybe he only calls in his backup monsters when the need arises.

I turn my focus to the nearest turnstile, one of twelve lined up underneath the six brown archways that stretch across the park entrance. The metal gates are open in front of each turnstile, so as long as I can get past this one, I'm free. There's a six-foot gap over each of the turnstiles. The kind you skip over at the subway when no cops are around. I could slide over and make a run for it, assuming Eddie can't use his telekinesis or whatever to slam the gates shut.

The turnstile locks between ticket scans, and only moves when the panel is illuminated. Right now, the panel is dark, which means the turnstile won't move if I try to dash through it. But then, as if reading my thoughts, the panel lights up. It doesn't make a sound, so Eddie doesn't notice. With the machine powered up, the turnstile might rotate with a little effort. Did *I* do that? I was certainly hoping a solution would present itself, but it's not like I just tried to use the Force or something. Unless that's exactly what I did. Well, if Eddie can manifest junk, why can't I? Eddie's facing away from me.

Here I go.

I waddle out from behind the ferns in a low crouch, then I start across the brick pavers of the entrance plaza in a casual stroll, like I'm trying to blend in. I quickly realize this is foolish given there's no one around me. Letting my panic take the steering wheel, the stroll morphs into a desperate dash. I train my gaze on the exit so I don't run face-first into a pole, but out of the corner of my eye, I see that Eddie's back remains turned and his attention is graciously diverted elsewhere. I pump the brakes when I actually meet the metal bar at groin-level and give it a light push. It gives way and, incredibly, without the gears making so much as a mouse squeak, I've made it through.

I run a few yards before I hazard a glance back. When I do, I half expect to see Eddie transform the entire gate into a mouth full of jagged, rusty teeth preparing to chomp down and gobble me up, but he's gone. In fact, so is the rest of Whirly World. The entrance area is intact but the buildings, signs, lamps, and roads on the other side have all vanished. There's nothing but a white, blank space, as if someone has yet to paint it. I feel a twinge of regret and fear, like I've made an awful mistake. Then I remember just seconds ago I was stuck in the park and now I'm free.

I take a breath and face the parking lot. The sky here is blank. No blue blanket or white clouds. The lot itself looks like it did while I was alive, mostly cracked concrete and patterns of white paint, but it extends into uncomfortable infinity. A walkway of faded red bricks runs through the middle of it. Every fifty feet is a blue sign with a white letter and number labeling each zone. The first two read A1 and A2, and so do hundreds past them, repeating forever. It doesn't seem like much can be gained from walking toward this wall of nothingness, but it's all I can think to do. A few cars are parked in scattered spaces. I search for my own. Driving into nothingness is faster than walking.

Loneliness overtakes me. My eyes get heavy with sadness. When I was alive, I preferred to be alone, but there was always someone there whenever I'd change my mind. I could stay over at April's, go see a movie with Mike, or call my sister. Now I've left their lives and they've left mine. The only friends I have now know nothing about me, and they have no one to talk to but each other. My only hope is that, despite my strongest impulses to the contrary, this is still a dream, and I can still wake up.

After about ten minutes putting one foot in front of the other, I notice that the cars are repeating. A pattern to give the suggestion that this is a parking lot in use. The weeds poking through the speckled and cracked concrete loop too, and, surprise surprise, my light-blue Ford Focus is nowhere in sight. I turn around to check the progress I've made, and discover, to my dismay, the gate is still directly behind me. I haven't moved at all. Damn.

I guess this is how being dead works. You are where you are and there's no going anywhere else. I suppose I should consider myself lucky. I have plenty of online friends that would probably pick the park as their eternal resting place, and I ended up here without even planning on it. There's a real problem in Whirly World of people spreading the ashes of their loved ones. It isn't permitted anywhere in the park. I can't remember if it's actually a health hazard or if management tries to keep it from getting out of control, but anyone that wants to is just going to do it anyway. What is park security going to do, scoop the ashes out of the air? What happens to those spirits? Where are my ashes going to end up? And which of my loved ones ended up with the task of scheduling my cremation?

Probably my mom. Parking lots always make me think of her. When I was younger, having a real estate agent for a mom was such an exotic proposition. While we drove around, and I first saw the world through the back of our brown Toyota Corolla, Mom would point out giant estates and important buildings that she or her colleagues had sold. I was wonderstruck. It sounded like my mom and her friends built absolutely everything, block by block.

Then, around the time I became a teenager and started resenting everything about my parents, my mom sold her biggest lot yet. The movie theater me and my friends always went to. The cineplex, where I saw Lord of the Rings, and Star Wars, was bulldozed to make way for a five-story parking structure, built in tandem with a new mall. Mom was so proud, but my social life was obliterated. Instead of taking my bike, I now had to bum a ride to see anything worth seeing, or tag along with my older sister and her friends. I lived in constant fear that one of the other kids in my class would figure out Sharon Green was responsible and a campaign would be launched to make sure no one ever talked to me again.

I resume walking, trying to push myself away from the bleak thoughts of the life I'm no longer a part of. There has to be a way to travel somewhere else. It's just a puzzle I have to solve. If this were the real world, I would have already walked past motels and restaurants. I would have crossed paths with hundreds of people, wondering if they were first timers or passholders, like me. Walking for this long would have probably put me back into the wilderness. I should be knee deep in tall grass and fallen trees, trudging through the nearby state forest.

That's one of the magical things about Whirly World. Worley

built it in the middle of nowhere, so its surroundings remain largely untouched. When you reach the crest of Timber Tracks at seventy miles per hour, the illusion of a ramshackle mountain railway falling apart at the seams isn't destroyed by rows of multi-story motels and convention centers. The inside of the park looks like the outside.

As I pass the signs reading A1 and A2 for about the hundredth time, I can't help but feel my insides succumb to loss and hopelessness. I slump down to my knees. Tears well up. I guess crying is one of the things that remains in the afterlife. Just so people know how sad you really are when your words fail you. I let a few tears out before I bother to wipe them away. I wonder what time it is back in the park. Did time elapse while I was gone? Am I expected to sleep here and do all of this again tomorrow?

"What on earth is the point of this place?" I scream as I flop on my back on the hard cement. I'm a grown-up toddler having a tantrum. I get good and worked up, tears, snot, the whole bit.

"Aww," someone says to my right.

I jump up in surprise. It's Kingston, the circus ringmaster. Barnum meets Bunyan, large and fantastical, in a striped tuxedo with tails. His hand is outstretched, holding a bright red handkerchief for me to grab. On impulse, I do. With a grand flourish, he spins his arm in a circle and several other colored tissues, tied to the first, come flying out of his sleeve. The sight is fascinating and funny but mostly disturbing. I get to my feet and take a step away from him. He pulls at the thread of hankies connected to my clutched hand and I let the red one go. *Should've wiped my face first,* I think, as I use the corner of my shirt instead.

"Feeling down?" he asks. "It looks like your ticket got punched." Then he pauses for the laugh. I give him a grim chuckle. Kingston is one of the park's mascots. My least favorite by a mile. I hate his big black hat and checkered vest and fancily embroidered boots. As he recoils his makeshift-rope of many colors, I reconnect to everything that irks me about the circus. Clowns and acrobats all maintain this bizarre attitude when they're performing. Like there's some joke they know that you don't and never will. This weirdo is full of that. He stuffs the puffy cluster of hankies into his vest pocket. I find his presence here, in parking lot limbo, troubling. More unnerving than if I'd met him inside the park.

I'm also scouring my brain to remember if there was ever an actor that played Kingston who died in Whirly World. None that I know of, and that's saying something, since I wrote a widely shared article on my blog about all the deaths that had ever happened here. It got a remarkable number of views. Death sells. So who is talking to me right now?

"Welcome to the show, Jason!" Kingston shouts. Of course he knows my name. Beverly did. Am I wearing a tag or something? "I must ask, what are you doing so far outside? Did you forget where you parked your car?" He pulls a horn from another pocket and honks it. "Aooga!"

I examine his features. I realize this is a Kingston unlike any I've ever seen before. Several actors play him on any given day. There's the version that strolls around the circus area, the one that leads the afternoon parade, and another that hosts the big top show of animals and acrobats. The illusion that all three, or more depending on the day, are the same person is maintained by a massive, bushy brown beard. It disguises the performer in the same way that anyone can play Santa with the right amount of fluff stuck to their face.

But this guy's beard looks like the genuine article. The rosy greasepaint cheek circles that are usually painted on have been replaced by a livid ruddiness. He doesn't feel like an actor. He's giving me the impression that he believes his magic to be real and his circus isn't just some trashy extension to a theme park that didn't need it.

"What are you doing here?" I ask, realizing this fails to encapsulate my confusion.

"Why, looking for you," he exclaims. "And here you are. Lost and confused. Tut tut."

"I'm not…" I begin, about to say I'm not lost, but of course I am. "Well, I'm not confused. I'm trying to get out of here. I don't suppose you know where the exit is?"

He raises a gloved, white finger and traces it in the air back in the direction of the park's entrance. "Back there, my boy. You've already passed through it."

God I hate this guy. I feel like an infant trying to wobble my way out of pre-school, only to be steered back into class by a teacher.

"I mean the *real* exit," I tell him. "I've enjoyed my stay and I'm ready to go home."

Kingston stands up straight, looking genuinely perplexed. "No one's stopping you from leaving." He gestures to the wide-open nothingness around us. I wonder if he sees the same thing I do.

"My mistake," I tell him. "I guess I have more to do here." I take a few steps back toward the gate. My feet feel heavy. I walk slowly, like a prisoner soaking up sunshine before the guards shove him back in his cell.

Kingston puffs up with pride. "Why, there's nothing you can't do here with a little heart and a lot of imagination." A baton extends with a snap from his hand and he makes high steps like he's leading a procession of jugglers and unicycles behind us. "This world is your world, Jason. You can make it what you wish."

He leans into me and puts a hand on my shoulder. His voice is melodious, but under it all is a rasp of course gravel. His breath smells like weathered canvas and old cigars. "You've dreamed of this place, haven't you? If you could change one thing, what would it be?"

I don't have to think too hard for my answer. "I'd get rid of the circus, for starters."

I expect Kingston to be shocked by this response, and he does not disappoint. He steps back and clasps his hand to his chest dramatically, like he's run out of air. "Get rid of the circus?"

"Oh yeah," I reply. "Poof. Gone." Kingston is too startled for words. I can't tell if he's putting on an act or I've really offended him. "You know, the way circuses do. You pack up everything on a train and move onto the next town." I'm tempted to tell him all the reasons I avoid his stomping grounds whenever possible. To recite the blog post I wrote when Kingston's Circus was first erected, ranting about how a theme park focused on the wild frontier had no business building a home for something so silly within its borders. That the only reason they were considering it is because they had a new CEO that favored boatloads of money over preserving the park's history. Something no one would dare to suggest if the Worleys still had ownership.

"Well then," Kingston says, crestfallen. "Poof." He grabs the collars of his coat, nods his head forward with a blink, and disappears. A puff of red smoke and confetti swirls in the spot he was standing, then fades into the invisible air. Good riddance.

Get it together, Jason. If this new reality is bound by the confines of this park, then let's find out just what that means. I can't let an irate security guard and pompous showman keep me from testing this place. I just need to be smarter about how I search for answers. No more tears. No more desperation.

I hear a click. The main gates of the park open. Not the ticket turnstile, but the massive doors that are only ever open on special occasions. A giant W splits in half, inviting me inside. I walk away from the turnstiles toward the center of the entrance plaza. In front of me are eleven blocky, gigantic, capital letters.

WHIRLY WORLD.

I didn't open this gate. I didn't unlock that turnstile. I didn't choose to be here. But I'll be damned if I won't make the most of it.

Kingston was right. I used to dream big dreams in this park. When I was a child, this place made it feel like anything was possible. Well, if that's true now, why am I pausing before I step back inside?

Why did Eddie almost spray me with mace? How did Beverly know my name? How does Clarence remember me but not realize that he's dead? Somewhere in these four hundred and fifty-six acres are the answers, and if it takes forever, I'm going to find them.

Chapter 4

WW

Gizzard Lake

Just inside the gates I discover Eddie, sitting on a bench, much calmer than before. I try to radiate the warmth and excitement I always feel when I finally make it to this hallowed ground. I wave to Eddie, and he returns the gesture with a small salute. I guess the emergency has passed. His demeanor has changed completely. The light in the sky suggests it's late afternoon. Perhaps he just tired himself out or is enjoying his favorite time of day like I did. I'm tempted to ask him about these conditions, or why he supposes I'm the only guest around, but I count myself fortunate no one is chasing me and continue down Market Street, passing the storefronts.

When I reach the lake I circle around the park's central hub to the right, in the direction I saw that mysterious boy run earlier. I try to put him out of my thoughts for now. I'm hoping he's a manifestation of my mind, because otherwise, he's a ghost too and I don't want to think about that. I freaked him out when we first met. I'll have to be more patient if I'm lucky enough to see him again.

The first landmark I reach that I haven't viewed in the afterlife is Sunburst Gardens. It's one of the most fluid and fluctuating locations on the map. Its dimensions have never changed, but the flora contained within are always in flux. I see it here preserved as it must have been today, the day I died, if the two are even one in the same.

This iteration is not one of my favorites, embracing a lot of local native trees and plants. In my opinion, it looks too similar to the surrounding wilderness. I thought the point of this area was to transport visitors to another place and time. When I've gone inside the garden in recent years it's been because April insisted on it. My favorite landscape designers have always made the gardens stand out with bold colors and fantastical topiary. This version just looks like home, which is fine, I guess.

I wonder if April knows I'm dead yet. I guess she'll have to talk to my parents. She's never had a great relationship with my dad. Few have. But she was close to my mom, and I bet my untimely demise will force them even closer. I picture them crying together, and I swear I can almost hear them. I want so badly for them to move on from this, to forget about me quickly, but I don't know how you can ask that of anyone. My brain wants to imagine the grammatically stellar eulogy my dad will try to write, realizing how little he knows about what I like to do, but I don't want to waste the energy.

I remember one time soon after April and I started dating, sitting in the gardens just going at it like teenagers. She smelled enchantingly like her strawberry shampoo and turkey drumstick (don't knock it till you've tried it), and we stayed in the gardens until the fireworks started going off overhead. My reverie is broken when I sense someone looking at me. Between the thick branches and bushes I spot a human face, staring. Even though I am a ghost now, seeing another gives me a chill. This spirit dissolves into the air almost instantly. I didn't even smile or wave. But neither did she.

That was Nuwa Chen. Whirly World death number nine. A poisonous snake, a cottonmouth if I'm not mistaken, caught her by surprise seven years ago. Those that followed her story could never ascertain whether she died in the park or at the hospital, but I now have my answer. Oh the articles I could write now that I have the inside track. I'm sure, like Beverly and Eddie and Clarence, Nuwa has dozens of park stories a nerd like me could listen to for hours. But like that runaway kid, she'd rather not share them with a new recruit. I don't blame her.

I miss the gardens Nuwa made. She spread as much of her Chinese heritage around as park management would allow. With ride maintenance, food consumption, and new construction, there had never been a huge budget allocation for pretty flowers. I always appreciated that, coming to a theme park that largely celebrates "Americana" (aka the white settler experience), I would find inspirations from halfway around the world, carefully reconstructed and lovingly maintained. Sunburst Gardens wasn't the same without Nuwa. How sad that, now that she's stuck here, she has to watch it lose her heartfelt touches.

Past this collection of greenery, down a long dusty road to the east, is Buckthorn. The ghost town. The irony isn't lost on me. I never thought I'd be staring at one, or the modern-day idea of one, as an actual ghost. I picture all the people that have died here sitting at the counter in Nellie's Saloon, ending each day with a whiskey toast and a poker game. Hollow House, the playfully haunted estate across the path from Sawmill Splash, would be an even more appropriate place to find them. But no one died there, or in Buckthorn. No ghosts ended up where ghosts are supposed to be.

I turn north and look up at the towering top of Catlin Peak. From there I should be able to see the entire park. I could take the back road behind Sawmill Splash, climb up the tall staircase inside the Lucky Spelunker, or brave the longest trail straight into the forest, winding back and forth past Florence Falls. By the time I get to the top, the sun will probably be setting. There's no rush, I suppose. I'll have plenty of opportunities to see this fake sun drop behind the fake horizon. But I've got to know what that fake horizon looks like. Never ending trees, probably, just like the parking lot's never-ending spaces and sedans. But there's only one way to know for sure.

As I mull this over, I hear a gentle splash behind me. I don't have to look to guess who has made it. I turn around and see him step out of the water like a beach bum after a gnarly session of body surfing. Blake Owens. The Californian. He flicks his long hair from one side of his head to the other like he's in a shampoo commercial. His unbuttoned green flannel shirt flaps to the sides, revealing a T&C Surf Designs shirt, whatever that stands for. I have a powerful urge to laugh at his conventionality, but I don't want to offend him before I introduce myself. Probably my favorite accidental death here.

Blake snuck into the park after hours with a couple of his friends in '89 and drowned in Gizzard Lake because he was blitzed out of his mind on cheap beer and skunk weed. What a way to go. His friends thought he left without them, and they just went home. Fun fact: Guess who discovered his body the next day. Beverly Thompson. She was finishing her shift and probably wasn't expecting to clean up a corpse. I always thought the poor woman almost keeled over right then and there, but it seems like she's made of stronger stuff than that.

Blake became an instant celebrity. He embodied the rebellious spirit all troublemakers aspire to. Kids dressed up like him for Halloween. Blake should have been a lesson to the rest of us thrill seekers but eighteen years later I was caught doing basically the same thing. I know I shouldn't look up to a guy like this, but now that I have a chance to meet him, I'm star struck.

> *Blake, Blake, who died in a lake.*
> *The very last swim the boy did take.*
> *And there he stays, never to wake.*
> *His final drink was his last mistake.*

"New guy!" he yells at me. I'm so popular. "A little birdie told me we got someone fresh today." I could have sworn he was sopping wet a second ago. And now he's totally dry. Afterlife water works differently. Got it.

"Well then," I reply. "My reputation precedes me."

"Exactly," he says, but I'm not sure he understood. "I'm Blake." He reaches out a hand and I shake it instantly.

"I'm Jason. I never thought I'd get to meet you."

"I know! Isn't this place wild?"

"Well, I'm not exactly sure what this place is."

"Ohhh." Blake nods. "This is Whirly World."

"No, yes, I know." I need to talk slower and more clearly. "I mean, this version of Whirly World. The afterlife." I look at the spot where he must have stepped out of the water. Unlike the lake in real life, which tries to appear bottomless, this one actually seems so. Usually, you can see pipes or patches of muddy cement in parts, but here it's like staring into a void.

"Oh, right," Blake says. "I'm not sure either. I don't think any of us are." Finally, we're getting somewhere. Leave it to Blake to get right to the point.

"Okay," I say hurriedly. "You know the other ghosts in the park? You're friends? It seems like some people here are a little, how do I put it, confused?"

"You're not wrong," he admits. "Everyone has their own vibe here. We mind our own business." Blake motions to the lake in front of us. "This is where I like to chill, mostly."

"Swimming?" I ask. Is that enough to sustain a ghost for several decades?

"Yup. And *searching*." He slowly waves his hands in the air, mysteriously.

"Searching? What do you think is down there?"

"Whoa." Blake's jaw drops. "You don't know?"

If I don't, Blake, it probably doesn't exist. "I guess not," I say, pretending that what he's about to tell me will be awesome and shocking. "What's down there?"

"*Gold*," Blake says with a conspiratorial grin.

Oh, no. He's fallen for one of the earliest and most debunkable urban legends. Because this area used to be a "land of silver," a rumor was started that Worley didn't just inherit the land he built the park on, he also was bequeathed a chest full of silver and gold. And because Worley was eccentric and already wealthy, he supposedly sunk the treasure to the bottom of Gizzard Lake. This is, of course, untrue for a number of reasons. First off, no park employee ever publicly corroborated the story. Thousands of people have witnessed the lake after it had been drained of water on multiple occasions. The silver mining in this area was notoriously awful. And there's no place to hide it anyway.

"Are you sure it's down there?" I ask.

Blake chuckles. "Are you sure it's *not*?"

Debating this man is pointless. "You got me there."

"You've got a lot to learn, new guy." Blake jovially throws an arm around my shoulder and gives me a noogie. I cannot believe this is happening. "So, you wanna check it out?"

"Check what out?" I ask.

Blake points his thumb back toward the lake. "My pad."

"Well, actually..." I gesture in the opposite direction, up the mountain. I want to tell him that I have more pressing matters to attend to, but do I? If nothing ever changes here then everything will be where it is whenever I get around to discovering it. If my newfound friends keep vanishing, hiding, or running away from me, I should probably take advantage of the opportunities I'm given to learn more about them.

"You mean, like, you have a house down there, or something?" I ask him.

He grins again. Blake loves his secrets. "Kinda." He turns and takes one step toward the lake, but then spins back to me with a finger raised. "Wait, first things first."

"Take off my shoes?" I guess. His expression tells me he has no idea what I'm talking about. Again, I've lost him. *Stop being snarky,*

Jason. Listen.

"No, dude," he replies, perplexed. Blake takes a moment to remember what the first things were. "Right," he continues. "Follow me so you don't get lost. Don't go up or down any staircases. And try not to move anything. I got everything where I like it."

Blake turns again and puts one toe in the water. I notice he's not wearing shoes, and I don't see them anywhere on the shore. His foot lands on something just below the surface. Blake puts his other foot in and it descends just a bit deeper, like there's a set of stairs leading downward. I have spent plenty of living minutes staring into this lake, trying to see the pumps and vents underneath, and never have I ever seen any type of staircase or platform. Such infrastructure would tempt people to take a step in despite the outer fence.

Speaking of, the fence is gone. There is usually a waist high, metal fence surrounding the lake to keep daring children and dumb adults from taking an ill-advised plunge into the unknown. I was leaning on it earlier today, and now it's vanished. If I'm going to figure out a way to get out of here, or understand this place better, the last thing I need is for things to start appearing and disappearing like the ghosts do.

After a fifth step Blake is up to his chest in the water. The surface doesn't make way for his body, or ripple against his frame. It's like, to him, it's not even there. He gives me one last smile before the rest of him drops below the top of the water. I was on my way to climb a mountain and here I am taking a dip in the lake. Either way, I'm testing the boundaries of this place and that feels like progress.

All I can see on or through the surface of the water is the reflection of the sky above. Unless it was a trick, I saw Blake's foot hit something solid. It doesn't feel like he's trying to play a prank on me. He sounded legitimately excited to show me his aquatic hideout. I better catch up with him before he travels too far. Here goes nothing. I place my foot into the water and let my weight drop me to the first step.

Nope, no step. I put my hands forward as a reflex but when I should be falling face first into water, they touch nothing. The air whooshes past my cheeks and my legs pedal in circles. This is going to be bad. My eyes slam shut and I don't want to open them until I hit the floor. Then, I hit the floor. Face first.

I groan at the impact, and once the shock recedes, I push myself up to my hands and knees. I do a quick check of my face and body, and amazingly, I don't think I injured myself. But I sure felt the force of the fall. Okay, the lesson is sinking in: If you try to leave the park, you'll find nothing but cracked concrete. Try to escape to someone else's wonderland, you'll end up eating dirt. I feel stupid. I guess I should be grateful that I landed on the ground and didn't fall straight through the earth.

As I pick myself up, it becomes clear the area beneath the surface of the lake is just as I imagined it would be. The bottom is crisscrossed with tracks and plumbing, and that's it. No treasure chest in sight. Above me, I can still see the surface of the water. There's a faint blue-green haze over everything, but my eyes aren't fogged over. It's like the water is there but not there at the same time.

"Blake?" I yell. No response. The yell doesn't sound like I'm underwater. It's not warped and full of bubbles. I wait to see if he'll peek behind any of the walls or patches of pipes but all is silent. Either he got too far ahead of me, or Blake and I are in completely different places. The bad news is I can't see any way to get back up. At least not from where I'm standing.

The good news is this clumsy mistake has granted me unprecedented access to a part of Whirly World I don't think many people have seen before. I've only ever observed this area in pictures and on the off chance they'll drain it for cleaning or renovations. They put up a big wooden wall to keep people from spying or falling in, but you can peek through the cracks or, if you're tall enough, stretch a selfie stick over the top. Pictures don't let you truly comprehend the depth of the lake, though.

Now I'm actually standing on the bottom of Gizzard Lake, and it kinda feels like walking on the moon. Only now I don't need an oxygen tank or a special suit, and my vision isn't blocked by murky water. The coolest part to see up close is the main track for the giant raft. Passengers are supposed to get the impression that the wooden boat that takes you around the lake is doing so thanks to the careful steering of the guy with the big oar in back. The truth is, he's only there as a lifeguard in case someone ends up going overboard.

As I circle Stope Island, climbing over pipes, I can see the raft is still parked at Port Juniper. Its base is fastened securely to the track. While the top of the raft is built of old wood, the bottom is slick as a submarine. I love seeing where the careful illusion meets the raw reality of running a place like this to code. There's no point in making the underside of the raft and its track look like anything but the world's most boring rollercoaster.

As the raft doesn't seem to be in operation currently, much like the rest of the park, there appears to be no way to reach Worley Lodge. The two-room shack is the only structure on the island. It's not where I had planned to go, but I'm curious what the afterlife has done to it. It's one of the only places in the park that actually has a sideways connection to the supernatural, if in an overtly unproven and commercial way.

Before the original builders filled in the edges of the lake to make it a somewhat symmetrical circle, Worley himself lived in the cabin to oversee construction. Today's version of the building is a faithful recreation of that house, but not the actual roof that Worley lived under. Sometimes he would head out into the woods that skirt the park to camp or hunt and be gone for a fortnight.

Employees always knew when he had returned because they'd see smoke coming out of the fireplace of Worley Lodge. So at sunset, every day, they keep "relighting" the fire to pay tribute. The plumes come from a smoke machine below the park and not a homey fireplace, but the gesture is warm, respectful, and effective. It's one of those things where if you know, you know. I made it a habit to tip my hat (whether I was wearing one or not) toward the cabin when I'd see those first plumes of smoke in the evening. Because even though he's gone, he's still *here,* in the park he loved.

I should have made a plan like that with April. "If I die in Whirly World," I should have told her, "I will blink the light at this hot dog stand five times every Tuesday. That's how you'll know I'm still with you." But that would require her to keep visiting this place, which I can't imagine she'll want to do again soon, if ever. After the honeymoon phase of our four-year relationship, she grew reluctant to join me on the best of days. She had started giving excuses with an edge, things like, "I have a baby shower that I'm going to by myself I guess." Now that it's become my final resting place, she might cross it off her list for good.

I was expecting to find some kind of maintenance ladder near Stope Island, but after doing two laps around it I'm not seeing a way to get up there. It doesn't feel like I can swim or float in whatever element I'm surrounded by, but I make a few pitiful leaps at the surface just to be sure. I'll have to find another way to the island if I ever want to reach the lodge, I guess. Ground level first. Then Catlin Peak. Then, maybe later, Worley Lodge.

The only thing low enough to step on but high enough to climb up from is the boat track. From that high up, theoretically, I should be able to reach the dock on the south side of the lake. It's hard to keep track of what I can walk on and what I can't. Hours ago I was leaning on a metal fence that a few minutes ago was no longer there. I can see the surface of the water above me, but as I performed my unrehearsed stunt fall, my body passed through it like a beam of light. Yet, I didn't fall through the bottom of the lake. There has to be some logic to it, but I haven't cracked the system yet. I work my way up onto the track.

I decide to follow the track the whole way, to adhere to the visual cues that make sense. I drop to all fours and grasp the rails in my hands. The sides of the track feel firm against my palms. A good sign. My knees, my feet, and my elbows all feel the solidness of the track as well. I awkwardly shuffle forward, clinging to the metal borders like some smaller, fleshy boat. If I stand up on the track, I'd just peek above the "surface," but I don't want to risk another fall. What if the track disappears while I'm on it? I shimmy along, wishing I was actually subject to the natural laws of being submerged in water. Of being alive. I feel dumb and definitely look dumb. I spent most of my adult life in a desk chair, so finding myself bear crawling across a quarter mile of track is more physical fitness than I have ever willingly signed up for.

There's just enough space behind the raft for me to attempt to reach the dock. I urgently want to get out of the lake, but I take each shift of my weight deliberately, patiently. The track is slanting upwards now, to help the raft arrive level at the dock. I thank the weird logic of this place that the tracks aren't wet with water from the lake, or from my hands which should be sweaty, but aren't.

I reach the highest point and, slower than I've ever moved in my life, I stand up. I'm now balanced, my legs straddling the track, but in order to reach my full height, I need to move my legs together. Somewhere in the back of my mind I recall that I'm supposed to pull in my core for better balance. After a few wobbly attempts, I just go for it, and yank my back leg onto the track closest to the dock. I totter, sure I will fall, but I throw my arms over my head and slap the faux wooden surface with my open hands. My fingers clutch the edge of the dock like I'm hanging from a skyscraper. *Don't slip now.* I can't help spitting out a loud grunt as I pull myself up. I kick my legs a bit to balance my weight. I've never spent much time in a gym but I imagine this is one of those slow pull-ups. The ones you see Olympic athletes do to train their body for the impossible. I recall clinging to jungle gym bars as a kid, pretending that if I fell I'd sink into a bubbling volcano. It was thrilling to imagine then. This is much less fun.

My grip starts to give. I clench hard but my fingers fail me. I'm falling again. I look at my hands, hoping in vain that there's something else to grab. Then something grabs me. A hand slips through the top of the water and takes my wrist. I kick forward and try to run my legs up the side of the dock. I push and grunt and finally flop one leg over the edge of the lake. Whoever has me doesn't struggle, just keeps a firm grasp helping me climb ashore. I hope it's Blake.

When my head emerges into the open air I see that it is not. It's the last person I'd hoped for. Kingston. He's smiling. I suddenly feel like a fish on a hook. When my feet are both back on dry land, I tug my wrist away from Kingston's hand and he releases it freely.

"Lose your way?" he asks, condescending.

"No, I always wanted to take a walk down there. Refreshing."

"That's it, Jason. Live a little. I bet even a man of your dedication and ingenuity hasn't seen everything there is to see in this world. Just make sure that, wherever your imagination leads, you can always find your way out."

"I will." I wish I were talking to anyone else besides Kingston.

"And when you want to really have fun, come visit me and my friends at the greatest show on earth."

I hear a tinkle of circus music drift through the park and assault my ears. Kingston grins. "Maybe later," I say, then point up the mountain. "I'm going to head up there and look for a way to get the hell out of here."

"See you a-round," chortles Kingston as he pirouettes on the spot. He waves goodbye and trips down Market Street. Everything about his presence feels malicious to me, despite his cheery disposition and gentlemanly walk. I'll have to ask the other ghosts if they've ever seen this clown walking around, or if he's just here to taunt me.

That's it. No more making friends. If I can't get out of here I'll have all the time in the world to meet the locals. I need to see what it looks like outside this place. I need to try and piece together how this perverted limbo works. The other victims of Whirly World have already adjusted to it, in their own way. I have to stop playing around, otherwise I might get complacent as well. I turn and take in the view before starting my ascent all over again. I feel my mind pulling me north, but I still give myself a second to breathe. Because somehow after traversing the interior of the whole lake, I managed to emerge back in my favorite spot.

Chapter 5

Catlin Peak

Most attractions in Whirly World are just a few minutes' walk from the others. Ten minutes, tops. All except for Timber Tracks, or the "mountain coaster," for people that don't take the time to remember what it's actually called. There are three ways up. I take the long way today, as I'm prone to on any day, because I don't mind the hike. One of the fundamentals of proper park design is giving your patrons multiple ways to reach a given spot.

The trail through Linden Forest is both beloved and berated, depending on who you ask. Timber Tracks is the second most popular ride in the park. Most people expect access to the queue to be more accessible than it's always been.

You want to avoid what I call "choke points." If you have something fun at the end of a path, you're not leaving enough room for the four types of theme park attendees: People traveling to a point, people leaving that point, people with no immediate plans, and people who have no idea where they're going. People that head up the Linden trail with no idea where they're going are always surprised how long it takes to reach the top.

Personally, I love how long this road is. Too many corners at theme parks lead directly to another entrance or exit. There's no place to take in the scenery. Most designers are too afraid to let that section just speak for itself. I think that the longer it takes to get up the mountain, the more impressive the view will be when you get there.

The park calls this a "trail" and uses that term very loosely. This is a paved road made to look like dirt. There are no exposed roots to trip on or jagged rocks to twist your ankle like you would find on an actual wilderness trail. Like the rest of Whirly World, it offers travelers a taste of the outdoors without having to commit to any unnecessary deprivation. No need to carry a canteen or watch out for coyotes or poop in a bush here.

This length of the park also reminds me of camping with my family, one of the few times it felt like all four of us were equally enjoying a shared activity. The third and final time my father visited Whirly World, I took him up the Linden trail instead of taking the elevator inside the Lucky Spelunker. It was the only part of his day that I think put the closest thing to an actual smile on his face. He said "It's nice that they didn't touch this part of the park," and I agreed, neglecting to tell him how much grounds keeping was required to make something look like it hadn't been touched.

Around the easternmost corner, I come to one of the first rest spots, several hundred yards short of where you'd probably find one after starting your average, real-life trail. A wooden bench, just off the trail, with a view of the park below. It's lovely, but I'm not planning to stop here. Then I see who's sitting on the bench. Clarence leans back and gazes out at the lake and trail entrance. I don't see his treat cart anywhere. I've never seen him this relaxed before. It's like I've caught him on break. I hate to disturb him but I have to walk by to reach the top, and I don't want to startle him.

"Good afternoon," I say, cheerfully. I'm happy to see Clarence somewhere else. I also wasn't aware of my deadness the last time Clarence and I spoke. I must have sounded nuts to him. Clarence has one of those patient hearts that just accepts people however they are. I should try to do the same. "Sorry about earlier," I say, thrusting my hands in my pockets in embarrassment. "I hope I didn't scare you."

Clarence doesn't respond. He just stares into the scenery. Maybe he didn't hear me?

"Clarence, you okay?" I inquire. Again, his face doesn't twitch in recognition. I walk up to the bench and get a good look at him. His eyes are fixated on something in the distance, and he's breathing gently. "Clarence?" I try one more time. I might as well be talking to a tree. I'm not dialed into his wavelength right now, and that makes me feel a bit frightened and alone. It's not like I was ever able to talk to him about serious issues while he was alive, but both versions of him that I've met today seem depressingly disconnected.

The Clarence I'm used to is the consummate confectioner. He never breaks character. He pretends he makes the goods he sells, like his candies aren't prepackaged. But when you buy sweets from the guy, you'd swear you were living in the 19th century. And the treats from his cart always tasted better than from any other location. That's true theme park magic.

But now he looks frozen, like a powered down animatronic. I wave my arm in an awkward final greeting. Nothing. I give up.

"Enjoy the view, I guess." I shuffle back to the road and continue the slow climb. I'm way past presuming this is all a dream, but I can't reject the possibility that I'm in my own, personalized purgatory. Just because I've only seen the ghosts of people that died here, save for Kingston, doesn't mean that any of this is grounded in a set of rules.

I glance over my shoulder, expecting Clarence to have teleported into another dimension, but the nice old man is still sitting where I left him. Either Clarence has some waking up to do himself, or he's achieved an inner peace so complete that it shuts others out entirely. I can't say I blame him. Also, I can't assume all these disappearing ghosts see me when I see them. It's like we're all playing an abstract version of hide-and-seek. I feel like I'm losing.

I can tell I'm getting to a point where I can potentially see over the park walls, but as long as I'm taking the long road I might as well reach the peak before the payoff. The view beyond could be something cool like a giant monster crushing a bustling metropolis. Or it could be something tailored to mock me like a wallpaper that just says *Nice Try* over and over.

By this point in the climb, I'd usually be a little out of breath, and on a hot day, my shirt would be sticking to my skin under my backpack. But I'm not hungry or thirsty or hot. I don't feel my mouth drying up in anticipation of a gulp of water. My muscles don't feel fatigued, they're simply recognizing the increased angle of my ascent. They know that we're going up.

It's nice not to have branches to avoid on the smooth pavement, but those imperfections can also make a hike a little less monotonous. On a wild and dusty trail, every step that doesn't leave you flat on the ground is a tiny victory against mother nature. The mind can trick you into thinking you're one of the early pioneers, totally unaware of what lies past the trees that surround you. It's fun to fantasize that you're one of the only people that's ever been where you are, even when the trail is smothered in the footprints of countless others.

There are no footprints here. The estimation of how many people have visited Whirly World since it opened in 1965 is somewhere in the millions. But the streets are cleaned so regularly, not even their cigarette butts or Styrofoam cups can leave a trace.

As the trail finally loops around for the last time before I reach Timber Tracks, I want to promise myself to ride the damn thing on the way down. I've spent most of the day in this park and I haven't been on one ride. The living version of me would be appalled. Please oh please let the rides still work here. What a cruel fate that would be. No lines to suffer, no crowds to tolerate, but no thrills to be experienced. A Henry Bemis "Twilight Zone" level of suffering: *"That's not fair at all. There was time now. There was all the time I wanted."*

I can hopefully explore the interior of each ride at the very least. Once I understand how the boundaries of this place work, and if I'm truly stuck here forever, I can make a project of seeing all the places I never could. There were so many times in my life when I walked by an Employees Only door left unlocked and wondered how far I could get without being noticed. My buddy Mike once procured an official Whirly World sanitation uniform from an ex-girlfriend that had been recently fired, but I told him that any plots to get behind closed doors would be short lived. It didn't fit either of us anyway.

One time the big train got stuck in Gabbro Caverns and everyone aboard had to walk through a tunnel used exclusively by park operators. All the other riders were complaining, but I *loved* it. The staff apologized repeatedly but I was enthralled by every second of the impromptu backstage tour, even if it was just a bunch of beige walls and posters reminding all paid employees of various park policies. Some of those that have been daring, or dumb, enough to sneak past where patrons are allowed have documented their journeys and posted them online. I do not condone such egregious behavior, but I'd be lying if I claimed not to have watched all of those shaky-cam stunts over and over.

I round the last curve, and the ground levels out. I made it. The top of the mountain. Another bench like the one I found Clarence resting on greets me at the final lookout. I take a seat. The park is eerily quiet and devoid of movement except for gently waving trees over Sunburst Gardens. The lake is shining in the sun downing glow of early evening. In the distance, I see the big top tent, the train tracks, but no people anywhere. I wish I had binoculars, and close my eyes to see if I can make them materialize. No such luck.

When I ran out of the main gates of Whirly World this morning, I was stuck in an endless parking lot. Now, I can see the boundaries of that lot, along with everything else I could usually see whenever I gave myself the time to watch it from this bench. There are sadly no surprises from this elevation. I can see both the west and east employee areas that park builders tried their best to disguise with tall trees and green rooftops. Past the main gate is Porter Ave, which stretches west into the mountains, and east toward the interstate.

I've seen this view hundreds of times, but here, like with everything else, it looks different. It's not quite like the painted dome that covers a lot of video game environments, but it's not far off. It's not like a dream of mine either. Whoever built this afterlife got most of the details right. I guess that's why it's so sad to look at. When the sun sets it drops a huge shadow over the park from the west to the east, like a giant spaceship descending to Earth. It's one of my top five favorite parts of the day, and this wouldn't be an awful way to watch it.

This is, objectively, nice. I should be enjoying myself more, instead of moping about my death or pushing against my restraints. I always considered my ability to enjoy any aspect of Whirly World, regardless of cost or wait time, evidence that I love this park more than most. Not that it's a contest. But if it were, I'm fairly sure I'd win.

It makes me chuckle to think of little, twelve-year-old Jason, dragging his parents around from one attraction to the other, melting down at any speed bump or hitch that got in the way of his well-laid plans. My parents once enforced mandatory restrictions on my time here, or even my requests for more time. When they found out I was hoarding my allowance to pay for a ticket they threatened to withhold money until I promised to spend it on other things. Naturally, I spent most of it on park merchandise, and afterwards they made their demands more specific.

My folks later designated an admission ticket to this park as a reward for good grades, but that didn't work as they had planned because I just got straight-As. They were as good as their word but didn't repeat this tactic the following year, and I went back to my usual averages of C+ and B-, with the occasional A if I actually enjoyed the subject. English, creative writing, history, and basic coding were my natural As. The rest were just time wasters until I could get back to the park. When I got to high school, Whirly World started their annual pass program. I jumped at the opportunity to buy a whole year for pennies on the dollar considering how often I used it. By that time there was little my parents could do to restrict me. I inherited my sister's beat-up Volvo when she got a new car for college, and the rest is history.

The sun has begun crossing over the train tracks to the west. Soon it'll erase the circus from view. That is, until the lights turn on. I hope the lights still turn on. Maybe they're automatic, or there's a gang of ghostly oompa-loompas that whistle while they work. But for, what, a dozen or so dead people that have to watch it all whether they want to or not? Maybe we all turn the lights on with our imagination.

I'm not sure if I've moved at all for a few minutes. Despite my rage at discovering I had died, I feel an urge circling through me that wants me to calm down, to slow my movement and stay in the moment. To let the dream die. I don't know why I'm resisting it. It's like that chill inside me. My body wants to let it go, but I won't let it. I've been experiencing a strange relief that I haven't been able to identify until now. Sometimes in life something happens that solves a problem for you, even in the worst way.

When I was fifteen years old, my cousin Luke died in a car accident. I was inconsolable for days and days. It was my first brush with death, even though he lived miles away. When I started to consider how it would impact my life, I realized one potential positive. Luke had always sent me postcards from his family's travels. Luke's father, my Uncle Harris, was a travel agent and got discounts on all sorts of crazy vacations. While I loved seeing where the Davidson's had run off to every year, I never took the time to write Luke back.

I thanked him whenever we got together as a family, which wasn't that often, but I never responded in the fashion that Luke obviously preferred. Whenever he was in one of the most beautiful or fascinating places on the planet, like standing on the Great Wall of China, or living in a yurt in Mongolia, he still thought of me, his cousin, and wanted me to know how he was doing. Even stuck at home with less nomadic parents, I never took the time to return the sentiment. Not once. Maybe it was laziness, maybe insensitivity. Maybe all his travels made me feel inferior. The confines of my own life were so small, how could I have anything to say back to him?

When I was processing Luke being gone, I realized those postcards would cease. At that moment, I released all the guilt I had been accruing over not writing back. It felt gross to even consider, but his death made me feel relieved in that one, awful, selfish way.

When I discovered I was dead, the same thing happened to my entire life. Every college friend I'd lost touch with, every way I could disappoint my co-workers, every goal I'd set for myself but never accomplished, every plan I'd made with April, they were all obliterated. Rather than feel a rush of regret, I just let them go. It felt like there was no point in crying over something no one could blame me for, something no one can reverse. I've thought about the past all day today, but it doesn't feel like it's holding me back. Not anymore.

My ass is still on this bench, isn't it? The line of shadow marking the sun's descent has cut across Gabbro Caverns and is creeping up on the creepy grounds of Hollow House. The more I sit on this bench, the more I want to sit on this bench. I feel perfectly okay with everything right now. Before I died, my stupid living thoughts would get in the way of enjoying this view. I'd be thinking about when the park would close, the hour-and-a-half drive home or hitting one last ride on my way out. Many times, I'd be thinking about the next time I'd be back in the park again. Right now, even with the sun setting, I've got no place to be.

A tiny alarm begins to sound in my mind. I don't want to stand up, or walk anywhere, or visit the, um, which one was it? The mountain coaster? It doesn't matter, really. Whenever I decide to get up from this bench, it will still be there. This sunset will only last for a few more minutes, and I've never seen one like it. As night draws closer, I can officially log this as the weirdest day I've ever had in Whirly

World. The sun finally sinks below the horizon, and everything gets dark, and calm, and still.

"Hey," a voice cuts in. The sound reaches my ears but I don't want to acknowledge it. I don't recognize the voice. "Champ. Kid. Snap out of it!" I hear one or two claps and notice my head is looking around for the source. I'm coming back to myself. The noise is coming from my right, so I look behind my shoulder. There's a short man leaning over the bench. His hair is white and wild. Patches of stubble surround a scruffy mustache, thick as hand broom bristles. Brown suspenders hold up brown pants over brown shoes.

"Whoa. Who?" I manage to mumble.

"Frank!" he exclaims, thrusting his arm forward and yanking me off the bench. "Frank Young. Welcome, son. Thanks for making the climb. I saw someone come in today and I wasn't sure if I was going to get to say hello before the sun went down. Just made it. And here you are. Fantastic."

Wow, Frank Young. Look at him. I've only seen this man in pictures. Frank Young went out like he lived. Fixing a rollercoaster. A year after Josie Bean took a fatal swan dive off the rails of Timber Tracks, he spent weeks upgrading the entire ride. He put on new brake runs, raised the car doors by a foot, and put a big metal fence right where she bailed. Management didn't even pressure him. Then one summer night, he was crushed when a large portion of the track dislodged. The track didn't kill him instantly, a fact I found out in college. He was working after hours, and might have survived, if only he hadn't been on his own.

My roommate, Nick, showed me photos of the scene, posted on Rotten.com, which I embarrassingly didn't know were available. Frank was staring at the ceiling, which he had probably been doing for hours, and I was relieved to see a calm look on his face. Of all the victims of Whirly World, Frank's was the only corpse I saw. His skin looks much better now.

He smiles at me like I'm an old friend. "You with me?"

I blink a few times to get my eyeballs working again. "Yeah, I'm here. Thanks for bringing me back."

"Oh, yeah," he says in a cautious tone. "You gotta be careful when you sit down. The hours can go by in a blink." He snaps his fingers to drive the point home.

"Thanks for the warning. Good to see you, or meet you, Frank. I'm Jason." Frank smiles and stretches his hand out. I give him a good shake. His hand is strong and rough, as I imagined.

"Jason," he says, memorizing it. "Welcome to the nuthouse."

I laugh. I heard Frank was grandfatherly and direct, and his vibe is so refreshing after all I've dealt with today.

"Nuthouse?" I ask him. "Is that what this place is? Where are we exactly?"

Frank curls his thumbs around his suspenders. "We're in Heaven, kid," Frank says, as if that's just a place you can go. "Step inside my office, young man, and I'll tell you how this place works."

Chapter 6

Timber Tracks

Frank leads me along the side path past the ride entrance toward an Employees Only door. Knowing he's going to open the door and I'm going to step inside and just hang out for a while, is pretty rad. The side path could be easily missed amid the copious trees and bushes that add so much green to the otherwise brown and orange ride entrance. Even the most distracted patron would have to walk a long way past several warnings before they got to this restricted area.

I've seen the darkest parts of this mountain with the safety lights on, but I've never been inside the operation room. I've studied pictures and good old shaky video of it plenty of times, but seeing it, smelling it, really feeling how small or big or old or new a room can be, is a totally different thing.

To my surprise, the door is unmarked. It's not locked, or even closed. I was looking forward to Frank pulling a giant chain out of his pocket and selecting one of a hundred keys, but instead he saunters through like this door is always open.

"So, how did I die?" Frank asks.

Gulp. He doesn't know. But then, I don't know how I died. Maybe that's not something we're privy to here. I'm not sure I'm the right person to break this to Frank politely, but here we go. "Well," I begin, then decide to just blurt it out. "You bled to death after two tons of metal track collapsed and pinned you to the ground."

He laughs at this. The way a rowdy uncle laughs at one of his nephew's bawdy jokes. He must be in shock.

"I'm sorry to break it to you, but you should know."

Frank jerks his head back. "What? Oh, of course I knew. I just wanted to hear *you* describe it. Everyone I've met here has a different take on it. Did you read about it or what?" The hallway we're walking through is barely lit, but Frank obviously knows where he's going.

I follow his voice to avoid tripping. "I've seen pictures."

"Oh, really? From the police, I hope? Wow, that's morbid. I hope my family never had to see any of that stuff."

"Do you know how *I* died?"

"Ah, no, I can't see stuff that far away. Sorry, kid." We walk in silence for a few seconds. "What about technology? Last report I got was from Bev in two thousand twelve. Smartphones, tablets, all that good stuff. But I've missed a whole decade. Nuwa's not one to spill the beans, and I haven't been able to get a straight sentence out of Clarence. Poor guy still thinks he works here. So, what's new?"

I say the first thing that comes to me. "Streaming. The cloud."

"The cloud?" Frank asks.

That term must sound so silly.

"Ha, yeah. Everyone's data is all up in the air. Er, stored in large server farms. We hardly save anything on local drives anymore. And no one buys physical media. Books, magazines, DVDs, all those are collectors' items. Hobby stuff. LPs are coming back, though."

Frank lights up. "Really. I wonder how much I could get for my Willie Nelson collection these days. When are you from?"

"Two thousand twenty-three."

"Wow, so that'll be twenty-one years for me."

I can't imagine. "That must feel like a long time."

"You know, that's the funny thing. It doesn't. Hell, I'm not really sure what year it is until someone new shows up."

"You don't get seasons here?"

"Nope. We're all sunny days year-round. If you can call them 'years' anymore."

"That sounds dreary. I used to love rainy days, windy days." I sigh and realize that it's a relief to finally have a normal conversation with someone. Even a ghost someone. "I'll be honest with you, Frank. I'm having a hard time accepting that I'm going to be here forever." We come to a long staircase lit by flickering bare bulbs along the ceiling, and I follow Frank down.

"No, no," he says, sympathetically. "Don't think of it that way. Did I want to be more than a mechanic? You bet. Did I want to live in my home state my whole life? Absolutely not. But I'll take living anywhere over living nowhere. When I was bleeding out, all I could think of was, 'crap, I've blown my only chance at being alive.' Now that I'm here, I get another chance to make the best of things." We reach a double door at the bottom of the stairs. Frank grabs the doorknob but turns to me before opening it.

"Letting the days slip by ain't so bad," Frank says. "When you want to be in the park, it's here. When you want to let the hours, or the days, just vanish, you can do that too."

"I don't know. That's terrifying, like blacking out at a frat party."

"I wouldn't know. Never went to college."

Frank opens the door and I step into the control room at last. I'm elated at the view but then everything feels wrong. These places often seem different in scale when you see them in a video compared to the real thing, but this room is still too large. What should be rows of wooden flats and stacks of security monitors is instead a massive four-story room with a string of lights winding up into a cavern above, twisting like the swirl of an ice-cream cone.

"Wait, what?" It comes out in an awed whisper as I try to understand what I'm looking at. Parts of the track appear to cross through the ceiling above, and glowing lanterns descend from their iron siding. All along the walls, like cave paintings, are depictions of the park in its various incarnations. Concept art that always shows the park set to a scale that's impossible to achieve, but fun to dream about. My eye is pulled to a model of this ride's track in the corner. There are two separate trains running on it, full of tiny people with their hands in the air.

This isn't what the control room of Timber Tracks looks like in the real world, at all. Granted, I've never actually stood where I'm standing now, but I've seen enough photographs and blueprints to know that something is off. "This isn't, where are we?" I ask.

Frank is ready to answer. "Oh, this?" he says, grinning. He proudly gestures around him. "Do things look just a little bit different? Maybe better? Certainly bigger?"

I nod, too busy taking it in to respond.

"That's a little Frank Young magic at work. When I was living I always felt this room was dusty. Claustrophobic. So when I got here I wanted to change it so badly that eventually, I did. And here we are." Frank hops into a metal chair attached to its own track. It glides across the room. Frank spins it around with a silly smile that makes him look half his age.

"We can *change* this place?" I ask, shocked.

Frank shrugs his shoulders. "Well, *I* can. Some of the others can too. Those who can't, or don't, I'm not sure. Maybe they don't want to. Maybe they haven't figured it out."

"Yeah, about the others. How many are here? Do you talk to them often? Who's that little kid? Why was Nuwa hiding from me? Why was Clarence just sitting on that bench?" Finally someone can give me some answers.

"Hold on, kid. One thing at a time."

"Oh, I'm sorry. I can't help it. As a self-appointed expert of Whirly World, I've just got to know everything."

"Well, this place can get to you if you let it. To answer your first question, nine others, by my best estimation." Frank looks behind me and squints. Then his eyes flick from point to point as he mouths numbers. I realize he's seeing things that aren't in the room. "Yeah, eleven total."

"Wait. What was that? What did you just do?"

Frank looks up at me with another jovial smile. He's really enjoying my ignorance. "Oh that?" he says with an air of pride. "It's easy." Frank stands up, walks to me, and puts one hand on my shoulder. "You gotta stop pretending this place is the park you remember." He turns me around and points at the wall. "Imagine that every person here is like a lightbulb. If you look with the right kind of eyes, you can see them, all of them."

I squint, but it makes the room darker. "I don't get it."

Frank gives me a couple of firm pats between my shoulder blades. "C'mon, kid. You can do this." He shifts his weight around and I copy him. "You're trying to look closer at that wall, but that wall isn't there. None of it is. But we're here, all of us. The thing we're standing on doesn't generate electricity, but we do. We're made of it. That's what you're looking for. The same thing lighting you up from the inside."

I try again, pausing to look down at my hands first, but when I look up the wall is still the only thing I see. I shake my head at Frank, who lets out an exasperated huff.

Frank backs up and stretches his arms outward. "Okay, look at me first. Give up everything that's telling you that I'm a person. That I'm this tall and this fat. That I'm wearing these clothes. Shake all that nonsense out of your head." He moves his legs back and forth like he's about to run a relay, wiggling his wrists.

I take a deep breath. If he can do this, so can I. Maybe this is like one of those magic-eye drawings that pops out after your eyeballs kind of dive into it. I remember feeling like a prodigy when I was finally able to see one of those after all of my classmates struggled with them. This is probably something you can't just clench your butt cheeks and make happen. I need to relax. This requires patience, and that's been a hard feeling to maintain today.

I turn back to the wall with determination and shake my wrists back and forth to loosen up. Instead of scrunching my face, furrowing my brow, or even squinting, I just close my eyes altogether. I imagine what it's like to be a lightbulb. They're hot, like humans can be in the right conditions. They're singularly illuminated, but only because they're connected to a power source, and often, each other. I try to imagine I'm using infrared goggles, or holding a bulb so close to my eyes that I can see the filament burn.

I open my eyes, but only see the wall again. I rub my face in frustration. It's still just the wall. I shake my head side to side. Wall, wall, wall. In the middle of the wall is a painting of Market Street at night. It's full of lightbulbs, albeit not the ones Frank wants me to find. Although they're powered by electricity, they're built to look like real fire, as if someone came along and lit them all as the sun was setting. These lights are probably turning on right now. How eerie that street must feel at night here. All lit up with only a few souls to enjoy it. A thousand bulbs to every ghost.

As I let my mind wander down Market Street, one of the lights on the poster starts to shine brighter than the others. The magic eye drawing is taking shape. I squint, like Frank did, and at last, there it is. A tiny ball of light, sparkling straight through the painting, the wall, and the entirety of Whirly World. I turn back to Frank who has been patiently waiting for me to get a clue. I point at the wall and smile, and he gives me an affirming nod.

"I see it." I shout, like an elementary student picking up basic math. Spinning giddily back around, I spot a few more lights around me. I can't let my excitement block my ability to sense them. I take a breath and try to figure out exactly what direction I'm facing. The one that first came into focus must be on Market Street.

I point. "That's Beverly, right?"

"Yeah, by the shops. That's the old girl." He moves his finger to the left, around where the security office should be. "And that is?"

"Eddie. Grier. I already met those two, kinda." My eyes keep traveling to the left as another spirit star comes into focus. The one on the far left must be Nuwa Chen, safe inside her garden. But there's someone on the other side of Beverly. Right in the middle of the Palace Theater, if these other lights are shining where I think they are. "On the right, there. That's gotta be Reagan Butler."

Frank nods. "That's her. Keeping that theater spinning."

"On purpose? I'd imagine she'd be far away from that place."

Frank walks back to his metal chair. "Well, it's not that easy. There's something mighty compelling about the locations where we all died. Not much makes sense here, but when we go back there, it almost does. Or at least that's how I see it."

"What about our clothes? I notice you're wearing the same thing you died in."

"Yeah, I think it's the same principle at work. We can take something from a store and put it on if we want, but it just feels more natural to wear what we were wearing when we first showed up."

I look down at my shirt. "So I guess I died in this?"

"It would seem so."

I cross my fingers. "Can we leave?"

"Well, sure. We can go anywhere in Whirly World."

"No, *past* Whirly World. Can we escape? Move on?"

Frank grits his teeth. "Eh." He scratches his neck, thinking. "That's not something I would recommend. It's not possible, kid. Trust me. I've been here a while."

"So we're stuck here," I say, the realization landing hollowly in my stomach.

"Well, we were stuck our entire lives, right? But we made the most of it. You'll learn. This place ain't bad."

I suppose that depends on who you ask. I look back toward the Palace Theater and use my newfound perception to pick out the bright spot that is Reagan's ghost. This time the ability to tune in to the others' lights comes easily, like slipping on 3D goggles. Reagan's death haunts me. I wouldn't wish for any of the fatal accidents that took place here on my worst enemy, but what happened to her was truly unfair. She was responsible for operating the *Rowdy Rivet Review*, Market Street's big show that used to run three times a day. It was a celebration of scantily clad women throughout history. A kid-friendly version, at least. The stage would spin between numbers so a brand-new group of gals, frozen in the next set of poses and costumes, could be slowly turned into view.

One Tuesday in 2009, after the second performance, Reagan was standing somewhere on the edge of the stage when the whole thing began to spin. I have no idea why she didn't just jump out of the way. Maybe she was so used to the feeling of that stage moving that it didn't trigger an alarm in her mind. She would have glided right along with the large wooden beast if it weren't for the negligence of a construction worker whose name is escaping me at the moment. Anyway, it doesn't matter.

The idiot had moved a batch of furniture onto the crack that divided the front part of the stage from the rotating section, in order to clean up a puddle of projectile vomit from one of the younger viewers. He forgot to put the set pieces back in place before activating the stage spin and didn't think to check if anyone else was in the theater with him. When the far wall caught up to the furniture, it turned the pile over like a flood bulldozing a row of houses, and Reagan was caught in the deluge, crushed by a table, a desk, and stack of chairs.

I never saw photos of the scene online because there was nothing to see. By the time the construction worker - Phillips, that was his name, Trent Phillips - by the time he stopped the stage, Reagan was irrecoverable. The entire stage had to be demolished to remove her body from where it had smooshed and spread, like a dead bug under a boot. Including reconstruction, it set the park back $1.2 million. The construction worker was fired, then successfully sued, and then he vanished. Thank goodness social media wasn't around at the time or he would have been burned at the stake. What a moron.

The stage still spins, although it shut down for five long years. Now it has a guardrail in front, only rotates twice each performance, and a safety setting prevents it from being operated at night. There's also a sensor that stops the rotation if anything impacts the side wall, the way a garage door won't close if it detects motion. There are lots of wonderful regulations that make this park safer than it has ever been. But each one of those rules was established the hard way. The earliest rollercoasters in France and Russia didn't add mechanisms to secure a car onto its track until lots of people broke their arms, and sometimes necks, by testing the limits of each ride's painful geometry. I like to think that Reagan's death saved someone's life, but that's poor comfort for that kind of ending.

Below the first string of ghost lights, with Nuwa on the left and Reagan on the right, is obviously Blake. The other stars are barely moving, but Blake's is slowly rotating counterclockwise around the lake. To my far left, just down the mountain, Clarence is right where I left him. Over to my right, behind what I'm guessing is Gabbro Caverns, is Rubén Castillo, right where he should be. But he's not the ghost I'm looking for.

I turn back to Frank. "Where's the kid?"

Frank is sketching something on a large parchment. He's not too focused on it because he turns to me immediately. "Hmm, who?" He takes off his glasses and squints past me.

"When I first got here I saw a little boy." I raise my hand to my stomach. "He's about this tall. Black hair. Ten years old, maybe."

"Oh." Frank leans back in his chair. "That's Nolan. He's nine. Guess you never heard about him."

Excuse me? I mentally prepare myself to learn something about Whirly World that I was not previously aware of. This does not happen often. "No, I certainly did not." I walk over to Frank's desk and perk up my ears. A child died here, and I *never heard about it*? What a terrible thought. Children should be protected at all costs.

"Nolan," Frank begins, and then pauses for effect. "Nolan's lungs didn't work right. He lived two years longer than his parents thought he would. He loved this place like you wouldn't believe, and his parents would take him here as often as they could, between medical treatments and the like. Eventually, when it was clear he wasn't improving, they were here nearly every day. He died in two-thousand and six while watching a fireworks show. Isn't that sweet?"

Are you kidding me? "Hell no. That's awful."

Frank shrugs. "Really? I don't know. I guess when you've been dead as long as I have, you feel how inevitable it is that we're all gonna go sometime. Some people get crushed by furniture, or rollercoaster tracks, and some people watch the night become nothing but color."

"I thought I knew everything about this place. Certainly, everyone that died here. How did the park keep that under wraps?"

"Well, the park didn't have to, really. His parents got him to the medic without making much of a fuss, but Beverly says he had already passed by that point. With everything going on, his folks somehow had the fortitude to not make a scene. Maybe they knew he was close. Maybe this was how they hoped he'd go. I can't say what it takes to do that. I never had kids. Never wanted any."

"So, Beverly told you about this?"

"Yeah, when she showed up. I certainly don't want anyone else to die in this park if they don't have to, but it sure is nice to find out what's going on in the world every time someone does. Someone that's happy to talk about it, at least."

I look back through the wall, expecting to see Nolan's little light shining from where I found him, but there's nothing there. "Then where is he? Why can't I see him?"

Frank chuckles. "Oh, right. Nolan's a hard one to pin down. I can barely track him half the time. He scampers around too fast."

That reminds me of another burning question. "When I saw him earlier, he disappeared through a doorway I couldn't see. How'd that happen? How does it work when we see each other?"

Frank scratches his stubble. "Hmm. It's a mix of things. It depends on how well you know a person. Sometimes people don't want to be seen. Sometimes a person doesn't realize how far they've moved between themselves and another person. I think the reason you can see the room we're in right now is because I want to share it with you. And you want to see it too." Frank waves a hand behind him, gesturing to a million little details that make up this wonderful space. At the end of Frank's metal desk is a short stairway I didn't notice before.

When I see the door it leads to, I realize where we are in the mountain. Next door, if left unchanged, is the boarding queue for Timber Tracks. The end of the line and the start of the ride.

I run up the short steps to the door and check the doorknob. It's open. I glance back at Frank and he gives me a small nod. He's really letting me go everywhere. Well, it's not like I can break anything, right? I open the door. Frank has left the boarding area just like I remember it. Thick wooden beams burrow into the sloped mountain wall. Long cables descending from the rocky ceiling hold metal light fixtures painted to look rusty. I have seen this room in various levels of darkness, with all sorts of different sized groups, and even a few times with just a handful of employees waiting to send off the last train of the day. But I have never seen it looking like this. Even for an enthusiast like me, the emptiness is unsettling.

I miss the noise. The rumbling of the ride, the windy sound effects on loop, the creaking of the old metal building, the chatter of families and friends. Instead, it sounds like I'm in space, completely devoid of movement or mirth, like I stepped into a snapshot of this area instead of the actual place. Stranger still, there is no train loaded on the track for anyone to board. The track is empty, and the black void riders usually vanish into looks impossibly dark.

"Yeah, not much to do in here," Frank says from the door behind me. "Listen," he begins.

I think he's about to tell me a story but now that I'm a few feet from one of my favorite rides in the world I can't wait for him to finish it. I can ride this, or at least walk the track, as many times as I want. The dream.

I turn around and gesture to the track like I'm giving it away on *The Price is Right*. "Well, there is one thing I could do." After the day I've had, I could definitely go for clouds of dynamite smoke and a twenty-foot drop.

As I step to the edge of the platform, Frank's eyes widen. His body quivers like a bomb just went off. He raises one hand toward me and shouts. I don't have time to be alarmed by this gesture because a sharp jolt pulls at my midsection and my feet fly off the ground. Frank and the light of the landing area spiral into darkness before me.

Every sense I have is assaulted with information. Wind batters my cheeks. A crackling groan pushes my ears open. Sulfur scrapes at the inside of my nostrils. I can't close my eyes but something in the air makes it impossible to see. My legs and arms flail as I impulsively grab and kick for anything to hold onto. The first thought I can manage beyond abject terror is that I've simply boarded Timber Tracks. Buy the ticket, take the ride.

But there's no car. No track. No mountain. Anything I attempt to see feels miles away. My head is full of sound, but I can't tell where any of the roar is coming from. It's like it's all around me and inside my body all at once. Then something below comes into focus. Oh crud, it's lava. Some kind of fire river that winds through whatever ground my body is soaring over. Through. Whatever. It's made of something scalding because I can feel the waves of heat blast against my skin. The coldness inside of me pushes against it.

I'm spinning around like one of Timber Tracks' trains. Above me, the fire shines across the bottom of a sea of leathery wings. Bats, with monstrous wingspans flap across what should be the ceiling. Beyond them are patches of light I can't identify. Maybe they're stars. Maybe they're tiny cracks in the rock. I'm pulled upward. The void closes in around me.

I'm whirling through a cavern lined with torches. I'm not sure why, but I reach out for one. My hand somehow locks around a metal handle and pulls one free. I hold it away from me, astonished that my brain is trying to process what era it's from. Medieval? Gold rush? Is this real burning fire or something in the park tied to a jet that endlessly pumps out fuel? How is this thing still lit even though it feels like I'm flying at a hundred miles per hour?

Ahead, it looks like I'm finally catching up to an actual track. Some kind of thread appears that winds outward into the darkness. It might be a cable. Something attached to a life preserver. Maybe I should grab this too. My torch hand is closest. The sparks from the end of the torch inflame the edge of what now appears to be a massive piece of string. It erupts in a ball of yellow sparks that races along the string, turning the bits behind into ash.

This strand leads into a combustible web of dynamite that zigzags directly in front of me. The first stick blows, shattering the blocks of rock around me. Pebbles collide with other explosives as they pop. They go off like fireworks, turning the black background into a kaleidoscope of flame. Just when I think I've lost understanding of up and down, my body tells me that I have started to plummet.

Something solid emerges from the nothingness below. One boulder, then another. Rows of them. I try to control my descent but something's pulling me where it wants to. Walls of rock are headed toward my face and there's no way to avoid the collision. I let go of the torch and put both hands in front of me as if that'll do a damn thing. The first rock finds me.

WHAM. By the time I process the fact that I didn't really feel that crash, here comes the next one. WHAM. Again, no pain, just a crunching sensation against my elbows and knees. I brace for a third in the fetal position. WHAM. Pieces of each boulder are blasted into powder. It puffs through the air in dust clouds I can feel passing through my chest. Then, an opening.

I trip over the crest of a landslide spilling into infinity. A tidal wave of jagged brimstone. Part of me feels like this nightmare is supposed to thrill me like another rollercoaster. A larger part feels like I've made a terrible mistake. If the dead can die a second time, this might be it. I try to slide along the rumbling current of rock but another shift in gravity throws me back into the air. I think I can see a length of metal track, just like the real ride, but it's spinning through space like me. I can't believe I haven't thrown up a hundred times.

A new light appears on a horizon of chalky clouds. A crescent shape, maybe a moon. The track beside me is pulled toward it. It looks like someone punched a hole in this celestial volcano and the real world is shining through. The track snaps into it like a puzzle piece, and suddenly it feels like exactly where all of this has been leading to. The light crashes into me at full force.

I hit the platform and skid along the floor in front of Frank, who hasn't moved. Once I stop screaming, the silence of the boarding area returns to my ears. If it weren't for my insides racing, because that was completely batshit crazy, it's like none of it ever happened. Like I temporarily lost my wits but now I'm back. No harm done.

"Yeah," Frank says, apologetically. "I should put up a warning sign or something."

Chapter 7

WW

Palace Theater

"What was that!?" I scream into the cold floor. I push myself up off the ground and shake off whatever I just survived.

"That?" Frank says, pointing into the darkness. "That was Timber Tracks. Or whatever it's turned into. If you're not ready for how crazy this place gets, don't go stepping somewhere without asking about it."

"Oh, I'm sorry." I shout as soon as I can stand up straight. "I didn't realize that cozy rollercoaster had turned into a car crash."

"Hmm, that's one way to put it, I guess."

I walk toward him, staying a good number of paces away from the track. "Well. How would you put it?"

Frank puts his hands in his pockets. He looks like he's enjoying my shattered nerves. "Well, and this is just a guess, mind you. If you ask me, these rides bring their riders to the apex of human emotion. They make a person the most excited they can get, without having to do anything but sit in a chair. Maybe hold on to a bar or something." Frank walks past me and gestures from the floor up to the ceiling. "This waiting area? Not the same. It's dull. Sedentary. It's everything you expect it to be so that's what it is."

Frank can see me trying to catch up to this line of thinking, so he continues. "Add to that the frequency at which this baby churns out all that emotion. About two thousand people ride this sucker every hour. So that's twenty-four thousand people a day on average.

Hypothetically, if one person walking around a house for half their life generates enough spiritual mojo to project them doing so into the world of the living, then eight million people screaming through this thing a year will generate, I don't know, whatever the heck is going on in that mountain coaster."

I suddenly process a scary thought. "Wait, can the living see us? Do we, uh, haunt this place when we're just walking around?"

"No way to tell. I can't see the living, so I wouldn't even know it if they were reacting to my presence. And believe me, I've tried."

I look back to the empty entrance of Timber Tracks. "But there's not even a train on the track," I point out.

"No, of course not," Frank suggests, like it's obvious. "No need for it. You've got to stop thinking about yourself like you're a body that would need such a thing. The way you move, the way you see the world around you, all that stuff is an old habit, so to speak."

"Okay, I think I'm getting it," I tell Frank, although I'm really not. Frank's on to something, but clearly there's a set of rules that governs this place. Otherwise none of us could see each other or stand on what's supposed to be solid ground. "But I thought ghosts could walk through walls and stuff?"

"Oh, really?" Frank answers, sarcastically. "Is that what ghosts can do? Look, I've been trying to figure this cockamamie park out for over two decades and you probably have as many answers as I do. Sometimes we can do stuff that defies explanation, and sometimes this place prevents us from doing something that it feels like we should be able to do."

"Like leave?" It's the only thing I really want to do and a problem none of the people I've met here seem interested in solving. Maybe they've just given up. My question produces an expression on Frank's face that says as much.

"I don't think there's anywhere else to go, kid. I think this is it. And in my opinion, we're lucky to have it. I always figured everything would go black when I bought the farm. Boom. No lights. No angels. No nothin'. But here we are. Still talking, making friends." At this he gives me a goofy smile.

I guess that kind of acceptance comes with time. "I don't know," I say, politely. I really want to tell him that I don't believe that for a second. That I feel, in my gut, we've been tricked somehow. But he seems to be at peace with his assumptions. I don't have the heart to argue with him and, after flying uncontrollably through Catlin Peak, I don't have the energy either. I'll give him the benefit of doubt. I put my hands out as if blueprints to the park are in front of me on a table.

"What you're saying is," I start, like a student addressing his professor, "we can all occupy the same space, but that doesn't mean we are all looking at the same thing. We can show each other the things we're looking at, but only if we both agree on it."

Frank furrows his brow but then slowly nods in assent.

"And the ground is only here because of the same reason. It's something we all believe and agree upon, therefore it appears real and holds us in like it used to." I hop up and down on the paved floor. "So if I wanted to—"

On the third hop my feet drift through the floor. Frank reaches out for me again, like he did when Timber Tracks sucked me in, like a father watching a small child, just out of reach, trip and fall. But by the time I recognize his futile gesture my face has slipped through the floor. Whatever my stomach has become, lurches. I see a flurry of dark shapes. Losing my grip on the ground means I'm looking at whatever was underneath us, but it's so close to my eyeballs I can't make out any of it.

I get an impulse to grab on to something. My nerves clench as they decide when to try and stop my descent. Then I get a stronger urge not to become trapped in a solid structure like the tip of a nail, so I let myself keep dropping down, down, down. One of the only things scarier than death. Confinement. Maybe, in a few minutes, I'll pop out into a cave closer to the earth's core. Somewhere I can spend my forever days in complete darkness. Hopefully I can land on its rocky floor with a bit more confidence and control. Why did I have to question the very thing keeping me above ground? *Stop thinking so much, Jason, and accept what's going on.*

The gray and brown blur becomes blinding light and I recognize the sweet liberation of open air. I've dropped into a tunnel. Before I let myself wonder where I am my brain brings in the thought of solid ground like it's an absolute, necessary truth. Of course the ground is real. Why wouldn't it be? What kind of moron would think otherwise? Who wants to fall forever?

My feet hit the bottom of the tunnel. I stop in place, knees bent, arms outstretched. Part of me doesn't want to move another inch, but I pull myself up straight and keep the rest of my thoughts on the practicality of permanent objects. Ground is great. Hooray for the ground.

When my eyes adjust to the bright fluorescent glare I recognize where I am. I'm frazzled from the four-story inner-earth plunge, but also giddy at this unexpected opportunity. Like most of Whirly World's off-limits locations, I've seen photographs and footage of the underground tunnel system but few have ever walked its narrow halls. And here I am.

Some of the tunnels were initially dug by the people that worked in the actual mines eighty years before the park was built. When designers discovered there was infrastructure already in place for an underground system that could shuttle trucks delivering supplies and employees dodging the busy crowds, they poured concrete into two of the long, crisscrossing tunnels. Ready-made underground roads to preserve the theme-park "magic."

If you didn't know what they were, you'd dismiss them as vehicle routes through a power plant, or the mountain interior of an interstate. But once you realize there's a rollicking frontier above full of high-powered amusements, the long, hollow gaps seem impressive and mysterious. Thank goodness I dropped into the northwest corner of this system or the first tunnel I might have found would have been full of whatever the center of the Earth is made of.

It's also fortunate that the lights are on, otherwise my chances of getting out of here would be slim. If memory serves, it's drawn out in a near perfect X of which I'm at the top left. I'm looking down a long hallway, facing southeast. That means the long hallway ahead of me goes away from where I want to go, and the short hallway behind me should take me back upstairs to Frank. I expect him to glide down after me, but I'm still alone.

It's frigid down here. The coldness I keep feeling cuts deeper. I feel it in my ghostly bones, which is strange, because I'd always thought ghosts made things chilly, not the other way around. The air here is freezing and there's no escaping it. I should probably get out of here as soon as possible.

I find the exit at last, tucked out of sight into a corner. It's closed. I try the doorknob. It's locked. I'm pretty sure that's a fire code violation. And there's no keyhole on the door. No keypad to the side. Weird.

Then I notice the sign. It does not say Employees Only. There's no English at all. Instead, there's a symbol on the metal plate. A circle within a circle. There are four letters along the border: M, B, C, and S. Inside the middle circle is a mess of straight and squiggly lines. It looks like a government logo, something you'd print on paper money or coins. It's a perfect print, maybe stained with ink or a brand. It's red and crusted. I've never seen this door before, in person or in pictures, so I have no idea if this exists in the real Whirly World. The hairs rise up on my arms. I don't know what it means, and I don't like it.

I step away from the door reflexively. Yes, it's unnerving but it repulses me *physically*. The door couldn't be pushing me further away if it were alive and yelling at me. Still, I can't stop staring at it. Compared to Frank's whimsical control room, which had its own afterlife customizations but still belonged in the park, this door feels *wrong*. I decide to make tracks in the opposite direction.

It takes twenty-one minutes to walk from the top of Catlin Peak to the front gate on Market Street (I've timed it), and this tunnel cuts right through the park at an even elevation. The simple floor plan should let me find another open door without too much trouble. As I walk south-ish and approach the center of the X-shaped hallway, I instinctively think to go right, toward the entrance to Whirly World.

A sound stops me from walking any further. A rhythmic clanging, like a blacksmith fashioning a sword or a suit of armor. It's coming from behind me, to the north. So much of this park has felt empty, but now it definitely feels like someone's down here with me. The spooky thing is I can see in each of this tunnel's four directions, and I'm clearly the only one traveling through its linear, sterile passageways. It sounds like the ticking of a slow, giant clock. From the center hub, the sound seems to be coming from everywhere and nowhere, like maybe it's part of some hidden machine that helps keep the park up and running. Like a giant gear in perpetual motion. It's like something is in the walls, trying to get at me. I push on, heading south.

Mercifully, the bottom left door of the X is open. A dull, gray, industrial staircase waits for me inside. On the left side of the wall, running along with the stairs as they wind up, is a string of posters. Some of them are safety notices, or policy updates for the staff, or - and this is mostly why I stop - vintage art prints. Some that I've never seen. There's a poster of Florence Falls that looks like it's from the 80s, and a watercolor of the southern tip of Shaley Flats that was obliterated to make way for Kingston's Circus. They're beautifully tattered at the edges where the glue still holds, like someone designed them that way and this staircase is some kind of queue for a ride above. I think back to the feeling of contentment I had on the bench at Catlin Peak. I feel strangely privileged to be in this stairwell right now, taking in a bit of scenery money just can't buy at Whirly World.

Even though open air is just above me, my heart wants to stay below and see all the things I've never seen. All the restricted areas. All the smoke and mirrors. Generations of park employees made this place look the way it does. The details, however messy, tell their story. This park has generated some sensational headlines over the years, but my favorite gossip always comes from behind the scenes. The confessions you can't read in a book, magazine, or even a blog. You have to go to the source and catch an employee on a good day.

The door to street level is also open, so it appears my luck is improving. The sun has set, leaving the sky a splash of dark red and purple. One or two stars have come out. The streetlights are illuminated, and I'm momentarily sad that I just missed them flick on. They all spark at the same time, an effect that, while due to the way the power grid is set up and not so park operators could impress anyone, still elicits oohs and aahs when it happens each night.

North is the lake, my spot, and Worley Lodge. The lamps are on inside and it looks as cozy as ever over the waterfront. Then my heart sinks. There's no smoke coming from the chimney. The fireplace has gone out at last. Damn. I wasn't expecting it to, but it's still depressing seeing Worley's presence gone at the center of an empty Whirly World. I try to drain the sad thought from my head as I look at the lights of Market Street.

Just west of the shops is the Palace Theater, its sign immaculate. An homage to the amusement halls dating back a century, the looping letters on the white placard are surrounded by old Edison style bulbs, orange filaments issuing their warm and inviting light across the street below. Sometimes there's a burnt or flickering bulb but here they're all running perfectly in sequence. It always seemed to me like this theater was locked in time, and now it really is. Tons of brick. Lots of entrances and exits. As many lights as you can fit onto the exterior. Early zoos, pleasure gardens, and world fairs all had centerpieces like this grand old theater. That was back when there were no coasters and the only amusement you could find was listening to music or walking around and chatting with friends or strangers. Modern park goers would be so bored.

The front of the Palace Theater was one of the best places to grab a table for lunch, or just escape the hot sun under an umbrella. The tables are gone now, which makes the entrance area feel much larger. After talking with Frank, I wonder if my brain has made this change to the park, or if I'm witnessing the remodeling efforts of another resident ghost. I guess there's no need for a sea of plastic tables for a limited clientele with no real need to eat.

Standing in front of where the Palace Theater tables should be makes me immediately think of April. This is the site of perhaps our worst argument. It was certainly the loudest I ever spoke to her in public, and the biggest fight we had in Whirly World. It was right before we started eating. We were seated at a table just to the left of the theater entrance. April would always try whatever seasonal specials appeared on the menu, and I got what I always got: grilled cheese. Not something you'd find on the kids' menu. The bread was made on-site, a sort of fluffy concoction similar to brioche, but sturdy enough to stand up to the griddle. Then they piled on top grilled onions, a tomato jam, and three kinds of cheese: cheddar, swiss, and brie. A sprinkling of crumbled bacon on top of that, the second slice of bread, and a big fat pickle on top skewered with a toothpick that looks like a miner's ax. My mouth waters.

April had a fondness for gum. A doublemint loyalist. She would chew and chew, working on a piece long after it had lost its flavor. This meant she would dispose of a piece whenever we reached a spot where enjoying it was unsafe or inappropriate. It didn't usually bother me. Wrapping it in a napkin before she gobbled up a hot dog? Fine. Popping it into a trash can before we boarded a ride? No big deal.

But that day she did the absolutely unthinkable. In plain sight, she pulled it from her lips and *stuck it to the bottom of our table*. I was mortified. I said "Are you a child?" and asked her politely to clean it up. She told me "I don't see the issue," which was ridiculous. I could tell she was lying but she just didn't care. I believe she followed up with something like, "Isn't that what they have a maintenance crew for?" The worst part? April never backed down. *I* had to throw away the gum. I brought up the story every time we dined there after the fact, maybe six or seven times, and she never apologized.

Since then I've come to wonder if the move was somehow retaliatory. I vaguely remember having another disagreement, albeit less inflammatory, earlier that day. I have no idea what sparked it, but it was something about "value alignment." The subject is beside the point. She still did something immature and passive aggressive, and for what? The act reminded me that, as much as I thought we knew each other, there were parts of April that still mystified me. I wonder how long we would have stayed together if I hadn't kicked the bucket.

Through the middle entrance I can see the stage. The refreshment counter looks ready to pop some popcorn, and the sconces and chandeliers in the lobby appear to be at their brightest setting. I wished for this so many times, to be able to appreciate a section of this park without anyone standing in the way or distracting my brain with their endless chattering. Well, I got my wish, and it's all too unnatural to enjoy. I guess I favor the nonstop foot traffic more than I thought. There is definitely a puzzle piece missing here.

Despite the eerie silence, I relish the look of the lobby as I walk through it. Every bronze fixture looks like it was polished seconds ago. There are no cobwebs hiding in the corners. The carpet doesn't have moist, matted spots where a janitor just mopped up a kid's spilled drink or barf, or both. If only the architects could see it now.

"Refreshment?" a voice asks. Clarence smiles at me from behind the counter.

I'm not sure if I didn't notice him before or if he wafted in on the wind like the bartender in *The Shining*. Regardless, I'm happy to see him. For a moment I felt alive again.

I walk toward the counter. "No thanks. I was just going to poke my head inside."

"Not here for the show?"

"Oh, is it still running?"

"It's just about to start." Clarence winks.

"Well then, I got here just in time." The popcorn stand, which I swear was empty just seconds ago, is now filled with fluffy morsels of salty goodness. I'm not hungry, I'm not even craving a small snack, but there's always room for popcorn. "One small popcorn, please."

Clarence prepares it with a series of careful and deliberate gestures that make me ache with nostalgia. It was always comforting knowing certain parts of your theme park day would be punctuated by enjoying the perfect treat. Clarence hands me the crinkly bag with a genuine smile. The bag's warmth soaks into my fingers and I'm reminded they've harbored a chill all day that I just can't get rid of.

The popcorn feels real, and it makes this place feel real. I savor every sensation. I bring the bag to my face and let the butter and salt fill my nostrils. I close my eyes and picture the theater full of anxious fans. I pretend to hear the stampede of shoes on the carpet. It's difficult. This place isn't the same, no matter how hard it tries.

I open my eyes and look to Clarence, ready to thank him, but he's gone. I guess he did what he came to do and moved on. I look around the lobby, just in case I missed him walking past me, but he's pulled another disappearing act. David Copperfield, eat your heart out.

I also don't see or hear Reagan anywhere. I have to play this carefully. I don't think Reagan's going to be too happy to hear all the wonderful things I have to say about this park, and I've never been that good at first impressions. Two weeks after Reagan's death, her girlfriend, Tabitha, wrote a scathing letter to the park's administration. It was published online and I must have read it a thousand times.

The beginning of it struck a chord with me. Although the anger I felt couldn't possibly be judged in the same league as what Tabitha was going through, I too was mad that something like this could happen at a park I love so much.

I obviously trust the Skid Greaser with my life every time I go on it, knowing it barely passes its safety review each year. But Reagan was killed by the negligence of another employee and the company he worked for. It strikes at the issues of safety, regulation, and accessibility, the stuff that bloggers like me are supposed to keep people accountable for.

It was the end of the letter that made my eyebrows curl. Tabitha went after the very *idea* of attending a theme park. "Juvenile" was the first word that ticked me off. She was understandably mad that the woman she loved died doing something she didn't want to be doing, but I think it's a stretch to rope in the people being entertained by her efforts. I don't know what Tabitha's favorite thing to do is, but I could equally question its value based on age in another category, and round and round we go.

It's no secret that Reagan Butler hated Whirly World. Even the short article that announced the tragic event in the local newspaper mentioned she "disliked the whole thing, never attending the park on holidays or her days off." Not that I memorized that article. On purpose at least. I'm always hesitant to bring up Whirly World, or any park, to someone I don't know very well. I've met a lot of people that simply can't stand theme parks, and I get it. They can be a bit much.

There's the waiting, the noise, the inability to avoid some of the most annoying people in society, and in the summer the heat can be excruciating. What's really digging into my thoughts as I pass underneath the central chandelier is not just that Reagan died in such an awful way, but that I'm now learning she's been trapped inside of it since 2009. For some a forever park day is Heaven; for Reagan it has to be one of the deepest circles of Hell.

As I enter the auditorium, I imagine her watching this show over and over. Riling up the crowd beforehand and shepherding them out the door after it finished. Right on the border of a circus with a screaming coaster and chuckling clowns. Pure torture.

"Let me guess. You're Jason."

I jump and whirl around. Reagan is seated in the back row. Reclined, really, with her feet up on the seat back in front of her. She's dressed in her red and gold theater uniform, complete with the tiny red hat tilted to one side. I sought to find her here, but seeing Reagan casually killing time in the room that killed her is somber and strange. I keep winding up at Port Juniper. That's probably where I expired. I wonder when that spot will call me back again, summoned by an unseen force.

"Yes," I answer, politely. "How did you—"

"Beverly told me your name," she answers before I can finish. "The old lady gets so worked up whenever someone new comes to town. Has it hit you yet?"

"Hit me?"

"Yeah," Reagan says, like she's beaten me at cards. "That you're stuck here. That this is how you're going to spend the rest of it?"

"Uh, yeah. It's starting to sink in I guess."

"How'd you bite the big one?"

"Actually…" I start, realizing she's the first one here to ask me that today.

"Let me guess," she says, standing. "Attacked by an owl? Gunned down by a crazy cowboy? Poisoned by a plague squirrel?"

I shake my head after each guess.

"No? Well then, my next guess would be crushed. Some giant thing came along and turned you into a pancake. That it?" She crosses into the aisle and walks toward me.

"No," I say, almost apologizing. "I don't know how I died." And I'm realizing, I'd been so taken up by the park itself, I'd forgotten to even ask. Maybe I don't want to know.

"Well, you've got plenty of time to figure it out." She reaches out a hand. "I'm Reagan."

Reagan is tall, maybe five foot, eight inches, with dark brown hair that sweeps the top of her shoulders. She's angular, with a sharp chin and narrow hips, and she moves with a deliberate grace, like someone trained in classical dance. Her eyes are a hazel green, and she has one dimple on her left cheek. She is drop dead gorgeous. More beautiful than any of her photos could capture. The eagerness with which I grab and shake her hand surprises me. If this were a party at someone's apartment, I'd be the last person to make new acquaintances. I guess "Oh, you're dead too" is a decent icebreaker. That and I already feel like I know these people.

"Right, Reagan Butler. I'm familiar with your…" I point to the stage, completely unaware how I plan to finish that sentence.

"Talent for interior decorating?" she says, exercising an impressively morbid wit. "Good, I wasn't looking forward to coughing up that story one more time."

While I have a hundred questions I want to ask her, none of them qualify as polite small talk or something appropriate for an introduction. So instead I look all around me and state something painfully obvious. "This place looks great." *Fascinating, Jason. You should talk about the weather next.* Reagan looks at the theater like she just realized what room she was in.

"Sure," she agrees, politely. "If you're into places with all the lights turned on all the time. I hardly remember what this place used to look like."

"Well, there were always people in it, for starters."

Her eyes pop open. "Oh, that reminds me." Reagan runs past me and up the carpeted steps toward the vacant stage.

I get a jolt of panic watching her race toward the spot where she died, but she passes it without pausing and heads backstage. Then I realize she wants me to follow her.

I last saw the wings of this stage on a tour when I was twelve. That tour stopped visiting this location after Reagan's "accident." Although Whirly World could probably make a bundle running a ghost tour that hits each place where someone croaked, they've always respectfully restrained themselves from doing so. I wonder if that will change in time. I wonder if the spot where I died will one day become a gruesome tourist attraction. I know that, had I not been the one that died, I would have dug for every detail. I can hear tourists taking my sad story back home. "You'll never guess what exclusive attraction I got to enjoy on my vacation. A corpse!"

I expect the backstage area of the Palace Theater to be grand and expanded like Frank's living quarters, but it looks as cramped and uninspired as it was sixteen years ago. Reagan is standing at the control panel. She's turned the key to power the system and is pushing colored buttons. I can feel the guts of this place beneath my feet warming up. This is the first time I've seen someone actually operate something since I got here.

"This stuff still works?" I ask. "You can run it like before?"

Reagan acts like she didn't hear me and continues to work. The biggest red button lights up. Reagan walks over to a large, golden rope hanging in a loop and pulls at one side. The stage's main curtain reveals the first backdrop of *Tomorrow's Promise*, the new big show in the Palace Theater that currently runs three times a day. The show started five years after Reagan died. Beverly or Nuwa must have revealed it to her if she's able to run it here.

Several rows of flat wooden sets show a busy highway, city skyline, grassy hills, and tall mountains. When the show starts, a pair of spotlights in the back make it look like the sun is rising over it all. It's an old-fashioned special effect but still satisfying to watch. I wonder if there will be a band of faceless performers that appear when Reagan snaps her fingers. But there is just lights, flats, and backdrops.

"Do you run this all day?" I ask. "That's gotta get tiring."

"Dear God, no," Reagan says, finally hitting the big red button. "Just for him." She nods past me to the theater.

I turn, expecting to face a packed house, but it still looks empty. Then I see Nolan sitting in the seventh row. He has a chocolate covered ice cream bar in one hand and his eyes are glued to the stage.

Reagan grabs my arm and pulls me toward the backstage wall. "Careful," she jokes. "You don't want to get, you know, smashed to death or whatever."

The audio recording begins, and the show is underway. It's made to look like a big crew is hustling to make the sets move, and there definitely used to be in the sixties and seventies, but it's all automated now. There are no performers, but Nolan's eyes dart back and forth, as if the show is as real to him as it ever was. I'm jealous.

"You start this show just for Nolan?" I ask.

"Every night. He never misses it. I wish I had a tenth of that kid's love for this place. It would make eternity easier to handle."

As long as the show is running, I'm going to sit in the audience. Even if most of it isn't there. I gesture to the seats.

Reagan nods. "Be my guest."

I take a gamble and walk back to Nolan's row. He's smiling. I wonder if he'll tolerate me more if he's in a better mood. He doesn't take his eyes off the stage as I shuffle down the line of red fabric and gold-painted metal. I pick a spot three seats away from him. Close enough to have a conversation, but far enough not to be distracting.

On stage a set of doors, painted to simulate the back of a magnificent ballroom, open wide to reveal another set of painted flats, this time faking a garden view and its surrounding forest. Usually, a new batch of dancers hops in through the door, but the stage is empty. Still, Nolan's eyes move back and forth, following what the show is supposed to be doing. I think back to what Frank said. *I want to share it with you. And you want to see it too.*

I try to see what Nolan sees. Instead of accepting the empty stage, I try to mentally fill it from side to side with performers. At this point in the show four pairs of swing dancers spin through a group of cowboys and girls lining up for a hoedown. My mind can understand they're supposed to be there, but all my eyeballs pick up are the lights and sets. I remember how the more I lost my patience with seeing the ghosts from Timber Tracks, the harder it became. I've never been patient when it comes to learning new things. I give up too quickly.

What would a nine-year-old think of *Tomorrow's Promise*? I was twenty-one when it premiered. I came to see it with my girlfriend of two months, Wendy Baker, and probably watched her more than the show. I look over at Nolan. I want to raise my enthusiasm to his level, but I can't even fake it. There's too much else going on in my afterlife at the moment. Two walls of fake pipes painted a rusty brown slide in, and there should be a bunch of engineers banging their hammers in the air to the beating drums in the music. So what if there aren't? I can still enjoy this moment with Nolan. Once again, I'm trying too hard.

Then I see something. Clouds of colored wisps that move like spirits, swirling as if keeping up with the choreography. I can't see anyone dancing, but I see the trail they're leaving behind, like they're covered in glitter and throwing it off with each spin. These ghostly projections continue through the next song and the finale. It's fascinating to watch, but the show never completely takes shape. Nolan stands and applauds when the music finishes. I think of the cast taking their bows but whatever phenomena I saw fades into the air.

"How many times have you seen this show?" I ask him.

"I dunno." He turns to face me. "Does it matter?"

"I guess not," I admit. It used to be terribly important, at least to me. I lost count over the years but used to take tremendous pride in telling people, while boarding Timber Tracks, "it's not hyperbole, I have been on this ride over a hundred times." I'm proud of those numbers but they don't add up to much now. If Nolan's been here for seventeen years, with no lines, he's probably passed through Timber Tracks more times than I can comprehend.

"How long have you been here?" I ask him.

He looks confused. "In the theater?"

"No, in the park. Are you gonna do the same stuff tomorrow?" I ask this in a tone that sounds patronizing. I don't know why I can't just talk to Nolan like a normal person.

"I dunno," he says again. "Whatever feels like fun."

"That is a wonderful attitude, Nolan. I'm Jason."

"Yeah, I know. I heard people talking about you."

"Oh really. Good things, I hope."

Nolan shrugs. "I dunno."

"Well, Nolan, I had fun watching this. Is it cool if I come back tomorrow?"

Nolan thinks about it. He takes a look around the theater. "Sure." He smiles. Actually, it's more like a smirk, but I'll take it.

"Thanks," I tell him.

"Bye, Reagan!" he yells backstage.

"Bye, Nolan!" Reagan screams back.

Nolan runs out of the theater. After a few steps he becomes nearly invisible. Reagan steps out onto the stage. The lights have dimmed. The curtain lowers behind her.

"That's a nice thing you do for him," I tell her.

"Yeah. What can I say? I'm a saint."

"What do you do when you're not, you know, here?"

"There's not much *to* do. Not everyone spends their days riding rides a hundred times."

I think back to spinning through the fiery chasms of Timber Tracks, wondering if I'd ever touch solid ground again. "Especially when they throw you around like a piece of dust swirling through a vacuum cleaner."

"What are you talking about?" Reagan asks.

"Timber Tracks. What happens when *you* ride it?"

"The mountain coaster? What do you mean what happens? I ride it and it goes whee. What happens when you ride it?"

It would seem my imagination got the better of me. "Nothing." I say, embarrassed. I search for another subject. "If there's only one show a day, what else is there for you?"

"You sure like asking questions."

"Oh, sorry. I like asking employees for their favorites in case there's anything I missed. I might be spending eternity here and I'd like to keep my options open."

"Well, there's not much. Sometimes I go jogging. Sometimes I sunbathe on the roof. Anything to feel remotely normal. Oh, and there's the fireworks at night."

"*Fireworks*?" I exclaim.

Reagan motions for me to be quiet. I almost repeat the question, with less intensity, then realize why that show has gone on. "Rubén handles that, I assume?"

"The one and only," Reagan confirms.

Rubén Castillo died because of a computer glitch. So many fail safes had to be skipped to create such a freak occurrence. One, the computer running the show had to spontaneously restart following an operating system update. Two, the software that operated each show had to launch automatically without any prompt from a user. And three, a glitch within said software had to launch not just one, but every single explosive in the sequence all at once.

Rubén was the first employee to die because something electronic in the park malfunctioned, no user error involved. He had been working at Whirly World ever since he graduated college and designed the nightly show for six years. He was responsible for incorporating pop music into the show instead of the outdated, patriotic cheesiness that ran since the park's opening. One time, before he left for vacation, Rubén almost got fired for blasting Hendrix's version of the national anthem, which apparently matched the show quite well. Sadly, no recording of it exists online. If only he'd been designing it in the era of smartphones and YouTube.

"Well, that's almost everyone then," I realize out loud.

Reagan looks at me, confused.

"I've almost met everyone here."

Reagan smiles and tries to look impressed.

"Wow, congrats," she says, eyes wide. "Get autographs?"

"Ha, ha." I return her sarcasm with equal measure. "Everyone but Josie's."

"Oh, totally. Good luck with that."

"Why? Is she not here?"

"No, she's here. She, like Ms. Chen, chooses not to spend her days with the rest of us ghosties. And, you know what? I don't blame either of them."

"And how does Josie manage that?"

"Easy. Josie can fly."

Chapter 8

WW

Fireworks

I sprint outside the front doors of the Palace Theater and look up into the night sky. Staring toward the stars the way Frank taught me reveals the last ball of light I've been looking for. What I assume is the spirit of Josie Bean, Timber Track's first victim, is circling above like a seagull coasting on an ocean breeze. No wonder I couldn't see her before. I didn't look up.

Frank took her death to heart but, if you ask me, Josie's to blame for what happened. According to her friends, she wiggled free of the ride's restraints, then flew from the car when there was nothing to hold her down. Why would someone do such a thing?

"Wonderful, isn't she?" Beverly says, stepping out of the shadows. She looks up at the sky, beaming like a mother watching her daughter in a school play. Her blue gray hair wisps around her kind face, making her look even more ethereal than usual.

I look up at Josie. "She's something. How is she doing that?"

"If I knew I'd be up there with her."

"Are you here for the fireworks show?"

"Of course. I wouldn't miss it."

"I didn't think such a thing was possible," I admit. "Fireworks, or the show at the Palace. I thought this place," I say, gesturing at the park around us, "was just a memory."

"There's a lot more happening here than you realize, Jason."

Beverly walks over to me and gives me a thoughtful stare. "How are you holding up, dear?"

"Who, me?" I ask, pretending everything is okay. "Fine, all things considered." Beverly's stare continues, unconvinced. She's intense, but I guess I was too the last time we spoke. "Beverly, I want to apologize for the way I acted this morning. I just couldn't believe what was happening. Truth is, I'm still having trouble accepting it."

"No one can truly 'accept it' on their first day, sweetheart. I didn't even leave the bathroom, the place of my passing, until the following night when I heard the fireworks. When I emerged, I walked to the lake. There I met Reagan, and Frank, and Rubén, and Blake." She looks at Buckthorn, to the east. "Later that night I visited the chapel, St. Charles, and I prayed for guidance." Beverly takes a deep breath and her chest swells. "I was instantly filled with gratitude. I realized that I had left my world behind. That was a simple fact. But it was also true that death was no more. 'Neither shall there be mourning, nor crying, nor pain anymore, for the former things have passed away.'"

"I don't know if praying will give me the answers I'm looking for," I mutter.

"It takes time." She puts a hand on my arm.

The gesture is soothing. For a moment, I stop feeling like I'm an insect trapped in a jar. It feels like I'm just at the park, talking to a friendly employee while I wait for the big show in the sky. I feel her friendliness rush through me.

I crook my elbow like I'm ushering her to a dance floor. "Well, time is all we have now."

She smiles and accepts. The two of us stroll, arm in arm, up Market Street.

Beverly inhales the night air. "Oh, there's so much more, Jason. We've each been given a tremendous gift. You'll soon come to realize yours. What He expects of you."

I'm trying to be respectful, but I can't help but feel like I'm losing her whenever she expresses her faith. Then again, I can't claim to have all the answers. "Is this what you expected?" I ask, instantly afraid that I've offended her in some way. It's too late to stop now. "Did you ever think you'd wind up here in the end?"

"When I walked the Earth I followed His word, but I never knew where it was going to take me. The good book says 'In my father's house are many rooms' and so I hold on to where I am until another door opens."

"I love that, Beverly. You've got a handle on this place, huh?"

"I'm sorry?" She scrunches the wrinkles on her forehead.

"You seem to understand what's going on here," I clarify. "You seem calm."

It's clear Beverly isn't sure whether to take that as a compliment or not, so instead she graces me with another tender smile. We've reached Port Juniper.

My spot. Hello, again.

"I'll leave you here, Madame," I say, as gentlemanly as I can. I gesture to Beverly as if expecting her to step gracefully out of a gilded carriage. She smiles, then looks bemused again.

"You're not watching the show tonight?"

"Oh, hell yeah. I mean, *yes*." I stammer, just catching myself before I blaspheme even more. "I'm going to say hello to Rubén."

"That's good," Beverly says, her smile coming back. "You should meet everyone. 'Let each one of you speak the truth with his neighbor, for we are members of one another.'"

I smile and nod, then turn to walk away before my inner skeptic makes another appearance. I spot Clarence, with his cart drawn up to the fence, like before.

"Anything before the show?" he asks.

I see an orange creamsicle in his hand. I could totally go for an orange creamsicle right now. Yes, Clarence. Good idea. "Yes, of course," I tell him, and reach for the popsicle.

Clarence gives me a grin that, like Beverly's hand on my arm, fills me with warmth, making this hollow place feel whole for a second. He hands me the treat like it's exactly what he wants to be doing at this moment, and for eternity. I open it at once, remove a third of it in one bite, thank Clarence, and walk on.

Whirly World makes a lot of their frozen desserts, but not creamsicles. These are bought in a factory. Delicious, but not as fresh or rich as the homemade stuff. Still, this creamsicle is incredible. The outer shell is all crumbly and the inside has just the right amount of softness. I can't tell if Clarence did something special to it, or this is just how things taste here. I didn't need food. I haven't been hungry all day. I just craved it. And, holy cow, I'm glad I did. For the first time today, I wonder if maybe this really is Heaven. When I finish it I drop the orange-coated stick into the nearest trash can.

The quickest way to get to where Rubén is likely setting up is the weirdest street in the whole park. The west road away from Gizzard Lake splits in three. North takes you to an expansive desert, south takes you to a circus, and the central road runs through these two themes that have nothing to do with each other.

The greatest parks can go to extremes when it comes to placing one area against another, thematically speaking. The reason I cringe looking at Kingston's Circus is not that I don't like circuses (clowns don't even bother me, honest), it's that the tented monstrosity looks like it crashed into the park unexpectedly. Like a rift appeared to another dimension and something pushed a giant big top through it. When you're on this center road with no name, you look right and it's like you're in the wildest parts of Arizona. Snakes, tumbleweeds, cacti, and a couple of trains chugging through. You look left and see an assault of red and white patterns. Ugh.

I plan to trespass a little bit, which I'm looking forward to. I could wind around the path under the Hooper Looper that leads to the staff exit, but it'd be quicker to hop the fence around Shaley Flats and walk across the sand. I guess it's not trespassing in this place since it's my home now; I'm just walking from one spot to another.

I think it's a ten-foot drop behind Gangway Grotto but falling doesn't seem to be a problem here. If I understand the layout of the employee break area, Rubén should be just a few staircases away. If he's permitted to personally launch fireworks in this version of Whirly World, instead of with a computer program, I imagine I'll find Rubén in a pretty good mood. A grieving friend told the papers that when Rubén launched his first explosive at the age of nine, he knew he'd never want to do anything else ever again.

When I was a kid, the fireworks looked so far away that I couldn't figure out where they were fired from. It wasn't until I happened to catch the show while riding Gangway Grotto that I saw the trails shooting up over the caverns. Grotto is an excellent ride to watch the show from, but you have to time it right. Get aboard too late and the fireworks will explode after the train has already gone underground (For this and more best places to view fireworks, consult one of my top ten favorite parks blog posts, called Most Bang For Your Buck).

Once you get completely backstage, behind all the walls and skyward façades, the employee area is sorrowfully bland. Maybe it was designed as a respite from the cacophony of a theme park in full operation, but the place where workers can get a meal and store their stuff has about as much character as an oil refinery.

After walking down the wrong puke green hallway twice I finally find the right staircase. I know I'm getting closer because I can hear Rubén humming, what I assume is a guitar solo, to himself. I reach the top of the building and step over a system of wires.

"Careful, buddy," Rubén warns me without looking up.

"Sorry, I didn't mean to sneak up on you. I'm Jason."

Rubén pulls himself away from his work and looks me over. He looks like a roadie for Megadeth. Tight black jeans, white shirt, brown leather vest. His mustache is puffed up into an impressive handlebar, and his curly, ear-length black hair falls down around his eyes. He pushes it back with one hand. "Nice to meet you, Jason," Rubén says, courteously. "Sorry you died, man."

"Oh, no worries. Dying gave me a chance to meet the infamous Rubén Castillo, so it's not a total loss."

He blushes. "Infamous, huh?" he says, smirking. "I like that. Infamous, ha."

"I was too young to see any of your shows, but I heard from everyone that they were amazing."

"Oh yeah?" he says, standing up from his work. "You a big fan of the park?" I figure I might unnerve the guy if I tell him exactly how big of a fan I am. It feels weird to care about such things now that we've all shuffled off this mortal coil, but I'm too afraid to embarrass myself. "I visit every now and then, sure." A *considerable* understatement.

"And you got stuck here, huh? Bummer. It's not often that we get a Blinky that didn't work here. Sorry you didn't die somewhere cool like Gorge or Red Rocks. I wonder if it's possible to float around places like that."

"I'm sorry," I interject. "Blinky?"

"Oh, ha," Rubén chuckles. "You know. The little Pac-Man ghosts. The red one."

"Oh, right." One of the ghosts. I should have known. Nothing ingratiates me to a stranger quicker than a nerdy reference. Especially one that I don't understand right away.

Rubén nods politely then returns to his work.

"I think it's awesome that you still do this," I say.

"Do what?" he replies without looking up.

"The fireworks. I didn't think that would work here."

"Oh, yeah," Rubén says. "Me neither. I didn't even try for a long time. At first I didn't know what the hell was going on, man. Those first couple of years were dark." He shudders.

Of course. I can't imagine what that must have been like for him.

When Rubén showed up it would have just been Eddie and Blake here to keep him company.

"Then Frank showed up," Rubén continues. "He realized we can, you know, change stuff. So I stopped moping around and got back to work. We gotta stay occupied or we'll lose it."

"So, how do you do it? The fireworks, I mean. Where do you get the supplies?"

"They're here every day," he says, gesturing to a pile of explosives. "Whenever I crack open these babies in the afternoon, everything I need is inside. Like magic."

"That's cool." But it's also creepy. A taxi didn't pull up the moment I got the urge to leave this place. Not every wish is granted here. Something or someone does that. "If you can fire these off, then can you blow up other stuff?" I ask.

Rubén looks up at me with a devilish grin. "Why? What did you have in mind?"

I shrug my shoulders and smile. "Just curious. I'm trying to figure this place out."

"There's not much to it, man," Rubén says as he loads a few more rockets into place. "The sun goes up, we do our thing, the sun goes down, rinse and repeat." He stands up and surveys his work, clapping his hands together in satisfaction. "Okay, you better find someplace to watch this thing. It's gonna get really loud right here."

I wouldn't mind feeling the full force of this array launching into the air, but not tonight. I promised Beverly I'd join her, and I'd like to see who else shows up. "Sure thing. Nice to meet you, Rubén."

"Yeah, guy. Sure, sure. Enjoy the show."

Now that I'm more familiar with the northwest backstage area, it takes me half the time to jog back to Gizzard Lake. Beverly sits where I left her. The lights around the middle of the park have dimmed so as not to pull focus from the imminent spectacle above.

Clarence is chatting with Reagan at the west edge of the lake.

She's started on an ice cream cone and is chatting happily with the old man. It's sweet to see, and it gives me a little relief that Reagan isn't having her patience tested all the time. I consider that my teeth will fall out if I keep eating dessert and nothing else, then realize how silly that sounds. With pleasures such as these still at our fingertips, maybe being trapped in Whirly World forever really is the best thing that could have happened to me. The others seem to have grown used to it.

"There he is." Frank rounds the lake to my left, arms in the air. "I was worried about you. How did that fall treat ya? Let me guess, you wound up in the tunnels and couldn't get back up? Classic beginner lesson. Happened to the best of us. And by that I mean, all of us."

"Yeah. Staying on the ground is harder than I thought."

"Ha ha," Reagan says, mockingly.

I look at her to confirm that was directed at me. It was.

Reagan crosses her arms. "What? It's funny. I bet you were really freaked out."

"I'll take your finest frozen lemonade, my good man." Frank says to Clarence, smacking him on the back.

Clarence opens the lid, reaches inside, and procures that exact treat without looking. Almost as if a small person inside the freezer held it up, waiting.

"I couldn't get up at first because that one door was cursed or something," I inform the group thinking of my unscheduled plunge earlier. "There was a weird symbol painted on it. Or burned." I expect the mention of this oddity to draw everyone's attention, but they all continue to enjoy their desserts. "Is that normal?"

Reagan takes a big chunk out of her ice cream cone. "Well, that depends largely on what you consider 'normal,' Jason." She puts a little derogative weight on my name. I start to feel like I'm a fraternity pledge or it's my first day in prison and I'm being hazed. I definitely have a lot to figure out before I take things as casually as the rest of these ghosts.

"I don't know about strange symbols," Frank says, "but I've definitely come across doors here that I couldn't open. I figured for all the things I can tweak in this place it would make sense that there are some places that are off limits."

"That doesn't bother you at all?" I ask.

BOOM. The first firework explodes above our heads. The assembled ghosts hush and our eyes shoot upward. I guess I'll have to ask the group about the symbol later. I hear a triumphant yell from across the lake to the north and see Blake jump up and down in excitement. Another boom, even though I'm expecting it, gives me a jolt so hard it makes my shoulders jump. It sends a dazzling green brocade across half the sky, with yellow sparklers scattering within. Then another boom, yellow and orange. My muscles and ears start to adjust to the powerful display.

A song steals over the loudspeakers that I don't immediately recognize. It's definitely nothing that's been played under a fireworks show here before. A string instrument squeaks out a sustained high note. A viola, or a theremin? As more strings back up the first note, I realize what I'm listening to. It's *Good Night*, by The Beatles. Ringo starts singing and the dazzling show swoons with the campy lullaby.

It's an appropriate pick for the nightly fireworks, which is typically the last show most kids see before they head home. There's no way management could have afforded the royalties to play this song every night back in the land of the living. I guess petty things like music rights don't matter when only the dead are around to listen.

Similar to whatever Clarence did to make that creamsicle dance on my taste buds, Rubén is pulling out all the stops. The array is mesmerizing. Each time one of the rockets erupts it seems to splinter off into a chain reaction, then another. I'm starting to lose track of which cluster of lights are coming from which rocket. It's common to see fireworks that explode into the shape of a familiar image, but these are animating in ways I didn't know were possible.

Green sparkles create the illusion of a forest, and somehow Rubén makes the leaves sway. A ring appears, which is suddenly covered in fire, before a horse leaps through it. A train exits a tunnel in a blaze of red bursts. A stack of cards shuffles and deals itself. A line of can-can dancers locks arms and kicks. Two cowboys are locked in a shootout, each bullet followed by a glistening silver trail. I can feel something inside of me lift each time I see a rocket sail into position, ready to burst and add another splash to the tidal wave of colors. Ringo hums and the violins bounce on playful scales. I notice these beats are flashing in the background, audio waveforms pulsing with the tempo, another layer of light against the stars.

Each cluster seems closer than the show usually is. I wonder what the minimum safe distance is between a sea of smiling families and deadly explosives playfully being tossed above their flammable heads. Then I reflect that safety isn't a factor now. Each color ricochets around Linden Forest, coating the branches in a glow that vanishes seconds before being replaced by another. I can feel each explosion as a rumble that shakes not just my form, but something deeper and more essential.

One of the rockets that has yet to burst is now looping around the general area of the show. Then it clicks. That's not a firework. That's Josie. She's descended so much that I can clearly see she's extended her arms outward and is spinning like a corkscrew. She's unafraid of the chaos up there, but then I can't imagine what a person like that *would* be afraid of. Another pop and the sky turns into Nellie's Saloon. Josie soars through its bright red doors.

As I look down at the enraptured faces of my newfound friends, my eyeline meets Sunburst Gardens, and I see Nuwa leaning against the metal railing on the other side of the road. She's not quite blissful, like the others, but appears relaxed. She's still dressed in her work uniform. Heavy gloves are tucked into her large, leather belt. She holds a wide, circular hat in her hands, and as I watch, she reaches up to release the tight knot of hair from the back of her head. It flows over her shoulders like black vines, dappled by the lights above. It isn't until the next loud explosion that I realize I've been staring and pull my gaze back to the show.

I wonder what Eddie thinks of all this. I stroll over to the corner of Market Street. I've never seen each firework bounce light off the road like this. I'm so used to standing on this street when it's flooded with park goers. I can almost picture them now, blocking the view, their bodies soaking up all the flashing hues.

By the entrance, gazing up at the brilliant night sky, Eddie looks much happier now. He sways back and forth slightly to the song. In his calmer state, I'm tempted to re-introduce myself, but I can't bother anyone now. While the brilliant spectacle illuminates the sky, everyone here seems perfectly content. Even with the strangeness that has irrefutably taken over my existence, I'm feeling pretty good, too.

I don't see Nolan anywhere, which seems at odds with what little I know of him. My confusion fades as I spot him on the rooftop of the Calliope Arcade. He's leaning against the edge of the building, arms extending, pushing himself up as close to the fireworks as possible. His face is frozen in a beaming smile. His head rocks side to side as he follows each of the show's twists and turns.

His level of happiness makes my insides swell. He's enjoying this more than all of us combined. I don't know how he managed. Here I am, barely coming to terms with what's happened to me today, or whenever it was when I died, and I'm thirty-three. And there's Nolan, robbed of his life so young, trapped in Whirly World for well over a decade, watching one of potentially thousands of fireworks shows since he arrived. But he looks like this one is his first. One of the most uplifting things to see in a theme park, or concert, or trip to the museum, is a person you don't know who loves it just as much as you do. Maybe more.

At this moment, everyone seems to be genuinely happy. They all have dramatically different ways of dealing with being here, day after day, but this show seems like the thing all of them agree on. I would bet money that none of them knows what month, or even day of the week it is, but then I don't either. All we know is, in Ringo's words, "It's time to say good night."

I always get sad when a fireworks show ends. They have big final acts but the last hurrah bums me out because I know everything is about to get normal again, and the fun of the day is done. I wouldn't be surprised if Rubén kept this going all night, but the commotion above is clearly building to a finale. A row of battleships blast each other upon a rough sea, azure cascades dripping down to dapple the surface of the lake. Through the chaos emerges Rubén's face, smiling, shining, and gigantic against the darkening blue. As the caricature winks, a barrage of what must be a hundred different rockets spill out into the smoky sky. All sense of what blast or glow comes from where is gone. The final explosion crackles to silence, and after an awed moment, we all holler and clap into the dead quiet that remains. I can't wait to see it again. My urge to leave dwindles a little bit.

But just a bit.

Chapter 9

Kingston's Carnival

When our applause dies down, I glimpse Nuwa as she turns back to Sunburst Gardens. Maybe it was just the fading fireworks, but I swear I could see flowers bloom, burst, and close as she stepped between the trees. I look up to check if Nolan's on his rooftop but the boy has departed as well. The front gate is similarly empty as Eddie has adjourned to wherever he spends his time. I turn back to the lake, and everyone else is drifting off in separate directions.

I wave my arm in the air. "Wait. What now?"

Clarence, Beverly, Reagan, Frank, and Blake turn to me.

Beverly is closest. "What do you mean, dear?"

"What does everyone want to do?" The others stare at me like students who got caught not paying attention. "It's just us, no curfew, no closing time. We can do anything we want."

No one matches my enthusiasm.

Then they applaud, looking past me. I turn to see Rubén, hands held high, approaching the lake like a celebrity walking out of the curtain on a late night talk show. I join them in audibly recognizing his achievement. I'm not sure I have adequate words to describe his sensational spectacular.

Reagan talks first. "Jason saw your show and he's bored."

I make a pleading gesture to Rubén but I can tell he knows Reagan is just playing around. Still, I want to be clear. "No, I, Reagan, that's not it. I'm just - inquiring - what everyone usually does each night. Are we supposed to sleep? Or clean the place up? Or what?" I look Rubén in the eyes. "And that was, I'm speechless. How did you do that? That was a sweet show."

"Sweet? I don't know about 'sweet.'" Rubén shrugs his shoulders like a magician pretending it all just "happened."

"No, really." I think of a time period-appropriate superlative. "It was, uh, excellent. How did you get The Beatles to play?"

"Oh, I'm glad you could hear that. It only works if you've heard the song before, so I try to pick songs a lot of people might have heard. Who doesn't know The Beatles, right?"

"I guess. My dad probably hasn't heard *Good Night*."

"Well, he's missing out."

"If you could play any song what would you play?"

"*Rock and Roll* by Zeppelin," Rubén answers. "And I've done it before. I know everyone's favorites." Rubén points at Beverly. "Perry Como." Then to Frank. "Willie Nelson." Then to Blake. "Grateful Dead. And so on."

"You just think about it and it plays?"

"I would call it 'feeling it' rather than 'thinking about it,' but yeah." I take a moment to imagine how that works. "Why? What would you play?"

"Men Without Hats." I answer immediately.

Rubén chuckles. "The Safety Dance guys?"

"Yes. *Exactly*." I always thought that song would work perfectly with a fireworks show. It's exuberant, with precise punctuational beats for each firework. "I mean, with your talent you could spell out each letter and make it spectacular."

Rubén nods sagely. "Noted."

Blake trots over to us from the north side of the lake. "Yo, what are we talking about? Excellent show, by the way." Blake forms both hands into pistols and fires a few fake shots at Rubén, who bows.

Frank slaps his hand on my shoulder and squeezes, hard. "This guy is about to run around the park all night. I'm gonna head home and turn in. Night, folks."

"Wait," I interject. "Aren't you going to eat, or sleep?"

The ghosts look uncomfortable. There is obviously something I'm not getting here and none of them wants to be the one to tell me. As they pass the same pitiful expression back and forth, I realize Clarence and his cart have vanished.

Frank clears his throat. "We, all of us and you, don't have to worry about any of that now. I don't get hungry, personally, but if you want to eat, go into any of the restaurants and grab something. If you want to sleep, close your eyes and you'll still be here in the morning. And if you don't, well, that's all right too." Frank is trying to comfort me, allay any lingering confusion as to how a person is supposed to act here, but it's having the opposite effect.

Ruben approaches me. "I get it, Jason. I felt the same way when I first got here. 'What am I supposed to do, man?'" he shouts into the air, as if asking God. "Am I really just gonna pretend I still work here? Making shows for a pissed off cop and a stoner?" Rubén turns to Blake and raises a hand in acknowledgment. "No offense."

Blake smiles. "None taken, dude."

"Then I realized what I'm supposed to do here," Rubén says, sounding at peace.

"What's that?" I ask, hearing more sadness in my voice than I realize I'm feeling.

Rubén's face brightens. "Blow stuff up."

"Right," I say, looking down.

Rubén gives me a friendly smack on my arm. "No, seriously. The first time I started messing around with powder and fuses again, it all came back to me. I don't care if anyone watches the stuff I make every night. I know it's up there. I do it for me."

I sigh. "I hear what you're saying. Having a hobby in prison makes the days pass easier, but when all is said and done, you're still in prison."

Reagan snorts at this. "To be honest, this place felt like a prison before. At least here I don't have to worry about finding lost kids or my boss telling me to change my attitude."

The group murmurs in agreement. I can't fathom their contentment. It feels like they all just gave up.

"So that's it?" I shout, feeling my mood grating on them. "We just wait around for more people to reach the end of their rope so we can have more people to talk to? That sucks."

Frank waves his hands at me. "Hey, hey. Calm down, buddy. Give it time."

Rubén shrugs. "It's just the way this place works,"

Reagan shakes her head to toss her hair out of her eyes. "Yeah. Complaining about it's not gonna change anything."

"Says the person who complains," I say before I can stop myself.

"*Excuse me*? You've known me for three hours. You're not in a position to bitch about this to any of us. We've been here for years. *Years*."

Frank steps in. "I think what she's trying to say is—"

"I can speak for myself, *Frank*." Frank steps back. "Jason, you're a theme park nerd that got to live in a theme park forever. It is mind-boggling why you have a problem with that."

"Well," I start, before Reagan holds up her hand.

"Never mind. I do not care." Reagan walks away.

Frank claps his hands together. "All right, kids. I'm done." He walks toward Catlin Peak like a coach that just lost the big game.

I'm annoyed that he has nothing more to say about this, given his enthusiasm for solving this park's problems. I don't think I'm asking too much. "Wait, Frank."

He stops.

"About those symbols…"

"Tomorrow. There's always tomorrow, and tomorrow." He leaves.

"And tomorrow," I say to myself. "Creeping in its petty pace."

Beverly approaches me, and her sweet face lightens my mood slightly. "You'll feel better in the morning, Jason. And if you don't, you know where to find me."

She walks back to Market Street. I turn to *Rubén* and see him heading toward the desert. The youthful vibe we all just shared, punctuated by a megaton barrage of sizzling color in the sky, is now reduced to a depressing nothingness. I've never felt more alone.

"Yo!" Blake yells at me.

I jump. I didn't realize he was still here.

"I'm up for whatever, man. I didn't sleep much when I was alive so I'm sure as hell not going to waste time doing it here."

His enthusiasm is exactly what I need right now. "Thanks, Blake. What do you do when you're…" I look at Gizzard Lake, remembering my failed attempt at exploring his underwater fantasy. "Topside, I guess?"

"Everything, my good man." He puts one hand on his chest and swings the other in a circle around him, gesturing to the park in its entirety. "I clash with God's angel and conquer new souls, consuming all that I can."

Did Blake just quote a poem? No, that must have been a song lyric. I'm usually good at identifying stuff like that, if not the song then the band, but the reference eludes me. That's the second time today I've lost the context of a nerdy conversation. I'm losing my touch. "So you've been everywhere? Seen all there is to see?"

Blake puffs up his chest, confidently, but I can tell he's not entirely sure. "I hope so," he exclaims. "Did you have somewhere in mind?"

Do I? I've never pondered a Whirly World sleepover with Blake Owens before. He seemed like such a loose cannon. The opposite of what I'd seek in a friend. Someone that couldn't possibly take a place as heavy as the afterlife seriously. It never occurred to me that his fearlessness is the perfect thing to cut through the mental fog that seems to permeate this place.

"Have you ever been to the parking lot?" I ask.

Blake is pacing back and forth in front of Port Juniper, starting at his feet. He pops his head up, smiles, then looks confused. "Which one? The one here?"

"Yes," I answer, my patience tested. "The one here. The one down there." I point down Market Street, with its thousands of lightbulbs still lit.

Blake moans. "Eh, once or twice, I guess. It's not that interesting. Just a bunch of spaces that go on forever. A few cars that you can't even break into. Plus you have to get past Eddie which can be a pain."

"Yeah, that's what I saw. But I also met someone. Kingston."

Blake stops walking. His eyes widen. "The circus guy?" he says excitedly, as if referring to a pop star.

"Yeah. The mascot of—"

"That's it. The circus, dude!"

"Yes, the circus 'dude.' That guy. It was weird to—"

"No, I mean we gotta go to the circus. It's the best."

No, Blake. Please. Anywhere but there. I wasn't planning to avoid that place forever, but I'm not keen for a visit on my first day. "The circus is your *favorite*? That kills me."

"My absolute favorite, no joke. It has this whole row of games you can play. Beating my high scores has made many a dull day fly by, believe me. And I'm super curious to see how good you handle them. It's a *right of passage*."

He accentuates those last three words as if they appeared in the air in front of him. He's practically quivering at the chance to get me into the circus. I sigh. "Sure, why not? Lead the way."

Then it hits me. The park broke ground on the circus in 2002, fourteen years after Blake died. How does he know it even exists? I think of what Rubén said, about how he can project the idea of a song, and if the others have heard it in their lifetime, they'll be able to hear it during the fireworks show. Could the circus work like that? He waves me over and I have to jog to follow him down Market Street.

"How long have you been going to the circus?" I ask.

"Ever since the little guy showed up. Nolan. I kept seeing him zip around the place. It was wacko, man. Looked like the twerp was just flying around in thin air. So one time he let me follow him. POW. There it was. Circus Land."

I guess it's like Frank said. The only reason I saw the control room inside Timber Tracks is because he wanted me to. I wonder if I'm making the park appear different for anyone else. Or is that something I have to be conscious of doing?

We turn right at the first road ahead of the park gate. Blake starts singing *Entrance of the Gladiators*, the song most people associate with juggling hoops and clown cars. Thinking about the tune always makes me laugh inside because the original composer wrote it as a military march and didn't secure the rights to it. If only he'd known how many circuses would end up using it to start their shows he could have made a ridiculous amount of royalties.

Blake faces me. "Have you ever been in love?"

This abrupt inquiry stops me in my tracks. "You mean, like, with a person? Sure."

"Did that person love you back?"

"Yeah, I think so. She said so."

"Exactly. That's the problem. How do you really know? How do you know someone really enjoys being around you or they're just being nice because they're nice?"

"Where is this coming from? Were you in love?"

"I was. I still am. But we could never be together."

The thought bums Blake out for a moment, then we round the corner into Kingston's Circus and it's like he's twelve years old all over again. I wish I could share in his affection. This circus is just as harsh on my eyes here as it was in the life I left behind. String lights swoop around the main plaza, harshly illuminating the scene. Large, flat, wooden clowns with red noses, yellow wigs, and rainbow coats rise above the red and white tarp encircling the area, flanked by white statues of horses and elephants standing on their back legs.

A nearby plaster replica of a pipe organ poorly conceals speakers playing the hokey soundtrack that doesn't let up for a second. Other places in the park have collections of themes on loop, pumped into the air from carefully disguised speakers. They're broadcast at a measured volume so they don't overpower the mood. The music here is inescapable.

But Blake, God love him, is in Heaven. He's running the perimeter of the plaza, arms spread wide like an airplane. It's like he's showing me just how fun this place can be.

The carnival is so audibly rowdy, and Blake's energy is so distracting, that it takes a minute before I realize we're not alone. Someone is waiting by the first game, a milk jug throw, leaning against the weathered wood. His cream-colored shirt is tucked into short gray pants held up by red suspenders. A brown newsie cap and bowtie gives him an air of charm and significance, which is overshadowed by a smugness emanating from the smirk at the edge of his mouth.

He's dressed just like employees would be in Kingston's Carnival, but there's something about him that gives me pause. I guess an attendant should be here to operate these games, keep score, hand out prizes, etc. Blake obviously trusts this guy because he walks up to the counter, grabs a handful of balls, and winds up to make his first throw. Instead of helping Blake, this old-timey attendant keeps his eyes on me. His smirk widens. I can feel my anxiety bubble a bit. That now familiar chill sinks back into my bones. Blake makes a toss and misses. Just as the creep factor hits a new high, the carny winks at me, then tosses Blake another set of balls.

Is this guy a ghost? Someone who, like Nolan, slipped through my ledger of Whirly World accidents. Or is he like Kingston? A facsimile that the park somehow requires to operate, or at least pretend like it's business as usual. I look around for other attendants, or clowns, or performers. It's just me, Blake, and our new friend here. He gestures for me to play.

I shake my head no. "Who are you?"

He points to his chest as if to say "Who, me?" His cockiness is unsettling, but I try not to let it affect me.

I nod. Yeah, *you.*

"I'm Earl." At least, that's what I think he said. His big city accent is thick. Earl puts his hands in his pockets. "You Jason?"

"Yeah. You work here?"

He bobs his head back and forth, thinking. "Whenever somebody wants to play."

Blake makes a third toss and hits his mark. He pumps his elbow back. "Yesss." Blake hurries down the row of spinning stools to the neighboring kiosk. It's a water gun race, where you try to hold a stream of water onto a target, propelling a boat from left to right as fast as possible. Everyone I've ever "competed" with at this game is able to hit the target with minimal effort, making the conditions for victory entirely dependent on however the game has been rigged.

Blake doesn't realize this or doesn't care. He grabs a gun and starts blasting. Competing against no one, he's guaranteed to win. I guess it's not a waste of time if I'm making Blake happy, so I pick the next stool over and arm myself with a metal gun attached to a rigid rubber hose. Blake has a commanding lead, so I'll consider this match forfeit and really "try" during the next one. When the starter pistol sounds for the second match, I lean into my pistol, really giving it my all. My boat zooms ahead of Blake's, and I'm starting to anticipate the sweetness of victory, when to my amazement, the stream of water from Blake's pistol splits in two. The second stream hits a second target, and a second boat starts to move. Blake looks at me and waggles his eyebrows, showing off.

So not only can my new buddy, Blake, disappear into a body of water, he can manipulate it as well. I watch as the first boat glides across the finish line and the buzzer goes off. In a packed park that sound would get drowned out by the din passing by, but in this lonely part of town it's ear-piercing.

My competitive spirit is getting the better of me. "All right, partner, let's do this. Best three out of five." I get ready for the game to reset, but Blake continues to fire his pistol.

Blake's expression is frozen in delight. In fact, his whole body is locked in place, like Clarence on the mountain bench, content with a sunset and nothing else.

"Blake? Blake?" He keeps blasting away. I clap my hands in front of his face, jostle his shoulders, but he's immovable. I consider for a moment that he's wasting water, but this isn't water. This isn't even a theme park. Blake is trapped somewhere I can't reach. "C'mon, Blake. I thought you wanted to show me the circus."

He keeps firing. In spite of his creepy vibe, my best chance for help is our mutual acquaintance, Earl.

"Can't you do anything about this?" I ask the carnie.

Earl shrugs. "He wants to play, he's playin'."

"Who do you work for?" I ask him.

Earl jerks his thumb behind him to the giant tent.

I'm assuming he means whoever I'll find inside. I feel childish, like someone asking to see a manager because their cappuccino wasn't hot enough.

Like everywhere else, this grand tent, this spectacle of color and light, is meant to be occupied by people coming and going. Even in the P.T. Barnum era it's trying to evoke, the place would be flooded with noise. But now, the carousel isn't spinning. There are no cars careening through the Hooper Looper. I look back to Earl, but he's no longer at his station. The large flaps at the front of the tent are open, and a welcoming orange glow spills out onto the pavement outside. The circus show always ends in the big top. I guess now is the time.

Through the tent entrance, past the stairs and stands, in the middle of the lit ring, I see him. Not Earl. Kingston. Or whatever this park has created to play the part. He's looking down at the sandy floor of the ring, leaning on his cane. He looks ready to start the opening number for a packed house, but I'm the only one invited.

I didn't get this kind of a welcome from any of the lands I've visited today. So why here? Whirly World has three mascots. Why didn't the Rootin' Ranger say hello when I passed by Buckthorn? Where was Phineas the Sasquatch, or Phuzzy, when I took an uneventful hike through Linden Forest?

We're all dead but in the tent, "The show must go on." Looking at Kingston, I feel a mix of dread and pity. It's such an unpleasant thing to see this fake person trying desperately to get me to hang out with him. I grab the first seat closest to the exit. The farthest I can possibly sit from the ring.

Kingston raises his head and arms into the air. "Ladies and gentlemen. Boys and girls. Children of all ages." He drops his face to meet my eyes. "Jason." He gestures to a crowd of empty chairs. "We are all here assembled to see the greatest spectacles and impossible dreams made manifest." He spins in a circle, addressing each section of the absent audience. "If I may have a few minutes of your attention, I guarantee you will leave this tent in a frame of mind to believe that anything in this world is possible."

I'm confronted with the horrible reality that Kingston is about to sing. To me. Directly.

"Maestro," he shouts. A spotlight cuts through the haze and catches the white makeup on Kingston's face. Even at this distance I can see he's given his lips a red accent. The spotlight is unmanned, operating via invisible hands. The elaborately lit organ on the other side of the round room similarly erupts in sound all by itself. I can see the keys strike all the right notes. Even the stool looks like it's rolling back and forth under the weight of an unseen musician. Kingston points his cane at me and I brace for the first line.

> *Friend! Come along with me.*
> *I promise you will see*
> *the finest show you'll ever know*
> *and that's a guarantee.*
> *Now Kingston is my name.*
> *Of oddities I claim.*
> *You fill my till and nothing will*
> *forever be the same.*

I wonder why he's singing the original tune. This was replaced in 2010 by a new show that was more 21st than 19th century. I didn't make a lot of time to see any of the five iterations of this show, and I didn't write much about them either. They're fine. The weird thing is Kingston doesn't play a big role in the current version. Of all the versions to subject me to, why this?

> *For when the lights go down,*
> *if you can trust a clown.*
> *And take a bet you won't regret,*
> *we'll soon upturn that frown.*

A stream of circus folk glides out of the back curtains, running counter clockwise around the arena, something I was not expecting. One is standing on a horse. Another is balancing on a unicycle. Several are juggling what appear to be tools like chainsaws and mining picks, strangely replacing the colored balls and bowling pins from the usual show. The last in line pulls an elephant through the curtain. An acrobat on its back spins a drum around with their feet. The sight almost takes my breath away before I realize each person is not a person, and that elephant is not an elephant. Their faces are made of rolled clay, just like the crew of wax figures backing up Eddie Grier, and the gray behemoth is nothing more than an eyeless stack of dun-colored blobs. Their routine is carefully choreographed, and their movements align beautifully, but the effect is more monstrous than anything else.

> *Performers such as these,*
> *whose follies aim to please.*
> *Will mystify as they fly by,*
> *a breeze on the trapeze.*

One or two more verses. Almost there. It's remarkable to me how quickly you can turn this park into a horror show. Something can go from family friendly to emotionally scarring in a heartbeat. I hope Nolan doesn't hang out here too much.

> *Let the cavalcade commence,*
> *and for a small expense,*
> *You will declare 'extraordinaire!'*
> *and laugh off all pretense.*

The cast collects in front of the back curtains and closes ranks for a final pose. A big half-circle curved around the elephant at the center. The shorter performers kneel forward and the taller bodies in back stretch their hands into the air.

> *So if we make you smile,*
> *and you applaud our style.*
> *Then sit right there and, friend,*
> *prepare to clap and stay a while.*

They all bow. I applaud. I'm scared to find out what will happen if I don't. The performers file out through the back curtain.

Kingston walks to the edge of the ring. Despite singing at me for five minutes, he isn't out of breath at all. "Welcome," he yells.

"I wish more people could have seen that," I yell back, even though we could hear each other at half the volume. I'm not sure what to say. If he's just a projection of a living aspect of Whirly World, something that robotically repeats the script, then I don't see the point in asking him questions. But if he's something more, another ghost, spiritual energy made sentient, I don't know. If that's what he is then, yeah, I have a couple of things I'd like to ask.

"We cater to audiences of all sizes," Kingston says.

"What's your real name?" A question that hadn't come to me in our prior meetings. I'll base my questioning on his response.

He takes off his hat and bows. "Kingston Cornelius Reed." Strike one against him not being a robot. He wasn't based on a real person.

"Where do you live?" I wonder if this personal line of questioning will bring about an unpredictable response, or short wire his programming. He pulls his head back and shrivels his brow. "I ran away from the circus at seven, and ever since I've been in Heaven."

Wait, I remember that from the character's short "biography" on the Whirly World website. It doesn't really answer my question. Strike two, but I think I'm calling him out already. He's definitely a creepy pre-programmed afterlife robot, or whatever.

I turn, abruptly. "Well, tell everyone this was swell, Kingston." I've spent a gracious amount of time here, I think. I instinctively walk behind the row of chairs opposite the aisle to reach the exit somewhere around the tent, when I remember I was sitting right by the way out. That opening is now a solid wall of striped canvas. A clever trick.

So he likes to play games. I scan the outer wall of the ring for wherever he's moved the exit. The wall is absolute. No way in or out. No windows and no doors. Yuk, yuk. It's late, and I'm out of patience.

I couldn't tolerate this guy, this place, when I wasn't dead. On my first day here, I'm not going to spend an ounce of energy on this prank.

I cross my arms and stare, waiting for him to make the next move. He pretends to be shocked, twisting his face at me as if he doesn't understand what's going on. *I'm not moving. I'd like to go now.*

He holds the expression for a few moments more, then smiles. "Going somewhere?"

"I was figuring out how to get as far away from this place as possible. It's late. I think the park is closed now." I point to the empty stage. "The show's over, Kingston."

"But that's just it," he barks. "What if the show never ended, good man? What if you could really live in the spotlight? What if the magic of the circus never left?"

"Everything ends," I tell Kingston, again curious if it'll throw him off his game. Maybe my snarkiness will shorten his response time or cause his eye to twitch.

But he seems different now. He's aware. It looks like he's restraining himself. "Jason," he says, like a parent explaining something for the eleventh time.

His new tone really pisses me off. Of all the dim-witted charlatans to tell me where to go and what to do. I wonder what punching this guy would achieve. Would he even feel it?

"Jason," he repeats. "In all of human history there are only a shockingly infinitesimal number of people that have been given the chance I'm going to give you now. I know you're someone who wants to make his world just the way it could be. It should be. I know a lot about you, Jason. I know what it is you seek."

I feel like I'm talking to a telemarketer and I'm somehow incapable of hanging up or turning off the speaker. And how does he know my name? If I have to figure everything out on my own, how come everyone reads me like a book? Am I allowed any privacy here? An air of mystery to make myself appear interesting. Am I doomed to an eternity of everyone acting like they're more capable than me?

"Oh, you know me, do you?" I'm letting my agitation show, which is probably a bad idea. "How do you know who I am, Kingston? You're a mascot played by a variety of local community theater actors. Joke's over. Open the tent." He's just slowing me down.

The stage lights go dark. Everything turns black around us except for an electric torch burning on the post to my right. Kingston has vanished into the darkness as well, but then his boots appear in the dim circle of the torch's light, and he continues talking. "Jason, you're dead, you're a ghost," he says somberly, looking at the floor.

I can't tell if he's trying to help me understand this, or he doesn't think I know.

"You don't have a lot of options now." He looks up at me, and his eyes have changed. Not in appearance, but the robotic ringmaster that had been prancing behind them has now been replaced with someone that feels as real as Frank or Beverly.

I stand tall. "I have more options than a puppet on a stage."

Kingston smiles. It feels like some sort of ruse has ended. He's dropped character. "I'm not sure why you're doing this. You seem to have gravely misunderstood your position."

"Where?" I jest, trying not to let him intimidate me. "In this tent?" Kingston doesn't even recognize that remark as a joke. I've crossed some sort of line with him.

"Don't worry, Jason. Everyone needs to be taught. You're just one of those special students, those independent thinkers. You need a bit more attention, is all."

Above me a giant ripping sound cuts him off. Moonlight fills the top of the tent as it tears itself open. The giant poles supporting it splinter into pieces. It falls toward me, billowing. *It's all a show*, I say to myself as the roof of this place collapses.

"Welcome to the big time," Kingston says, before we're enveloped in darkness.

Chapter 10

WW

Kingston's Circus

My feet are still on solid ground, but everything around me is gone. At first I can't tell the difference between my eyes being open or closed. I bring my hands up in an attempt to block Kingston if he tries to attack, but there's nothing in front of me. It's not dark, just gray emptiness.

I pick a direction and start walking. I'm being played with, or tested, or both. Kingston seems to hold all the cards, at least as long as I'm in his tent, so I have to play along. Today I hiked up to Timber Tracks, and circled Gizzard Lake multiple times. I can stand a little stroll through the shadows. *No big deal*, I tell myself, hoping I'll believe it.

If this is a game, it's not fun. I wonder if I broke some rule earlier when I went into the parking lot, subjecting myself to its infinite horizon, like a teenager getting grounded for sneaking out at night. Maybe this is penance for trespassing in the underground tunnels. I can't be the only one who's been subjected to this. This might explain why everyone else is so nonchalant about their imprisonment. If someone steps out of line, they spend some time here. What do you threaten a ghost with when you can't kill them a second time? Boredom.

The first thing I can see in the void as I approach it is a floor-length mirror, lit by a candle on a small table at its side. I recognize it instantly as a funhouse amusement, but this one's shape isn't warped to create the illusion that I'm taller or wider or otherwise goofier looking than usual. I can't even see myself in the reflection.

Two figures step into the frame, like they're on the other side of a glass door. It's my parents, smiling. My dad's arm is draped around my mom's shoulder, like they're posing for a magazine, or starring in a commercial for prescription medication. The image before me would be strange on its own but is particularly unsettling because my parents divorced a decade ago.

I can't recall the last time the three of us were in the same room. I suppose my untimely death will bring them together in an awkward way. They'll be forced to sort through my affairs and belongings. I feel bad for them. and sympathy is not an emotion I typically associate with my parents. I loved them. I still love them. I operated on the assumption that we had a lot more time to say goodbye, and that my parents would meet their end before I even got close. I guess I could be spiteful that they never made the effort to understand me when they had the chance, but I feel like an idiot for letting that get in the way.

"Tell me, Jason," Kingston says, from nowhere in particular. "If you could make your life here anything you wanted it to be, what would it look like?"

Now that I don't have to look at him, I can focus on his voice. Every time an actor plays him, they sound like a cross between W.C. Fields and Burt Reynolds. Over the top, but also trying to entice those looking for a bit of spectacle. This Kingston has a third, sinister element. It doesn't blend.

A second candle illuminates, revealing another tall mirror. I cross in front of it and wait for someone else to present themselves. This time it's Jennifer, my sister, looking much younger than when I last saw her. My guess is this Jen is in high school. This isn't a real version of her, but it's nice to see her again. My sister always cared about me. She was patient when I made mistakes, tolerant when I demanded attention, and had a genuine interest in my hobbies, even if she faked it. Mirror Jen bows and begins to dance. My sister teaches ballet to little kids, but I don't think that's what I'm looking at. This feels like a big performance. No music accompanies her movements, and her outfit is more theatrical than something Jen wears to class.

She has on a brown and black leotard. The top is stitched with swirls of green and yellow sequins that glisten in the spotlight following her around an empty stage. A thin green scarf is draped along both of her arms, and it flows beautifully as she undulates her shoulders. She looks like a flower, or a tree. Actually, I know she's a tree, because I realize now what this is.

When I was thirteen, I went through a phase where I wanted to use the arts to save the environment, which is ironic given my love affair with the fabricated wilderness I currently cannot escape. At the time this illusion is suggesting, Jen was dating a musician. After she had read a few of my embarrassingly amateur plays, Jen floated the idea of us producing a short musical together. I pitched the journey of a young sprout that blossoms into adulthood, only to be cut down by some villainous land development project.

Jen loved the idea, and her violinist boyfriend started composing it. It never really got off the ground, of course, because I moved on to other things that I never finished. Jen eventually repurposed the work into a choreography showcase that helped her get into a respectable conservatory, but we never really *collaborated* on it. It was totally my fault. I flaked. We never had another opportunity like it.

"Okay, I see what you're trying to do," I say to the vacant air. "You're showing me what could have been. Bravo, Ghost of Circus Past." Or maybe Kingston is shaming me with mistakes that could have otherwise brought me closer to the people I claim to care about. Well, what the hell does he know? Is he suggesting that I was responsible for my parents' separation? That ship sailed a long time ago. Did the job my sister adores fall short of an unrealized dream because I didn't have the patience to finish a forgettable student production?

"What is a dream but a life unlived?" Kingston asks, somewhere inside my ear. "Why do you keep running? Where are you trying to go? What are you afraid of?"

"I'm afraid I'm going to spend eternity in the circus, you overblown windbag."

Another mirror appears. Kingston's going to run out of these pretty quick. I don't have that many friends. In this third frame, April approaches. Like my parents and my sister, April brings with her an unrealized goal. Something we often talked about but never achieved. Our child.

A baby is laughing and cooing in her arms, wrapped in a white blanket. April's happier than I've ever seen her. He has my nose, and her eyes. There's a multicolored butterfly on his onesie, one of April's favorite things. They're all over her apartment. I could see her hanging a mobile of them over this boy's crib, whatever his name is. *Henry*, the name comes into my head unbidden. That was the name we'd batted around late nights, cuddling in bed, talking about the future. The little guy notices me and extends one of his chubby arms with a smile.

I feel a surge of satisfaction that must come from leaving something behind that can actually live on and on, unlike me. I have to turn the pleasant notion away because the beautiful baby I'm looking at doesn't exist. Will never exist. When that idea is gone, all that remains is an aching regret. I struggle against a surge of longing but it overtakes me. It's pointless to wallow in this morbid speculation, but whatever Kingston's trying to do is finally working. He's found the pressure points in my heart and he's squeezing tight. I take a deep breath to let the pain pass through me.

I can shrug off the flaws in my parents' marriage, and I actually enjoy seeing my sister perform our unfinished musical, but this is hard to watch. The topic of starting a family was always the quickest way to start an argument. I didn't want to deal with the stress of raising a child. Now that I think about it, now that I've died, that child would have had to grow up without a father so I'm positive I made the right decision by waiting. Still, did April make the right decision by staying with me? Did I possibly deny her this much happiness for so long?

I'd turn away but that feels like giving Kingston what he wants. All I have to do is stare at these things and he'll let me go, right? That seems like the game we're playing here. But these people are gone, or I am. What does he expect me to do? Make clay versions of all my loved ones? Rearrange my greatest regrets in some sort of perverse dollhouse?

"You can't imagine all that you deny yourself," Kingston continues. "There is nothing greater in this world than the power of imagination." I'm not sure what world he's referring to.

"Well," I answer, finally, "that's my decision to make. What's it to you? I turn around and say the last part into the darkness. "What do you want?" I discover Kingston standing behind me, like he's been there this whole time.

"I like to put on a big show. It's in my nature."

"That's great, Kingston. But this isn't a show. This is my life." I point behind me, but the mirrors are gone. "Or it was my life."

"And you never wanted to make it more than what it was?"

"I don't see how that's any of your business," I spit back at him. "You just keep your little monster children dancing and I'll be on my way, thank you." My hands are on my hips, expressing my impatience, I suppose. I'm not sure what good that will do.

"No," he says, and my stomach drops. "There is still *soooo* much you need to see." That elongated *soooo* comes across his lips with a guttural reverberation. He's smiling now in an awful way, like I'm standing on a trap door or under a falling piano. The word "fear" means something different now. It always felt it meant self-preservation, the avoidance of demise.

Now I'm most afraid of failure. Of making a mistake that will literally haunt me forever. Why did I think for a moment that I was more powerful than this place? I'm not sure if Kingston is real, or just a projection, but he definitely has a plan for me. He's reveling in these moments like a cat sniffing a quivering mouse in its paws.

"Look again," he shouts, spreading his arms and fingers above his head like he's drawing a rainbow. Confetti shoots from his sleeves. Another mirror rises from the nothingness at his feet. Then another, and another. I'm suddenly in a hall of mirrors, twisting in ways I can't comprehend because of their confounding reflections.

I see myself everywhere. Jasons of all types. One is laughing and pointing derisively. Another weeps profusely into his hands. Another grasps his head in pain and falls to his knees. Another stands between my parents, or watches Jen from offstage, or pulls faces at the baby I never made. The silence is shattered by an army of Jasons talking over each other, arguing and debating. I can't make out any of it. I want to run but a surge of clarity stops me. I'll smack into one of these mirrors. I carefully put one foot in front of the other, waving my arms in front of me. The hallway turns right, then left, then right again. I've been in a few of these labyrinths and rarely enjoyed them.

"I'm lost, I got it. Congratulations, Kingston. You've achieved the painfully obvious, you hack of a clown." I say the last part under my breath, just in case pissing him off further is a bad idea. The path I've chosen has come to a dead end, I think. It's so hard to tell. I know I need to turn one hundred and eighty degrees and reorient myself. I look down to see if I've left footprints for me to track, but the ground has a spotless finish like I'm walking on glass. I can probably find the last turn I took incorrectly and trace invisible breadcrumbs back to where I'm supposed to be. But I don't want to give Kingston the satisfaction. I can imagine myself from above, a pathetic lab rat that won't stop scurrying. I feel Kingston's twisted satisfaction at seeing the big picture where I can only see myself, frantic and exhausted, duplicated in every frame forever.

"Enough!" I yell. My voice cracks and I wonder if I'll burst into tears soon. "If you want me to spend the rest of my time here then fine. But I'm not going to pretend like you're in charge. You're a mascot. A glorified jester. You're nothing." I brace myself for some physical or mental attack. I prepare responses for an argument. I'm ready to fight.

"I'm not afraid of you!" I scream as loud as I can. The words don't feel like they travel very far, and as soon as they leave my lips I realize how untrue they are. The mirrors are still in place. My situation has not changed. I can't believe that just a few hours earlier I was horrified at the prospect of permanently residing in my favorite place in the world. I didn't realize how good I had it.

Which is clearly what Kingston is trying to teach me. He might not be in charge here, but the park definitely is. He wants me to think that I hold no power, no significance. But then why is Kingston doing this? If I don't matter, why the effort? Who is more desperate, the rat that can't find a piece of cheese, or the scientist that can't find the answers they're looking for?

Kingston doesn't respond to my shouting. I've either struck a chord or he's long gone. Maybe he'll return in a few hours and torture me some more. Staring into the shadowy nothingness over my head, past the top of the mirrors, I wonder if I'm even in the park anymore. Maybe I got my wish. I found the way out, only to enter a realm far bleaker. My anger gets the best of me and I erupt in a wordless scream, clenching every muscle in my body, or whatever strands of emotional impulse a ghost is made of.

CRACK. One of the sheets breaks. A lightning bolt pattern has split through one of many mirrors. Did I do that? I scream again, a weak, pensive noise that sounds like it has a question mark at the end. The mirror sheet doesn't budge. No, it's not me. It's Kingston. This is the next phase of the experiment.

WHAM. Another crack appears. A spiderweb, stretching out from a single point of impact. It looks like something just punched the mirror from the other side. I step back. Run, my senses tell me, but I think better of it. Fleeing is pointless. I'll head face-first into a sneaky mirror, or whatever force is about to break through will just find me again. All I can do is brace myself for the next prank and hope it isn't too much for my mind to handle.

CLANK. The third strike has less impact than before, but it creates a new line that connects to the lightning bolt crack. I can see the texture along the inside of the fracture, the edges that are slowly splitting the mirror into pieces. I'm tempted to kick the mirror from my side, but I might do it right when the whole thing comes crashing down on my leg, so I step further back. I cross my arms in front of my face, hoping the tiniest piece of reflective glass doesn't pass through and end up in the middle of my eye when the levee breaks.

SMASH. The mirror explodes. I'm standing way too close. I fall back into the wall behind me and barely manage to stay on my feet. My shocked reaction reflects in the chunks of mirror as they collapse to the wooden floor. Something is waving its arms through the wreckage. There's a heavy object in its hands. It's a sledgehammer. The something holding it is Frank.

"Come on, kid," Frank hollers at me, holding one of his big, hairy hands through the exposed frame. I'm so relieved that he's not a killer clown that I thrust my hand forward without really thinking and let Frank yank me through to the other side.

"This way," Frank shouts, but I can't figure which "way" he's referring to. The walls around us are jet black and featureless. Frank runs away, and my eyes slowly focus on what appears to be a tight hallway. I try to grab his shirt, fearful that he'll disappear like so many have before, whether they intend to or not. He runs too fast. All I can do is follow at top speed, hoping he knows where he's going.

Blissfully, there is some sort of exit ahead of us. Maybe an open door. Yellow light angles in from outside, revealing the faintest of textures on the wall and ceiling. How long have I been here? I've caught up to Frank and have to slow down to avoid knocking him over. I put a hand up and push him in the square of his back. *Sorry, Frank, but you gotta move.*

The light, the open air, the soft ground. It all hits me at once. Frank stumbles and I try to hold him steady without breaking either of our strides as we tumble outside. We've made it. I notice a patch of cacti. I'm not even in Whirly World anymore, I realize. Frank has figured it out. We've broken through somewhere in the open desert and we're free. Stranded, maybe, but better than an endless funhouse. The sky is almost light, but the sun hasn't breached the horizon yet. I can see it just trying to peek over some ancient train tracks.

Wait, no. This is Shaley Flats. The wasteland outside of Gabbro Caverns. Those are the ride's train tracks. I glance quickly behind me without slowing. We bolted out of a maintenance exit along the desolate road between the circus and the desert. The road with no name. We're clear of Kingston's domain, but Frank keeps running. There's a franticness to his gait that he didn't even express when I was vacuumed into Timber Tracks. Frank's more afraid than I am.

I see, or maybe just sense, someone far to my right. It's Beverly, standing a hundred feet away on Market Street. Her hands are calmly clasped at her waist.

"Beverly, you should get out of here," I shout as I turn back to the desert. I don't stop to see if she takes my advice. On top of a sand dune, I see what Frank's gunning for. One of the Gangway Grotto trains is parked just ahead of us. Steam lingers about the smokestack. No one stands at the controls but this baby is ready to roll. Frank jumps into the sand and starts to stomp his way up the incline. I know the sand's going to slow us down, so I leap as far as my body will let me and prepare to scamper up the dune like a lizard.

Frank waves his left arm, pointing me toward the only passenger car behind the engine. As he reaches the cab, he hops through the open door and seizes the reverser handle. I grab one of the poles dividing the rows of benches in the first car and swing myself inside. My body falls flat on the bench. I expect the train to blast off at maximum velocity after our sprint to safety. But of course, after Frank throws the lever, the train needs a minute to build momentum.

I hear a roar of anger. I sit up and look back at the circus. The door Frank threw wide, the window into the black void, is still open. I can see the hallway beyond more clearly because a light is slowly emerging from the other end. It's red. Glowing. Growing closer and closer. I felt rescued for a moment, but there are obviously no hiding places here. I've really done it now. I poked the bear and now he's going to feast on everyone in the park.

Kingston tears out of the open door like an Olympian doing the hundred meter dash. Initially he looks silly, bounding forward in a flashy costume that doesn't exactly lend itself to long-distance running. But then he resembles a raging beast. His eyes have turned red. Sparks of fire are spitting from his fingertips and scraping away from his heels. He's gritting his teeth so fiercely it looks like he's about to crunch them into a thousand pieces.

We roll away from Kingston as fast as the train will take us. I look back at Frank in the cab. He's looking at the window, watching Kingston gradually catch up to us. I search the passenger car for something to chuck at him. It's empty and immaculate. Part of me wants to throw myself from the back of the train onto Kingston, to save Frank. But Frank yells from the cab as I begin to climb forward over the benches.

"Hold on," Frank shouts.

The train isn't moving that fast, Frank. Grotto isn't a rollercoaster by any means. It's for little kids and big families. If we were on Timber Tracks we'd have left Kingston in the dust. Then, if we were "on" Timber Tracks, I'd be sucked up into the coaster's sense memory whirlwind. But this locomotive, even with the pedal to the floor, moves at a recreational speed that isn't going to keep us from this charging psychopath for long.

Kingston loses his hat to the wind. The fire from his hands catches on his jacket. Pieces float away in the morning air. He seems to be genuinely exerting himself. He's looking right at me, panting. The satisfaction I get out of the strain he's putting on himself is immediately supplanted by terror. He's just a few feet from the car. This will all be over soon.

Then he realizes, about the same time as I do, that we've crossed over a cluster of things tied to the track. A pile of small boxes that he's just about to step on. I turn back to Frank in confusion, and he ducks behind the cab's wall. I swing my head back to see Kingston reach his arms forward as if hoping they'll stretch the length of space between us. Sparks drip from his fingers in great streams, falling onto the pile of boxes. The boxes are marked "dynamite."

KABOOM. All I see is fire, and yet I feel no heat. A shockwave bounces through my ears. When they start working again, all they detect is the sound of the air zipping past. My limbs flail. I'm flying somewhere. North, I think. A building comes into my view, upside down. Or am I? I want my body to turn, and it does. I can see more clearly where I'm going now. I spot the likely point of impact.

Images of flight safety manuals flash through my brain. I move to grab my knees and curl into a ball. I think I will roll on the pavement when I land on the road just west of Hollow House. I have no idea where Frank is. I seem to be intact, so I imagine he's been turned into a missile, like me. As the ground lunges up at me I think *This must be how Josie felt in the end.*

WHAM. I sense a massive impact, but there's no pain. I bounce and bounce down the road but I don't feel damaged, just out of control. After I've slid to a halt, a stunt that would have shredded me to the bone if I was in the real park, I stay still for a while. I'm not sure exactly what just happened, and Kingston's whereabouts are unknown, but I'm not ready to think about that just yet. I'm just glad that Whirly World isn't whirling anymore.

I slowly get to my feet. Everything looks surprisingly calm. The engine and its car both dropped back into the desert. They came to rest at the southern edge of the road, severing the northeast curve of the track and leaving two dark trenches of sand. A cloud of dust lingers. I scare myself into thinking that Kingston is going to come soaring through it like a helicopter, but he's gone.

"Now that…" Rubén says. He stands to my right, near the queue to Gangway Grotto.

I see that Frank punched a hole through the south side of the building's rooftop, and now hangs, ass first, out of a freshly made window. He kicks his legs, so I know he's okay.

Rubén looks at the wreckage with his arms crossed. He seems pleased with himself. "*That* was a sweet show."

Chapter 11

Gabbro Caverns

"It was four years after I got here," Frank begins. "Mostly spent that time inside of the mountain. Soaring through the ride. Seeing how big those chasms really were. Making the track do things I could never make it do before. There were no deadlines to keep. No people to keep safe. It was a playground. I couldn't get enough."

Rubén checks the desert from the entrance of Gabbro Caverns, then looks back at me and shakes his head. Ever since we sprinted over and tucked ourselves into this improvised hiding place, I've been waiting to hear Kingston's cackle before he traps us inside. But he's left us alone. For now. Maybe we blew him into another theme park. A guy can hope.

I lean my back against the coolness of the rock and breathe in the particular aroma. This cave, just like any indoor ride, has its own funk. It reminds me of the inside of a rubber Halloween mask. My local library had a perfume that made me think of Hollow House if I closed my eyes, and the tang of the swimming pool at my high school was a dead ringer for the soaked interior of Sawmill Splash.

Through a viewing window I can see the tracks running through the old cave. Animatronic bats hang from the ceiling, and plaster stalactites and stalagmites line the ride's path, like jagged teeth.

"But one day," Frank continues. "I started really digging. I attached a drill bit to the front of an electric train."

I raise my hand, but Frank dismisses me.

"Don't ask me how. It's a blur, kid. Anyway, I'd run the drill as I was laying track and I kept that engine going for, oh, a few days? At least? Nothing else really mattered to me at the time." Frank walks to the edge of the cavern and points north, to the mountains. "At some point I figured that I should have shot out of the hillside. The mountains look like they go up for a while, but they really drop into a creek on the opposite..." I must have been nodding because Frank stops his sentence. "Ugh, what am I telling *you* this for?"

"Oh, I'm sorry," I say. But I'm not. I could draw Frank a topographical map that goes for miles. I've studied this landscape more than any neighborhood I've ever lived in.

"The point is the mountain goes up then it goes down," Frank says sharply. "Not quite sea level, mind you, but enough that I shouldn't have been in the mountains as long as I was. I started pushing the track upward to compensate and that's when I finally hit the surface." Frank slams one hand into the other, pushing it out toward me with a "whoosh."

"What did you find?" Rubén asks.

Frank has the two of us on the edge of our seats.

Frank laughs. "Trees. Lots and lots of trees." The laugh fades into a sigh. Frank steps back inside and finds a flat rock to sit on. "And something else. A presence. Out there with me. Wherever I went I could feel it behind me. All around."

Rubén and I look at each other, guessing which way this story will go with our eyes.

Frank shakes his head. "And then, no this is stupid..."

"No, no," I interject. "Things are no longer stupid in this place. Anything goes."

Frank smiles. "Well," he says, facing the absurdity of this memory, "it was Phineas."

"You mean, Phuzzy? The sasquatch?"

Frank shakes his head. "Eh, I don't call him that. That's, that's a fan name. I don't call him that." I suppose, on this point, he and I will respectfully disagree.

Phuzzy is the park's sole animal, or half-animal, mascot. He's a seven-foot ape person. The bastard child of Bigfoot and Donkey Kong. I've met people that relay fond memories of embodying him during normal park hours. I've also met people that say his sweltering costume, cumbersome boots, misbalancing foam pads, and restrictive eyeholes are insufferable. The park named him Phineas, presumably after the P in P.T. Barnum, but fans instantly renamed him. He's Phuzzy. I won't hear any of this Phineas nonsense.

Phuzzy is on a bunch of signage and promotional material, and the guy in the suit appears during parades, photo shoots, and special events. On extremely rare occasions, for maximum hilarity, the actor actually roams through the backwoods of Linden Forest. These sightings are rare, making the hurried photos that exist of the phenomena so damn funny. He gets all upset when he sees litter and sometimes throws it back at guests. Phuzzy's the best.

"Anyway, Phineas," Frank continues, "comes tearing out of the darkness and carries me away. Literally, carries me." Frank circles his hands around his midsection, simulating the size of Phuzzy's grasp. "He scoops me up, throws me over his shoulder, and takes me back here. I couldn't move, I couldn't fight back, I…" Frank is really bothered by this. It's hard to imagine anyone carrying Frank with ease. He's not a tall man, probably a few inches shorter than I am, but he must weigh over two hundred pounds. I have yet to see him at a loss for words, but Frank's struggling to tell us the rest.

"It's okay," Rubén says, reassuringly. "We believe you. We've all seen crazy stuff. Right, Jason?"

I nod several times. "Crazy is all I've seen today. That's all this place is."

Frank nods like he's hearing us, but stares somewhere in front of him, reliving that powerless moment.

I think of Kingston's confidence when he was trapping me inside the tent. I can't imagine the terror of a beast hunting you through a forest, treating you like a bear treats a leaping fish.

"Anyway," Frank sighs, "I know what this park will do to keep us here. Believe me, kid. I know how hard it is to accept it. But we're stuck. I should have just laid it out for you earlier. I didn't know how bad you wanted to leave."

"To be honest, until I ran into Kingston again, *I* didn't know how badly I wanted to leave." I shrug and turn to Rubén. "You've never seen anything like this before?"

Rubén shakes his head. "Kidnapping psycho-mascots? Nope. But then again, I never tried too hard to get out of here. I just thought we were stuck and that was that. Full lockdown."

"It just seems like we should be able to leave," I reply, stating it as clearly as I can. "The existence of these barriers, Kingston, Phuzzy, Eddie, suggests the existence of a manager. And I'm not talking about some benevolent angel watching over our dearly departed souls. Someone that's controlling all of it, just like how someone manages the real park every day."

Rubén interrupts. "I think we just haunt this place, you know, classic style. We're here because we died here. Simple as that."

I push myself off the faux rock wall, my anxiety driving me into motion. "Right, but how does that work? Aren't you curious? I never really believed in ghosts, not really, but if I had to explain it, the idea of someone's spirit being trapped in a house, contained within the walls, windows, and doors, makes a lot more sense than being trapped in something as big as this park. All those entrances and exits? All that open air?"

Frank rubs his hands together. "Well, if you're going to get scientific, what are we? Us ghosts, I mean. Bags of energy? Walking circuit boards? If just a handful of people living in a house or apartment can generate enough juice to let a spirit stick around after their bodies fail, imagine how supercharged Whirly World is. Or any theme park. Maybe the space just has to have a border somewhere. This park has a lot of open air, but no one can enjoy it without a badge or a ticket."

"If you think we're stuck here, that there's no hope, why did you help me?"

"Well, Rubén saw you head into the circus and the door slam shut behind you, so to speak. He came to get me, thinking you might be in trouble. Not real trouble, but more than you could handle on your first day."

I smile at Rubén.

He waves me off, as if to say, "No big deal."

Frank continues. "The tent openings vanished, and the fabric had gone more rigid than rock. We couldn't seem to get inside. Which, for me, is weird. To not be able to tear open something as flimsy as a tent or rip the ropes holding the whole thing together. It felt off. Different."

"How long did it take you to get to me?" I ask.

"Hours," Ruben says. "You were in there all night."

"Yeah, also different," Frank adds. "So I got to thinking we could pull the support ropes off with the train from the caverns. I loaded one up, took it round the bottom of the desert, and parked it by the lake."

"Lemme guess, don't ask how you can power trains?" I ask.

"You're catching on." Frank laughs, then sees the dissatisfaction on my face. "I've always loved locomotives. I guess they just make sense to me here. Anyway, I get off the train and meet Rubén north of the circus. And then…"

"And then what?" I ask.

"Then we heard you scream," Rubén says.

Frank shivers. "Never heard anything like it. Not here. It sounded like you'd really gotten yourself into a tight spot. I ran to the back of the tent, and I'm not entirely sure how, but I just found a way in. I saw a handle and I pulled it."

"What about the explosives?" I ask Rubén. "Where'd that idea come from?"

"Well," Rubén says with a smile. "I thought if the train didn't work then maybe we could blast our way in there. While Frank was getting the train together, I cooked up some powder that's heavier than what I usually make. When I saw that wacko come tearing out of that tent, I dunno. I figured I'd even the odds. Fight fire with fire."

"He's not a wacko. I think it's more sinister than that. The thing that just chased us? That was malevolent. That had an agenda."

Rubén stops to think about this. Frank is quiet, still not looking up at either of us.

I don't know why I'm so confident. These two have been here so much longer than I have. I should just shut up and listen, but I can't. "Whatever is pretending to be Kingston will find us again, if it doesn't already know where we are. Maybe it's biding its time?"

Frank wipes his huge sandpapery hands across his face, then looks me in the eye. "Yeah, kid, you might be right. You just got here, so you couldn't know. But this all feels different."

"We need to get everyone together. I think we're stronger as a group. Do we know where everyone is? Where they hang out?"

"Wait, what are you saying?" Rubén asks. "Stronger? What does that mean?"

"I mean he's not messing with us right now and I'm trying to figure out why before he starts picking on us again."

"Look, kid," Frank says to me, "I'm sorry I didn't warn you about how this place can push back. But you're thinking about this all wrong. It's like a storm. There's no fighting it. You batten down the hatches and you wait it out."

I stand and walk toward Ruben, pointing at the scene of our spectacular train crash. "But you, what you did. That was way more than just some pretty sparkles. You knocked that jerk into the next zip code. He couldn't contain it. Who knows what else you can do?"

Rubén shrugs.

I keep going. "You all can change things here. I've seen Reagan power the attractions. Blake can manipulate water. Josie is literally flying above our heads right now. You can all do amazing things, and whatever just chased us feels threatened by that."

Frank shakes his head no. "I think you're giving Kingston way too much credit. He's just an egomaniac that wants us all to run away to the circus with him all day. That's it. I don't think he has the capacity to feel threatened. These people here that aren't, you know, us." Frank motions to Rubén and myself. "I think they're just trying to keep this park running." I strongly disagree but it's more of a feeling than something I can put into words.

"I told you, kid," Frank says. "There's nothing past the park. Bangin' our skulls against the walls here is only going to give us a headache. I know the prospect of being here forever is a lot to take in right now, especially after everything you've seen so far, but you've just, you've got to settle into a rhythm. Right, Rubén?"

Rubén has been looking down at the train track that runs through the cavern this whole time. He's tapping his fingers like he's solving a math problem in the air.

"Rubén?" Frank asks again.

"How *did* I do that?" Rubén wonders aloud. He points his finger at me. "When you asked me about those crates, the ones I get my powder from, I said they just appeared every morning. Which is true. But I never really thought about it until now." Rubén looks west, toward where his launch platform is, just beyond the walls of Gabbro Caverns. "It just always made sense to me. If I could make this stuff when I was alive, and I have all the supplies I need to make them here, then why shouldn't I be able to do it, right?"

I nod to show I'm listening.

"But I've never made dynamite before. I've certainly never tried to blow someone up before. Well, unless you count shooting Roman candles at my cousins." Rubén snickers.

"What are you getting at?" Frank asks.

"I just think the new guy is on to something."

Frank curves a pessimistic brow at me. "Or someone just got here a day ago and still has a lot to learn about this place."

I really want to get to the bottom of this, but it feels like this chat is devolving into an argument. "Fine. If it wasn't for you two, I would still be stuck inside that circus tent. You smashed through Kingston's illusion, and Rubén blasted him so far away he's thinking twice about messing with us again. But all of that is just the new normal and I'm sure I'll get used to it." I'm terrible at diffusing arguments.

Frank throws his hands in the air and marches out of the tunnel. "If you want to bait that thing into pestering you for the rest of existence, then be my guest. I won't be a part of it."

I don't understand why he's so opposed to this idea. Maybe he needs this place to be one way and can't accept it being anything else. I'm still learning how all this works, true. But that makes me the perfect person to ask these questions. There has to be a part of this that Frank, that all of these ghosts, haven't considered yet. There has to be a way out of here.

"Ah!" Frank screams.

Rubén and I both snap to attention. I skid out of the entrance, sliding on the sandy surface, half expecting Kingston to come swinging toward us, riding a bouquet of balloons. But it's not him. It's not even Phuzzy. It's Beverly.

Frank lets out a sigh of relief. "Ugh, sorry Bev."

Beverly is standing beside the train tracks, hands clasped at her waist, waiting peacefully. How long has she been there? It's really good to see her. I realize Beverly's comforting presence, even from thirty feet away, calms me like before. *Stronger together.*

"You okay?" Rubén asks.

The two of us approach her. I can't tell if she was looking for us or if she happened to cross our path on a morning walk. There's a stoic serenity always hanging about her that I wish I could emulate. Here we are, Rubén, Frank, and me, hiding in a cave, quaking in our boots. While Beverly doesn't seem to have a care in the world.

"Fine," Beverly says to Rubén. "I didn't mean to startle you, dear," she says to Frank. "My feet can sometimes fall a little lighter than I realize."

Frank's calming down. All the questions I wanted to ask, the problems I wanted to solve, can wait. It's impossible to be frustrated around this woman. She's as trustworthy as a favorite teddy bear or a security blanket.

"I'm sorry if we scared *you* earlier," I say. "When we were running away. We were…" I have no idea how to describe it. Rubén and Frank turn to me, equally curious what words I'll choose. "Running from something."

"Not something," Beverly corrects me. "Someone."

"Right, Kingston, of course. You probably saw him too. Although I'm not sure it was him, really."

"No, of course not." Beverly says, succinctly.

"Of course not?" Frank responds. "How do you know? Who do you think that was?"

"Oh, don't you know?" She makes the same face she made when she realized I was unaware of my own death. She looks as if she holds a piece of information we're not ready to hear, and is burdened by the responsibility of telling us the truth. She looks up, searching her thoughts, or the heavens. "The father of lies."

"Satan?" Rubén curls the fingers in his right hand into a sign of the horns, two fingers raised. Devil horns. "Satan," Rubén states again, plainly.

Beverly nods, like a teacher encouraging a struggling student.

"The deceiver," Beverly says, as if there are other Satans.

Frank turns to me. I look at Rubén. The three of us are speechless.

This is obviously an exaggeration on her part, but the words have weight. Maybe it's just the way that anything sounds when you quote it from scripture, like it should not and cannot be disputed. The ultimate argument-enders. The four of us stand there for a full minute, considering this.

"Well," Rubén says. "That's pretty metal."

"Look, Beverly," Frank says, indelicately.

It sounds like he's about to correct her. I have an impulse to get ahead of him so as not to offend Beverly and turn her away. I'm not sure what I'm hoping she'll say but I really want to hear her out. "No, let her finish."

Frank looks at me and rolls his eyes so dramatically they almost fall out of his head. Rubén looks similarly skeptical.

"You two aren't the least bit curious where she's going with this?" Discussing the netherworld might not lend a ton of credibility to the points I was trying to make earlier, but I like my odds better with Beverly on my side. I don't think Kingston, or Phuzzy, is Satan himself, but I do think these beings are keeping us here and we deserve to know why.

"When you say Satan," I say to Beverly, choosing my words with care. "Do you mean the actual Satan, as in the devil? Or just like, someone mean and powerful?" Beverly is delighted at my curiosity. I suppose she doesn't get asked these questions a lot.

She smiles. "It is not my place to proclaim so, but…"

Frank leans in. "Buuuuuuut?"

"But he has bequeathed upon himself a royal majesty that is not deserved, that is not given. We must test each spirit lest they be false prophets."

She lost me. Frank and Rubén are barely following as well.

Beverly recognizes our confusion. "Sorry, dears." She bites her lip and thinks. "He should not be able to do the things he can do in this place. Not only that, he uses his lawless power to control others. There are many of these signs."

I remain dubious, but it's been a while since I went to Sunday School. Holy cow, I hope she's wrong about this.

Rubén makes air quotes with his fingers. "When you say 'this place,' where do you think we are?"

"After we die, we face judgment. This altar of souls is our place to rest. Each day that passes brings us closer to His will."

"This is heavy. I don't know, man. I get to eat ice cream all day, without getting fat, and blow stuff up at night. I thought this was Heaven."

Beverly rests a hand on Rubén's shoulder. "It is not. That kingdom awaits."

"Oh, nice." Ruben smiles at us. "I made the cut, guys."

"So it's like if a ride breaks down," I say, "but you stay in line anyway?"

Beverly smiles, amused by this analogy.

Frank grumbles. "Eh, I don't, agh," He flops his hands forward like he's pushing these devout notions to the ground. "I think this place, just like a real theme park, has hazards. And we need to avoid them or we wind up in the wrong place at the wrong time."

I'm trying to see Frank's side of this, to believe that Beverly is misinterpreting this situation but then I recall wisps of fire burning through the skin on Kingston's fingers. I remember the dark hallway filling with bright red light before that monster raced out of it. And I recall the chill I feel whenever I am away from other ghosts.

I point to Frank. "You didn't call it a hazard before. You called it a presence. You can't just say that you were scooped up by Phuzzy in the backwoods of those mountains and then compare that experience to a guard rail or some security tape."

Beverly blinks. "Phineas scooped you up, Frank?"

"That's not important right now," Frank says, embarrassed. He walks away from us and into the flat desert, grumbling incoherently.

I turn to Beverly. "If the devil-in-a-top-hat just tried to kidnap us, why aren't you afraid?"

"I believe that if he truly wanted us to be in bondage, we would be. He has a need for us. We're employed to prevent some eventual tribulation. Until then, I pray."

Frank turns back to us and yells. "If he's got that much power, why doesn't he dance back over here and drag us to Hell?"

I feel like I keep repeating myself. "You showed him how strong you can be, because you and Rubén teamed up. He wasn't expecting that. Beverly thinks that Kingston, or Satan, is using us for something. Maybe we're both right?"

Frank sighs in disagreement but doesn't offer a cleaner explanation.

Rubén nods. "Well, let's get the band back together. Who else do we need?"

Finally, we're getting somewhere. "Everybody. Let's get everyone's take on this. Is the fireworks show the only thing you all come out for?"

"Most nights. But I don't know if I can wait that long."

"Then maybe there's a way we can call a meeting. Are we one hundred percent that there are just a few of us here? The four of us and seven others?"

Beverly turns to Frank. "There's one way. Right, Frank?"

Rubén and I look at Frank, waiting for a response.

At first he doesn't appear to know what Beverly is talking about, but then he extends his hand, palm facing downward, and rocks it back and forth. "Eh, kinda."

"What is it?" I ask. "Don't hold out on me, Frank."

Frank steps back over the tracks and approaches us. "It's risky. And we'll need Reagan."

"Risky?" Beverly says, sweetly. "Oh, Frank, you're being modest. A few years ago, Frank figured out a way to see where everyone in the park is at any given moment."

I nod. "Frank showed me. The lightbulb-eye trick."

Frank shakes his head. "No, this is different." He doesn't sound excited about it. "I showed you something we can all do inside of our heads. This requires more power."

"Well, what are we waiting for? Let's try it."

"I wish it were that easy, kid. To broadcast like that we'll need to use the main security office. And that can be hard to access."

"Is it locked? One of those symbol locks?"

"No, but it's guarded. By Eddie Grier."

Chapter 12

Employees Only

Apparently the ghosts rarely make plans to see one another. Their days are so repetitive, and they're used to crossing each other's paths so often, that the prospect of finding someone at a specific time is a low priority at best, and an annoyance at worst. I imagine it's like living with roommates you didn't get to pick. Even if you all get along, you spend so much time in close proximity that you have to take breaks to preserve your sanity. Everyone needs their privacy. Blake, for example, is probably floating around Gizzard Lake, but summoning him is easier said than done.

So I'm not surprised that Reagan is nowhere inside or outside of the Palace Theater. She told me she only comes back here to set up the show for Nolan. Still, Frank, Rubén, and Beverly all confessed an unusual and unexplainable desire to stay close to where they died. It sounds comforting, like being in your own room with your own stuff. We're guessing if we just wait here Reagan will return eventually.

This wait is going to be difficult, but I'm glad we all stuck together. Beverly grabbed a broom and is sweeping up the lobby, which doesn't look like it needs it. Rubén is in the front row, snacking on some Red Vines he got from Clarence. Frank and I are downstairs, running checks on the gears that keep the stage spinning.

Frank twists one of the bolts. "You know, if I hadn't been knocked out by that chunk of track, Reagan wouldn't be here. If the same safety measures had been in place here that were on all of the rides, that accident just wouldn't have been possible. I'd been pushing to make the whole park safer, but then I ran out of time."

This will be terribly rude of me, but I'm too curious. "Um, not that it's any of my business, but if the safety measures were in place, how did that part of the track get dislodged?"

Frank doesn't seem offended, just tired. He drops his wrench into a toolbox. "Yeah, not one of my finer moments. I guess our last one rarely is." Frank raps his knuckles against the vertical pipes that line the basement wall. "I love this place. I'm proud of the work I did here. But I tell ya, it's a wonder this world hasn't taken more lives."

"Because it's breaking down?"

"No. Well, sure, everything breaks down. But the top brass left too much to chance. I kept telling them, for years, to put different safety restraints on Timber Tracks. To make it so people couldn't get free of those bars. But they didn't care. They said the park had gone on like that for almost forty years. Why fix it if it ain't broke?"

I heard rumors as a kid that there was a way to slip through the restraints on Timber Tracks, but I was only eleven when Josie died and none of my friends were dumb enough to try it. "Why do you think Josie tried to get free?"

Frank shakes his head. "Not a clue. Even after she took a dive off that thing, the powers that be were still slow to make changes, which is why I took it upon myself. They said she made the decision to break the rules and she suffered the consequences."

I'll play devil's advocate. "Well, didn't she?"

"That's not the point. It was our responsibility to save people from themselves. From being so stupid they don't realize they're playing with their own lives."

"So why did the track fall?"

"Because I didn't secure it properly, Sherlock." Frank throws his hands in the air and walks a few steps away. "Because I was in a hurry trying to keep people safe. Management only closed the ride for a month. I wanted to try and add more of a curve on the bigger turns, but nights were the only time I could work. I got tired, sloppy. There's no one to blame but me. Is that what you want to hear?"

"No, no, I'm sorry, Frank. I just, you know, I'm curious. No one talks honestly about this stuff. And I never thought I'd actually get to ask you about it."

"Almost every death that's taken place here was preventable. What kind of jerks build a place like this and let people get run over by it just because they're statistical anomalies?"

"Well, I died here and I have zero regrets." Not a complete truth, but I'm trying to make Frank feel better. I suppose it's easy for me since I don't know how I died. "Accidents happen, Frank. No matter how hard you try to prevent them."

"Thanks, kid. It just gets to me. The randomness of it all."

It can be heartless to brush off the mortality rate here, but it's not that high. If you consider the thousands of employees that have worked here, and the millions of people that passed through the gate since opening day, far less than one percent lost their lives doing so.

I look behind me at the metal frame that holds the revolving stage. I contemplate how many variables must have been in play for Reagan to be where she was standing seconds before she died. If she had gone to the bathroom, or taken that day off, or chose something else to do with her summer, she'd be at the beach. Wait, that's it.

"I know where Reagan is. How do I get to the roof?"

Frank leads me to a maintenance ladder that stretches up the back of the theater. The lights are dim behind the heavy curtain at the front of the stage, so the sunlight is blinding when I push open the roof hatch. The metal squeals as the compression cylinders release and the door swings upward on its hinges.

The view from the roof is a real treat. It totally spoils the illusion of a turn-of-the-century marketplace to see all the spotlights and air-conditioning machines, but I never get tired of backstage access like this. It puts the struggle of maintaining a modern theme park into perspective. It takes a lot of money to make something look like it didn't cost a lot of money.

Reagan's uniform is draped over an exhaust vent. I become alarmingly aware that I have inadvertently crossed into her personal space, and yet I still look around like a stupid, flesh-and-blood man. Reagan, in her underwear, is sunbathing on a lawn chair that she's apparently dragged from Port Juniper and somehow hoisted up here.

And now I'm standing here slack jawed and have no idea what to do with myself. "Oh, I, uh, you're, hello." I'm incapable of starting a sentence. I look anywhere except at her. When that feels too awkward, I try looking only at her face. Can ghosts blush? If so, I am.

Reagan doesn't move a muscle. "Look who it is." She has dark shades on so I can't see if her eyes are closed or not. "What's the matter? Were the other rooftops occupied?"

"No, why would, oh, ha," I chirp back at her. I've always assumed I have a quick and educated wit, but I cannot compete with this woman. To be honest, my brain isn't the part of my body doing the thinking.

She turns her head to me and nudges her glasses down to the edge of her nose. Her eyes watch mine as I struggle to maintain direct contact. I feel like a prepubescent teen in a raunchy 80s movie and she's the sexy babysitter that's come to teach me a painful lesson about rejection.

Reagan pushes her sunglasses back up. "Well then, why are we having a conversation?"

"Oh, right, yes." I suddenly remember everything up to this point. "I need you. I mean, we need you. Your help. The gang. And I. They're downstairs, and I figured you'd be up here after you said you do this sometimes."

"That's great. That's really great. I'm proud of you."

"Frank says there's a way to check if we know everyone that's here in the park. That it's just the eleven of us. But we need your help to..." Actually, Frank didn't specifically say what Reagan would be doing. "Turn it on, I guess."

I wonder if she'd care to know more. I'm not sure if it's my responsibility to tell her that Kingston went on a rampage and tried to trap me in the circus and then light me on fire.

"Did you hear anything unusual this morning?" I ask.

"Not really." She sounds bored. "I mean, there was that explosion but one of you weirdos is usually doing something you shouldn't be doing. Why, breaking stuff already?"

It's so, so hard to focus on anything but the flower pattern on her underwear. I opt to look straight at the sun instead. Much more comfortable. "Kinda. Can you help us? Just for a second. Then you can get back to…"

"Not being bothered? Sure, sounds fun. Give me a second."

"Right, right, of course." I make an about-face and march away. I notice her uniform again, lying flat like she just flew out of it. I figured she was getting a tan but realize that must be impossible here. Even standing in direct sunlight, my insides are still clutching that all-encompassing cold that's been with me since yesterday. This question will likely annoy her further but I'm too curious. "Are you warm right now? Is that why you come up here?"

Reagan shuffles her body. "It feels a little different, yeah."

I'm envious. If I can't get out of here I'll probably have to find my own rooftop somewhere. "Sorry to bother you." I head down the ladder. Of course I notice that she has an absolutely dynamite pair of legs, but that results in me nearly losing my footing, and I'm relieved when I'm back in the quiet darkness of the theater.

Frank is at the bottom of the ladder. "Find her?"

"More than I was expecting."

The main security office lies in the middle of the southeastern employee area. This side is mostly for maintenance and storage. It's where rail cars go to get repaired, where people get in costume for the shows, and where troublemakers are sent if they get caught.

It's also where lost kids wait to be reunited with their parents, which is why it's a restricted area of Whirly World that I've actually been in before. When I was six years old, and my fixation on this park was reaching a fever pitch that never really subsided, I foolishly ran away from my parents when they told me we had to leave the park early. An astute security guard (her name was Samantha if I'm not mistaken) deduced that I had evaded my family after spotting me enjoying the review at Nellie's Saloon without proper supervision.

My childish excuses for being alone failed to convince them so I was sent to the adolescent detention area, which is actually quite cheerful. There's a mural of the park that's painted all around the room, and lots of toys, books, and magazines to help pass the time. I thought the place was cool, so I was grateful to Samantha for taking me there. I saw her a second time a few years later and thanked her again for the rare "behind-the-scenes tour" but she had no idea who I was or what I was talking about.

Eddie Grier has claimed this whole zone as his personal domain. He clearly hasn't come to terms with his death or the nature of his existence, so the hub of this park's security is probably where he feels he needs to be. It seems like Eddie spends his day making the rounds, so I hope whatever we have to do won't take long. I don't like the idea of him catching us invading his headquarters. Even though I feel much more confident about facing him with four other ghosts at my side, underestimating the awful things that this park can summon has gotten me in trouble more than once already.

We take the road that cuts through the middle of Market Street east. Frank pushes open the employee door like he probably has a hundred times. There's one big road that winds around the triangle shaped building in the center of the area, wide enough for large trucks to pass each other, side by side. Thankfully, it's clear. No Eddie. No clay face security guards.

As we reach the main building, I register the mood of the other ghosts. Beverly seems cheerful and unaffected. I wish I could have some of whatever she's having. Reagan seems confident as well, but I can sense a bit of uncertainty beneath the surface. Frank and Rubén are positively spooked, necks twisting back and forth to spot danger approaching from every direction. I'm mixed. Excited to make progress but scared of the unknown.

I speak up. "None of you have talked to Eddie in all this time?"

The four exchange glances and Frank talks first. "Well, sure. You can talk to him. He's got lots to say about how this park should operate. Oh, and he's full of amazing stories." Frank opens the door for the group and we all pass him on the way in. "You ever hear the one about the kid who flicked a cigarette out of the train car on Gangway and Grier flicked it right back at 'em? Landed right in the kid's shirt pocket. Classic."

I've heard it multiple times, but I've never heard Frank tell it, so I let him start rattling off the amusing details. I try to stay focused on the story, but as I glance through the first door on the left I notice all sorts of designs and prototypes I've only seen in pictures. In my anxious anticipation of coming here, I forgot this is where the illustrators and architects that conceive of the park's next phases come to work when they're on the grounds. Home of Whirly World's "imagineers." I know I'll get an earful from Reagan if I take a sudden detour so I try to absorb as much of it as I can in a few seconds. There's a paddle boat design from before my time, a self-propelled eight-seater that never went into production. On the table next to it is a lakeside restaurant called The Salty Gullet that was supposed to replace half of Port Juniper. The illustrations on the wall behind them are also from the last century. The room is some kind of museum.

The hallways are painted a sterile blue, like a dentist's office. My sneakers squeak on glossy white tile. The walls are lined with a series of retro posters promoting cleanliness and safety. There are a couple of them that I've never seen before. Given their vintage value, I'm surprised they're not framed. They're just push-pinned to the wall.

The best of the bunch has a Schoolhouse-Rock-looking kid winking while dropping a piece of trash into a can. The Rootin' Ranger is behind the can, cheering, underneath the word *BULLSEYE!* I make a mental note to check how much it's worth online, then realize that's not a thing I can do anymore. Shame. It would look amazing in my apartment. I picture April's reaction to me bringing home more theme park art. It hits me like a wallop in the stomach, and Frank seems to notice the shift in my energy, pausing to look back at me.

"You okay, kid?" His walrus-y mustache and twinkly eyes give him the look of Santa's brother. He can't help but look kind.

I wave away his concern. "Yeah, yeah of course. Just anxious. Finish your story."

We reach a staircase on the south side of the building and Frank wraps up his tale. "So this idiot gets off the train with ash on his face and a hole burnt through his fancy jacket, and then asks for a refund. Grier threatened to sue him because he almost torched the place, and then kicked him right out the front gate. 'It's a non-smoking park.'" Frank chuckles to himself and then notices the staircase. "Here we are. One flight up. Second door to the right."

The old-school posters, which I'm guessing are from the mid-eighties, continue on the walls along the stairs. When I reach the top I realize they're not displayed as a throwback to a bygone era. This building is somehow trapped in that time period. I look through the window at the first second-floor office, and it's like I'm staring into the past. The desks, chairs, telephones, they're all from forty years ago at least. If I had to place a bet, I'd say 1983 exactly. The year Eddie died.

"Are you all seeing what I'm seeing?" I ask. Beverly is the last to reach the second floor. "Everything's from the eighties."

Reagan joins me at the window and looks through it. "Oh yeah, look at that. Neato."

"Well, why is that? Everything else I've seen in the park is updated. Current. How come this place is stuck in the past?"

"It's like I told you," Frank says. "Things change if you want them to change. I guess it's real important for Eddie to keep this place looking like it did when, well, you know."

"When he was murdered?" Reagan asks.

The rest of us nod.

"Poor guy is having such a hard time accepting what happened that he's bending the world to his will."

She's right, and if we don't hurry he might start bending us as well. I pick up the pace. "Then we should probably get this over with before he gets back, yeah?"

"Right you are," Frank says.

As Frank makes a move for the doorknob, Rubén waves his hand in the air. "Actually, guys. I'm going to wait outside." We all turn to him, surprised. "You know, to see if Eddie shows up." I hadn't thought of that strategy and it feels like neither did the others.

"Good idea," I tell Rubén.

Without pausing, he turns and walks down the stairs.

Frank opens the door marked CCTV and I follow everyone inside. On the back wall, and on a wide desk in front of it, stand the largest assembly of monitors I've ever seen. They're all black-and-white RCAs with curved edges and old-school twisty knobs. The lights are dimmed. I impulsively reach out to turn on the lights and even though I can feel the switches under my fingers, nothing happens. Reagan snorts and then flips a series of switches near the door and each screen illuminates. Dozens of camera angles blip into view. Some are in places I never realized had surveillance. How does this work?

"How come only you can do that?" I ask Reagan. She looks to the switches she just operated with ease, and then up at me.

"Because I'm cooler than you."

That's probably true. I turn to investigate the switches, but now they're gone. Or maybe I never saw them to begin with. I run my hand along the section of wall I saw Reagan reach for, and all my fingers touch is dried paint. I wonder when these ghosts learned to do the things that they can do. I wonder when I'll figure out what my special power is, if I even have one.

Frank leans onto the main desk like he's supervising a shuttle launch. "Okay, let's see what we can see." He taps the keyboard a few times and maneuvers a small joystick so each camera turns back and forth, up and down. "Good, it's working."

Reagan steps close to the monitors and surveys each of the glowing boxes that pulls the park into focus. "I can't see anybody." She taps one of the screens with her finger.

A few keyboard strokes bring up a shot of Sunburst Gardens. "Nuwa's in the greenhouse, as usual, staying out of sight." He taps away and the screen now points to a bench in Linden Forest. Clarence is sitting there, like before, enjoying the scenery.

"I saw Clarence there yesterday," I tell the group.

Beverly sighs. "That's where he died."

I take a step back. I should have known. It's probably his favorite spot. No one else in the room seems affected by this revelation so I try to regain focus on the task at hand.

Frank leans toward the monitors. "And Nolan's so damn hard to track on this thing, wait," Frank shouts, jabbing a finger at one of the squares.

I see what he's pointing at. Nolan is looking up at Hollow House, a few feet from its front door. There's a fuzziness around him, like the pixels that make up each image are having a hard time figuring out where he starts and stops. Then, just as soon as I noticed him, he's gone. Frank grunts. "Damn. That kid is fast. Well, there was Nolan."

Frank presses keys and twists the camera controls some more. "I don't see Blake anywhere. That's not good."

"Wouldn't he be underneath Gizzard Lake?" I ask. "Or inside of it, wherever he goes?"

"Maybe. If he was, I'd still be able to see something going on there. Some kind of something he left behind."

I turn to my left, roughly where I expect the lake to be, and squint. Nuwa's ball of light is tucked away in Sunburst Gardens, but just beyond it, Gizzard Lake is dark. I shouldn't have left Blake alone outside the tent. Why was I in such a hurry to see Kingston?

Frank takes a step away from the monitors. "Well, I've seen all I can see with these." He turns to Beverly who's occupied with the screens focused on Market Street. "Okay, Bev. Do your stuff. Let's see who else we can see."

Beverly has stuff? Beverly nods to Frank and turns to the group. She reaches out both hands like she's drawing us into a circle. Frank grabs her right hand. Reagan lets in a deep breath and takes Beverly's left hand. The three of them gesture for me to join. I'm not sure what praying will do at this point but I guess it's worth a shot.

The difference between Frank and Reagan's hands is stark. Frank's skin feels like burlap, where Reagan's soft fingers glide effortlessly into my palm. I'm not sure what I'm supposed to do now. Bow my head? Repeat what Beverly says in unison with the others?

Frank gives my left hand a squeeze. "Buckle up, kid. This is gonna get weird."

I recall being yoinked into Timber Tracks despite Frank's warning and have a sudden impulse to let go, but then the sensation is upon me. A pulse of energy flows from Beverly and passes through our arms. I can sense it continuing through the walls, and then out through the park, like the wake of a massive wave. Then I can feel it. The park. The whole damn thing. And not just the frozen limbo we're trapped in. I can feel the people. The living, hundreds of them, going about their day.

"How is this happening?" I wonder aloud.

Beverly shushes me.

It's not like I can feel everyone at once. I think that would be too much to handle. But wherever my thoughts go, my senses follow, and there are beating hearts all around us. I can hear the faint shouts of a large family arguing as they wait for the Lucky Spelunker. I can feel a mother's hunger as she waits for her favorite meal, the barbeque chicken at Nellie's. I can sense the rush of anticipation as a ten-year-old crosses through the front gates on her first visit.

Frank mumbles. "Something's wrong with Hollow House."

My omnipresent gaze floats over to the attraction, and instantly it's like I'm shoulder to shoulder with two teenage girls as they erupt into a screaming fit. The final basement scare triggers, a row of skeleton hands rocketing out of the ground as the grim reaper appears above them. Their brains tell them to run for the exit but their feet can't move.

It seems operational to me. "Why did something break?"

Reagan stomps on my right foot and for a moment I'm back in the monitoring room. "Not the people. You're too close. Zoom out."

I have no idea what that means.

Frank squeezes my hand. "It's the whole area, kid. Something funny there."

I pretend my brain is a camera and try to cast a wider net on what I'm feeling there. I can't sense the whole building, like I can tap into the emotions of the people walking through it, but I know very well what it looks like and I try to picture the mansion in my mind.

As my imagination brings the image to life, an orange glow starts to surround it, like dull lamplight seeping through drawn curtains. It flickers with movement, a luminous field of insects, and I realize it's coming from the crowd of people inside and outside the attraction. This is unlike the lightbulb projection of ghosts I can see from a distance. It's fainter, less accessible. A realm I can no longer touch. The living.

"Oh, cool. I see it," I shout to the group.

"Great," Reagan says, coldly. "Now shut up and keep looking." I can feel Reagan's shoulders twitch. "That looks weird. I've never seen anything like it."

I can't see what they see but I don't want to express my frustration. I take a deep breath and try again. It's obvious that clenching my muscles or otherwise straining myself is not the ticket here. I release my need to immediately understand this and just observe what I can. I'm not sure if we're all supposed to be seeing the same thing or if these impressions look different for each of us. If I describe what I'm seeing to the group, they might poke fun at me for stating the obvious or chide me for not analyzing it correctly.

"The mountain has it too," Frank says. "Deep below. Under the ride. See that?"

Reagan and Beverly make agreeable murmurs as they follow Frank's direction. I stay silent. We can't spend all day here. I need to figure this out as soon as possible.

Okay, what am I looking at, exactly? I can see Hollow House. I can see this orange glimmer that covers each tiny person. Focusing on one or the other reminds me of watching the busy street below my apartment through the screen on my bedroom window. The eye seems to forget there's a panel of black mesh right in front of your face unless you command it to pull back and take in the rows and rows of crisscrossed fiberglass.

What is my eye forgetting right now? I try to push in and out of the picture. My view wanders from Hollow House and I start to track people walking around Gizzard Lake, entering the queue for Sawmill Splash, eating an early meal at Port Juniper. They all look the same, like tiny orange fireflies. My shoulders are tense. My whole upper body curves forward in my attempt to see what I'm supposed to see. I stand up straight and remember to keep breathing.

"The circus too," Beverly adds. "That odd purple mist."

Okay, purple. Got it. Whatever they're talking about isn't showing up yet. I breathe in and let my breath out slowly, relax my stomach and then, there it is. Somewhere underneath Hollow House is another source of light. I'm grateful to see that it appears purple to me as well. It's not moving like the other lights. It doesn't seem to be restricted by the walls or fences around the building, and it leaves a trail behind it, like someone drawing with neon.

And this looks "weird" to them? They've had this standing seance with Beverly before and it's never shown them this? I open my eyes and see Frank, Reagan, and Beverly before me. At arm's length, they don't appear to radiate the yellow star shine that I can see from across the park, but when I squint there's definitely something there that's not human. I look past Frank, to the north, and see Clarence's light in Linden Forest. I close my eyes again and now I can see all three colors at once. Yellow means ghost. Orange means human. And purple means, what?

The door bursts open behind me. With a bang I remember where we are and what we're looking for. Rubén's back. Time to go. But the shocked expression on Frank's face tells me it's not Rubén. Reagan's eyes widen and fill my insides with dread. I turn.

Eddie Grier stands in the doorway, blocking the only exit. He's as surprised to see us as we are to see him.

We're trapped.

Chapter 13

WW

Security

"You're not supposed to be in here," Eddie yells, like we're a bunch of wily kids. The principal caught us sneaking into his office.

"We're screwed," Reagan states plainly.

It's clear Frank has no idea what to say. "Eddie…"

All I can think to do is put my hands up like a spooked bank teller. I feel a hand on my shoulder. I turn to it and its wrinkled flesh instantly tells me it belongs to Beverly. The warm fuzzies her touch engenders are like a cup of cocoa and diminish my spiking anxiety. She steps in front of me and I'm tempted to crouch behind her.

Eddie wouldn't hurt an old lady, would he?

"None of you are authorized to be here." Eddie says.

Reagan swears behind me, the kind of curse April reserved for spiders. I turn and notice the chair at the monitoring station is now occupied. One of Eddie's faceless buddies has appeared in it and seems to be surprised to find us standing so close. I hear footsteps at the door and see two more nondescript security officers rush in. Eddie puts one thumb behind his belt buckle and takes a few steps toward us.

Eddie smiles as he advances. "Does one of you want to tell me what you're doing in an off-limits security office?"

Frank offers up his hands, a placating gesture. "We all work in the park, you see. And, well, we thought there might be a threat."

Eddie scoffs. "That's security business. What are you, a mechanic?

From where I'm standing, you're breaking and entering."

The faceless security officers have all risen to their feet and are pushing in toward us, herding us into the center of the room. Even without features, each one of them oozes menace. I look to Frank, then Reagan, without any idea of what to do or say myself.

Then Beverly steps toward him. I instinctively reach out a hand to stop her, protect her, but she shuffles past. She raises her right hand, and places it in the middle of Eddie's chest. I gasp. I think Reagan does too. The motion is so sudden Eddie doesn't react until it's over. Eddie raises his right hand and gently grabs hold of Beverly's wrist, but she doesn't budge.

"Ma'am," Eddie says politely. "What are you…" Eddie freezes. His eyes nearly pop out of their sockets in surprise. His eyes dart around the room, seeing something we can't. Eddie stumbles a bit and Beverly puts her hand on his shoulder to steady him. The room goes quiet. Even Eddie's backup seems too stunned to move.

For a second it looks like Eddie has run out of breath. He finally takes in a gulp of air that sounds like a sob. Tears start to well at the base of his eyelids. "Sheila?" Eddie reaches out his hand. "Can you hear me? Sheila."

"She can't," Beverly tells him.

"What is this? What are you…?"

"It's three weeks ago."

Eddie scrunches his eyebrows in disbelief. "What? How?"

Good questions, Eddie. I look at Frank and Reagan to see if they're as surprised as me, but they look more concerned than confused. Frank nods to me in assurance. Reagan keeps her eyes on Eddie. I first assumed Beverly hit him with a view of the park like we just tranced our way through. Now I'm not sure what she's doing, exactly. Wasn't his wife named Sheila?

Eddie appears more and more shocked by the second. He reaches both hands out, trying to grab people we can't see, vaulting one emotional hurdle after another. The three mannequin-men Eddie called in for backup remain graciously immobile. I'm not sure if they're waiting on Eddie to make a move, or if he controls them and presently can't manage Beverly's trick and his own at the same time. I'm hoping it's the latter.

"Philip? That can't be…" Eddie says, and I see the whole reality of our situation land on his brain like a ton of bricks, his eyes locked in another place. Has he really been gone all this time? Has Beverly performed this parlor magic on someone else here? I have to assume she knows more about me than I thought. Eddie reaches his hand out to hold something. A face, judging by the height.

"He doesn't see or feel you," Beverly says, like she's guiding him through an acid trip.

Philip. His son. It's been so long since I read anything on Eddie Grier. The details are hazy. Philip was about eight or nine when his father was fatally stabbed in the park in 1983. That would put him in his early fifties. Sheila would be in her seventies by now.

Eddie begins to cry. First a whimper, then a wail. Reagan puts her hands over her heart and her eyes well up. "How didn't I know?" Eddie sobs. "I thought, if I can just make it through one more shift. Whatever's going on here will work itself out. We'll find that kid."

"They found her," Frank says. "You helped her get back to her parents. You slowed down the guys responsible so they could be caught. You saved the day. You're a hero, Eddie."

Eddie opens his eyes. Tears stream down his cheeks. "Where is she now?"

"She grew up," Beverly says.

Eddie pushes away from Beverly's face and tissue-soft hands and fixes the television monitors with a distant stare. His breathing is ragged as a series of emotions march their way across his face. Finally he wipes away tears and missed years in one swipe.

"What year is it?" Eddie asks, his voice regaining some of its typical regimentation.

"Two thousand and twenty-three," I blurt. It comes out before I really plan to speak.

Frank's jaw drops, and Reagan punches me in the arm, like I just spoke from an audience to an actor playing a character on stage. Hey, it's my year. I feel it's up to me to tell Eddie about it just like I've updated the other ghosts on the last few years or decades. Forty years in Eddie's case. Eddie shakes his head and looks right into my eyes. We're finally seeing each other for the first time.

"Two thousand and twenty-three?" Eddie replies. He looks like he just finished a marathon. I'm still embarrassed from having shoved my way into this powerful moment so I give myself a few more seconds to think up a considered and respectful response. Frank gracefully steps in and backs me up.

"Two thousand twenty-three," Frank puts a dramatic space between the numbers. Beverly holds out her hand to Eddie again and he takes it gingerly.

"Thank you, I suppose," Eddie rasps at Beverly, like he's thanking his dentist for a root canal. He sounds grateful, but also a little beat up.

"I'm Reagan." She waves. "I died in two thousand nine."

Frank nods. "Frank Young. Two thousand two."

I look at Reagan and Frank's smile and notice that Eddie's creepy friends are now gone. All three of them. My reaction to it prompts Reagan and Frank to also notice. I guess Eddie doesn't need them anymore. The weight of what Beverly just did starts to sag on my shoulders. His unjustified death, his treatment in this cursed version of the park.

Eddie eases into a chair and takes a deep breath. "Sorry, folks. I need a moment."

All four of us chuckle. I immediately feel awkward about finding it funny, but it feels like a nervous laugh that exists purely to dispel any residual awkwardness from a profoundly uncomfortable situation.

Eddie, apparently also seeking levity, smiles at our reaction. "That's a long time."

We all nod.

"A very long time," Beverly says. "I'm sorry I wasn't able to help you sooner."

Eddie searches for the words. "Ma'am, how did you…"

"Mysterious ways. Don't worry about that now."

Frank moves forward and leans onto the desk in front of Eddie. "What do you remember? What was going on all that time?"

Eddie is staring out into space as if the whole of his afterlife is suspended before him. "I don't recall it being a long time, is the thing. I mean, I knew days were going by but nothing else mattered besides finding that lost girl. What is this place? Where are we?"

I defer to the others. After experiencing the last thirty or so hours I don't know how I would classify this place. I know it so well in the real world, but here I can barely put it into words. I look around the room, clear in my intent not to engage in this part of the discussion.

Frank takes a stab at it. "Well, it ain't Whirly World. We left all that behind. It's someplace that looks like it and all we can figure is it's better than no-place. At least here we have each other."

"Does my family know?" Eddie asks.

"Know what?"

"That I'm here. That I can see them."

Reagan steps forward. "They know you died. But there's no way to contact them. Or anyone. We've tried."

Eddie looks up at her with despair.

Reagan puts her hand to her forehead and takes a breath before she responds. "It's confusing, I know. I couldn't get out of the theater for a week when I first got here."

Frank looks surprised. A little ghost lore slipped past him.

"I couldn't even get upstairs for two days. I kept feeling the walls closing in on me and I got lost in the basement. I never knew how I got down there, or how I got out. But I did, and I met Beverly, and Blake, and Frank, and everyone else that's died here. And we got through it."

"Hello, Beverly," Eddie says to her, and I realize I haven't introduced myself.

"I'm Jason. I died yesterday so it's new to me too." I try to sound comforting but end up sounding weird.

"He's the new kid," Reagan adds. "And there are more of us. I'm sure they'd love to meet you, Eddie."

Eddie nods to each of us in turn. Now that the pleasantries are out of the way, we all stand still, collectively unaware of where this moment should take us.

There's so much more I have to tell Eddie, but I imagine he's having enough trouble just sitting in that chair and accepting what happened to him. But I do have a few choice questions for Mrs. Beverly Thompson. "Beverly. What did you just do? If you don't mind my asking."

"Well, if you want to know," Beverly answers. "What I just did was a little forward and altogether inappropriate. I really shouldn't have shown him that without his permission." Beverly turns to Eddie. "You've been through enough. Take your time."

"How come you haven't done this before? Why'd you wait so long?" I realize it sounds accusatory, like I'm blaming her in some way, but I really want to know. And actually, maybe I am blaming her. It feels cruel that he was stuck for so long with no one to help him understand his circumstances.

"I tried, but I've never been this close to him." Her eyes brighten, excited at the prospect of what she's just done. "He was always disappearing on me."

Frank steps closer. "What did you show him?"

Beverly shrugs, as if it could have been anything. "Sheila and Phillip at the park. Laughing. I tried to think of a happy moment, but there are so many to choose from."

"So, you can see anything that's happened?" I ask her. "And show it to others? Us?"

"Anything *here* that has, is, or maybe will happen."

"*Will?* You can see into the *future?*"

"Of this park, yes, sometimes," Beverly is cool as a cucumber.

For a moment the reality that I could have someone explain to me the future of this park beyond my own lifespan thrills me with possibility. But then I remember how much I hate leaks and spoilers. That was always one way I was at odds with my passion and profession. For as much as I love gossiping about theme parks, I prefer to leave the surprises behind closed doors. It makes the act of experiencing them for the first time so much sweeter. So maybe I don't want to hear about the future. At least not yet.

"Cool," I answer. The award for most underplayed reaction of all time goes to…

Rubén bursts through the office door and we all shout. Reagan kicks the desk in shock. "Knock, Rubén. My God."

Beverly "tsks" at Reagan, and I notice Frank mindfully unclenching his fists.

"I haven't seen any—" Rubén starts. "Eddie it's Eddie!" Rubén shouts, then quickly realizes we're aware of Eddie's presence.

"Who are you?" Eddie asks Rubén.

Rubén looks at the rest of us.

"It's okay," Frank says. "He's come around. He's had a profound revelation."

Rubén smiles. "Well then, Rubén Castillo, at your service."

"Nineteen ninety-five," Reagan adds. Rubén looks at her in confusion. "It's when you died. We're bringing Eddie up to speed."

Rubén approaches Eddie. "We've actually met. Not here, but back there. When we were alive. When I was a lot younger. I don't know if you…"

"Castillo, yeah," Eddie says. His eyes warm at the memory.

"You're Diego's brother."

Rubén smiles. "Yeah. Bingo."

"How's your brother doing?"

"He's dead," Rubén says, glumly. "But we are too."

"I'm sorry to hear that. You worked here when you weren't at school." Eddie looks Rubén up and down. "You got old."

"We all did," Frank tells Eddie.

"Pardon me," Eddie says to the group. "But what are you all doing here? In this room. How come I haven't found you here before?"

I expect Frank to answer, but he appears unable to phrase it at the moment. Beverly still looks embarrassed. She reacted so quickly it looked like she does this stuff all the time, but now she seems embarrassed about brazenly jumping into Eddie's mind.

I'll try to explain. "We're looking for people. We want to make sure that we know everyone who's here, in the park. So it's actually fortunate that we met up with you. Although I imagine you're having a really lousy hangover right now."

"How many of you are there?" Eddie asks.

"Eleven, we think," I answer before anyone else, like I'm trying to win a game show.

"Well, I'd like to meet the rest of you."

"Which brings us to the next item on our list," Frank says. That could be one of many things now that we've seen dark, shadow-purple, demon zones pulsing in this park, and waking up Eddie Grier, making him face the four decades of the life he lost.

Frank slaps his hands together. "We gotta find Nuwa."

"Who's Nuwa?" Eddie asks.

"One of the rare people here more introverted than you, Mr. Grier," Reagan says.

"I've never spoken more than a sentence to her," Frank says. He looks to Rubén who nods and shrugs in reply. We look to Reagan.

"What?" she answers, annoyed. "I don't know her. She wants

to hang out in her garden paradise all day, fine. I don't blame her. Whatever it takes to make the years go by."

Eddie looks north of us. "Sunburst Gardens?"

"By the lake, yeah," Frank says. "She's not someone you make an appointment with."

"Maybe she's lost. We should wake her up too."

"No, she's awake," Reagan says. "She just has healthy boundaries unlike the rest of us."

"Eleven people," Eddie says. "In forty years. How terrible."

"Yeah, that's life. And life isn't fair."

Frank pats Eddie on the shoulder. "That's all behind us, buddy," Frank says like he's addressing an old college chum.   " W h a t ' s done is done. We're still around. Somewhat."

Eddie smiles at Frank but it's forced. It's still all sinking in, but I'm amazed at how quickly Eddie has been able to come to terms with being dead for such a long time. I think I'm doing okay with all of this, but I didn't have a few hundred weeks go unaccounted for. I think we'll need all the friends we can get if we're going to be able to stand up to whatever's controlling Whirly World, but it might be too much for Eddie to deal with currently.

I thought Eddie might have been a victim of his own trauma, but now I think a more sinister power is responsible. Someone, or something, did this to him. I wonder if this is keeping Nuwa from speaking to the rest of us. Getting more answers from Eddie would help us all understand this better, but we shouldn't be in a rush. Not today. I understand now that we truly have a chance to get out of here. We just have to overcome anything meant to keep us apart.

"I'll do it," I say to the group. "I'll go talk to Nuwa."

"What?" Reagan says. "We're *all* going to do it."

"I don't know. I think that's aggressive, all of us crowding in there. I think one of us should tell her what's what and let her decide."

"And why should that be you?"

"Well, I've never tried it before, for one thing. She doesn't know *not* to trust me, I don't think. I only saw her when I first got here and then when she watched the fireworks. And I used to spend a lot of time in the gardens." I don't add that I was only there so much because of April, but the truth is that I likely spent more time in them than most parkgoers. The room feels unconvinced aside from Eddie who's barely following along. But no one else volunteers.

Frank shrugs. "It's worth a shot, I guess. I think it's a longshot either way."

"What could it hurt?" I ask.

Eddie stands up. "No matter what you all do, I'm going to get some fresh air. This room was only supposed to have two to three people in it, tops."

"I'm not sure if that's air out there," Reagan interjects.

Eddie nudges Frank and me to the side as he leaves the room. "Well, whatever it is, I'm going to breathe a ton of it. Thank you again, Beverly." He nods to her.

Beverly nods back. "Of course, Eddie."

Frank follows Eddie outside, starting the first of what I imagine will be a series of questions.

Reagan watches them go, then turns back to me. "Well, on your way then. No time to waste, right?"

"Absolutely" I answer with confidence. "Just one thing first." I turn to Beverly. "If you can show Eddie his family, can you show me how I died?"

Beverly's blue eyes catch the light from the monitors as she takes in the seriousness of my expression.

"I think, before I take any more steps to move on from this place, I should figure that part out. I don't have time to wait around for someone else to die in this park and tell me on the off chance that they live nearby and saw the sad story on the evening news. It wouldn't necessarily change anything about my circumstances, but it'd be comforting to know what happened."

"Oh, man," Rubén says, sympathetically. "You don't know?"

"Nope. How would I? Did you, right away?"

"No, not exactly. I mean, I figured I was going to blow myself up one way or another. I had plenty of close calls. So it wasn't a huge shock when I found out I got burnt to a crisp. But it was still tough to watch. You sure you're ready for this?"

"Well, I might not get another chance. If we break out of here, how do I know I'll get to talk to Beverly or any of you again? I gotta do it. You two have done this before, right?"

Both Rubén and Reagan nod.

Reagan breathes in through her teeth. "Yeah, that's not something I want to do again." She gives me a bump on the shoulder with her fist. "Good luck, you're gonna need it." She walks out of the control room. What's that supposed to mean? Reagan is gone before I think to ask. My anxiety spikes.

Rubén takes Reagan's cue and follows, nodding encouragingly as he leaves. I turn back to Beverly, trying to knock away any thoughts telling me to do this later.

Beverly reaches out her hand. "I can describe it to you first. How you passed, I mean. If that will make it easier."

That's sweet. "No thanks. I'm pretty sure I want to be in the front row for this."

Chapter 14

WW

Sawmill Splash

As my hand reaches for Beverly's I echo my one wish regarding however it was that I died.

Please don't let this be embarrassing.

Seeing anything that I don't recall after the fact has to be extremely weird, let alone me falling over dead. So many memories flash before me of times when I could have seen someone else in a life-threatening emergency. Would I help? Would I know how to dislodge something from someone's throat? Do I remember CPR? Did someone help me?

I take Beverly's hand, using the same will as I would if I had to jump into a freezing lake. At first, I just feel her wrinkled hand and long fingernails. After a few seconds the here and now fades to black. And then I'm there, as if the last two days never happened. My favorite spot. I hear birds, footsteps, dozens of overlapping conversations. A hundred sounds have returned to the air. I'm back in Whirly World. I've missed it so much.

I'm standing next to myself. The other me is walking north. I need a shave. I'm alone, thank goodness. April doesn't have to watch this. My family doesn't have to drag me out of here. It's early, and the sunrise looks warm and inviting. I can't feel it. All I can feel is Beverly's hand and the coldness that's been creeping around inside me since yesterday. I'm finishing off a large pretzel, scraping up the last bite of cheese sauce from the plastic dipping cup. A dab of cheese remains on my chin, and part of my hair is sticking up. It's like I haven't looked in a mirror all day. I'm headed for Sawmill Splash, something I would never do at this early hour unless it was unreasonably hot, and it seems to be. People are wearing shorts and sandals, and a few are using umbrellas for shade.

A sign outside of Sunburst Gardens is advertising its next theme: The Aura of Autumn. Market Street is beginning to fill with pumpkins and garlands of leaves in preparation for Halloween. The full effect is way too much to install in one night so the staff starts trickling out decorations day by day, starting in September. A few more weeks and over half the park will shut down for the season. The coasters will close, turning the park into a shopping mall with a garden and a killer view. Attendance will go into hibernation.

The line for Splash looks to be over an hour long, but I use my Marshal's Badge to take the express lane. Even along the expedited path, there are a lot of fun details to see. I take my time through the queue and appreciate them. I'm proud of myself. This is the last time I'll ride Sawmill Splash, and I seem to be savoring it.

Splash's story operates under the guise that everything on the ride is happening because of one dangerous mistake made by a bumbling lumberjack. The park never named him, but fans call him "Jim," after Jim Larson, the guy who built the ride. Jim, the lumberjack, knocks over a lantern that kicks off a Rube Goldberg machine that leads to you getting drenched in a log canoe. When the park first opened, Jim was clearly intoxicated, something that was funny at the time but eventually replaced. In '82 he went from "drunk" funny to just "clumsy" funny. It's such a small thing to care about but I lament never being able to experience the original.

Twenty minutes later, I reach the boarding platform. As I watch myself climb into the back of Splash's four-seater log behind a mother and her son, I remember I'm here to watch myself die, possibly on this ride. I would be the first. As the log slides off the boarding ramp,

I naturally move along with it, like a guardian angel, floating in the air as the log shuffles up the first incline. Overhead, a crane knocks a large gear that spins down two rows of pipes, sending off the tiniest sparks as it grinds to a halt just before we dive down the first drop.

I can't feel the ride directly, but I can tap into each sensation through my memories. The vibration in my feet as the log scrapes against the bottom of the flume. The tug at my waist as my seat slams into the side of the track. The errant spray that dampens my shirt and tickles my cheeks. And those drops. Those wonderful, stomach-churning drops. My mind says I'm safe but my heart fears the worst as the bubbling crest of the fall draws near.

It's a great run. A worthy "last ride." Everything works. Even the tiny jeep that drives through the side of the warehouse, that only shows up around a third of the time. The lady ahead of me, holding her son down by his shoulders, screams at the top of her lungs on the last perilous plunge. I'm not much of a social screamer, so I'm always grateful to those that are, when it's appropriate. A really good scream can make a ride sing, and this poor lady is going all out.

By the time we disembark, she's all smiles. The two of them took most of the last splash, leaving me moderately dry considering how much the ride can really soak you. I exit safely, so I suppose Splash's safety record is certified for another day. I wobble south toward my favorite spot like a man who is wearing wet pants. I stop and look at the sun. One of the rafts on the lake disturbs a pair of ducks that take to the air and fly past me, quacking in disapproval.

Then it starts. I can see it in my eyes. Something's wrong. I expect a heart attack, thinking of all the double cheeseburgers I've stuffed into my face in my thirty years. But my left arm reaches suddenly for my forehead, and I start to put it together. An aneurysm. Me, at my age. That's absolutely what this is. My eyes swirl frantically, looking for the cause.

I guess I should be scared as well but all I can feel is empathy for this person who's about to feel the world slip away. The other me shakes his left hand and it jumps to his forehead in a clumsy slap. I think of April's uncle who died suddenly from a stroke. Will that loss make mine easier or harder for her?

Now I just want this to stop. I imagine only seconds have passed since this started but it feels like he's taking forever to succumb. Did I know what was happening like I do now? Was I drinking in the last moments of my life like a milkshake through a giant straw? I don't remember. Did the horror of this consume me as the inevitability or our fragile decay took hold of the last functioning parts of my brain? Or maybe things just got blurry for a bit and then I collapsed?

I would have thought a lifetime of watching horror movies would have prepared me for this. But it isn't shocking or scary. It's sad. Why did I subject myself to this? I could have had Beverly just say "you got a real nasty headache and died," and I could have moved on. How am I to erase this image from my memory? How can I forget that it all ended here, for all of Whirly World to see?

Then, I slump. I fall to my knees for a split-second then most of me gives out. Like I just lost a boxing match, my head and shoulders crumple into the metal fence. It's not a position I'm necessarily proud of, but it could have been so much worse. I could have made a loud splash in Gizzard Lake. I could have been splayed out like a cartoon chalk outline.

Well, that's it. I'm not moving any more. I'm a corpse. I've seen a lot of things pretending to be dead in this place. The ghosts of Hollow House. Costumed teenagers at Halloween. But this is real and it's me and there's nothing I can do to stop it. My head is turned away so I step around and kneel to look myself in the eyes. They're closed. My face is peaceful. I want to feel that peace as well but my insides are quaking.

I wonder if I woke up in this instance, thinking I was having a dream about an empty park on an otherwise perfect day? Or did it take time? Did I have to go somewhere else first before my eternity-long sentence was carried out?

Then I see something even more awful than my death. Twenty feet or so behind me, a man - a father - is throwing a stack of napkins into a trash can when he looks over and notices me. His two kids, a boy and a girl, come running up behind him. They're shouting something with smiling faces but I can't hear anything anymore.

I am about to ruin this man's day. I'm about to haunt these kids, what, forever? As his eyes go from curious to worried to panicked, I try to pull myself out of this vision but I forget how I got into this thing in the first place. Then I feel five wrinkled fingers slip out of my hand and there's Beverly. I'm back. We're in the CCTV room. That was just a memory.

I feel awful. Not for me. I had a good life. Sure, there are things I'm not proud of, moments that I'd do over if I could. There are things I had to suffer that I wish I hadn't, but I've never seen someone die and I can't believe I volunteered to do so. Why did I stain this happy place with what I just saw? I want to go back. I want more time.

"Who else found me?" I ask. "How long was I there?"

Beverly hugs me. These questions yell at my muscles to push her away but they don't listen. I stop talking and let her embrace linger.

"That's all for now." Beverly sets me upright and grabs my shoulders. "It's never easy. For anyone. Sometimes we're called to see something or help someone. That's His way. It's no one's fault." For Beverly's sake, I want that to make me feel better, but I can't fake it. I'm crushed. "You didn't ruin his day," she continues, like she read my mind. I guess she did.

Chapter 15

Sunburst Gardens

The archway leading into Sunburst Gardens is covered with thick, old ivy and crowned with a large copper sign that reads SUNBURST in filigreed capital letters. In one step, the rough flat concrete turns into artfully laid brick lined in squares of twenty or so, joined by ceramic tiles in a rainbow of colors. The wild west rowdiness of the park fades into background noise as you walk under the verdant canopy of trees. So much of this park is pleasing to the eye because it's pretending to be something else. But this garden is legitimately beautiful, featuring wild animal topiaries, wrought iron benches, and tinkling fountains.

It was, and hopefully still is, April's favorite spot.

April always had an affinity for plants, a passion I could never keep up with. She'd point at something on a walk or hike together and ask if I knew what it was. In our four-year relationship, I don't think I ever got it right. I didn't even hazard a guess half the time. That must have been what it felt like whenever I quizzed her about this park. How could I ever have expected her to follow my obsessions if I never took the time to study hers?

We'd walk through the garden and she'd call out what everything was, and when we walked out I'd check the tags to see if she was right. Even when she was wrong, she never failed to take a guess. I can't even make a bad impression of it now. I'm not sure how many flowers I could write down in a list if I was forced to.

The current garden, however pretty, feels off. Nuwa never designed it. She died seven years ago and the garden has been revamped five times since then. Management kept her last design for an additional year after she died, but that was about it for park tributes. She didn't get a plaque, bust, poster, or anything. Right before Clarence, she was one of the last people to die here and I bet everyone in the park today has no idea what her name is. It's not fair.

As I assumed, Nuwa is nowhere to be seen. The garden rarely got what I would call "crowded" but it still is disheartening to see all of the benches empty. The speakers, usually filling the air with classical music suited for a picnic, are silent. The walls are so stuffed with greenery that, while light still seeps through here and there, the outside park cannot be seen. I spin around slowly and study every vine and strip of bark for Nuwa's eyes but find nothing.

In this version of Whirly World, Sunset Gardens is Nuwa's home, so I should be respectful. I stop to think about the most appropriate questions to ask her. Perhaps a compliment will work? I should introduce myself first.

"Hi. I'm Jason. I, uh, got here yesterday." I'm not expecting a response and I get none, so I continue. "I was talking to the others. The other ghosts, I mean. The other people here. And we thought it was worth coming over and saying hello."

Nothing. Just total stillness, without even a breeze to rustle the leaves. I might as well plunge forward. "We think there's something that's keeping us all here and if we work together we might be able to break free."

Honesty is probably the best policy here. "Or, rather, I believe that and I'm slowly convincing them of it, I hope. So, yeah, that's why I'm here."

Silence. It's weird not to hear birds, which have always loved to stop by Sunburst. I wonder vaguely if there are any ghost birds and then dismiss the notion. There is a possibility that Nuwa's not even here. I could just be talking to myself, which wouldn't be a first at Whirly World. I guess there's no harm in telling her my life's story if we're going to be here for a while.

"I've always loved this park." I turn back toward the entrance in case Nuwa's over there and can't hear me from where she's hiding. "I saw all fourteen of your designs in the time you worked here. I confess I didn't know who'd made them until you died. But then I learned how long you'd been here and realized that it all made sense."

Zero response.

"My girlfriend April loved it here. She only came here three times when she was a little girl, before we met. But when I told April about your death, she said she remembered the name Nuwa Chen. She said your gardens 'told a story.'"

I'm finding this confession oddly comforting. It's like talking to a therapist that doesn't butt in or ask you more questions. I've heard people say that flowers like to hear people talking, that it helps them grow. I guess it works both ways. I wonder if Nuwa spends her dead days walking the length of this place and delivering her own soliloquies. She hasn't asked me to leave yet so she's either not listening or not talking.

"April, that's my girlfriend, would walk back and forth saying 'mhmm' and 'of course' when she saw each of the displays lined up, like she knew where the designer was going with all of it. I used to make fun of her but maybe she really connected with them somehow. I won't lie, Nuwa, Sunburst was not my favorite place to visit in this park, but I was always glad it was here. Not many theme parks dedicate this much space to something that's naturally gorgeous. So, thanks, I guess, for all the time you spent here making it that way."

The words float out of my mouth and are lost as they drift away. If she's here with me, biding her time until I leave, her stealthiness matches her green thumb in equal measure. I keep expecting to hear a rustle of leaves or see her face slip past behind the fence. But the evidence suggests that there's no one here but me. Well, I have more I want to say.

"I'm sorry that you died. I mean, I'm sorry that everyone died here, obviously, but what happened to you must have been really frustrating."

The reporting on Nuwa's death didn't say much about how long she suffered, but my research told me that snake venom can take a few hours to run its course. The bite could have been close to a major artery, otherwise she might have been able to get help. My theory is that it wasn't just the bite. She could have injured herself in a struggle and either knocked herself unconscious or inhibited her movement, preventing her from seeking medical attention. There are also several theories on how a cottonmouth even got into the park in the first place, but who needs a theory? We're near the woods, where the snakes live, and one decided that snacking on after hour rats that were plump from eating park trash seemed like a better kind of life. There is an animal control team but they mostly work on prohibiting people from overfeeding the ducks in the pond or keeping pigeons from dumping on all the parked cars.

Nuwa's case was not only the first snake bite in Whirly World, it was the first animal attack of any kind in fifty-one years of operation. That's a pretty good record, in my opinion. But in her case, it was still one bite too many. They drained the lake and brought in a snake catcher to see if there was a nest, but no snake was ever discovered. In the end it just seemed like a fluke. Like nature had it in for Nuwa that day. Anyway, back to my monologue.

"I'm not sure how that snake got in here but it shouldn't have. I'm sorry." I had nothing to do with it. I wasn't even here that week. But I still feel like the need to keep this place looking fresh takes its toll on people. It's hard to justify it taking someone's life, though.

Out of the stillness a voice jumps at me and I scream.

"It was my fault."

Once my insides calm from her expertly timed scare, I turn to Nuwa. Up close I realize that her overalls are one of the only things I've seen today with a little wear and tear. It's faint, scraped with waves of brown and green, but you can tell Nuwa's been working. She looks like she has more to tell me, so I just give her a tiny wave to say hello.

Nuwa goes on. "I was looking for a kitten I heard meowing the day before. Animal control didn't have the best reputation of processing cats appropriately. There were rumors they were being put down instead of being put up for adoption. I didn't want it to end up in a kill shelter somewhere so I looked for it after my shift was over. That's when I got nailed by that snake, that lurking little shit. He got hold of my arm before I even saw him."

"So what did I do?" she asks, but I know she's not going to wait for me to answer. "What did I do? I reached for my shears so I could split the thing in two. Only I was in shock from the bite and my muscles were twitchy, so I dropped them onto my calf."

I wince and she nods as if I gave her the correct response. She brings her left hand down on the bottom of her left leg with a "Whack." She had an accident. I knew it. I'm proud of my powers of deduction in the manner of her death but I keep that personal victory to myself.

"Ouch," I say out loud.

"I didn't know where to put pressure. I stood there like a dummy and stared at my arm getting poisoned and my leg getting emptied and I froze. By the time I had the sense to run for the gate I could barely breathe and my leg gave up after a few seconds. I don't remember it but I guess I hit the bricks and blacked out."

"Did Beverly show you?"

"No she did not, thank you very much," Nuwa says, disgusted at the idea. "It's bad enough that we have to spend forever here. I don't need that visual in my head if the powers that be had the sense to not put it there in the first place. She told me that the staff disposed of the snake but beyond that I told Beverly to mind her own business."

She's got a point. I should have asked Beverly to describe mine. Oh well. Too late.

I have to sell this to her, somehow. "What if we don't have to spend forever here."

Nuwa puts her hands on her hips.

That sounded like a crummy sales pitch. "I think the powers that be, as you put it, are keeping us here against our will. I think they're malevolent. I think we're trapped in some elaborate scheme that we can't see the size of because we're right in the middle of it. I think you feel it too."

Nuwa cocks her head to one side. "You've got this all figured out after just one day?"

"I don't think they can mess with us if we're all working together, as a team."

Nuwa looks around her. "No one bothers me here."

"That may be. But that's my point. However this place was built, it gave you the power to hide from everyone. As long as you keep doing that you'll never know how much power you wield against whoever holds the key."

"Are you talking about the Ranger?"

"The Rootin' Ranger?" Buckthorn's Sheriff-of-sorts. Keeper of the peace and peddler of barbecue chips and beef jerky. When the park first opened his costume was topped with a mortifying looking fake cowboy head. It had a giant jaw and dead eyes. It was hideous. Everyone came to their senses and the park just let an actor play him starting in '87.

"I did wonder about that," Nuwa says, pensively. "He's part of the reason I learned how to hide in the first place. After I got here and came to terms with what happened to me, he started stopping by and asking questions. They seemed like considerate requests at first. He wanted to know what I enjoyed doing and how I came up with my designs. But I stopped talking to him because he's not real, right?"

"No, I don't think so. And the others have also had unfortunate encounters with mascots. Frank saw Phuzzy, or Phineas. You know, the sasquatch? The big furry guy?"

Her face is deadpan. "I am aware of who Phuzzy is, yes."

Of course. Obviously. I continue. "And I saw Kingston, from the circus. Like you, he came after me right when I got here. He told me that there were things that I could do in this park that I'd never dreamed of before. I think he was referring to everyone's special gifts. I don't think you all have those by chance."

"If these creeps want us to stay here," Nuwa says, sounding doubtful, "then why would they make it so we could do the things we can do?"

"That's an excellent question. I'm not sure."

The two of us stand silent, thinking this over. There are plenty of things about this place that don't add up. If Kingston gives out these powers, can he take them away? Was he chasing us to capture or hurt us, or was he just scaring us?

I look to the surrounding trees and plants for inspiration and realize that they have completely changed. Thick pines have been replaced with bending palms. I can see Gizzard Lake over the garden fence and large bushes with blue flowers bursting from them.

"Neat trick," I tell Nuwa, gesturing around me toward the pleasant scenery. She looks unsure of what I'm referencing. I motion with more emphasis and she smiles.

"Oh, right. You probably saw only what you could see on your own. Whatever theme they have in whatever year it is."

"Two thousand twenty-three," I tell her.

She shrugs, like she doesn't care.

"Actually, some of the new ones have been—"

Nuwa puts up her hand to stop me from speaking. "*This* is the new stuff. Plumeria. Hibiscus. Bird of Paradise. If I can't go to the tropics anymore, at least I can pretend."

"Wow." I read the new markers on each exhibit. "People are missing out."

Nuwa chuckles. "Most people wouldn't know careful landscaping if it whipped them in the ass. But that's kind of you." Nuwa gracefully raises one arm toward a batch of flowers bursting out of a nearby shrub. Plumerias, I think she called them. She opens up her fist and spreads her fingers, and the petals roll open and change from orange to pink. I'm impressed, but I think she just did it for her own edification. She closes her fist and the petals retreat.

"Is this how you're able to hide?" I ask. "Pull the vines over our eyes, so to speak? Not that there's anything wrong with that. Believe me, I get it. I came to this park to get away from the real world. Sometimes we need to be separate from everyone else."

"No. *This* is how." Nuwa lowers both hands to her sides, then lifts them upwards while folding her fingers inward. The bricks on the path beneath her move aside and shields of bark climb up out of the soil, surrounding her. They clasp together with a crunch, and then as easily as they shot upward, they dive into the dirt and Nuwa's gone.

"Ah," I say, and can think of nothing else to add. After a moment I realize my mouth is still hanging open. Right when I think she's left me on my own again, the seed of large, wooden plates emerges from the ground again, opens, and Nuwa steps out like she's traveled here in some strange, earthen UFO. Or like Venus stepping out of a clamshell. Goddess-like.

"I wish I could do something cool like that," I tell her, honestly. "I keep waiting for some special power to show itself but all I seem to be good at is getting up in everyone's business."

"You can't help it. It's who you are." I can't tell if that's a compliment or Nuwa is just stating a fact. She turns and walks toward the gazebo in the back of the gardens.

"So, will you join us?" I ask again. "We're going to put our heads together and see—"

"I heard you the first time." She stops and turns toward me. "No." She has more to say but lets that rejection hang in the air for a few beats. "I don't believe there's a way out of here. I think people fear the afterlife, fear death, because they don't know who they are. I know who I am. This is where I'm supposed to be."

Okay, I'll try harder. "But haven't you ever—"

"Jason. Stop."

At the risk of her going full-subterranean, I back off. She appreciates my silence, gives me a warm but final smile, and walks away. The tropical plants and trees seem to inhale as she walks nearer to them, bursting into a frenzied bloom, a technicolor miracle. I take a moment to appreciate the updated Sunburst Gardens, and then leave Nuwa to tend to it. Or however she spends her time here.

The sun is almost directly above the lake now. I look around to see if anyone else has finished their assignment. Frank said other than that one bench on Catlin Peak, or behind his dessert-cart on Market Street, Clarence can be found in the employee area to the west, restocking his supply from the freezers there. The old man doesn't need to do this, as it's unlikely he runs out of supplies on a daily basis. Clarence only has a handful of potential customers here, but he seems to be committed to restocking his cart out of habit.

After asking Eddie about everything from his taste in music to his son's favorite ride in the park, Frank headed west to track down Clarence and see if convening with the rest of us was something he was interested in or could even perceive the benefit of. As much as I love him, I have to assume that Clarence is operating on a completely different wavelength from the rest of us. As nice as he is to have around, he likely won't be much help in the challenges to come.

Rubén couldn't wait to check out Hollow House after we recognized that strange, purple aura glowing inside of it. Apparently it's his favorite ride, which I would not have guessed. He seems like a Hooper Looper kinda guy, but I guess his tastes are somewhat dark.

The prospect of Whirly World's haunted house actually possessing a supernatural presence sent him jogging north of the lake. He must still be in there because I can't see him now.

Reagan said she'd wait at the Palace Theater for Nolan, which seems like the best way to track down that squirrely kid. He doesn't keep to a schedule outside of watching that one show in the late afternoon and then the fireworks at night. Like Clarence, I don't predict Nolan will want to hang out with a bunch of serious adults, but it doesn't hurt to ask. Hopefully one of those three will have better luck making progress than I just did.

I'm not sure where Eddie is right now. We left him on Market Street, absentmindedly staring into one of the shop windows. He's got a lot of catching up to do, and that's before we really sit him down and tell him what we think is going on. What I think, at least. I can't fathom the depths of his loss and confusion right now. We yanked away his coping mechanism against the unrelenting monotony of this park, and none of us can make that right.

I'll just stare at the sun for a little while. I don't have to worry about ultraviolet light flooding my retinas and doing permanent damage. I don't need to wear sunscreen. I can barely feel its warmth. It's not at all the same as being alive. There are no minute fluctuations in the waves of heat that cascade down on me, but it does feel like the temperature is higher now than it was last night. Still, there's the matter of that chill I can't seem to shake. That's still there, lingering inside whatever spectral skeleton is holding me upright.

Then I see something. An object directly between me and the sun. I hold up my hand to block the light and get a good look at it, but it's completely silhouetted. It's not something wrong with my vision. I never got eye floaters but my sister used to complain about them. This is definitely there, and it's moving. It's getting closer, like it's aiming to land on top of me.

Wait, are those *wings*? Oh, God. Whatever it is looks human.

But there's something behind it. It's a human-shaped thing with arms drawn to its side, and some shape behind that keeps cutting through the sun's rays. *This is it*, I say to myself. *Time to get smited by an angel for your lack of faith.* Whatever it is, whoever it is, the visage looks more and more like a person as it gets closer. Someone suspended from something, dropping to Earth in slow motion.

I'm shocked when it floats closer and it's actually Beverly. She's flying down at me in her janitorial uniform, smiling. Like every other impossible thing I've seen lately, I have to take this at face value. I didn't know Beverly could fly too, but then a few hours ago I didn't know she could see into the park on any day, month, or year, so maybe I haven't been paying attention. Then I see who's holding her.

Josie Bean places Beverly down gently, like Superman dropping off Lois Lane. Josie's wearing blue overalls with the bottom hem curled up a few times over her calves. Her curly, bright blonde hair bounces with every subtle movement, like happiness made human.

She has on the official 1997 Whirlyween shirt. It's light brown with a deranged fisherman drawn on the front, bursting out of a tidal wave crashing into Gizzard Lake. I Know What You Did Last Summer came out that year and the park leaned on the seaside horror theme for their fall festivities as much as they could without paying royalties.

I was four years old and obviously did not attend Whirlyween that year. My first Halloween-themed visit was in 2008 when I was fifteen. I lied to my parents and told them that I was going to Mike's. He told me he would go along with the lie but ended up going to an R.E.M. concert that night and not telling his parents anything. When they realized they didn't know where their son was, his parents called my parents and the gig was up. I got two weeks alone in my room and one month without allowance for that stunt. It was worth it.

Josie, who a moment ago looked like an angel descending from the pearly gates, puts her tiny hands in her large pockets and hops up and down like a giddy kid. Beverly stands there, smiling at the both of us, clearly taken with Josie's energy.

"Hey there," Josie says to me with a light drawl, enough to guess where she's from. She waves at me back and forth, rotating her hand like she's wiping a window clean.

"I'm Josie Bean." If you count the time she's been stuck here in the afterlife, this woman is eleven years older than I am, but doesn't act a day older than twenty.

"You can fly," I say back to her. Obvious, but still amazing.

She lights up at the observation and jumps up into the air, reaching both arms into the sky. "I can. I know!" she shouts. More jumping. "I love it, love it." When she stops jumping Josie looks at me funny and bobs her head to one side. "I don't know you."

"No, that would be impossible. You've been up there, and I've been down here." I motion toward her home in the clouds and then the ground I'm stuck to. "I'm Jason."

"Right, right. How long you been here?"

"Since yesterday. I think. Who knows?"

I shrug my shoulders and so does Josie. The absurdity of it all makes her laugh.

"Josie," Beverly says. "Tell Jason what you told me."

Josie looks confused, then her eyes widen. She smacks her lips and points at Beverly like she just answered a trivia question correctly. "Right, right." She turns to me. "He wants to talk to you."

"Who?" I hold back a chortle because Josie expects me to know.

"You know, 'the big guy,'" Josie says, pointing her thumb behind her. I look at Beverly, hoping she'll have more information, but she just nods and smiles. "The old guy."

"Clarence?" I ask.

"Clarence?" Josie curves her eyebrows at each other, puzzled. Then she giggles. "Oh, not Clarence. No."

"God?" I guess.

Beverly laughs a kindhearted laugh.

"Worley," Beverly says.

The name gets knocked around in my head a few times before I can grab hold of it and realize who she means. Josie's backward gesture was directed at Worley Lodge.

Beverly gives me another knowing nod. "Yes, him."

Chapter 16

Worley Lodge

"Warren Worley?" I ask, bewildered. That's impossible. According to the laws that I am cobbling together about this place, you have to have died here to be here. The man who built this theme park died of pneumonia in 1973 at his home in Hendersonville, Tennessee, which is definitively not here. If he's *here* then my understanding of how this purgatory functions completely falls apart. How could Warren have a presence here, miles away from where he died? Let alone one that "wants to talk to me."

"No, *Whirly*," Josie says, correcting me. "In the cabin." She points across the lake.

Whirly? Ha, a common misconception. I doubt "Worley World" would have been as easy to advertise. I've read tons of emails, press releases, tweets, and articles that have spelled Warren's last name incorrectly and it makes me chuckle every time. I imagine he would have found his calling at a much younger age had his last name been directly associated with things that spin around for one's amusement. But I let Josie have this one.

"Sorry, my bad," I tell Josie, then turn to Beverly. "How is that possible? If he's shacked up in that cabin then how come I couldn't sense him? How come we couldn't see him?"

"Well, it's not really him," Beverly answers. "Not like you and me. You'll see."

Josie runs to me and tries to circle her arms around my waist.

I'm not used to having pretty blondes dash at me, so I shout "Ah!" and involuntarily leap out of the way.

"Whatsa matter?" Josie asks. "Let's go."

"Wait," I say, losing a bit of breath. "Go? What, now? You just grab me and we go?" I point my finger up into the sky.

"Of course, silly. It ain't nothin' to be afraid of." She punches me in the chest. It's playful but has a bit more heft behind it than I anticipated.

"That's easy for you to say. I've never flown before. At least, not like this." I look out at the gap of water between us and the island. I would guess the distance to be about a hundred feet. I've been thrown around a lot recently and haven't suffered a scratch, so I'm not sure what I'm afraid of. Maybe I'm more anxious about meeting Worley. Or whatever is waiting for me in that cabin.

"Okay, I…" I start to say, before realizing Josie has walked up to my side. I take a step back, surprised. She extends her hand, like she's asking to dance. "Heh," I utter, nervously. "Just try not to drop me in the water. It's not easy getting out of there."

I take her hand, like Wendy grasping Peter Pan's, and at once Josie floats upward. She glides effortlessly through the air, but her hand is small and delicate. I have to close my fingers tightly around her wrist so I don't slip and fall. We only travel a few feet off the ground, but I can't help getting twitchy, my legs wiggling as they lose the comfort of solid ground. It feels less like we're both flying and more like Josie's dangling me over the edge of a cliff. I think of a happy thought, just in case it might help. It does not.

Like before, I can't see the bottom of Gizzard Lake. Below me the water looks like the heart of an open sea. I wonder what it looks like below the surface right now. I wonder where Blake is. More than anything, I wonder who is in that cabin, and what he wants with me. Is this Worley just another mascot of this park trying to run us ragged?

Once my shoes land in the grass on the island, and I wobble to my knees despite my best efforts not to, Josie glides downward with the grace of a ballerina. She walks up to the cabin before me and looks in the front window. I take a few more seconds with each step to give the moment some space. I'm about to talk to someone that I never, not in my often exaggerated imagination, thought I'd ever talk to.

I could tell him about all the amazing experiences I've had at Whirly World in my lifetime, all occurring long after he died. I've probably spent more days inside the park than he did. I could try to dazzle him with technological advancements and attendance records. Or would that just confuse him? I imagine Frank or Josie or whoever has done that already.

I've been to this island hundreds of times, albeit via boat and not by flying here. I've looked through this porch window each time and wondered what the inside of this cabin smells like. What it feels like to sit on its big couch. How warm it could get on winter nights with a roaring fireplace. And here I am, stopping by like I am walking into the house of a relative or dear friend. An invited guest.

Now, through the window, I see him. His hand is resting on the mantle, and his eyes are lost in the burning logs at his feet. He's wearing the green vest and dark jeans he wore on opening day. He walked out of this small building and stepped up to a podium erected at the island's edge. A huge crowd surrounded him on all sides of the body of water he built, and for a moment he had the social status of a politician, far from being the son of a poor silver miner.

He gave, and I mean this literally, a weird speech. I memorized it, of course, thinking that would impress a lot of people. It did not, although Mike gave me a knowing nod and tolerated it whenever we came here in the morning, around ten o'clock, the time when Warren addressed the crowd decades before. It took a long time to commit the whole thing to memory because it's hard to follow.

He kept saying "for he" over and over as if addressing the type of person best suited to enjoying the park, or maybe he was talking about himself. Hard to say. "For he who fears no challenge undone," stuff like that. It was a bit cheesy and confusing. Afterward, people started thinking of Worley as the face of the park instead of the voice. Instead of the guy who created it. He wasn't asked to make speeches after that.

The hardest line to remember was "for he that tries and toils to hide in the rolling shadow and the forever frontier, see it and know it and dare to dream the dream he needs to dream." Like, what? I love the man and cherish the gift he has given this world, but he was not someone known for his words. But Whirly World, and other amazing theme parks, could only have been built by an odd duck. Walt Disney, for all his eloquence, still loved trains so much he built one behind his house so he could sit on it and go choo-choo through his backyard. That's one notch beyond kooky in my book.

As I reach the front door, Josie twirls on her heel, waves goodbye with a chirpy "See ya," and flies away. I don't wave back. I'm kind of locked in a jolt of mystification because I've never had someone fly away from me before. I just watch her zip upward like Supergirl. Before I move to enter the cabin, I notice again that the fireplace is lit, so the chimney must be spewing smoke. But it's not. Whatever is burning those logs is only working inside of Worley Lodge.

Unlike during normal park operating hours, the handle on the cabin door turns and it opens inward with a slight push. Worley himself looks up at me as I walk in. But he otherwise barely acknowledges my presence, mumbling something to himself. After a few words I recognize the speech. He's rehearsing. I'm getting a rush just watching the man speaking these infamous words to himself that I can't bring myself to stop him.

He finally focuses on me. Here I am, standing in the doorway, mid stride, waiting in vain for my brain to tell me what to say. His face splits into a wide grin. He's happy to see me. There's an expectant look in his eyes, along with some nervous fluttering as if it's hard to let go of the words he'd been reciting moments ago. His gray hair, typically unkempt, is parted and drawn tightly to either side. A similar effort has been made to straighten his goatee, but scattered hairs still stick out in all directions under his crooked nose. Age has sunken his eyes into his bony brow, but they're still warm and bright.

I wrote Worley a letter once, when I was ten. I knew he was long gone, but we had an assignment in school that asked us to address someone in history, living or dead. My fellow students mostly picked the obvious - living politicians, celebrities, astronauts - but I wanted to communicate with someone that was dead. Someone fun. The last question I asked was "What did it feel like to die?" I remember my mom's look when I put that one on the fridge.

Even standing in the room with him, not saying a word, juggling ideas for how to start a conversation with this legend, is inspiring. Just as I settle in for a staring contest, Worley perks up, shaking off whatever haze he was trapped in.

"We ready?" he asks, enthusiastically. "Is it time?"

Ready for the speech? I look behind me, expecting to see his personal assistant waving him through the door, but it's just me. "Uh, sure," I manage, realizing that's officially the first thing I say to him. Ugh.

"Great, great," he says, wringing his hands in contemplation. Worley is at the height of anticipation, like a novice magician about to pull a tablecloth out from under a set of dishes. If he thinks it's the morning of the big speech, then it appears he's in a trance, like Clarence. Like Eddie was before Beverly brought him back. *Not like you and me*, Beverly said.

"Do you have a moment?" I ask.

His face drops. "What, why? Is something wrong?"

"No," I squawk, putting a hand up to calm him. "Nothing like that. I just wanted to introduce myself, and to, thank you." He looks very confused. "Josie sent me, the flying girl." I glide my hand in the air like a plane and make whooshing sounds.

He looks worried. "Josie? Is she from costumes?"

"No. Never mind." I take a deep breath and change tactics. "I think you're going to do great today, and I think you've built something really special here. This place. Whirly World." I gesture around me like this cabin is Whirly World. He looks unsure where I'm going with this, and I'm not sure what point I'm getting at either.

Worley smiles. "That's a nice thing for you to say, uh…" He leans forward and presents his hand, palm up, like I need to place something there. *Introduce yourself.* Duh.

"Jason," I say, proud I got it right. "Green. Jason Green. That's me, sorry." I take two steps forward to, I don't know, shake his hand, but before I get to him Worley closes his hand and stands upright, like he grabbed my name out of the air.

"Jason," he says. It's the oddest thing to hear my name in Worley's voice. Now that I'm closer to him I can see the sunspots along his cheeks, the tobacco yellowing of his teeth and mustache. And the brightness of delight in his flecked green eyes. "It's a pleasure to meet you, Jason Green, but if you don't mind…" he gestures to the door behind me. "I have a date with destiny." He winks. "And I'm sure you're needed elsewhere."

Outside the cabin I swear I hear a crowd beginning to cheer. Is it actually May 7th, 1965 in this room? Have I stepped into the past, or is part of Worley stuck here? A memory we can replay like putting on a record? *He wants to talk to you.*

"You didn't send for me?" I ask. "You didn't want to talk?" He looks sympathetic to my needs but clearly has no idea what I'm talking about. This is all so bizarre and silly. How can I expect him to make any sense of this? This man has a speech to make.

I gesture through the doorway with a smile. "My mistake. On with the show."

Worley pokes his index finger into the air and makes a clicking sound in his cheek. Then he skips once, beginning a cartoonish march toward me, leaning back, like someone leading a small brass band. What a goofball. I've never seen this side of him from film or photographs. Spry for his age. I step to the side and watch Worley stroll out the door. Is he going to give his speech? One that only I can hear because I'm on this island? Or maybe everyone can hear it and I've rebooted him somehow? I put the needle back on the record. I fall in behind him, eager to hear this speech up close.

Before I leave the cabin though, I need to get another good look at this place. Maybe sit on the couch for a few seconds. I turn back and on the other side of the cabin, there's Worley again, standing by the fireplace, running lines. I check to see if there's a Worley in front of me, but no, he's gone.

"Oh, hi," I say, surprised. This in turn surprises him, and he snaps out of his funk. The record has skipped back. He's in a loop. I guess we both are now. Maybe he did ask Josie to come get me but forgot seconds later. How long can I keep him in here, I wonder?

"We ready?" he asks again. "Is it time?"

"Um, I just came in to, uh…" I say, dropping my voice an octave and trying to sound official. "They're having trouble with the sound…" C'mon, brain, give me one piece of audio equipment to name. Just one. "Stuff, the equipment. The *microphone*. Yes."

"You mean something else has broken?" A gravely laugh tells me he's not surprised. "Murphy's Law of theme parks, it would seem."

It feels gross to lie to him or make him worry. "But it'll be ready, Mr. Worley." I say, with an air of assurance. "It'll all be perfect." H e guffaws. "Ha. If I wanted perfection I wouldn't have tried to build this place. Do you realize how many people I have to employ to make this park run right?"

"Approximately seven thousand, eight hundred," I fire back. No, wait, that's not right. "No, that's wrong. That was your operating staff during your first year. You only had five thousand today, give or take, because you didn't have the Skid Greaser running yet and your liquor license hadn't cleared yet and…"

Worley looks baffled. "I'm sorry, do I *know* you?"

"You do not." He's going to forget me in a minute. I might as well tell him straight. "My name is Jason Green, and it's the year two thousand and twenty-three, and I'm dead and we're both stuck here in your theme park."

He stares at me. I think I broke him. A smile creeps onto his cheeks. He probably thinks I'm joking. I definitely sound more sure of what's going on than I actually am. Who knows what powers are really at play at this moment? What he and I are made of? Where our thoughts come from?

Worley doesn't humor me for long. He looks impatient. "Well, I'm sorry to hear that, Jason Green." He nods. "You tell me when that microphone is ready and we'll open this place properly, how's that?"

I can hear in his voice the tone someone might take with a crazy person or wild animal. I nod, but don't move or respond. I'll think of the right thing to say. I just have to keep trying, and it doesn't seem like there are any wrong answers if I'm talking to an answering machine. "If you could change one thing about this park, what would it be?" The first question on ten-year-old Jason's letter.

"I would get one of my five-thousand friends outside to fix my micropone," he jokes.

"Do you believe in ghosts?" I definitely didn't write that one when I was ten.

"Ghosts?" As if the word is in another language.

"Ghosts," I echo back.

Worley puts his hands in his pockets. "I built a haunted house, didn't I?"

His prideful boast makes me chuckle. "Yes, you did. In more ways than one." He doesn't know what that means and I'm not pausing to explain it. "But do you really believe in them? Ghosts? I know this is a strange thing to ask, right now, of all times, but I need to know."

Worley looks at the fireplace in contemplation. "I am a man of an occasional, spiritual persuasion, yes." He looks dreamily at the smoldering logs. "Is this about those dreams?"

The what? "Dreams?" I ask. "What dreams? About ghosts?"

He looks up at me and I brace for the answer.

"We ready?" Worley says. "Is it time?"

Dammit, I lost him.

"You mentioned something about 'those dreams.'" I say with force. "What dreams?"

"Dreams? What are you on about? Do you work here?"

The mystery of the man starts to melt away, and now I look at him as someone I need to press for answers. I have him for sixty seconds at a time, it would seem, so I need to crack the padlock around his consciousness to see if he knows what's going on here.

"Does the name Kingston Reed mean anything to you? Is that what you dreamed about? The circus? The devil? Does any of that ring a bell?"

His eyes seem to slip back into the haze for a second, but he continues looking at me. I'm worried that I broke him a second time but he keeps talking, almost as if I'm pulling off some form of amateur hypnosis.

"Not the devil, a demon. How do you know that?"

"Because I've had those dreams too." More lies. "About Kingston. The man with the red eyes and fingertips of fire." I hope this will land, but he doesn't seem to be following this line of questioning. "The demon you said. What did he look like?"

"I never saw him," he replies, still in the haze. "In my dreams, I mean. He was just a voice." Worley cleans up a few of the cobwebs upstairs and looks at me with more clarity. He appears less playful than the man that marched past me a minute ago. "And I don't know who this Kingston fella is, mister. The demon's name was Babbadon."

I'm not sure I heard that right. "Babbadon?"

"Abbadon," Worley says sharply. "Abbadon."

I have the strangest feeling. Ice passes between my muscles and the outer membrane of my bones. The chill I can't seem to lose pulsates through my body and I start to shiver. It feels like I've heard that name before. I've played enough D&D to know how many demon names people have dreamed up. They've never scared me though.

But *that* name. Something sounded every time Worley said it. A ring of truth. It was like Beverly telling me I'm dead all over again. Something I already knew but forgot. Of course it's "Abbadon." Who else could it be? The weirder things get around here, the closer I get to discovering the truth.

Worley goes on. "I normally don't believe in that kind of thing, but you're not the first person to ask me about it." He looks out the window. "Other people on staff told me they've been having dreams too. It's the oddest thing."

"What did it say in your dream? The demon."

Worley looks up and I realize he's hit the end of his film reel. "We ready? Is it time?"

No time to waste. "You've been having dreams about Abbadon. I've been having them too. What did he tell you in your dreams?"

I really spooked him with that.

"What?" he says, with dread.

"Sorry. The employees and I were talking about it."

"Is this about the speech today?" He's getting off track.

"No, the speech is fine." It's ridiculous, actually, but that's not the point right now.

"Because what I wrote is all mine," he says with pride. "He just put the idea in there. He planted the seed of the thing. Those words."

I can see Worley's speech in front of me, written in his handwriting, and I think of a former colleague, a witty conspiracy theorist named Otto. He wrote an article a few years back about his theory that Worley was speaking in code. Communicating beyond the iron curtain or some other spy nonsense. Worley said some weird stuff but he never seemed like something was slowing him down.

I thought Otto was being silly, but now that I'm looking at Worley and picturing him giving that bonkers speech just outside this cabin, I shudder at the possibility that Otto was right. Not about the spy stuff, but did a demon write that speech for Warren Worley? That's outrageous. This place is pure joy. Something so magical it could never be dreamt up by a being that vile and destructive.

"What do those words mean?" I ask him.

"The speech?" He looks worried.

"Yeah, the words. Do they have a deeper significance?"

Worley comes back to himself, to 1965. "Well, whoever you are, why don't you wait a few minutes and find out for yourself. I haven't given it yet."

"You did. I heard it. It was fifty-eight years ago. What did it mean?" I raise my voice a little, which feels insensitive, but he won't remember it anyway.

"Young man. I have no idea what you're talking about."

I let the line of questioning go. I'm going to lose him in a few seconds so I might as well think of a better way to get at this. He looks at me for more clarification but I ignore him. His speech is not the most important issue right now. Worley might have spoken to the nutball that chased me out of the circus. The mountain monster that grabbed Frank. The real version of him.

"We ready? Is it time?"

"Abbadon," I begin. Worley's expression changes instantaneously. "What do you think he looked like when he talked to you? Did his voice sound familiar at all?"

Worley stares at me in silence. Waiting through each cycle for him to catch up is exhausting. I might not be able to get the answers I need. Maybe Beverly would be better at this. Maybe she's already asked him about this, but if so, why didn't she bring this up before?

Worley looks into the fire. "His voice? I didn't recognize it, no." He turns back to me and all warmth has left his face. He looks sullen and tired. "But then I've never talked to a demon before." He shakes his head. "But they were dreams. I have a speech to make."

"A speech that he wrote?" I ask, knowing this will set him off. "Abbadon?"

Worley's face goes red and he huffs. "Look, I don't know who he is and he didn't write that speech, and I don't know who you are either. Can I have one moment to myself, for crying out loud? Are there so many people working here that I can't have that?"

I'm not sure I have the stamina to spin in these circles anymore. I need to talk to the others. Maybe one of them knows that name. Or has had these dreams. Or got these answers from this looping-Worley before. Maybe this new development is common knowledge and I'm just being the "new guy" again.

"Of course," I say, reassuringly. "My apologies." Worley takes a few breaths to calm down. I shrug. "We're just stuck here, and it's awful. And I think you know why." Worley looks profoundly confused and I don't expect him to be anything else.

"We?"

"Yeah, you, me and the others. I don't think they believe me, that there's something we can do about it, that we can escape. And I don't really expect you to understand." Because how could he know what would happen in the future of his park? I sigh out a breath I hadn't realized I'd been holding and give Worley one more plaintive look. "Is there anything you know that could help us?"

It looks like Worley's trying, and I appreciate that. Then his eyes go blank. "We ready? Is it time?" The film reel loops again, and I'm out of ways to question him.

I smile. What a wonderful opportunity I've been given. What a gift. I straighten up and gesture to the door. "We're ready, Mr. Worley,"

I say, like a dutiful employee. "It's time."

Worley pokes his finger into the air and makes a clicking sound in his cheek. He leans back and skips into his funny march. I offer my hand to him as he approaches and he grabs it. We shake for what feels like forever. He pulls away and I regretfully let go.

"Thank you, Warren Worley," I say. My voice catches, and I can feel my eyes prick with tears. "Thanks, for everything. You changed my life in ways I don't have time to tell you."

He stops his stride, dumbstruck. Then he smiles his effortless smile. "Easy son. It's just a theme park." He gives me a brotherly smack on my shoulder and walks out of the cabin.

The closer he gets to the edge of the island, the more transparent he becomes. The way a ghost is supposed to look, I think. He waves at an invisible crowd on the other end of the lake and approaches a podium that isn't there. Is this what he did on opening day? Or have I changed him, somehow? Imposed my memory on this location. Either way, he's gone. I look into the cabin, and he's back where he should be. He doesn't look up as I close the door.

Josie gives me a boisterous wave from across the lake at Port Juniper before coasting through the air and offering to take me back to shore. While I'm still nervous that her skinny forearm isn't enough to hold on to, the trip is a lot easier than climbing up on the track that hides beneath the waterline. I thank her when we land and look around for anyone else.

"Do you know where Beverly went?" I ask.

Josie shrugs. "Not a clue. That lady is a mystery."

I use the right kind of eyes and spin around, taking in the entirety of Whirly World. I stop when I spot four lightbulbs on the northside of Gizzard Lake. They're clustered before the next spot on my itinerary. The palatial estate with the purple glow. The only ride that Worley mentioned when I asked him if he believed in ghosts.

Hollow House.

Chapter 17

WW

Hollow House

My opinion, which I have gone into at length in my blog, is that Hollow House is the best haunted mansion experience of any theme park, period. Maybe it's due to the fact that it's closest to where I grew up. The place where I lost my "scare virginity" so to speak. You never forget your first time. For starters, there's no track. You get to walk through the whole thing, so it's a continuously active experience. It's the age-old horror-maze model, but a much classier version than the ones that pop up at parks today for a month-and-a-half each year. It's four stories high and about fifteen minutes long. And they only brought it up to accessibility and fire code standards in the last few years, which meant that it always felt a little unsafe to simply be inside the building. I love it.

It's built to resemble an actual house, not just a series of vignettes that suggest the passage through a dark and stormy estate. You wind around the building, climbing up each cobwebby and smoke-filled floor until you reach the attic where a shadowy panel opens to reveal a colossal staircase stretching all the way down to the basement. Then you have to make your descent for the big final scare, after which you exit through the best gift shop in the park. Hollow House sustains its tension without resorting to gore or cheap thrills, through an accomplished blend of music, sound effects, lighting, and other practical magics.

I love that it rests on the northwestern corner of Gizzard Lake, so whenever you take in Whirly World's central body of water, a broken-down house infested with the dead is always in view. The exterior's trim and molding is exquisitely detailed from the hand rail leading to the front door up to the tallest spire on the fourth floor. The property doesn't feel sinister at first, but standing closer you can see the crookedness of the tree branches and the massive cemetery in the backyard. It looks as if Dracula moved into the Biltmore Estate.

When I told Josie where I was going, she took off and returned home to her castle in the clouds. Not a fan, I guess. Standing in front of Hollow House are Frank and Reagan. They look up at the second story windows as if they're expecting someone to call out from upstairs.

"Hey, you two," I say, and Reagan jumps.

She groans. "Ugh."

"Sorry, didn't mean to alarm you." I raise my fingers to both of them like I'm casting a spell. "If you want to be truly frightened," my voice deepens, "you'll have to keep walking a little further." An oft-repeated line from the ride.

Frank and Reagan are not amused.

"Wow, nice," Reagan says, calm again. "I bet you can do the whole thing."

I shoot back a confident smile. "I can."

"You talk to Nuwa?" Frank asks.

"Yep." Frank raises his eyebrows at me. "She said no and walked away. Maybe I wasn't the right person to talk to her after all." I look at Reagan apologetically. She doesn't reply.

"Ah, well, you tried," Frank says.

"Did you find Clarence?" I ask Frank.

"No," Reagan says. "And I didn't find Nolan. That kid is fast but it's not like him to disappear for this long. It feels like something's keeping us apart."

"Some *thing*? Not some *one*? Where's Beverly?"

Frank motions toward Buckthorn. "In the church. Praying or whatever she does in there when she's alone."

"And Rubén?" I ask.

Reagan motions toward Hollow House. "In there."

It's not uncommon to hear a gang of students or siblings screaming through the front of the house from all the way across the yard, or one of the louder selections on the audio track like a crash of lightning. The walls aren't that thick, but now the house is quiet.

"And neither one of you wanted to check?" I ask.

They both look at me, defensively.

"I was about to," Frank says, but I don't buy it.

"We were waiting for you," Reagan says, which is more plausible.

Still, I'd put my money on them being scared. Because I'm terrified. If Timber Tracks suddenly turned into some sort of hellish space volcano when I got too close, what will Hollow House become once we turn the knob on the front door and let ourselves inside?

Without warning, that door opens and Rubén stumbles out. We all jump.

He blinks at the sunlight with a startled wince that suggests he was not planning to stand where he's standing. "¿Qué carajo? How did I get out here?"

"Oh great," Reagan says, crossing her arms. "We're all doing amazing right now."

I walk toward Rubén. "What's it like in there? Did you get lost? Are you hurt?"

"Nah, man," Rubén replies. "Just turned around. I thought I was upstairs."

"Maybe we oughta go in as a group," Frank suggests.

Reagan stirs. "And what are we looking for, exactly?" She says it to all of us, but I have a feeling it's directed at me.

Frank scratches his head. "Well, we saw the property stinking of that purple whatever-it-was glow. There has to be something making it. Something that broke the place."

"Have any of you ever been inside Hollow House?" I ask. "Here, I mean?"

Frank rolls his eyes. "Psssh, plenty of times."

Rubén nods.

"I haven't," Reagan says. I can't help but look shocked. I'm a bit offended. *After all this time?* Reagan reads my expression and scowls. "Yes, Jason. Imagine that. I don't care about going into this dime-store carnival funhouse, even fourteen years after I got here. Deal with it."

I put my hands up, defensively. "I didn't say anything."

"Well, I just went in there," Ruben says. "And it's just Hollow House. No purple spewing monsters. Nada."

"What's there to be afraid of?" Reagan asks. "Let's just get this over with."

"If you're in such a hurry, why are you waiting out here?" I ask with a laugh.

"Because we were waiting for you." Reagan yells.

"Fine," I say, putting my hands up in surrender. "I'm here. After you." I gesture for both Frank and Reagan to enter before me.

Neither of them moves.

Reagan points to the door. "You love it so much? Why don't you lead the way?"

I will myself to move toward the door. My feet don't budge.

"I'll go first," a voice cuts in from behind us. We turn and there's Eddie. His hands are on his hips, and he looks up at Hollow House with relaxed authority. None of us question his sudden appearance. He gives off major dad energy; he'd been letting us test our autonomy, but now he's here to save the day. We all stare at him.

Eddie walks to the front stoop. Rubén steps to the side of the front door. Eddie looks all around the front of Hollow House like he's planning to buy it. With his back turned, Reagan, Frank and I exchange glances. Reagan's surprised. Frank's intrigued. The more, the merrier.

I'm happy to enter this booby-trapped building behind park security. Still, Eddie's a bit unpredictable right now. I hope he's up for this. I hope we all are.

Eddie pushes the door and it opens with a satisfying creak. From his belt Eddie unsnaps one of the largest flashlights I have ever seen. No joke, it's nearly two feet long and probably weighs eight pounds. He clicks it on and blasts the beam inside the first room. My nerd-fueled curiosity kicks in and I skip up the front steps, hopping on one foot after the other. I can hear Reagan behind me snort at my exuberance but I ignore her. Rubén and I meet at the doorway and step inside Hollow House behind Eddie, with Reagan and Frank bringing up the rear.

The entrance leads directly into a wide living room with two lounge chairs, a small table on a dark red oval rug, and a brick fireplace that rises up through the center of the house. To our left is a full laid out dining room. A flowing white tablecloth rests under a procession of plates, glasses, and silverware, with an elegant, elongated chandelier hanging above. Diaphanous cobwebs cling to the crystal facets, hang off the chair backs, and drip down from each corner. There's only one problem. All of it is hiding in complete darkness, save for Eddie's megawatt flashlight.

Reagan shuffles past me and approaches the back wall. To my amazement, she flips open a panel hidden behind a painting. Just like her other technical tricks, I can't tell if that panel exists in the real world or if these access points are things that just appear to Reagan when she needs them. Behind is a heavy-duty power switch. Reagan bends her knees, pushes her palm into the rubber handle, and puts her whole weight into flipping it upward.

The building instantly jolts to life. What has always appeared to be a dark and moody interior hits me with so much light and noise that I briefly shut my eyes and cover my ears. The wings on the gargoyle sconces start to flap, the cutlery in the dining room dances up and down, and parts of the floorboard snap and bend. Good. Everything's as it should be.

Reagan closes the large, metal panel, returning the framed art to its normal position. That painting is one of my least favorite sights in Hollow House. It's one of the things I find legitimately unsettling, and not in a pleasurable way like the rest of the haunting effects. It's four feet wide and two feet tall, with a black background, and one giant, bloodshot eye.

It doesn't blink. It doesn't look around. It stares straight forward and yet, from the day I first entered this house at nine years of age, I've felt like it followed me around the room. The orange skin around it looks rotted, covered in bright purple veins that appear to pulsate even though no such effect is applied. Its menacing gaze is off putting, and yet you also can't look away. It appears desperate. Panicked. Like it's imprisoned and can only look out at the living world.

I've had nightmares about it. Granted, it freaked me out when I was a kid much more than it does now, but I can still see it when I close my eyes, even as I pass through the rest of the house. At this moment, however, its existence is oddly comforting. If it's here, in this version of Hollow House, then maybe this place will remain just as I remember it. Scary, but predictable.

"You okay?" Rubén asks me.

I snap to attention and remember why we're here. "Yeah. Just your run-of-the-mill haunted house, right?"

Rubén smiles. "Right. I ain't afraid of no ghost."

Eddie leans over the security railing which blocks us from entering the dining room and searches inside. Finding nothing of interest, he stands straight and turns to walk through the living room. Reagan, Rubén, and I watch him, following wherever he points his beam of light, which bores through the ride's atmospheric lighting, showing the raw textures underneath. In its gaze, cobwebs and dust become plywood, nylon, and synthetic rubber.

Frank steps into the front doorway. "Honey, I'm hooooome." His shout drowns out the looping track of whooshes and groans, but then the sounds reclaim the room. The five of us look around like the house is about to answer. "Looks like Hollow House."

The door slams shut behind Frank with a bang. The knob catches Frank in the rear and he skips out of the way. Eddie snaps around to see, blinding me with his overpowered light. I blink repeatedly. The room comes back into view, and I discover, to my horror, that it's not a room anymore. The walls are gone. I'm standing in a field of smoke. My newfound friends have all disappeared as well. There is no sound.

"Guys?" I yell. No response. Dammit.

I spin around and look for anything solid, but there's just dirt at my feet. We're so stupid. Why did we even bother coming in here? It's obviously a trap. Painfully obvious now that I'm in it. And yet the five of us walked right into it, like we were begging to be caught. Like I didn't have enough fun stumbling through Kingston's mirrors. I had to come here. I couldn't stay away.

I hold myself in place, trying to remember where I was standing. Eddie was to my right, just about to step into the back hallway that curves around behind the living room, ending in the staircase that guides people up to the second floor. I take a few cautious steps in that direction.

Out of the fog appears a hallway. Not like the one I'm looking for, but it's something. The walls don't look like they were built by humans. They're like a blank void shaped into a flat surface, visible only by the lack of fog passing through them. They remind me of the faceless acrobats in the circus performance. Something totally alien tried to make a face, or in this case, a hallway. The hallway curves to the left, just like the east wing of Hollow House, so I walk forward with a bit more confidence.

Around the corner the hall widens out in a way that doesn't resemble the actual Hollow House at all. At its end is another corner.

I turn to look behind me and just see more fog. I don't like being strung along like this, but it would seem I have no choice, again. As you pass through this leg of the real Hollow House, clusters of smoky light fly past the openings, blasting air into the hallway, while a passing "spirit" shrieks and giggles. The hallway, now barren, usually has cracked openings in the back wall, through which you can see a bit of the backyard. Well, the fake backyard that's propped up by flat silhouettes of trees and fences.

But *this* version of the hallway, like the last, is formed of some unknowable material that seems to absorb light and the darkness forms the shape of a hall that I know in my gut isn't a hallway at all. There are no cracks along the surface, no glimpses of "outside," and no blasts of air to scare me. It doesn't matter. I'm already terrified.

At this point the floor is supposed to start rising under my feet in subtle waves, one of my favorite sensory illusions. The simple effect is achieved by rotating bars on a conveyor, like rolling pins brushing from your toe to your heel, and the floorboards are rubber that's molded to look like wood, allowing the bars to undulate underfoot. They rise off the floor enough to notice, but not too much that they throw off your balance. While your eyes are pulled toward the end of the hallway to guard from anything that might jump out, you're gently tapped from below by rows of things beneath the carpet. It's genius.

But not here, now. Here, there's nothing. Total silence, like I'm in a vacuum. Not even my footsteps sound on the floor. If only the real attraction could pull off a hallucination like this. The impossible hallway that never ends.

I hear a voice. I think it's Frank, but it reaches me as a dying echo.

"Frank?" I shout, but my voice is muffled. Weak. Swallowed up by the blackness.

I hear a different voice. Reagan's. I can make out words. "No, not you," she shrieks. "You're not real."

"Where are you?" I yell. My voice is barely audible.

"Stop!" Another shout, likely Eddie's. "Come back, please."

They all sound lost, confused. Like they're in a theater and yelling at the screen, well aware that the movie can't talk back. I guess I'm lost too, but I'm becoming less scared and more annoyed. If any harm could happen to us, it would have happened already. We've given ourselves over to whatever controls this place and now we just have to wait and see what it wants. If it wants to mess with us, we let it. There's no other option. No way to fight back.

I walk. The end of the hallway doesn't appear like it's getting closer, but after a few paces I start gaining traction. I reach out and touch the wall, dragging my fingers along it. It doesn't feel like anything, just a force pushing my hand away. It's like my brain knows there's a barrier there but my eyes can't see it to study it.

Eddie screams from somewhere in the dark. "Sheila, wait." He's calling to his wife. I guess he sees her. I look behind me to make sure I'm not being followed.

"Don't move." Frank yells. "You're going to break your neck, ya jerk." I'm not sure who Frank is seeing but he must have succumbed to another apparition. A ghost haunted by the living. But this place is just make believe. None of the scares are real in the actual Hollow House, and none of them are real here either. Hold your ground, Jason. Don't fall for it. I reach the end of the hall and peer around the corner.

Someone's there. As I come closer I see the brownish-gray tweed jacket with leather elbow pads. The kind he wears when he teaches. The worn corduroy pants. And I smell bitter black coffee, shaving cream, and pencil shavings. His face is just as I remember last seeing it, with deep creases in his forehead, his graying brown hair combed backwards, embracing his receding hairline. Neat and tidy and disappointed. It's my father. He's looking at me like I just came home with a mediocre report card. I'm about to get a lesson.

"So," he says. "This is where you've ended up." At first I think he means Hollow House. Then I realize he's referring to Whirly World.

It's a name he utters with a particular tone of disdain. He joined me at this park exactly three times in my life. The third was on my sixteenth birthday. All I wanted in the world was to stay at the local hotel, something that never made much sense on any of my regular visits. My mother agreed on the condition that we'd go as a family. My father reluctantly joined us.

He had such a miserable time, and was so vocal about it, that I vowed never to come here with him ever again. I wasn't expecting him to enjoy himself or understand why I had such a good time here, but it was still a letdown that he couldn't at least pretend to have fun on the event of my milestone birthday. So it'd be weird to see him at Whirly World under normal circumstances, let alone inside this version of Hollow House.

This phantasm, whatever it's made of, knows right where to hit me. I can feel this weak spot, somewhere deep in my intestines, start to twist. But this isn't real. My dad isn't here. I know this. I try to push the nasty sensation along like I just ate something disagreeable. Somehow that only makes the feeling twist harder, like a crocodile in a death roll.

"Nice try," I say. The words give me a bit of confidence.

"What a screw up," he tells me. "You couldn't even make it to, what, almost half my age? And what do you have to show for it?"

"You're not real."

"Not real? Is that what comes from living in a fantasy world all the time? You're starting to lose track of what's right before you?"

I want to argue. I want to outwit this version of my father. To catch him in a lie. But the more I talk to it, the more I feel like he's actually here. His words are setting off all the insecurities I had when I was still living under his roof, forced to justify every dollar I spent, every decision I made.

I feel myself tugging at the bottom of my shirt, to cover up my slightly pudgy stomach that my dad always judged, something I taught myself to stop doing in my twenties. Just remembering the willpower it took to stop apologizing for my body, makes my hands snap away from my shirt hem, and with that action I see him change.

He's thinking. As I examine his expression, the image of him standing there starts to transform. It flickers, and for a second it's like I can see past it, through it. My dad's balding brown head suddenly becomes red in a flash that's nearly imperceptible. His eyes are strained. He's exerting himself.

Another flash and he appears shorter, then snaps back to his original height. This isn't just a projection of my dad, or some accusing phantasm. This is something pretending to be my dad. Someone, perhaps.

"I'm happy with where I ended up," I tell my phantom father, "because I know who I am. Who are you?" The image flinches. I'm getting somewhere. The walls of Hollow House start to fade in around me. I hear Frank again.

"Where'd you go?" Frank yelps. "Get back here."

Fake Dad heard this as well. His eyes dart to the side, then back at me. His hair once again fluctuates between brown and red, short and long. That's not just anyone's red locks. I'd recognize that shoulder-length cut anywhere.

"April?" I ask whatever I'm looking at. Again, they flinch. My dad vanishes and is replaced by my girlfriend. Former girlfriend. She carries the same strained expression as my dad. Like she's losing a staring contest. I feel a strong desire to communicate with her, to reach her somehow. I want to tell her I'm sorry I was too afraid to get married, to have kids. I want to warn her that I died. Better to get the news from me than a cop or a tweet.

April takes a deep breath, smiles, and turns away from me. A pang of regret pulls me toward her. I open the door to the greenhouse at the back of Sunburst Gardens and let her inside. Blinding sunlight ricochets through the glass dome. A magnificent cypress rises up out of a man-made marsh in the center, and its winding branches nearly scrape the ceiling. There's no one here but us. It's cold inside, which is odd. This room is usually warm, even in the fall.

"Did you know," April says, like a tour guide, "That this is the second largest bald cypress in the state? It's over a hundred feet tall and over eight hundred years old."

"I was not aware of that fact," I joke. She tells me this every time we enter here. I could recite the rest of her monologue, about how tragic it is that the tree is locked up inside this enclosure and not out in the wild, but it's one of the only times that April stops to tell *me* something about Whirly World, and I never get sick of it.

April continues her speech. "It was struck by lightning in nineteen ninety-three and would have died if not for a team of conservationists that brought it here, recreated its habitat, and nursed it back to health." April raises her arms wide to emphasize the pool of muddy water as she circles around it. "They could have left it where they found it, letting the big beauty get reclaimed by the forest floor, providing housing for birds or small amphibians, or nutrients for new saplings to suck on. But we have to sell tickets, don't we?"

"Yes. We definitely do." I try to get close to her, but April keeps circling the middle of the room, looking up at the huge tree. A shiver runs through me. I rub the upper parts of my arms to warm myself up. It doesn't work.

April sighs. "Why can't the rest of the park be like this?"

"Are you kidding me? There are trees all over the place. It's built into an actual forest."

"Yeah, but they had to cut down so many to put in all the rides. Imagine what it must have looked like a hundred years ago."

"It was a disgusting mining camp full of mud and smoke. You know this."

April nods. "Okay, okay. Two-hundred years ago then."

I feel like we've already had this conversation. It's rehearsed instead of playful. I suddenly have an itch to ride the Skid Greaser. "Let's get out of here and check the wait time on one of those tree-killing rides." I always try to keep my options open when I'm here with April. I don't want to spoil a good thing. But something is inviting me back outside. Time's a wastin'.

April shakes her head no, letting her sunlight-glazed hair sway around her ears like a curtain, and returns her gaze to the tree. I'm taken by her beauty, but the movement feels showy, which is so unlike her. She's up to something. She's stalling, but that's silly. She never spends a second longer in this park than she has to.

She gives me a look that can only mean one thing. *But we're in public, April.* I have no idea what I've done to get her in this state. I point at myself in mock disbelief, my default joke whenever she gets randy or romantic. Hopefully she's just joking too. I've seen so many people making out in this park and it's always horribly inappropriate. There's a time and place.

April's not letting up. She bats her eyes at me, those unforgettable eyes, and I inadvertently lower my defenses. As she gets closer, I pick up her perfume that I can never remember the name of. Citrus blossoms and sea water. I let my hands wrap around her waist and bury my nose in her neck, inhaling deeply. She smells wonderful. I can't recall a single time she wore that or anything like it to the park. Unless…

This isn't real. I'm not actually here. I'm dreaming. No, we've been through this Jason, you're dead. You're in a haunted house in a haunted park. April sees my expression change and starts to squirm. She suddenly seems repulsive.

"Who *are* you?" I demand. April looks forlorn. Lost. I push her away and cross my arms, resisting the urge to apologize or reach out to her. "I can do this all day."

April's frown turns upside down. Her pouting becomes playfulness. It's a look I've *never* seen her make. She's showing too many teeth. She begins to clap, slowly. The image of the woman I love melts like a candle. The form morphs into something much shorter. I'm expecting it to become another persona from my past, my sister as a child, perhaps. But what it's becoming I don't recognize at all.

It has pointy ears and a long, crooked nose. It has large, glassy eyes the size of my fist. Its wide smile takes up the width of its squashed head, and as it continues to smirk, two rows of sharp, pointed teeth emerge from its crescent grin. Its arms drag the floor, and its knees bend backwards, like a bird's. Oh, and it's naked. I try not to look.

I lunge forward to grab it, desperate for answers, and it runs, pushing open a doorway that wasn't there a second ago. I chase the thing like a street urchin that just stole my wallet. Through the doorway is a small bedroom with an adjoining bathroom that leads into another bedroom. The little monster hops over a pile of clothes on the ground. Those are my clothes. This is my college dorm room. I push through the strangeness of this abrupt transition and race through the bathroom.

It runs into the next bedroom, curving wide around a bed pushed up to the edge of the doorway. I step on the edge of the bed and jump into the air. The door to the hallway isn't wide enough for the thing to escape. As I crash to the ground, I manage to grab it by the ankle. Its skin is slimy and warm, and its toes are long and wiggly. The grossness of it makes me retract and let go. It flings the door open and scampers through it.

Past the door is a hallway. I see a framed photograph of April's family, the Moores, taken when April was seventeen, all standing together in white pants and sweaters. Around the corner is the Moore's living room.

April's dad, Felix, is standing behind the couch. He's surprised to see me. "Jason. What are you—"

I spring off the couch cushion and throw myself at him. We tumble into the house's entryway, and I manage to land on top. He wiggles a bit but I think I have him now. He, or it, shrinks back to its tinier frame. My knees move to dig into its feet. I try to put all my upper body strength into pinning its arms.

The ground is slick. We're back in the empty hallway.

"Well done, hotshot," it snarls, struggling. Its voice is high-pitched and warped, as if on the verge of a cackle.

At first I assume this is the presence I met before, the demonic Kingston that chased me from the nightmare circus. But this creature doesn't seem as proud or controlling. This little goblin is just a trickster, and I've caught him mid-prank.

"*Who are you?*" I ask again in a commanding tone.

"Me?" His tone is shrill, a growl. "Oh, we've met." He morphs into the body of a man.

My hands almost lose their grip as his arms grow twice in size. Beneath me, in his gray cap, is the gentleman from the circus games. The carny.

"Earl,' I say, recognizing him.

He switches back to being a little monster. "Murl," he says, correcting me. Ah, Murl. Not "I'm Earl."

"Murl," I say, correctly.

He smiles as big as he can. "Yes," he replies, really stretching out that last "s." "You catch on quick. You don't go for it the way the others do. Less fun." He pulls an arm free but I grab it again and slam it to the floor.

"What are you?" I yell, but I know what he is. "A demon?"

"In your premature language?" he pauses, then nods. "Sure. I'm a demon."

"What are you doing? What is all this?" I can't tell if I'm finally going to get some answers about this place, talking to an honest to goodness denizen of the underworld, or if I now have twice the number of questions to ask.

The halls of Hollow House have now returned to normal. Behind

Murl is the staircase I was searching for earlier. A faint red light creeps in through the open door at the top. A shadow steps into the doorway, someone or something large and hunched looking.

"Hey, Green." It's Frank. "That you down there?"

"Yeah, it's me," I exhale, relieved I'm not about to meet another unexpected spirit.

Frank makes his way down the stairs, gripping the rail for support. "And what's that?" He pauses after a few steps.

"This is Murl." I point at the demon underneath me. "Have you met Murl before, Frank?"

Frank ignores me and keeps his eyes locked on Murl. Frank looks puzzled but bemused. "What in the Sam Hill? What are you supposed to be?"

Murl mockingly repeats Frank's last question.

"So I'll take that as a no," I tell Frank.

"You know, I had a feeling," Frank muses. "You get to fixing so many machines that catastrophically break down over the years that were running perfectly just seconds earlier, before it almost feels like something is playing with you."

Murl grimaces. "What machines? What are you talking about, human?"

"You're a gremlin, that's what you are."

"How dare you," squeaks Murl, lolling out his pointed tongue in a grotesque raspberry.

I cut Frank off before he can retort. "What's the point of all this, Murl?"

Murl snickers. "Humans are fun to play with. You're so predictable. And you're so close."

"Close to what?"

"You think you can get out of this place, but you get trapped again and again. Like Worley. Like Grier. Like Mitchell. He won't give you up, ever." Who is Mitchell?

"*He* won't? Abbadon?"

Murl's left eye twitches. That hit a nerve. "You caught on quick. Smarter than most, but you don't know what it is you seek, where this will end."

"I want to get out of here, Murl. It's that simple."

Murl grins. "Only one way out of here. Through him."

"What does Abbadon want?"

Murl chuckles. "You, of course." The little twerp bears all of his teeth and sinks them into my forearm.

It doesn't hurt but the sight is so sudden and horrifying I yelp and release him. Murl jumps to his feet, shoves past Frank, and darts up the stairs. I don't bother following him, and neither does Frank. Right before Murl reaches the red doorway, Eddie steps through it. His eyes burst open in alarm and he swings his flashlight instinctively. Murl does a backward flip and pushes off of Eddie's stomach, arcing over the flashlight, and landing on his long feet.

"Aah!" Eddie screams.

Murl runs for a newly formed door. It has a symbol on it that I recognize, and a chill floods my bones. Murl has no trouble swinging the door open and slamming it shut behind him. I jump and run toward it, but there isn't even a doorknob to grab. It's locked.

"What the hell was that?" Eddie yells. "You see that?"

"Yeah, yeah," Frank mutters. "Gremlin."

"Scared the shit out of me."

"This," I say to them, pointing at the door. "This is the symbol I was talking about."

Frank walks over to investigate. "What symbol?"

"The one on the door." I'm getting agitated. That demon got under my skin.

"I don't see a symbol. What are you going on about?"

I turn to the door and see it still, clear as day. I poke it with my finger. "That." Frank shrugs. "Oh, come on. It's right there."

"I don't see it either," Eddie says, joining us. "But that doesn't seem that strange anymore. We keep seeing things here that other people can't."

This is different. It doesn't add up. I pause to process it.

Frank puts his arm on my shoulder. "We'll figure it out later. We gotta find the others."

I nod and follow them up the staircase. The second floor of Hollow House is a giant ballroom. You walk down a roped-off path that runs through the room diagonally. Bright blue projections cover a thick bed of artificial smoke. The projections alternate and flicker, never giving you a complete picture of the whole space at once.

Sometimes the effect of the room is lessened by the occasional lack of smoke, but it can be chilling when the shape of two men having a fencing duel, or a ballerina spinning, suddenly emerges from the darkness, then vanishes seconds later. But there are no shapes cutting through the smoke today. Just us. We're the projections.

Reagan's voice cuts through the haze. "So did you three lose it for a bit there, like you were seeing things, or was that just me?"

"Yeah, a bit. You okay?" Eddie asks.

"I'm fine." She sounds both flattered and annoyed Eddie would ask. "Are you okay? You just screamed like a banshee. What's up?"

"Big news," I tell Reagan. "We met a demon."

She looks at me quizzically.

"Well, the demon did a backflip over Eddie's head. Technically Frank and I met him."

Frank points at the door that Murl escaped through. "Is he the purple cloud? What's his name?"

"Murl. And I don't know. All I know is he can change his appearance, as well as the appearance of our surroundings. And he knows who Abbadon is. And he said something about someone named Mitchell."

"You met a demon?" Reagan asks. "Not a bad person but an

actual demon. From Hell."

"None of us knows what's really going on. Demon is just a word. Whatever it is knows what's going on. Right, Frank?"

Frank's mind is elsewhere. He jerks his head at me. "What? Oh, yeah. Sure."

Reagan approaches us. "Are we going to waste time trying to catch him in this place or are we going to go see where the others are?"

"I don't know," I confess. "On one hand, Murl is a part of this, somehow. On the other, he doesn't seem like the type of being that's prone to honesty. There's no way I could truly trust him, and he did try to imprison us here." Nods all around. "I can't explain why, but it feels like Abbadon's not here. This is Murl's house."

Reagan raises an eyebrow. "Who's Abbadon?"

"It's a name Worley mentioned when I talked to him."

"Worley? You actually wasted time talking to him?"

"I think he's wrapped up in all of this. I think he heard the voice of the thing keeping us here and it, Abbadon, tricked or influenced him somehow."

Eddie looks around. "Where's Rubén?"

I'm hit with an urge to reach the third floor. Selfishly, this is the closest I've come today to experiencing any of the park's attractions. The third floor is a library. It's packed with books and the building's highest concentration of jump scares. Wicked spooks pop up out of open chests, from behind couches, and through trap doors or secret exits. Hollow House waits until you ascend two floors before it starts making things leap up and scream at you. Most people let their guard down when they see the cozy interior with soft carpets and a roaring fireplace and then wham, the shrieks begin.

"Hello. Earth to Jason," Reagan chides.

I snap out of my reverie. "Sorry, let's move."

I lead the way to the third floor. Whatever Reagan has done to this place is keeping the mechanical boogeymen in the library at bay.

She claims that Timber Tracks runs for her just like any other ride, so maybe this is the way she prefers Hollow House to be. Sans scares. I can see a few of the fake ghosts hiding in a crouched position, ready to pounce. In the fireplace there is usually a crackling fire with an angry man's face yelling inside of it. Seated in a nearby chair, a dummy holds up his hands in terror and his arms shake back and forth. But this has also been deactivated. The fire is a projection set against a ceramic mold, and the seated man is frozen in place.

Another path winds through the room. A thick, waist-high rope keeps people from wandering off. I gleefully step over it for the first time, feeling like a rule-breaker. Behind the chair stands Rubén, staring intently at the fire.

"Find anything?" I ask him. He doesn't respond. His eyes seem stuck on the fake flames. I walk toward him, waving my hands around in front of me to grab his attention. Again, no response, so I step in between him and the fire. His expression doesn't change a bit.

"Rubén." Eddie's voice booms behind me. "You happen to see a demon running through here a second ago?" Rubén doesn't acknowledge the question. Like Clarence, like Blake, he's here but not here. I look back at Eddie. "This place can really get you, huh?" he says to me. "One minute you're with us and the next you're off in your own dream somewhere."

Then, Rubén speaks, his voice barely more than a croak. I jump at the sound.

"The Chevy flipped over when it drove off the road. I could have reached him, but there was too much, too much. Something sparked the tank when we hit the tree. It pinched the driver door shut, and the engine popped into the front seat and lit up. Manny got thrown out the passenger window. But Diego was trapped. I guess I could have tried to grab him, but then what? I was nine years old."

No one speaks.

Rubén looks up. "Sorry. I just saw my dead brother for the first time in fifty years."

"No worries," Eddie says. "I just chased my wife and kid through a haunted house. They wouldn't turn back, wouldn't even acknowledge me, except that I terrified them. It doesn't take much to scare the crap out of me in this place."

Rubén looks back into the fire. "After that I had a hard time around fire, you know? My mom told me to face it, the fear, head on, and I did. I took it a little too far, actually. I got addicted. I couldn't stop getting my hands on things that burned. And it's not like the fear went away. I just learned how to get a rush from it. But that fear was always there. Even here, seeing my brother on fire, it got me, even after all this time."

"This place freaks me out too," I tell Rubén. "All of it. But that's nuts, right? We know we can't get hurt here. We're already dead. So why should any of us be afraid?"

Reagan lays a hand on Rubén's shoulder and pats him in a motherly sort of way. "I don't know what you dummies are all afraid of either. We're the ghosts in this ghost house."

Then Rubén's mouth twitches, and so does Frank's, and before I realize it, we're all laughing.

Rubén gives a last look to the flames before he turns. "We getting out of here or what?"

I point to the attic. "The quickest way would be through the long staircase in the back."

Reagan eyes me suspiciously. "You just want to see the rest of the ride."

"First, it's not a 'ride.' Second, yes. Yes I do."

Reagan waves me away. "Go ahead, get lost, see if I care. Frank and I are going to round up the others and see if anyone knows anything about Murl, or this Mitchell."

"You mean David Mitchell?" Rubén asks.

We all turn to him.

"He didn't say," I tell Rubén. "Who's David Mitchell?"

Rubén looks more like himself now. "One of those two miners. From the Pollman Mine."

Two miners. The story comes rattling back out of the dark recesses of my memories. As I process the details, I look at the clueless other faces in the room.

"The trapped miners," Rubén continues. "The guys buried in the mountain."

Chapter 18

WW

Pollman Silver Mine

Whirly World wouldn't exist had the Pollman Silver Mine not collapsed in 1883. I read a few newspaper articles about it in high school, but my research and interest ended there. It's a sad tale, but the most interesting parts of Whirly World's history involve the land war that followed. The property passed through banks and billionaires before losing over half its value and falling into the hands of Worley's grandfather in the 1940s.

By Rubén's account, or that of his great-great-great-grandfather who worked the mine, David Mitchell and Floyd Petersen rescued sixty-eight workers before themselves getting trapped. The two got split up during the evacuation and re-entered the mines to look for each other, and never resurfaced. People spread rumors that parts of Timber Tracks run through the old Pollman Mine, but that's impossible. The mine, or what's left of it, is a hundred or so feet below the lowest curve of the coaster.

As much as I enjoy unearthing more of the park's past, I fail to see what this has to do with Murl, or Abbadon, or our chances of getting out of here. Did the demons crush that mine? Is Mitchell, or Petersen, trapped here with the rest of us? If so, how come we can't see them or their lights beneath the ground? Why did Murl give us Mitchell's name?

Of course, Frank has theories. "Mitchell's gotta be a key. It's all connected," he says as we reconvene in front of Hollow House.

While the others retraced their steps back to the entrance, I left the way the designers intended: up into the attic, down the back staircase, through the basement, and finally out of the family crypt in the backyard. All the audio cues and animatronics were inactive, like the previous rooms, but it was still nice to visit an old friend. Reagan rolls her eyes at me as I emerge from the back of the house. I can't help but grin.

Frank puts his hands out like he's holding a sandwich together. "All the layers of this park are stacked on top of each other. Ground level, tracks, tunnels, mines." He moves his hands down, emphasizing each level. "We just gotta dig."

"How?" I ask. "You said there are some places that are impossible to reach."

"Maybe we could float through, like you did." Everyone looks at me. "Twinkle-toes over here dropped from my workshop into the tunnels yesterday." He makes a descending whistle while flapping two fingers to the ground.

"Floated? More like plummeted. I was lucky those tunnels are even there. No, I'm not going to do that again, thank you. But any of you are welcome to try."

Reagan scoffs. "That sounds like a great way to get lost. Anyone have a plan that might actually work?"

I feel a low rumble beneath my feet. I guess the others feel it too because we all look at the ground.

"Earthquake?" Eddie asks. "Do we get those here?"

I shake my head from side to side, but then I realize I have felt these vibrations before. In Sunburst Gardens.

Nuwa's protective pod breaks the surface of the pavement to my left and rises up. It cracks open like a pistachio shell and she steps out into the group. Judging by everyone's body language, this is something most of us have seen before, but Nuwa's entrance is still unexpected.

This is the furthest I've seen her from Sunburst.

She nods. "Sorry. I've been listening."

"Oh, no," Frank says. "Drop in any time."

Eddie looks amazed. "That's some trick."

Nuwa turns to Eddie, who looks like he's still processing her magic. "Hello, Eddie. My name is Nuwa." She reaches out her hand and Eddie takes it.

"Nice to meet you. Are you a plant person, or a ghost person?"

Nuwa smiles. "A little of both, actually."

Eddie looks at all of us. "I can't believe you all can do the things you can do."

"Really," Reagan says. "Have you noticed the thing that you can do, Mr. Grier?"

Eddie looks confused. "You mean forty-year naps?"

All of us look at each other. Who wants to tell him?

"You mean," she goes on, "you haven't noticed that you can make people appear out of nowhere? People that work here. Or something."

Eddie looks to the rest of us to make sure she's not joking. We all nod. "You mean…?" Eddie steps away from us. "No, that couldn't…" Eddie looks at the bridge to Sawmill Splash. "They were just in my mind. They couldn't…"

On cue three of Eddie's creations walk out of the ride's exit. It looks like a family - a father, a mother, and a young boy - fresh from running through the log flume and headed to the next part of their day. The father is wearing Bermuda shorts, the mother is pulling suntan lotion out of her small backpack, and the kid is swinging a bag of merchandise in circles. Judging by their dark skin, and the relative height of the father, my guess would be that this is Eddie's family. Whether he planned to create them or not. The mother and child go running off into Buckthorn, but the father, upon noticing Eddie in his path, walks over to him.

"I thought I was in a dream. You know? When I woke up, when I saw this place, the way you all see it, I figured I just stopped dreaming. But..." Eddie's double stops a few feet from himself. Eddie reaches up a finger and pokes the faceless man in the chest, and the double mirrors his movements. "But they were here this whole time." Eddie looks at us, his face serious. "They didn't hurt anyone, did they?"

"We can't get hurt," Frank tells Eddie. "Not in that way."

"They were freaky though," Reagan adds in her usual manner.

"You just dealt with it your own way, Eddie," Nuwa says. "We all did. There's no right or wrong way to be dead."

I step forward. "If it's worth anything. I think what you can do is really cool."

Eddie looks at the ground. "If those men are down there. Like you said, those miners, we have to find a way to get them out of there. We can't let them lose any more time."

"I can take you to him," Nuwa says.

"What?" Reagan shouts. "So they're still down there?"

"Just one. Just Mitchell, I think. There's not much down there. He just wanders back and forth, pounding at the walls. He talks to himself. Sometimes, I listen."

"But you've never met him?" Frank asks.

"No, no, no. Never."

"Poor guy," Rubén says. "Man, I think I've been here for a long time. That guy's been down there, what, for over a century? What does that kind of thing do to a person?"

Reagan shakes her head. "He's not a person anymore. None of us are."

"Why hasn't he left?" I ask.

"Maybe he doesn't know how," Rubén says.

Frank takes a few steps toward us. "Well, one of us should go, you know, talk to him."

I point to Rubén. "You know his story best."

"First?" Rubén replies. He leans back. "I ain't going down there.

Especially not in that weird walnut-shaped torpedo. No offense."

"None taken," Nuwa replies.

"Then the kid should go," Frank says. At first I think he means Nolan, the smallest of us, but as I consider the reasoning behind that choice, I notice that everyone is looking at me.

Frank points. "Yeah you. The *big* kid."

I raise my hands. "Wait, this is happening kind of fast. What should I say to him?"

Reagan crosses her arms. "This was your idea in the first place."

Was it? "I mean, I suggested we all group up, that we were stronger that way. Beverly was the one that suggested visiting the surveillance room. And then we all saw the ominous shadows at Hollow House. I thought we were in this thing together."

"Of course we are," Frank says. "Right everybody?"

Rubén gives me a thumbs up. Reagan and Eddie do not.

"I'll admit," Reagan says. "I got a kick out of almost meeting a demon, and I'm curious what this 'Mitchell' has been up to, but our chances of getting out of Whirly purgatory still suck."

"Wait," Eddie says. "What do you mean 'getting out of here?' Out of Whirly World?"

Frank points to the outer walls. "I don't know if you've tried yet, Eddie, but we can't get very far. This is all there is. All that's left."

Reagan gestures to me. "But Jason here thinks we can, I don't know, push our way out, or something. We haven't really gotten to that part yet."

I turn to Eddie. "I think there's something, or someone, keeping us here. You saw that little guy, Murl, the demon, or whatever you want to call it."

"Yeah, up close and personal," Eddie says.

"I think he works for someone. A demon Worley called Abbadon."

"Wait, you talked to Worley? He's here?"

"Not really. A memory of him. It's a lot to explain. I'm sorry."

Eddie shrugs. "Nah, I get it. But you should probably be the one heading downstairs, if you know what I mean. You seem to be the one out to get the answers."

He's not wrong. Everyone goes quiet which tells me they agree.

"I know I'm new here, and that I've been asking a lot. Questions yes, but of all of you. I'm sorry if I've made your afterlives harder. Thanks for trusting me." I look from one face to the next, and no one looks away.

I glance at Nuwa. "Okay, how do we do this?"

"Gradually," Nuwa answers. "I've only done this by myself."

Great, no pressure. I take a few steps toward her.

"Wait," Eddie yells. "It's gonna be pitch black down there." Eddie runs over, removes his massive flashlight from his belt, and hands it to me.

I smile at him. "Thanks. I'm glad you're here with us, Eddie."

"Yeah? I'm not so sure. Things were a lot simpler before."

The ground beneath us starts to rumble. Nuwa raises her hands, palms faced toward me, and I step closer to her doing the same. Even holding my hands a few inches from hers, I can feel energy shaking every nearby molecule. I look down into Nuwa's focused eyes and wait for the next prompt.

The earthen carapace emerges from the crumbling gravel. I've been thrown around so much lately you'd think I'd feel virtually invincible, but I still shudder as it envelops us. Bits of dirt fall from the edges as the two halves crunch together. I can't help but smile nervously when the last bits of sunlight disappear and the two of us are in complete darkness. I wonder if my breath smells all right.

I'm not sure if we're supposed to hold hands so I opt to stand completely still. We begin to descend like a rickety elevator. I push against the sides to avoid losing my balance. The walls of this weird egg feel like the bark of a tree, as if I'm buried inside of one, pushing my way out. My fingertips detect chunks of dirt rolling past us.

My permanent vacation in this ethereal version of Whirly World has taken me to some unexpected places. I've laid eyes on backstage areas I thought were forever out of reach, but now I'm about to set foot somewhere that few have seen for a hundred and forty years. Our momentum shifts in another direction. Sideways, I think. I'm tempted to ask Nuwa how long this will take but I don't want to break her concentration. I'm not even sure she can hear me over the rumbling.

Faster than I expected, I sense the change in our location. If I'm judging these sensations correctly, we just emerged into the open air. I can hear the shell split open, yet we remain in total darkness. I can't see the walls of the mine, Nuwa, or my hand in front of my face. I fumble for the button to turn on the flashlight. With a click the powerful beam shoots directly into Nuwa's eyes. She winces violently.

"Oh, sorry!" I move the light past her, to the curved walls of the cave. There's not much to see. We popped out at the end of a long hallway. Thick, wooden beams hold up the ceiling just inches above my head. My imagination begins to play with the idea of being trapped down here if there was another collapse. Hopefully Nuwa can find me if we get lost.

"You heard him talking before?" I ask her. "Hear anything now?"

Nuwa concentrates. "Footsteps. Faint."

At first I assumed we stood in complete silence, but now I'm picking up all sorts of subtle sounds. Our shared breathing is mixed with a light whooshing coming up from the chasms ahead. Tiny grains of rock trickle down the cave walls. My ears scan for more when I pick up the unmistakable tapping of boots on stone. I click the flashlight off. Maybe this was a mistake. Why has my hunger for answers led me into another dark, enclosed space, placing me at the mercy of a potentially deranged spirit?

"What are you doing?" Nuwa asks.

A dim light appears at the end of the passage.

"Who's that?" a voice calls out. The light, from an open flame, probably a lantern, swings back and forth. "Petersen? That you?"

Nuwa takes a few steps back and bumps into me. "I'll be back." Abruptly, her protective shell bursts from the cave floor. Immediately upon being covered, she plummets into the ground, leaving me completely alone.

I yell "Wait," but she's gone.

"Who is that?" David Mitchell yells down the hall. "How many of you are there?"

"It's just me," I say. I suppress an impulse to turn my flashlight back on. The man approaching me died two centuries ago. An electric light of this magnitude, let alone one that can fit in my hand, might scare the hell out of him. But where do I put it? And what will he say when he sees what I'm wearing? I did not think this through at all.

David reaches me and holds up his lantern. Sure enough, he freezes in disbelief at my appearance. He's wearing a long-sleeve shirt tucked into tattered pants. His clothes appear to have been, at one point, different colors, but through a century of abuse they're saturated in the same grime that coats the rocks around us. Soot stains his skin, making the whites of his eyes pop out in alarm as he tries to understand what he's looking at. "How on earth…?"

"My name is Jason."

"How did you get down here? Where are the others? Are we getting out?"

He looks supernaturally exhausted. Past just losing sleep or otherwise physically overexerting yourself, David looks like he had his soul drained like an old well. His muscles look atrophied. His posture is locked in a painful hunch.

"There are no others." I tell him. "Well, no one that you're expecting. They're all gone."

"Gone? No." David shakes his head. His lantern rattles. "We got them out."

"Yes. You did. You saved so many men. You're a hero."

"A hero?" His face twists in confusion. "If you know what happened to my men then how did you get back inside? Where's Petersen? What caused the collapse?"

"I don't know. Any of it. I wish I did."

David lowers his lantern. His eyes are sullen and lost. Vacant. "Am I dreaming?"

That's not a bad place to start. "Yes. This is a dream."

He sighs. Sadness floods into him. "Then I succumbed? There's no more air?"

"What's the last thing you remember, David?"

"Petersen. He was here." David looks past me.

"Where? In the mines, with you? Where did he go?"

He lurches at me. "You think I'd be shoutin' like this if I knew, dammit?"

I try to think of a quick way to calm him, but he recedes.

He staggers backward and slumps against the wall. "I tried. I swear, I tried. I looked, I called, but no one answered. I chipped and I chipped but I can't seem to get anywhere. I tried. I tried so damn hard." He holds up his other hand and I notice it wields a battered pickaxe. The front edge of the spiked tool, slash weapon, is glowing with a red sizzle like it was just used to scrape lava.

I need answers. "Where did you last see Petersen?"

A wave of fatigue pushes his hunch even lower. "I couldn't reach him. He started talking all crazy and then I lost him. That was, eh, a few days ago, I think." He pinches his nose like he's stifling a migraine. "I don't know how I can still breathe in here."

"What was Petersen talking about?" I'm not sure he's listening.

David raises his head. "He said he found a way out, but only he knew where it was. He went searchin', but I…" He looks down the hallway, concealed in darkness. "I lost him."

"You don't remember anyone else?"

David straightens up. "What?"

I think we're finally talking to each other.

"There was no one else in here with you after the collapse?"

"No, that's just it. I couldn't find anyone else."

This feels like a bust. Damn. I may be more trapped down here than I've been this whole time. Maybe searching for answers, for an escape, is just going to make the terms of my internment irreversible. We have to get David out of here.

"What if…" I begin, but David looks like he's about to say something.

His eyes open as the realization comes. "There *was* another fellow. The one Petersen talked about."

"Wait, what, who? What was their name?"

It looks like the pieces are falling in place. The pickaxe begins to slip out of his hand. I take a step toward him and suddenly the ground begins to rumble. An incredible blast of rock and wind explodes behind me. Clods of dirt ricochet off my back. David jumps to his feet and swings the pickaxe into an attack position. I turn to see Nuwa's travel pod standing upright. The borders split and Frank comes charging out.

"I'm here, kid. What did I miss?" Frank notices David. "Whoa. This him? You him?"

I'm too shocked to answer. My hand quivers at David, hoping he'll ease down.

"Easy there," Frank warns. "You're not in Kansas anymore."

"*Frank*," I interject. "Give him a second. He's really mixed up."

"Oh, sure. I just got excited." Frank steps back.

David keeps the pickaxe raised between us.

"I mean, I'm a big fan," Frank continues. "Of your work, Mitchell. Miners in general. You guys had it real tough back then, I mean now, whenever you are, or were. The hours, the conditions, wow. Anyway, the point is, you got the job done. You got a lot of good stuff out of this mountain. It's a damn shame what happened."

David lowers his pickaxe but is having trouble keeping up.

Nuwa steps around Frank. "We should take him to the surface."

I nod in agreement. "My thoughts exactly."

David steps backward. "Surface? What surface?"

"We can get you out of here, pal." Frank shouts. "Think about that. What a ride."

David looks terrified. "No. I need to find Petersen."

Frank dismisses this with a pff. "We can find Petersen for you. You should see what this gal can do." Frank points to Nuwa, who blushes uncomfortably.

I turn to David. "Chances are, Petersen isn't somewhere you can reach, David." I take a risk and put my hand on his shoulder.

Once, when I was six years old, I placed both my hands on a pot that my mother had been using to cook macaroni and cheese. It was still piping hot, and after a quick second I screamed and dropped it. I got second-degree burns and had to wear mittens to school for two weeks. It scarred me emotionally for a few years. I stopped helping my mom in the kitchen. I got weird around cafeterias and restaurants, using double layers of napkins on everything.

The heat surging from David's shoulder puts all that to shame. I feel as if my palm is melting into him, fusing our skin together. I yank my hand away after what feels like forever and scream. Everyone else then screams. Frank almost falls over. Nuwa raises her shields briefly, holding her hands at her hips, the tops of her pod doors slowly protruding from the cave floor.

David jerks away from me, dusting his shoulder with his hand as if I imprinted something on him. But there's no mark, no burn, nothing. I look down at my hand and, although I'm feeling an excruciating pain pulsating from the center of it, there's no redness on me either.

"What's the matter with you?" David grunts.

"You burned me," I blurt in surprise. Nuwa reaches out to check my hand but I wave her off. "I can feel it, but I'm not hurt. But I don't think you want to carry him anywhere."

"What was that?" Frank asks me.

"I don't know, Frank." I turn to Nuwa. "Maybe you should go back up and get everyone else."

"No one else wanted to come down," Frank says. "They're not as dumb as we are."

Nuwa steps up toward David with deliberate slowness. "I'm sorry. For everything."

"What do you want from me?" David asks, exasperated.

I try to keep my voice calm. "I want to help you find Petersen." This cheers David up a little. "I want to find a way to get you and him out of this cave, and then out of this park."

"Park?" David asks. "What park?"

The coolest place ever, David. "Whirly World."

"What world?" David asks, bewildered.

While I'd argue that, in ten minutes or so, I could successfully bring David Mitchell up to speed on the history of amusement parks and coasters in the United States, now is probably not the time.

I turn to Frank. "Why can't I touch him? It's like my hand was going to melt off."

"Well," Frank answers. "In my professional opinion, if it's too hot to touch, it's not supposed to be touched. You gotta figure out what's supplying the heat." Frank walks up to me. "Gimme your flashlight. I want to see how deep this place is."

"Flashlight?" David asks.

I manage to say, "Frank, I—" before he grabs it from my hand. Frank clicks it on and is unfazed by the beam's power.

David, however, is stunned to silence at a source so bright as to make the tunnel look like a steam train is passing through. Frank walks past.

David looks at me. "What surface are you from again?"

"The future," Frank says, before I can stop him.

"I'm sorry," I say to David.

David seems amused. "Then you're not a dream. And I'm not breathing." His face turns to anger. "Petersen, what have you done?"

"What did he say before you lost him?"

"He said he'd do anything to get out of here. He knew we had a few hours, minutes maybe, before there'd be nothin' in here we could breathe. He started speaking gibberish."

"What did he say?"

"You know, I'd tell ya. But I think it's dawned on me that it's been more than a couple of days since I last spoke to someone. My memory ain't what it used to be. I ran out of air, didn't I?" David looks up at us. "All of us ran out of air."

Nuwa nods. "One way or another. Yeah."

"It's a dead end," Frank yells. He is so far away all I can see is the flashlight's beam.

"Tell your friend to be careful," David says to me. "It's real easy to get lost in here." He looks down at my hand. "You got burnt just touchin' me?"

I flex my fingers. "It sure felt like it. Is there anything else you remember? Anything."

"Petersen told me," David says, distracted.

I nod vigorously. I don't want to lose him again.

"He knew they didn't have the money to keep this place stable. But I told him." David looks up at me, his eyes wanting desperately for me to believe him. "I told him, if management gets kicked out, we're next in line. Something goes wrong, we benefit in the end." David looks around him and resumes his broken hunch. "But this is the end we got. He was angry. Lord, was he angry."

"Angry? Who?"

"Petersen," David answers. "He was all set to go west. I stole the man's dream, telling him it would pay off to stay. And now he's gone, I don't know where."

"He never mentioned an Abbadon? Or Murl?" The pitiful and

confused look on David's face tells me no.

"We can't move Mitchell," Nuwa says. "But at least I know we can find him."

Frank makes his way back through the tunnel. "Hoo, these mines are something else. It's one thing to lay down ten stories of steel, but you sandwich tons of unstable rock in between all that, you got some pretty unpredictable working conditions."

I raise my hand to block the beam of the light. "Any ideas how to get David topside?"

"If none of us can touch him? No, I got nothing."

David tightens the grip on his pickaxe. "I gotta get back to looking." He stands, gathering the lantern, and walks past Frank down the tunnel.

It feels like failure to watch him vanish into the darkness, but I can't think what to ask him, or do with him, that will matter. It seems like whatever this place does to us, this chronic apathy, it's done to David ten times over.

I look at Nuwa. "Maybe, if we find a way out of here, we can come back for him."

Nuwa nods.

Frank gives me a thumbs up. "He'd do the same for us, if he really knew what the hell was going on around here."

Nuwa raises her hands, preparing to do her magic. "I don't want to spend any more time down here than we need to. The energy in this place is unbalanced. I don't like it."

"You see that tool he had?" Frank says. "It looked like he'd been peckin' at the center of the earth with that thing."

I step in front of Nuwa. "Thanks for bringing us here."

The distinctive clang of metal on rock comes ringing out of the tunnel. One strike, then another, then another. Frank aims the flashlight down the hallway, but there's no sign of David or the yellow glow of his lantern. He's gone back to work. Who am I to stop him? It's just what Clarence and Eddie did. Forget it all. Work. That might be my destiny too. I'll manifest my own laptop here and find some cozy table to sink into while I write articles about Whirly World that no one will ever read, using an internet connection that doesn't exist.

Over the sound of the stone chips and metal clangs, David's singing voice floats through the tunnel. The tone is tired and dreary, and at first I can't make out the words. It sounds like one of those ballads that were written while digging caves or building bridges. Each line ends with a swing of David's pickaxe.

"What's he saying?" Frank asks.

I hold my hand up to quiet him and listen.

Two lines finally stand out. After a few repetitions, I'm able to decipher part of David's song, presumably the chorus.

> *And give me strength to see the light,*
> *and know what's right and true.*
> *Or all I'll see is eternal night,*
> *when the devil gets his due.*

Chapter 19

St Charles Church

"He sounds crazy," Eddie says after we bring him up to speed. "The man lost his mind, plain and simple. I don't blame him. I went through the same thing and I'm barely hanging on. If I hadn't seen daylight for a hundred years, I'd probably be beyond reach." Then he whirls and points to me, a sudden idea lighting up his face. "Maybe Beverly can do her thing to him. You know." Eddie slaps his hand against his chest and makes his eyes bug out.

"We can't touch him?" I tell Eddie. "I tried."

"Wait, what were you doing touching the guy?"

"I don't know. I felt bad for him. It was an impulse."

Frank is ahead of us, and points to Buckthorn. "Whether she can help him or not, I want Bev's take on this."

Reagan and Rubén are waiting for us at the Buckthorn Post Office. It's the first building on the sandy cement path that stretches from the center of Whirly World to the eastern wall. Although the "ghost town" effect that Buckthorn achieves is one of the park's best motifs, I've never seen it as empty as it appears in the afterlife. It fits the aesthetic, but is surreal nonetheless.

Buckthorn wasn't built, mostly. It was assembled. It runs along the same path that split the miners' tent camp Mitchell and Petersen occupied, back in the day. The smaller buildings were carried in on flatbed trucks from dozens of abandoned settlements across the United

States. Worley pilfered standing structures from any site that wasn't declared historic and off-limits.

Anything here that was erected on the spot came from lumber reclaimed after the mine collapsed. The land was sold almost immediately, but no one came to pick up the pieces. Using materials most contractors would flinch at, Worley used the built-in character they provided and fabricated something that looks like it's always been here.

It actually fooled a lot of people in the 60s. Apparently waves of history buffs attended the first weekend after it opened thinking they were going to visit the actual Pollman mine. Even with a name like "Whirly World," there were still people thinking they were going to get a backstage tour of one of the state's most infamous tragic accidents. I wonder if they left right away after they found out what they paid for, or if they figured "what the heck" and got on a coaster.

Beverly likes to spend time in St. Charles Church. Most people just call it "the chapel." I never considered it a place of any spiritual significance. It exists mostly for show; something you'd expect to see in a ghost town. The tall spire and sturdy cross that rests on top add a nice feature to Buckthorn's roofline, but the building's interior is simple and small. It's a nice place to get some shade, or park a stroller, or use the bathrooms in the front, but I've never seen or heard of any actual services held there. One time I joked to April that we should get married there. She didn't find it funny.

Walking down the dusty center street, we look like a posse ready to stir up trouble. Reagan examines the windows of the various shops. None of the lights appear to be on inside. Rubén squints as he looks up into the cloudless, midday sun. Frank puts his arm up and stops me from walking, then gestures down the road. Everyone slows down.

In the middle of the street, facing us, stands the Rootin' Ranger. Not a statue, or a cut-out, but the actual cowboy mascot. At first I think he's just part of the scenery, but his hand rests ever so aggressively on his holstered pistol. I think I see him smiling.

"You gotta be kidding me," Frank says. "That who I think it is?"

Although he's trying to look mean, I can't bring myself to fear the Rootin' Ranger. I don't care if it's another thing this park is throwing at us to slow us down. I've seen this guy make balloon animals. I dressed up like him for Halloween in fourth grade. I take a couple more steps toward him, hoping I'm as unafraid as I feel.

"You new 'round these parts?" the Ranger asks. His voice sounds familiar.

"I've been here more than three hundred days, cowboy."

"That's funny. I don't recall seeing your face before." He spits at his feet.

I want to get a closer look at him, so I keep walking. Now that I've experienced the sensation of flying off an exploding train, I wonder what taking a bullet feels like. Am I ready to do that, so we can escape? Or am I all talk?

Based on past experience, this could be a lesser demon, regular demon, a time-trapped memory, or the devil himself. That narrows things down. As I get closer, most of his features match those of the man on the poster, just like Kingston. Leather-brown weathered skin, stubbled cheeks, and a ten-gallon hat. It's like I'm staring at the person the character was based on. The "real" Ranger.

He taps his pistol. "You lookin' to start a fight?"

I ran from guys like this while I was alive. Bullies. But here, it's different. Whatever is beyond those park walls is where we're meant to be. I feel it in my soul. I keep walking.

His facial features are finally clear to me. I definitely recognize this guy, but it's more than that. Somewhere beneath the Ranger's snarled lip and gritted teeth is the same clown I met yesterday. The bully that locked me in the circus. He looks like the Ranger, sure, but it's the same guy. He's playing games with us because he thinks we're going to lose. The Rootin' Ranger throws his legs wide, like the full extension of a sumo wrestler, and comically holds his hand directly over his holster. I look to my waist and am, alas, unarmed.

I raise my hands. "You wouldn't shoot an unarmed man, would you, Ranger?"

The Ranger grins. Someone grabs my shoulder. I turn and Eddie is standing behind me. The rest of the crew slowly catches up.

He pushes me aside. "I got this."

The Rootin' Ranger is amused. "Oooh, look who showed up. The sheriff."

Eddie walks ahead of me. "I remember you."

"Who? Me?"

"Yeah, you're the guy from my nightmare."

I notice that instead of a taser, Eddie now has a vintage pistol holstered at his waist.

"The Rootin' Ranger? In a nightmare?" The Ranger laughs.

"Nah, not him," Eddie says. "*You.* I can see you past that costume. You're that smart mouth guy. The one that kept me locked up in my mind for forty years, thinking my wife and kid were waiting at home for me when they knew I was dead." Eddie lets some rage loose with that last word. "You're that demon." Eddie looks back at me. "Agamon?"

I shake my head. "Abbadon."

"Yeah, Abbadon." Eddie says back to the Rootin' Ranger. "In a funny cowboy suit."

At the recitation of his name, Abbadon drops the act and laughs violently, as if Eddie just said the funniest thing anyone has ever said. "You talk of things you know nothing about." Abbadon's voice is lower; further away from us. "You say these words like they mean something to you, humans, when you haven't the power to understand how things work."

Eddie cocks his head to one side. "Draw."

"Please. Let's not waste time. It's so precious here."

A little farther down the road, a man steps out of the Rootin BBQ, rubbing his hands on a dirty cloth. He looks familiar, but then I notice he has no face. He's an employee of Eddie's imagination. A chef, palms plastered with grease.

Reagan nudges me from behind. "Look."

I turn to my left and see a woman and child walk out of the general store, also faceless. The boy runs ahead to the edge of the wooden sidewalk. The mother grabs at the boy's arm, holding him back. She's dressed like every woman from every fifties western I've ever seen. White dress, straw bonnet. The boy is dressed like Tom Sawyer and turns directly to Eddie. Others appear from every doorway in Buckthorn. A priest leaves St. Charles, a gravedigger walks through the rusted gate leading into Harriet's Rest, and a buxom beauty with wavy auburn hair in a frilly red dress steps out of Nellie's Saloon.

"Draw," Eddie repeats, tapping his gun.

Abbadon stops smiling. "All right." I blink and miss the draw. Abbadon has a six-shooter, but somehow unleashes twenty shots at us. I want to be brave, but I instantly flinch my whole body.

I see Eddie get one shot off before he takes half of the bullets in his chest. Eddie's shot passes through right where Abbadon's heart should be, as if he's not really there. Eddie and I fall to the ground. The Ranger stops firing, so I look up. He blows the smoke encircling the end of his pistol, twirls it three times, tucks it into his holster, and vanishes.

I look over to Eddie, lying in the dirt. His torso is covered in purple marks that pulsate with light beneath his uniform. He tries to lift himself up with his elbows, but his wounds flare up and he drops back down.

I run to him. "Oh no. Does that hurt?"

Eddie grunts. "Hurt, no. They're just tugging at my arms. Like I pulled something."

The woman in the white dress walks up to Eddie and extends her hand. The priest walks up behind her and gently puts his arm under Eddie's to help him up.

"I appreciate it," he says to his friends. "But if one of you had armed yourself that could have gone a lot differently."

Frank lends a hand. "You can't control those people?"

"People?" Eddie says, getting to his feet. "I don't know what these are." He looks at the group of a half-dozen walking dummies surrounding us.

Reagan watches the redhead walk back into the saloon. "Well, you were the first here. You made friends. Just like Frank makes rooms."

Rubén walks up. "I think you're just spooked by them because they're spooky."

We all nod.

I chuckle. "And what's with them not having faces?"

Everyone turns to me like I said that backwards.

"What?" Reagan asks.

I point to Eddie. "The friends you make. They don't have faces. Please tell me I'm not the only one who sees them without faces."

Frank coughs. "You're the only one that sees them without faces."

"Wait," Reagan says. "Normal bodies - two arms, two legs, etc. - but no faces?"

"Correct," I tell her. "Like a mannequin. It's very unsettling."

Eddie looks at the faceless group. "Sounds like it."

"I saw the same thing in the circus. When Kingston put on his show just for me. A bunch of clowns and acrobats with no faces, marching in a parade."

Reagan laughs. I look at her in desperation.

"Sorry," she says. "That just sounds like a nightmare."

"Well, it was kind of boring, if I'm being honest. But thinking back on it now, yes, it was positively nightmarish. What does it mean? What's wrong with me?"

No one answers. Frank walks up and pats me on my shoulder.

"Nothing's wrong with you, kid. We just all see this place differently."

"What about the Ranger? Nuwa told me that he came to see her a few times. Anyone ever seen him in Buckthorn?"

Everyone nods.

Reagan looks at Eddie's wounds. "He's never shot at me. That's for sure."

The faceless crowd disperses. Rubén approaches Eddie. "What was that about? You didn't get a chance to hit him."

"And he didn't stick around," Frank observes. "Why doesn't he just take us out?"

Eddie grunts. "I hit him, dammit. But it didn't do anything."

I check the windows and rooftops, in case the Ranger is spying somewhere. "He's messing with us. This is all a big game."

Reagan puts her hands on her hips. "And how do you plan to win that game?"

"I don't know. I have no idea. Okay?"

Reagan walks past me. "Let's go find Beverly."

I can tell that her faith in me is nearly at its limit. I rub my neck in frustration and follow her, the others falling in behind me.

Reagan is the first of us to reach the eastern edge of Buckthorn. The town square. The chapel is on the northern side. Also in the square, which is really a circle, are Hipshot Canyon, Dally Ranch, the Skid Greaser, and the Marshal's Jail.

The doors to the chapel are open. I do a quick three-sixty to make sure no one is following us, ready to defend myself against a homicidal cowboy, a demented ringleader, or a raging sasquatch. I see nothing of the sort, so I follow Reagan through the chapel doors.

The tall windows above the entrance are letting in a dazzling amount of light. It's strangely brighter here than it was outside in the open sun. A rugged red carpet separates the dozen or so rows of pews. Beverly is seated in the second row. She looks up at the altar with serene reverence. It's so peaceful here, I'd hate to break the mood.

Reagan does it for me. "Hey, Beverly." Her voice echoes to the high ceiling.

Beverly looks back at us like she was expecting the group to arrive at precisely this moment. "Back from the mines already?"

"How did you...?" I begin to ask, then stop myself. Beverly proved this morning that she could see anything, anytime, within the walls of this place. "Did you know about the mines?"

"I knew they were there, yes, but I've never seen them. Something stops me from getting near that place in my mind. Such a sad story. Those two men. She looks up toward the giant cross-shaped window that looms over the chapel stage.

I swear she's done something to this place, but it looks structurally the same as in my memory. I never took an ounce of spiritual inspiration from this building during the many times I passed through it, but now it feels like someplace that might actually let you speak to the almighty.

Nuwa walks in behind me. Beverly nods to her. "I also didn't know you could travel so far down there."

"Hi, Beverly," Nuwa says. "And thank you for that."

It looks like they share a moment. It's none of my business, but I can't help myself.

"Thank you for what?" I ask.

Nuwa welcomes the question. "When Beverly first showed me the things she can do, the way she watches people, I made her promise never to spy on me. Even if I was in trouble." Beverly smiles. "And, I'm not sure why, but it feels like she's kept it."

"Well, look at us." Beverly says. "Almost all together."

I turn and notice Frank, Eddie, and Rubén standing in the vestibule. Beverly's right. This is the largest congregation of ghosts I've seen since the fireworks last night. But it's not the whole crew, and that worries me.

"Yeah, almost," I agree.

Frank starts to count. "We're missing Josie, Clarence, Nolan, and

Blake. Those first three I can probably account for, but I'd love to know where Blake went."

Beverly stands. "He's in jail."

All of our heads snap in her direction.

"Marshal's Jail?" I ask.

Beverly nods. "In the basement."

"Really?"

"Doing what?" Frank asks.

"Being imprisoned," Beverly answers.

That doesn't make sense. "Are you sure?"

The Marshal's Jail sounds imposing but is not what I would call maximum security. The ground floor is a retail shop, and the basement is a museum.

Beverly nods. Huh, okay. There are a few cells downstairs, but they're only sturdy enough to keep tourists from stealing a collection of antiques. They switch things up for Halloween, adding morbid items like a cowboy-dummy swinging from a gallows or a pair of well-placed actors, in the darkness, waiting to charge and scare the piss out of someone.

But at its scariest, Marshal's Jail looks like it could be knocked over by a raging toddler. In fact, all of Buckthorn looks like it's one violent breeze away from falling over. It's frail, either because of the creator's intent or it's just maintained poorly. Its state of disrepair is one of the reasons I love walking around it. How did Blake get trapped in a place like that?

Beverly walks back down the aisle and out into the sunlight. "Let's go break him out."

We fall in behind her, like the end of a church service.

The street is empty, thankfully, as we make our way back through the middle of town. The jail is a twenty-two-foot stack of faded, dark-red bricks. Unlike the church behind us, which radiates a warm glow that says "welcome," the jail has a cold gloom that says "enter at your own risk." The door is closed. The windows are shuttered. It looks like you're not supposed to go inside, like the door handle is just for show.

Eddie stops and surveys the building. "Anybody got a set of keys to this place?"

"No," Frank says. "I can try to take that door off its hinges."

Reagan pats the door, and the thin metal sends a rattling echo through the first floor inside. "I could see if there's a power supply somewhere. Was this manually locked?"

"All of Buckthorn is. It's kind of like time-traveling, this place."

Rubén walks to the door. "Hey. Crazy idea. Why don't we…" Rubén tries the doorknob and it opens easily. He pushes the door with a flourish. "See if it's open."

We all nervously make our way inside. Eddie wanders through the gift shop, taking in the decorations and souvenirs for sale. He picks up a kid's plastic rifle with a bright orange tip. He smiles, feels the weight in his hands, and looks down the tiny targeting sight. We leave him there and descend into the basement.

The lights are on, which is a good sign. The place doesn't seem decorated for any annual celebration, be it Halloween or Christmas. The first wall of bars is open. Maps and photographs of the Pollman Silver Mine cover the wall over a Civil War era writing desk. Mannequins sit on the other side of the low fence keeping us from touching these things, adorned in late-nineteenth-century apparel. They rest in chairs that line the back wall. The three prison cells are at the end of a long hallway to our right.

Faint sobbing echoes from the cell to the south.

"Blake?" I call out. I turn to Nuwa and Frank, standing at my side, and the two seem to hear it as well. There has to be some way that this scenario is booby-trapped. Abbadon loves his surprises. I look for hinges hiding a trap door, or a sign that the bars are electrified. But it looks like it always does.

When I get to Blake's cell, he's seated on a wooden chair in the middle of the room. His head is in his hands. His elbows rest on his knees. At the foot of the chair is a puddle of water, being fed from an impossible torrent of tears pouring from Blake's eyes. The stream is soaking his jeans, and his shoes are halfway submerged. He heaves in miserable sobs.

We all gather in front of his cell, but I can't tell if he knows we're here. We stare at him as he weeps profusely. I have no idea how to alert him to our presence, and the silence from the group tells me no one else does either.

Finally, Reagan walks to the bars. "Blake? It's Reagan. Can you hear me?"

Blake continues to cry. I look to the others. Nuwa's eyes are also wet. Frank scratches his mustache like he's staring at a tricky crossword puzzle.

Rubén claps his hands together. "Blake," he yells.

Blake jumps out of his chair, slips on the drenched floor, and falls over. All of us look at Rubén in surprise, but he ignores us and taps on the cell door. "You stuck in there?"

"How'd you guys find me?" Blake asks.

I step closer so Blake can hear me. "Beverly told us. Who put you in here?"

"There was a guy. The cowboy guy."

"The Rootin' Ranger?"

"What?" He cocks his head to the side like a puppy.

I put my feet apart like a gunslinger at the ready, hand at my hip. "The mascot. Of the park. You know. Tall guy, leather chaps, ten-gallon hat."

"Oh, right, right. Yeah, that guy. But there was *another* guy." Blake's eyes drift off, like he can see a person standing in front of him.

"What?" Frank says. "Who?"

"Or, was it the same guy?" Blake wonders aloud.

"That doesn't matter," Reagan says. "We have to get you out."

Blake starts crying again. He backs up against the wall and slides to the floor. Tears dump out of his eyes like two faucets. Reagan squeezes her forehead in frustration.

"Don't worry, Blake," I tell him. "We're going to find a way to get you out." I remember the upstairs door being unlocked and give the door to the cell a tentative pull. Sadly, locked. I gesture to the group. "Reagan can hotwire anything in this park." I point to Frank. "Frank here is building rooms that didn't exist before. Nuwa can pull you out through the floor."

"Nope," Nuwa says, confidently. "This place is a block of ice. I've always avoided it."

"And I can turn some stuff on, yes," Reagan says. "But I'm not a locksmith."

Everyone in this basement is in dire need of a pep talk, which is not a skill I excel at.

"Okay, then, Frank will get you out," I say desperately.

Frank has moved to the edge of the metal wall, where it meets the brick. "I'd need some tools." He does not look optimistic. "I don't know, kid. This baby looks heavy."

"And Blake, what about you?" He's the Aquaman in our Justice League. That has to count for something. But it's not like he can swim out of here.

"What *about* Blake?" Reagan asks.

"He has powers too. I've seen this guy do several weird things with water and I've only been here for two days."

Blake stops crying for a moment and looks down at his hands. "Powers?"

Nuwa laughs. "Yeah, Jason has the notion that we're all superheroes."

"That sounds cool."

"Look, we're not stopping crimes, but it's undeniable that you all can do extraordinary things here. There has to be someone who can break in, or a way that Blake can break out. Some way we haven't thought of."

The group stops to think. Even Beverly looks like she doesn't have an easy answer.

Blake looks at his hands. "I don't have any powers."

"What are you talking about?" I say in disbelief. "You live underneath a lake." I pause for a moment, then add a "dude," to try and speak his language.

He chuckles at this, but his smile immediately fades away. "I don't know."

"Well, I do." I'm hopefully getting more convincing at this pep talk thing. "Rubén over here can make fireworks appear out of thin air. You've all seen it. Nolan can sprint through every ride in this park in under ten minutes. And Josie?" I point upward. "Is probably doing barrel rolls through the clouds right now."

Josie's name brings a smile back to Blake's lips. He blushes. "I can't fly."

"No, only she can. That's the point. You're different. You can do stuff with water I've never seen before."

"Well, how is water supposed to get me out of here?"

I'll admit, I don't have an answer to that. But it feels like Blake is holding back. I walk to the door and push against it, testing its stability. It's solid. I move my hand away from the metal plate in the center of the door and notice a faint impression on its surface.

I've seen it before. I walked away from it in the tunnels. It stopped me from getting back to Frank in Timber Tracks. It's keeping us from rescuing Blake. Unlike the symbol on the tunnel door, this insignia has no color. It's the same shade as the bars, only visible in the right light. I take a step back. I refuse to give up. We can't just leave Blake here.

"Frank," I say, and he turns my way. "We can't bend these bars, but they're just stuck into the bricks. Can we move them around?"

Frank sighs. "Believe me, I'm trying to think of a way. I don't make a habit of changing too many things in this park. I just like to tweak things here and there. Nothing too intense."

Blake walks to one of the brick walls and puts his hand on it. "I've been banging on these walls ever since I got in here. Why do you think I'm crying, dude? It's impossible." This reminder starts another round of weeping, although Blake is running out of energy. He starts to cough, like he's gagging on his emotions.

Then, the wall changes. A wave of gray spreads through the cracks between each red brick around Blake's hand. Reagan gasps. Beverly moves closer to Blake.

"Blake," I say.

He draws his hand away and the effect vanishes.

"Wait," Reagan shouts.

Blake recoils. "What? What did I do?"

"I don't know, but do it again."

I point to Blake's hand. "You were changing the wall. Like you were flooding it."

Blake looks down at his hand, then to me.

"Yeah. Try it."

Blake spreads his fingers and lunges at the wall. He pushes his hand into the brick with all his might. Nothing happens. He strains like a bodybuilder, spitting.

"Whoa, whoa," Rubén says. "Not like that."

Blake stops. "Well then how, man?"

"You were sad before. It was like you 'cried' into the wall."

This inspires Blake to give it another try. He puts his hands against the brick. Again, there's no change, but Blake keeps holding the position. He closes his eyes and takes a deep breath. Having never manipulated water myself, I can only guess what he's thinking.

"Just relax, Blake," Beverly says. "We're all here."

It seems like the smallest stimulus will shatter Blake's concentration, so the room goes quiet. I share a few nervous glances with the others. I can hear Frank breathing anxiously through his teeth. Rubén looks down at his feet. This might take a while.

It looks like Blake fell asleep, except for the fact that the wall is changing again. The cracks darken, and the wave - one centimeter a second - creeps out from Blake's hand.

Rubén claps. "Yeah, buddy. You're doing it."

It doesn't seem like Blake heard that. His mind is pouring into the wall. One of the bricks, about eye level with Blake, begins to vibrate. It slowly wiggles free. We all watch in astonishment as, after a half a minute, it fully emerges with a splash and lands on the floor. Blake doesn't acknowledge it and keeps focusing.

"Wow, he's really doing it," Rubén says.

Yes, he is, against all odds. I wasn't sure what to expect from Blake's ability, but this is incredible to watch. Concrete and brick shouldn't act like this, and yet, Blake is destabilizing the whole wall, brick by brick. The gray sludge in between them squishes into each open space as the damp spot expands.

That's when I realize how stupid this is. Blake could bring the two stories of Marshal's Jail down upon all of us. It might not hurt us, but I'm not sure how long it would take to dig ourselves out. I grab the bars and rattle them, trying to get his attention. The wall gives a bit and doesn't seem nearly as heavy as it looks.

I turn and look at Reagan. "I think we can move this."

Reagan grabs two bars to my right. Frank runs up at my left and counts. "Three, two, one, *pull*." I pull with everything I have. The three of us don't manage to dislodge the bars, but we're definitely getting somewhere. Another pull causes two bricks above to fly out into the hall. Nuwa has to move Beverly out of the way.

"Get back," Reagan shouts. The room clears except for me, Reagan, and Frank. None of this commotion reaches Blake, whose mind is committed to flooding that wall. Frank counts and we tug. It's definitely going to fall from the top. One more yank should do it.

Another pull and the top row of bars becomes dislodged. Frank starts to furiously shake his arms back and forth. Reagan also rattles the bars, trying to free them, but I take my hands away and look up at the crumbling interior. It doesn't look like Blake's cell was a load bearing part of this basement. That's a relief. The more it disassembles, the more it looks like plastic.

Rubén joins Frank and Reagan for the final pull. A row of bricks tears from the ceiling. They catch the wall before it collapses on them. As a unit, they slide their hands up the bars as it leans downward and let it crash to the ground when they're clear. The clatter finally wakes Blake from his magical stupor. Like a sponge, he instantly soaks up all the water in the wall. The remaining bricks and globs of cement freeze in place.

Blake wipes the last tears from his eyes. "Cowabunga."

Everyone holds still as the pieces of the building settle. The wall of bars, now bent from the struggle, rocks back and forth on the floor. The strange symbol can also be seen on the backside, but it looks etched into the metal, rather than protruding from it. It gives the image a dimension it didn't have before. The grooves add depth, shadow.

Staring at it, upside down, I realize what it is. It's like someone took an outline of the roads and scribbled a symbol on them, an X with a circle at the top and center, and a little squiggly line at the bottom. It's unmistakable. I can't believe I didn't spot it earlier. Even altered in such a way, you'd think I'd be able to spot a map of Whirly World.

Chapter 20

Nellie's Saloon

Blake looks up to the sun. "When did it become morning?" We step out of Marshal's Jail and into the center of town. It must be two or three o'clock in the afternoon.

Reagan does a silent head count. "Okay, this is everyone. Oh, wait." She cups her hand over her mouth and yells up at the sky. "Josie! We're having a very important meeting down here. Do you want to join us?" No response. I wasn't expecting one, and neither was Reagan. "Yup, this is everyone you're gonna get."

I try to ignore the sarcasm. "Let's go into Nellie's and get out of the sun."

Nellie's is decorated like a saloon but is actually the second largest restaurant in the park. I push open the swinging double doors, like a deputy making a dramatic entrance before a rabble of drunk outlaws. The twenty tables and one-hundred-plus chairs are all empty. On each wall is an array of tall, thin paintings depicting each of the park's main attractions as if they were being advertised in the early 19th century.

I walk to the bar and wait for everyone else to enter and settle down. Frank is right behind me. He walks behind the bar, reaches under the surface, removes a bottle of Jim Beam, pops off the cap, and takes a healthy swig.

I'm intrigued. "That stuff work here? Alcohol, I mean?"

Frank finishes his sip and wipes his mouth on his sleeve. "Hard to say." He puts the bottle on the surface of the bar and looks at the label. "It does something. And not just something that I can trick my mind into doing. Although, I gotta make my way over here and drink up. Can't take the liquor out of the location." He takes another swig, coughing a bit. "Want some?"

I hold my hand up. "No thanks. Just asking new-kid questions."

Everyone sits at the two big tables closest to the bar, except for Reagan who holds the chair for Beverly and then remains standing. Everyone looks to me like I'm supposed to start talking, but I'd rather hear what they have to say. They met Abbadon. They saw what Blake can do. They know the stakes and what we stand to win.

"Well," I start. "What does everyone think?"

"I think we need a plan," Reagan answers.

"The plan is, or the best plan that I've come up with so far is, to start breaking stuff. We need to show Abbadon that we can change Whirly World too. That we're not afraid of him."

Nuwa raises her hand. I call on her like a schoolteacher. "I, for one, am afraid of him. I don't think we've seen the full extent of his abilities and I'm not eager to test them."

"Then why are you helping us?"

"I was curious to meet Mitchell. And then I wanted to help Blake. And I don't like bullies. I'm taking this one decision at a time. So much of this is unpredictable."

Rubén raises his hand.

I'm about to call on him but stop myself. "We're not in the principal's office. You can just speak up. There are only eight of us."

Rubén puts his hand down. "I've seen this guy shoot bullets and run down a locomotive. I'm with Reagan. We need to have a plan if we're going to piss him off again."

"But we walked away. And we're still here."

"That's just it," Reagan says. "Nothing changed."

"We know his name. We know who he is."

Reagan crosses her arms. "Really? Who is he, Jason?"

"He's a demon."

"And how many of those have you dealt with before?"

"I'm out of practice, Reagan. But that's not the point."

Frank puts his bottle down. "No, that's definitely the point. We don't know what we're up against. I don't want to spend the rest of eternity swinging a pickaxe like Mitchell."

Eddie leans back in his chair. "Yeah, I just found out what's going on. I don't want to throw that away."

I look at him. "But you stood up to Abbadon an hour ago."

"Right and look where that put me." Eddie shakes his head in defiance. "Straight on my ass. My bullet passed through him like it was nothing."

I walk around the tables near the bar and look into everyone's eyes. "I believe that if Abbadon wanted us to be trapped in a deep, dark cave, he'd have done it already. He needs to, I don't know, entertain us, or something. He wants us to be involved. He has a violent streak, yes. But I've also seen this hellspawn sing a musical number. He's a showman. And a showman needs an audience."

Frank dismisses this with his hands. "That was just Kingston being Kingston."

"*No*," I say, with too much emphasis. I'm getting riled up and it's not helping my case. "It's an act. He gets into it because he has a weird fascination with this place."

"Well, that makes two of you," Reagan says.

"What is that supposed to mean?"

Reagan chuckles. "Oh, come on. You love this place more than all of us combined. You keep marching around like a superfan, putting everyone in danger. If you hadn't gone into the circus with Blake, he would have never been grabbed by that jerk."

That seems both irrelevant and incorrect. "This is a special place.

How could it not be?" I glance from face to face. No one backs me up.

"It was a good job," Frank says. "One of the best I had. But that was it. A job."

"Okay, I get it. You all resent this place because you had to work here. But even if you were always on the clock, you have to admire what this park manages to accomplish."

Again, the room is quiet. After what feels like forever, Rubén speaks up. "I wouldn't keep putting those fireworks up in the air if I didn't think it was helping somebody."

Reagan furrows her brow. "Helping?"

Rubén nods. "Yeah, helping. Making their lives better. That always felt like what we were doing. I think people can hear me. Sense me. The ones on the other side."

Frank leans on the bar. "What are you talking about? You never told me that before."

"Well, there's no way to be sure. But it's like I can feel the show running, on the other side, and my show happens at the same time. And the two are, I don't know, going in sequence. It just feels like something I can do, so I do it. And me doing it, makes their fireworks better." Rubén turns to Reagan. "Why do you keep the shows running for Nolan?"

Reagan sighs in frustration, then searches for the right answer. "Because he wants me to, I guess, and that kid got a raw deal. Nothing's more unfair than that. He should be twenty-six, flexing his college degree and taking on the world. Instead he's racing around this place like there's no tomorrow and none of us can get him to slow down."

I can feel my temper going. "Why? What's wrong with loving this place?"

"Oh, grow up. You know, I remember you. That's right, from the real park, Jason. You came into the Palace Theater every week asking about some commemorative pin."

Not *some* pin. "The two thousand seven Christmas Parade Pin."

My family spent the holidays in New York and none of my friends came through with picking me up one or two. Then a freak bidding war started right as I was about to start my Junior year of high school. Anyway, it was important.

"Oh my god, whatever," Reagan drags out the "errr."

Beverly stands up. "What Reagan is trying to say—"

"*Can it*, grandma." Beverly sits back down. "*Two weeks*. That's how long I had. Two more stupid weeks and I would have been back at school, finishing my degree and finally paying for my own place. But no. Trent Phillips had a bad day and I was dead. No, not only dead, stuck. Stuck in the one place that I never wanted to come back to." Reagan's eyes fill with tears, and her fists are clenched in anger.

I regret pressing the issue. "Don't you want to break free?"

Reagan sighs again, exhausted. "You're so naive, Jason. You think two days being dead in this place is enough to turn it around? You think you have any idea how this purgatory really works? There's real life and then there's this place. It's that simple."

"Where are we?"

"Hell," she answers, immediately. "My summer job for eternity? That's *Hell*."

Frank tugs at his suspenders. "Well, we all got a different way of looking at that."

Reagan turns to Frank, and points at me. "Sure, Frank. But when Jason looks at things they tend to explode or get trapped in jail. I don't want to be next on his list and make this never-ending nightmare any worse than it already is."

Blake waves. "As the person who got trapped in jail, I would like to make it known that I would still have gone into the circus because the circus is awesome."

"Thanks, Blake. Thanks for clearing that up."

I calm myself down as much as possible. "I'm sorry, Reagan. I'm sorry that Whirly World brought you such misery, but some of us liked coming here. When I could only make a handful of friends or couldn't deal with the stress from keeping my job or understanding my parents, this place was there for me. I've seen too many smiles on too many faces to believe that this park doesn't bring some joy and good into this world."

Reagan looks at the floor. "You should have saved your money and gone to therapy."

"You're probably right. That's one of those things you don't realize until you're dead. So I realize that now. But I don't regret one minute I spent in traffic coming to this place. Not one ride that broke down while I was waiting in line. Or a pin I wanted because it was the only one missing from my favorite set. Not for a second."

Nuwa looks up at me. "If you love this place so much why do you want to leave it?"

That's a question I've been asking myself since I got here. "Because it's not the place that I love. I lost that place, just like I lost my life. And what's worse, some jackass is acting like he runs the show here and we have the power to kick him into the sun if we just work together."

Nuwa looks sympathetic. "Then what's the plan?"

I have everyone's undivided attention. *What exactly is your plan, genius?* It doesn't seem like anyone is enthusiastic about confronting Abbadon, but I can't let it go. I'll face him by myself if I have to. There has to be a way to stop him. We just have to try. "Well, let's focus on what we actually know. Rubén, you blew Abbadon up. That dynamite you created actually had an effect on him. So his power can be matched, and in some cases, beaten."

Rubén nods. "I don't see the whole picture yet, but, sure."

"We know that he uses symbols, re-drawn maps of the park, to stop us from going where he doesn't want us to go. And Blake proved that these things can be moved around."

Blake holds up a finger. "One. We moved *one* of them around.

Keep it real."

"Fine, Blake. One. But that's better than none. We also know that he never backs down from a challenge. He basically comes when we call him. So we can, I don't know, bait him." Everyone but Beverly and Nuwa laughs at this. "Or we could annoy him so much that he does what we tell him to do." Farfetched, true, but I'm the only one coming up with ideas.

Frank walks around the bar toward me. "Say by some blessed miracle, we do that. Where are we supposed to find this Abbadon? He could be listening to everything we say, waiting to sabotage us. We could be playing right into his hands."

"He's in the circus, waiting for you," a child's voice says at the saloon door.

We turn to see Nolan. None of us heard him come in.

"I was just there. He told me to invite you over."

Those are more words, ordered within sentences, that I've heard from Nolan in two days.

Reagan waves. "Hey."

Nolan waves back. "Hey." His face looks nine years old, but inside of his little mind is something else entirely. There's an assurance and directness in the way he talks, ringing with a maturity that cuts through the higher pitch of his voice.

I step toward him. "You want to come with us?"

Nolan shakes his head. "No. I'm doing stuff."

"Ah, of course."

Nolan turns his head to look down the road. He leans into a running stance, but before any of us can see him take his first step, he's a blur darting toward Gizzard Lake.

Frank walks up. "It's good that he won't be here for this."

"For what?" Reagan says. "We're actually going through with this?" She turns to Beverly. "You can see into the future, right? How do we win? What do we need to do?"

Beverly thinks. "I know this park goes on for many years. But the park for the living. I've never known the fate of our park. I can't see where *we're* going."

I look into Beverly's eyes. "Will you go with us?"

"No, that kind of thing is not for me. I'm not quick, like Nolan." She motions to Reagan. "Or strong, like you. My faith shows me a different path and it's never led me somewhere I wasn't needed."

"I think we need you. I think we need everybody."

"If it is to be, then everyone will know it to be so. You have spirit, Jason, but it's not for you to say what this Abbadon can or can't do."

I'm desperate. "Then what should I do, Beverly?"

She smiles. "Have faith. He will show you the path."

I again take stock of the ghosts around me. "Who's with me, then? Eddie? Frank?"

Blake puts his hands behind his head, getting comfortable. "I'm not sure if I'm ready to go back in the slammer just yet, my man. Know what I mean?"

That's unfortunate.

Frank nods to me. "Sure, kid. Let him chase us around some more. What's the worst that could happen?"

That's one.

Rubén waves. "I'm in. Believe me, I don't want to be. But if there's some way to get out of here, I don't want to miss the bus, you know? Maybe see my brother again."

That's two.

Eddie nods. "I'll walk you there. But no promises."

That's three, maybe.

Nuwa stands. "There is so much we don't know. I used to not care about it, the way things are run here, I mean. I had my garden. My silence. My privacy. Those are things I always wished for in life and I had to fight so hard to get them and then to keep them. Here, they were just mine. For me. And I thought there was nothing anyone could do to them. But I don't know for sure anymore."

I can't tell if that's a yes or a no. "Are you saying you'll fight for those things or you don't want to risk them?"

"I'll go. I don't think that weirdo could touch me even if he wanted to and I'm curious what will happen."

That's four.

Reagan walks over to the bar. Frank steps aside as she rummages through the shelves beneath the surface. It doesn't take long for her to find a bottle she likes, which looks like gin. Reagan takes a swig, gives us all the finger, and strolls out the back door.

Our band is assembled. Nuwa, Rubén, Eddie, Frank, and I walk past Gizzard Lake, toward Market Street. There are five of us, which is not terrible. There were only three of us when we blew up the train, and I wasn't even a part of that plan. Abbadon's hiding something, and in my gut I sense he's not as powerful as he'd like us to believe. I was scared of creepy magicians and gory movies when I was a kid, but then I learned it's all pretend. Abbadon's theatrics reveal a fatal flaw. His bite isn't as bad as his bark.

"Whirly Swirl?" I hear someone ask.

We all look behind us and there's Clarence with his cart. He's holding out Whirly World's signature dessert. A tall cup of soft-serve ice cream with a spiral of flavored jelly from top to bottom. It's like a frozen milkshake, but it stays creamy to the last bite. Somewhere around halfway through it the jelly and the ice cream get all mixed up and it's sublime.

There are only a handful of flavors on the cart's sign, but there are more for those in the know, and special variants they sell at seasonal events. My favorite flavor is blueberry. My least favorite is popcorn, which they thankfully only added to the menu one Halloween. It tasted like popcorn, sure, but it was a bad idea. That aftertaste. Hoo, boy.

Clarence's cart is open. The frost from inside turns to steam in the sun. He offers me the dessert directly. I check the flavor. Blueberry.

I smile. "You know what, Clarence? I would absolutely love a Whirly Swirl."

I grab it and dig in with a long, thin plastic spoon Clarence has thoughtfully poked into the top. I back away from the cart, in case the others are also in the mood for a snack. They are. Nuwa gets mint, Rubén gets hot cinnamon, and Eddie gets a Worleyberry, which the park claims is their own invention, but is obviously just boysenberry. Frank chooses Rum Punch, which is alcoholic and only sold at the hotel bar outside the park. Still, Clarence clearly makes the rules, and whatever ice cream he says goes.

Goodness gracious, this thing is incredible. Not only is it mixed and chilled to perfection, but it's also making me - what's the word - happier? That sounds silly, but it's true. I feel like everything I was worried about was just stuffed in a knapsack and I dropped it behind me somewhere. I can tell the others feel the same.

Rubén is inhaling his Swirl. He looks up. "Damn, this is out of control, Clarence. Anybody else feel like they can do anything right now or is it just me?"

Eddie nods. "This is the best damn free ice cream *I've* ever had. I don't want to think how long it's been since I had one of these. If I'm even having it now, or what. I don't care."

Nuwa mumbles something in approval.

Clarence is beaming. I don't think anything can shatter his mood right now so I figure I'll be honest with him. It might be my last chance. "Clarence?" I pause to get my words right. "Do you know what we're about to do?"

He looks past us to the south. "Well, it looks like you're headed down Market Street. My guess is you're going to do some shopping. It's way too early to be leaving the park."

Frank laughs. "No, it's about the perfect time, actually."

"Well, just in case," I continue. "Our 'shopping' might not go very well, and I want you to know that we're only doing it because we can't see any other way."

Clarence chuckles. "Your business is your business, Jason." He looks at Stope Island. "He liked lemon, you know."

After another bite I'm so blissed out I hardly hear Clarence. Then I realize who he's talking about. "Who, Warren Worley?"

"Yup. The man almost ate as much sugar as me. We used to say that it would kill us one day but that's not how things ended up for either of us, is it?"

I think I'm having my first, real, conversation with Clarence. I can't mess this up.

"You knew Worley?" I know he did. I want *him* to say it.

"I did, indeed. That man was unlike any I'd ever met in all my years. The vision he had, the things he talked about. He gave me and a lot of other kids jobs when no one else would. He wanted everyone to be as happy as he was, and I can't recall seeing one frown on Warren Worley's face. Not ever." He looks wistfully toward Worley Lodge.

I turn my head toward the rest of the group, still devouring their frosty treats. No one is looking up, and I'm too afraid to move or speak and dispel this one in a million conversation.

"Have you been to the island? Since you got here?"

Clarence looks down and smiles. "Once. It was nice to say hello, but that's not him. I haven't really talked to that man in…"

"Forty-eight years."

Clarence looks at me. "Is that right?" He looks down at his cart. His shoulders hunch a little, like his bones just got heavier. He's somewhere else now. Clarence grabs the handle and pushes himself up. "Have a wonderful evening, Jason." He gives me a nod, then wheels his cart away from us and heads north toward Catlin Peak.

When he's out of earshot, Eddie speaks up. "Is he, you know, how can I put this?"

Frank finishes his Whirly Swirl with a giant slurp. "A few scoops shy of a sundae?"

I shake my head. "That's a rough way of putting it, Frank. Maybe he's happier in the dream." I look over to Kingston's Circus. "I kind of envy him." I look down at my empty cup. "Did you have ice cream here before Clarence showed up?"

Frank throws his cup into a nearby trashcan. "Yeah. But it wasn't the same. It was just frozen milk. Whatever that man makes is from another world."

A dream world, I can't help but think. A place where every day is perfect and the sun is as shiny as a candied apple.

Market Street is empty. I scan the roofline for Nolan, but there isn't a soul in sight except us five. The sun is still hanging above the western mountains, but the shadows are getting longer. Now's our chance. In the light of day.

"Well, well, well," Abbadon says as he steps out of the Carnival onto Market Street. "It looks like the parade's about to start." He's not dressed like Kingston. He's wearing a solid black tuxedo like a gambler headed to the roulette table at a fancy casino. His hair is slicked straight back and his lips are curled in a knowing smile. He looks confident.

My stomach turns. Time to be intimidating, I guess. "We're not afraid of you anymore."

"Oh yeah? That's what you said the last time. And who's we? Where're the rest of you?" He's picked up a new accent. It doesn't have Kingston's grandiosity, or the Ranger's rugged drawl. "Why don't I go lock up all of your friends?"

"Because then there'd be no one else for you to play with. That's how this works, right? We're hamsters, running on wheels, and you clean the cage and refill the water?"

This analogy makes Abbadon chuckle. "This seems like an awful expense for just a handful of household pets."

"We're not your pets anymore. We're breaking out." I look to my left and right for a little encouragement from my compatriots.

Frank nods like he just remembered his lines. "Right. We're breaking out."

Abbadon's laugh grows. "And go where? This is it, pilgrims. The end of the line. Your paltry souls don't have the strength to last one minute in open space. Those areas, in between, aren't made for you. You're lucky I kept you here. I could have sent you out to evaporate. You could be lost in the cosmos, drifting into obscurity. But you're here. You're safe. You get to live somewhere people spend their whole lives trying to return to."

Rubén walks toward Abbadon like he's got nothing to lose. "You know, I used to think demons were cool. I threw up devil horns all the time. Gene Simmons and Dio were my heroes. This should be an epic moment for me, but there's nothing metal about you. You're pathetic, Blah-bbadon." Rubén puts his fingers on one hand together like a puppet, opening and closing its mouth. "Blah, blah, blah. That's you."

Abbadon's eyes narrow. If we wanted to piss him off, it's working. He puts his hands to his side and his feet lift off the floor. He slowly ascends and stops about twenty feet above us. Rubén continues to walk, looking straight up into the sky.

Abbadon looks at me. "You like theme parks, right?"

I nod, unsure and a bit afraid where he's going.

"Do you know why you can't go to Dreamland or Paradise Park anymore? Care to tell our friend Rubén here what happened to the Venice Pier?"

I know the answer, but before I can pass the information along to Rubén, it gets caught in my throat. Maybe I was lying to myself. Maybe Abbadon does scare me. Something in his tone tells me I've made a huge mistake.

"What?" Rubén yells up at Abbadon.

Abbadon looks down at Rubén, so pleased with himself it makes me nauseous.

"Fire."

In a whoosh of flame, Rubén becomes a blowtorch. Jets of fire shoot up from his feet, covering his whole body. He screams with an intensity so sudden it pushes against my chest. The pain locks Rubén in place. Neck snapped back, he howls in agony.

Eddie draws his weapon. A couple of well-aimed shots pass through Abbadon. Abbadon revels in Rubén's suffering, like an electric guitarist watching their instrument burn. I want to help, but what can I do? Frank runs at Rubén, raising his arms to grab him. It seems like a foolish gesture but I'm not moving so who am I to talk?

Before Frank can reach him, the flames pour out from beneath Rubén and wash up onto the storefronts of Market Street like an ocean wave crashing against the shore. In seconds the walls brown to a crisp. Rubén disappears into a tower of red heat. Frank falls backward. This is my fault. Abbadon's burning it down and I basically asked him to.

From a lazily outstretched finger, Abbadon shoots a missile of fire at us. The fire coasts over my head and lands at Nuwa's feet. Abbadon shoots another missile, and then another. Nuwa puts her shields up, planks of bark that bolt out of the concrete. They sizzle and don't catch fire, but the third knocks Nuwa down. She curls up in a ball and more tree roots cover her body. They pull her through the ground just as another firebolt strikes the metal fence that encircles Gizzard Lake. It ignites like the top is covered in kerosene. The flame loops around and meets Port Juniper, turning every plank in every wall into cinders. The lake water begins to bubble.

Whatever Abbadon is doing to this place is tampering with my capacity for rational thought. Fear of fire is instinctual, and even though my logical side tells me I can't be hurt by it, my animal brain is screaming.

Eddie holds up his hands and grimaces at the wall of fire. He's called backup. Security guard after security guard, faceless and awkward, emerge from a nearby alleyway. They each run past Eddie and, without flinching, throw themselves into the fire. They land at

Rubén's feet, melting like wax, but the poor guy continues to wail, immovable.

The only place that isn't on fire is Kingston's Carnival. I spot a small gap between the tall flames curving through the streets and regain control of my feet. Leaving everyone behind, I make a mad dash for the circus. *They'll be fine,* I tell myself. *We'll all be fine.* Abbadon likes to pretend he can hurt us, but this is all just a show. He has to run out of steam eventually.

The concrete below my feet cracks open and I throw myself to one side. I turn back to Market Street and see the quaint avenue collapse on itself. The buildings topple into the fire and plummet into a dark void beneath the ground. I can't see anyone.

I'm losing my balance. It's not just the ground that's moving, it's the park. With a crunch louder than any I've ever heard, Whirly World shifts against its borders. The whole of it, all four hundred and fifty-six acres, starts to spin like a top. The motion throws me off my feet toward the carousel at the edge of the circus. I manage to hook an elbow around one of the candy-cane poles holding up a pink and yellow horse, which at my touch begins to accelerate in speed.

The last blocks of concrete holding up the circus drop into the empty pit beneath the park. The carousel rotates like an out-of-control propeller and takes flight. As I climb into the sky, clinging to my fiberglass steed, I see the whole of Whirly World, turning like a record on a player the size of Rhode Island. As the fire spreads, the charred remains vanish into darkness.

I can't keep holding on to this thing. No ride here is rated for this speed. My feet are pulled into the open air. My left hand pops free, and my right clenches the slick metal as hard as it can, but it's nowhere near enough. My hand slips. I'm airborne.

There's nowhere to land, and anyway, I'm still on the ascent, flipping nauseatingly through the air. Below me Gizzard Lake drains downward like an inverted fountain. Worley Lodge plummets into nothingness, a silver dollar flipped into an endless well. I try to right myself, but I can't tell which way my head should be facing. I reach my hands toward what I think is the sky, praying that I'll stop spinning and figure out which way is down. I swing between a patch of white islands in a sea of blue and a growing blackness.

Something takes my hand. Someone. I see Josie's delicate fingers wrapping around mine. My arm snaps outward and the rest of my dangling limbs follow. She pulls me away from the black miasma consuming Whirly World and we soar into the clouds.

Chapter 21

Parade

We've landed, thank goodness, although I'm not sure exactly what I'm standing on. I can't see my feet anymore. The cloud vapor currently supporting my weight comes up to my thighs. The white, puffy threads coasting off it swirl as I wave my hands back and forth.

If Frank thinks Whirly World is Heaven, he never saw this place. It's like someone designed an exposition based entirely on Josie's mind, and then built it out of clouds. There are fountains, gazebos, bridges, and rolling hills. There are statues of people I don't recognize. She's made what looks like a copy of Timber Tracks, but it's just the coaster without the mountain that usually surrounds it.

Once I get used to the idea of walking on this stuff, I follow her into a giant park with cloud grass, cloud trees, and a cloud bench that Josie does a giant cartwheel over. She seems to have an impossible capacity for enthusiasm. Nothing slows her down. Since we got here Josie's been running around like she's never seen this place. I guess she doesn't get a lot of guests. She stops at another bench and sits down, allowing me to catch up.

"This place is amazing," I tell her.

"I know," she says, with a huge smile.

"Why did you bring me up here?"

"You were falling."

"Yes, I was. But, why me? Why not the others?"

"You're the one that Babylon was really mad at."

"Abbadon." I don't think she heard me.

"I thought he might shut you out."

"But he doesn't come up here? We're safe now?"

Josie looks around. "Yeah, up here is all mine."

"The others, did he shut them out?"

"No, they didn't leave. When you go into the dark parts you don't leave. Leaving isn't a thing you can do here."

"Will you help us?"

Josie stands up. "Help you with what?"

"Shut this place down." I point downward. "Well, *that* place."

If it's even there anymore. Where did my friends go? Am I going to have to rescue everyone from a new set of demonic prison cells?

Josie looks up. "You feel that too?"

"Feel what?"

"All the stuff *way* up there." Josie jumps as high as she can and points to the sky. "The voices. The music. It's all flying by like a freeway full of noisy semis and we're trying to hitch a ride but nobody's pulling over. And it's not even like we need roads or sidewalks or even hands or feet in that place. We can just fly around and see each other or don't see each other and make it what we want it to be all the time. But…" Josie stops walking.

"But what?"

"But every time it feels like I'm coasting out of here, I wind up back where I started."

"We can't leave because of Abbadon. Help us stop him."

Josie appears to give this a great deal of thought, and I give her all the time she needs to think it over. Then she turns to me. "I'm not really a fighter." Josie smiles and starts to skip.

"That's a shame. It would be a big help to have someone who can fly on our side."

Josie stops in front of her standalone version of Timber Tracks. It's sitting in an open field like a jungle gym in someone's backyard.

"I don't remember landing. All I remember is flying. Like I never stopped."

Oh. We're having *the talk*. "I don't remember anything from how I died. Beverly had to spell it out for me." I have an uncomfortable question to ask, but Josie seems open-minded. What the heck. "Why'd you get out of those restraints?"

"I had to kiss a guy," she says without a pause. She turns back at me and winks. "And I'm proud of it. It was a good kiss. I've always thought the more love, the better."

I can count the number of people I've kissed on one hand, so I can't really relate.

"Charlie Gillman," she recalls. "He's all grown up now with two kids. Or that's what Beverly tells me. He makes sure his kids' belts are tied on *tight*."

"You've been able to fly since you got here?" She nods. "Man, I wish I could fly."

"Why can't you? It's easy."

I laugh at her, but her face still seems legitimately perplexed. I suppose to an outside observer, all the reality-defying powers that everyone has here seem to require great skill and experience. Maybe the power just comes naturally. Maybe I didn't get one.

"Then teach me."

Josie leaps into the air, curving upward like a high jumper clearing a bar. She lands a few feet from me, kicking up some of the stringy vapor still floating at our feet.

"You know how to fall, right?"

"Fall?"

"Yeah, fall." Josie hops. "First you're up, then you're down."

"Yes, I know how to fall. Everything subjected to gravity does. It's the law."

Josie bows and gestures to the side with both arms, motioning for me to perform the stunt she just pulled off. "Well, that's all it is. When you fall, you go down. When you fly, you go up." Josie is going to explain this her own way, so I better learn her language.

"Okay, falling up," I say, and consider what this means. The last time I thought of my material relevance in relation to everything else in this park, I slipped through a mountain. So I've been doing my best to stay grounded. Being on a cloud doesn't help.

I jump up in the air, as high as I can, and perform as well as expected. I spin my shoulders around but otherwise don't change my posture much before my feet land. I am given zero extra lift thanks to an altered understanding about which direction gravity is supposed to be pulling.

Josie laughs. "You want to be on the ground *so bad*."

"It's worked for me so far. I'm rather fond of it."

"I never even notice the ground being there anymore." Josie walks to the edge of the cloud and looks down. "Nothing here feels like it should be where it is."

I can't muster the courage to stand next to her, even though I'm curious what she's looking at. "What do you see?"

"Same as it ever was."

I tiptoe to the edge and peek over. Sure enough, it's like nothing happened. No dimensional vacuum. Gizzard Lake, Market Street, Kingston's Circus, all there. Beyond the park, past the walls, hills and mountains covered in trees stretch as far as I can see.

"See, it's whatever he wants it to be," Josie says. "It's not Whirly World. It's not the same. The ground, the air, it's all different. Nothing has to be the way it looks."

Either she's passing me some divine wisdom or I'm having trouble following her logic. Probably both. I look down at the map below me, a perspective of this park I've only seen from drone or helicopter footage. It's most certainly not the same. This place was always a re-creation of nature. A fake. Not the real thing and I accepted it.

This version is just another re-creation. Something that was scanned and printed but not really understood or felt. This can't be where we're supposed to end up. And yet, I'm expecting everyone to go with my plans, asking them to let go of the reality they've depended on for decades, and I can't even let go of the ground.

I remember crashing into the entrance to Timber Tracks, then sliding into the pavement after that locomotive exploded, and later being thrown into the carousel. Beaten but not broken. Mitchell was trapped in the mines, but he kept moving. Something inside us gets back on its feet. Maybe that's what Abbadon needs. Our will. Well, he can have it. "Thanks, Josie," I tell her.

She smiles. "For what?"

"For giving me a second chance. I'm going to go back down there now. And I'm going to try again. And if that doesn't work, I'm going to try again. Because I believe in something. I can feel it with my whole self. I'm going to keep fighting."

Josie puts her hand out for me to take. I wave it off.

"No, I got this." Then I step off the cloud.

After the initial shock of the soles of my feet not finding ground, and the powerful lurch in my stomach, all I can feel is the rush of air blasting against my cheeks. I have to force my eyes open to see where I'm going. I've only gone skydiving in video games. You'd think I'd have gotten used to the sensation after my time here, but I still struggle to maintain control.

It feels like I'm falling, sure. But it also feels like I'm leaning into a massive painting of Whirly World that someone's hung on the wall. I'm pushing my face in, inch by inch, absorbing every miniscule detail until I'm nose to nose with it. If my feet can stand me up on the pavement, and on a cloud, what's stopping me from standing this way as well? Why don't I just stop here?

I try to allow that possibility to exist. If I think I'm going to hit the ground at a hundred miles an hour, then I will, and no amount of flailing will prevent that. I slow down. I allow my legs to droop, and now I'm gliding. It's not what I'd call "flight," but I'll take it.

I put my arms out in what must look like a ludicrous impression of a bird. I resist the urge to flap. The position allows me to modify my descent a bit. I aim for the front gates. With more grace than I knew I was capable of, I return to the surface of Whirly World. When my feet touch the ground, I remind them that it is solid.

I look at Market Street. It's empty. The calm before the storm. I take a breath and allow myself to be transported to the 1880s. The place and time you're supposed to be when you let the park take you there. Not a movie, not a song, not a good book. It's as close to the real deal as you'll ever see or touch. When I first arrived here I marveled at the chance to experience this place all by myself. No lines, no noise, no interruptions. Heaven. Now I'm risking eternal damnation to possibly say goodbye to it forever.

I turn and there's Abbadon. He's Kingston again, as if the costume dresses itself whenever he's near the circus.

He straightens his red coat and white cloves. "Round two?"

"I think we're up to round four. Round one was when Rubén blew you up. Round two was when you cheated at a gunfight. And round three was when you threw a temper tantrum and burned my favorite theme park down." He smiles. I am so sick of watching him smile. "Of course, there have probably been hundreds of rounds over the years. Like the time Frank tunneled his way out of here and you chased him dressed as a monkey."

"If you say so. It would seem I run this place."

"No, that's not the way I'd put it. Management runs this place, back on planet Earth. They open and close it each day and actually bring joy to the people that walk through those gates. You don't 'run' anything. Rubén, Reagan, even Clarence, they're the ones who keep that spirit alive here. You just take and take and throw tantrums when you don't get what you want."

I try to remember all the awful things that bullies used to tell me when I was in school, the stuff that really hurt. I think it takes a special kind of awfulness to look inside someone, see what really gets to them, and use that to your advantage. I'm glad I'm not very good at it. Am I the only one left to face him? Did everyone else get flushed down the drain?

I turn back to Market Street and see a familiar face: Nolan.

He scowls at Abbadon. "He's not nice," Nolan says to me.

I nod. "No. He's a big piece of poop. The worst."

I figure this might be worth a laugh, but Nolan looks serious. Determined. He raises up his two little fists like a boxer moving to the center of the ring.

Abbadon chuckles. "Oh, please. I think you're too short to go on this ride, kid."

I raise my fists too. "Whatta ya say, Nolan? Want to kick his butt with me?"

What Nolan does next is so incredibly fast I barely perceive it. The kid dashes forward, pushes Abbadon in the chest with both arms, and then zips behind him, placing his hands and knees on the ground, positioning himself to trip the demon as he stumbles backward. Whether Abbadon underestimated Nolan's strength, or was surprised at the kid's speed, it works.

Abbadon falls over Nolan, landing on his back. It's delightful. I laugh, heartily. The cheerful moment is brief, however. I imagine Abbadon's retribution will be swift. Sure enough, he springs to his feet. His hat has fallen off and his dark brown hair is tousled. Firelight burns behind his eyes. He looks around his feet but Nolan has vanished.

Then the nine-year-old bolts out of the Five-and-Dime. He slam dunks a ten-gallon hat made of yellow foam onto Abbadon's head and speeds away before the demon can react. Just when Abbadon looks up to see what it is, Nolan exits Maple Mart at full speed. He stamps a Rootin' Ranger sticker - a big, red bullseye - right on Kingston's red vest. I can hear Nolan snickering as he easily evades the swing of

Abbadon's outstretched arms.

I laugh again, and this time Abbadon hears me. He lets Nolan race about and makes his own desperate dash in my direction. I ponder how to defend myself when Abbadon grabs hold of my throat and lifts me into the air. Nolan returns with a bag of rock candy. He reaches in, grabs a handful, and throws it at Abbadon's head.

Abbadon swats Nolan away like a fly, sending the poor kid into a display stand of jackets which collapses to the floor. I try to call Abbadon a "coward" but the word sticks in his grip. He squeezes. I realize that cutting off my air supply is not something he can do, but I still feel helpless, and claw at his arm in an effort to break free.

Suddenly, the lights strung along the rooftops of Market Street all turn on simultaneously. They look brighter than usual, like they've multiplied. It's a strange sight to see before sundown. Anything that's supposed to flash or blink does so with an intensity I've never seen before. Abbadon notices but keeps me in his steel-like grasp. Reagan appears by Nolan, pulling piles of coats off the boy so he can stand back up.

Abbadon's head jerks in her direction. "You're wasting your time," he shouts, his voice deep and bubbling with rage.

Reagan throws Abbadon the bird and runs toward the shop's entrance. A switch appears there, against the wall. A broad, metal switch that Reagan just manifested. She puts all her weight into throwing it upward. A horrendous cacophony erupts from the speakers along Market Street. Every musical cue I've ever heard here, from hillbilly songs to emergency signals to the monologue that plays when the park closes, runs simultaneously.

My ears start ringing and Abbadon winces. His free hand starts to curl inward and I see a tiny ball of flame forming against his palm. I want to yell at Reagan to take cover but I can't. She's sprinting through the Five and Dime. The northern wall is covered in pipes that aren't usually there, and a bulky, rusted switch lies at the center.

Go, Reagan, go.

She has to hop off the ground to grab it and push her legs against the wall to bring it down. Sprinklers at the edge of all the rooftops around us explode. We're drenched. Abbadon's handmade fireball goes out, and his wet hair flops to the side of his head. He growls. I can feel his anger vibrate through his hand and into my neck. He swoops down to Reagan.

She yells at Abbadon. "Pick on someone your own size!"

"Impossible," he yells back. "No one's that big."

Reagan reaches the front of the store. A switch smashes through the plaster on the wall next to her. It's so big it looks like a ladder just cut the wall in half. Abbadon reaches his hand out, pushing against the air, and the switch retreats. Before it vanishes, Reagan throws her arm forward and grabs it. She yanks back, heaving, like She-Hulk holding on to a speeding car. With superhuman strength, she pulls the switch down. All of the entrances along Market Street close and security gates slam shut behind them.

"You're children," Abbadon screams. "All of you!" He takes off into the air, and I go with him, my neck hanging on his crooked fingers. I kick at him a bit but otherwise dangle, pathetic and powerless.

CRACK. A red burst of light pops in our faces. Abbadon releases me. The sparkling boom of Rubén's firework is deafening. I give up all hope of straightening myself out before I hit the ground. I see a road curve up at me and get a split second to raise my legs and curl into an awkward but momentum absorbing forward roll. I do another and another and crash into the western wall of Sunburst Gardens.

Abbadon is above me, dodging one colorful explosion after another, looking for Rubén. The next shot reveals Rubén, unburnt and furious, behind a patch of cacti in Shaley Flats, just west of the lake. He's firing off as many as he can bag and reload. Good for him, but he's about to get pummeled. Abbadon drops through the sky, landing in front of Rubén with a crunch that sends bits of dust and rock into the air. I run toward them, unsure of how I plan to help.

Rubén takes off running across the desert, a foolish move given who we're fighting. Then vines shoot out of the sand, creating a small canyon and splitting the train track in two. One snags Abbadon's leg and, sharply pulling him downward, slams him into a patch of cacti. A second wave of vines brings Nuwa up out of the ground. With a flick of her hand, two more vines take hold of Abbadon's body.

He's not happy about this. Like a welding gun, Abbadon's eyes become jets of flame. His skin turns red. From Nuwa's sudden pained expression, I'm guessing he's getting too hot to handle. Nuwa yanks Abbadon down again, and he's powerless to change course. He crashes into a pile of rocks and disappears into the cloud that forms when they're blasted into dust. Nuwa looks over her shoulder, and I see Frank.

Frank's leaning out of the cab of a locomotive bigger than any I've ever seen run through Gabbro Caverns, and it's churning toward me at an impossible speed. Nuwa reaches out with her vines and grabs Abbadon again. She cries out in pain, but pulls him back with the straining grunt of a weightlifter hitting their limit. She slams Abbadon's red, smoking body against the train's wheels. Charred pieces of bark coil around Abbadon's arms and legs, sewing him into the massive metal circles spinning along the track.

He tries to break free, but after a few revolutions, he's caught under the train and trampled repeatedly. It looks like something out of a deranged cartoon. Something an evil Road Runner would do to Wile E. Coyote. I'd be laughing if I wasn't mortified. It looks like Frank turned Abbadon into roadkill. I want to hope it's enough, that Abbadon can't walk away from this, but I know it's not.

A mighty groan roars from the bottom of Frank's train, which starts to lift on one side. I can see Abbadon beneath, running on the track in time with the train. A firework hits Abbadon, to no effect, and I notice Rubén has joined Nuwa. She shoots a vine that wraps around

Abbadon's waist, but it bursts into flame and she immediately pulls it back, screaming.

Abbadon jumps into the air, holding Frank's train above him. I'm starting to think we're not going to win this fight. With herculean strength, Abbadon chucks the train into the base of Catlin Peak. I think of Frank being flattened inside the iron cab, then see him jump from the locomotive before it smashes into the dirt and explodes.

Abbadon floats to the ground along the west edge of Gizzard Lake. He's heaving in and out. With each breath he puffs his chest and curls his fingers, as if a newfound power is coursing through him. He's also wearing something I've never seen him wear before.

It's not a costume. It's not flashy. There's hardly a speck of color on him, aside from his lurid skin. He's wearing light brown overalls, a gray cap, and a thick pair of workman's gloves. He doesn't look like a demon anymore. True, his eyes are lit like candles and his skin is the color of blood, but he looks like a man now. An angry man on the verge of losing it.

He sees me and points. I brace myself to be sent after Frank's train. Then a gunshot rings out. Abbadon's finger bursts. I follow the sound of the shot and see Eddie, two guns drawn, fingers on each trigger. Fire sizzles out of Abbadon's open knuckle. Abbadon screams, for a moment, but now he's laughing. Eddie fires two more shots, which smack Abbadon in the chest, and he shakes them off.

From behind us, dozens of faceless, uniformed officers rush past. Eddie's backup. Like warring ants they throw themselves onto Abbadon. He punches them away, one by one, deflecting each attack like Eddie is tossing teddy bears at him. Eddie runs out of officers. Abbadon has trouble composing himself but is clearly enjoying his inevitable victory.

Abbadon takes a step toward us and a thirty-foot tidal wave charges out of Gizzard Lake. It recedes, scooping up Abbadon and pulling him over the metal railing. The contents of the huge lake begin to slosh back and forth, like a pool after an earthquake. Abbadon's booming voice reverberates from beneath the surface, but I can't make out what he's yelling.

Rubén and Nuwa run up to meet Eddie and me. The four of us watch the water spectacular unfold. It's hard to tell who has the upper hand. Like an orca show at SeaWorld, rows of splashes soak the ground around us, but no one moves. A particularly intense wave stretching far above our heads crashes into the south wall and shreds Port Juniper. From this eruption of wooden planks and dirty water, Blake rolls to our feet, unconscious.

Abbadon hops out of the lake like a champion exiting the ring after a savage knockout. Eddie reaches Blake and tries, unsuccessfully, to get him on his feet. I guess I'm up next. Now that I've dragged everyone into this irreversible situation, is there anything I can do to Abbadon but bark foul language? Is Eddie saving bullets? Can Nuwa just grab him again? Will Rubén launch fireworks at him all day?

Abbadon points at Blake. "I'll destroy him. He'll be the first."

"You're not going to destroy anyone," Beverly says. Abbadon and the rest of us notice her crossing Market Street. She steps delicately around the scattered debris.

"You cannot stop me. It is not in your power."

"You will not end this man, because you need this man," Beverly says, pointing to Blake's limp body in Eddie's arms. "You're nothing without all of us."

"You think you can—"

"Confirm and preserve us in your holy service, Lord. Lift up our minds to heavenly desires. Deliver our souls from everlasting damnation." There's more, but it's drowned out by Abbadon screaming like a petulant brat. His skin begins to glow. Spit flecks off his lips as he hollers at Beverly. He sure likes to hear himself wail.

Abbadon stops to take a breath, lets out an exhausted grunt, and throws a fireball at Beverly's feet. It strikes something invisible in the air and fizzles. Beverly flinches but stays standing. "Grant eternal rest to all the faithful departed. Deliver us from evil."

Shocked, Abbadon throws another, then a handful. Each time they hit whatever golden glow is shielding Beverly, she holds her ground and prays, but I can see her legs start to shake. She looks down at her feet, ever so briefly. She can't keep this up.

I run to her. Abbadon sees me and sends a fireball my way. It misses but lands close enough to knock me over. I slide in front of Beverly like a runner stealing home base. She looks down at me for a split-second, then closes her eyes and commits to her words, recalling them like she's casting some sort of spell. But this doesn't feel like magic. This feels like Whirly World is coming undone. Like we're between two halves of a coin being flipped.

Abbadon shoots a continuous jet of flame at Beverly, pushing her back a few feet. I run behind her and grab her by the shoulders, shoving my weight in the opposite direction. The second my hands touch her, Whirly World changes. I'm surrounded by tourists. The stores are full of shoppers. The rides are running. Birds fly in the air. This isn't a memory, or the future. This is now. I'm looking at the park in real time. *I made it. I escaped!*

Then I hear screaming. Everyone is running. It's chaos. The earth is quaking. The lake is sloshing. Windows are breaking. It's like the climax of a Godzilla movie. Whatever Abbadon is doing has bled into the real world. No one sees me. They pass through me like I'm not even here. Because I'm dead. I haven't escaped. I can still feel Beverly's shoulders. I can still hear the demon yelling. If I let go, this will disappear.

Then I hear that clanging again. The sound from the tunnels. That echoing in my ears from down below. I don't know how I can hear it through Abbadon's cries of frustration, but the beats pulse against my eardrums. I feel like it's been there this whole time, and I've just never stopped to notice it. I have an idea.

I release Beverly's shoulders and look around. The tourists, the bustle and panic, the birds, are sucked away from me instantaneously, and I'm back in the other Whirly World. I spot the place where Frank's locomotive collided with Catlin Peak and it left a deep impression. I step away from Beverly, through her bubble of righteousness, and run toward Nuwa.

"Hey!" I yell, trying to get Nuwa's attention. She can't hear me but sees me waving my arms like a crazy person. "The mountain, we have to open it." I point to the remains of the train and the giant hole it left behind.

"What, how?" she yells.

I can barely hear her, mostly reading her lips. I reach her and choose different words. "Well, when I say we, I really mean you. *You* have to open Catlin Peak."

She laughs, but she knows I'm not joking. "Jason, that's a *mountain*."

"Yes. And you're a *superhero*. That's what superheroes do. They move mountains. *You can do this!*"

Nuwa's not convinced. I start to think of another way to inspire her, then notice she's looking over my shoulder to the east. We both see Abbadon lift the entire, two-story building queue for Gangway Grotto into the air, like Darth Vader using the force, and aim it at Beverly, who's still chanting. Can her faith absorb a building?

I turn back to Nuwa. "You told me you fought so hard to get a place of your own, and that you finally had it here. Do you really want some asshole like him to take it all away?"

Nuwa turns to Catlin Peak, bends her arms back like she's about to shove something heavy, and spreads her fingers into a powerful forward thrust. A strand of dirt, covered in tall trees, like the tail of a Stegosaurus, draws up from the earth and snaps down into the mountain. Nuwa flexes her arms slowly to her right, like she's rolling over a dresser, and the mighty strand of gravel and bark rips through the soil like a saw blade.

Another clang sounds, not as muffled as before. Then another. Abbadon hears this and drops Gangway Grotto to the ground. The next clang rings out into the open air as the tear Nuwa created splits open. A glint of fiery metal shoots out, soaring above our heads on the edge of David Mitchell's pickaxe. The miner holds on as it carries him through the air like Thor gripping his hammer. Abbadon turns but fails to defend himself.

David buries the pickaxe in the underside of Abbadon's jaw and swings upward. Abbadon's knocked away like a golf ball, crashing into Calliope Arcade on Market Street. Wood splinters and glass shatters. I wince, thinking about the rows of delicate pinball machines that just got demolished, whether they were real or not.

Abbadon launches himself from the rubble like a rocket. David blocks with his pickaxe. Abbadon seizes the weapon by the edge and squeezes, clenching his teeth in hatred.

"You couldn't stay buried, could you?" Abbadon yells.

David doesn't answer.

The ground shakes. Windows break. We stumble. My first thought is the park is going to start spinning again, but these vibrations are coming from everywhere, pushing against us from every direction. Something is rattling us like a bottle of soda. Beverly holds her ground.

Out of deep space, beyond the clouds, comes a voice so powerful it feels like a hailstorm of sound. Beverly doesn't flinch, but Eddie and Nuwa cover their ears. Rubén ducks.

"*Your power is forfeit,*" is what I think the voice is saying. I can't catch every syllable as it reverberates throughout the entirety of Whirly World. It's the loudest thing I've ever heard and seems to employ every language at once. It's louder than concert speakers at peak volume.

At this voice, Abbadon freezes. The blazing furnace within him goes out. I hear wood cracking and turn to Hollow House.

The front of the building splits open and Murl jumps out. He lands on the fenced entrance to the front yard, points a finger at Abbadon, and laughs. "You've done it," he cackles. "You forgot the balance. He won't stand for it. I knew you would lose control. You've done it. Just wait and see."

"*Your lands are forfeit.*" Behind Abbadon, a purple tear appears in the open air. It spreads like a lightning bolt and Murl zips through it. "*Our deal is forfeit.*"

A massive purple hand bursts forth from the web of light and seizes Abbadon like a human hand snatching a baby bird. Only this hand is not human. Pulsing veins protrude from the scaly surface of the skin. The fingers end in sharp, black nails that scrape together as the towering fingers crunch their victim. As quickly as the hand emerged, it vanishes back into the crack in the air. In a flash of light all of it is gone. A whip crack rips through the sky like a bolt of lightning just passed. Then everything is quiet.

None of us can speak. Eddie drops Blake to the ground. Beverly opens her eyes.

Frank races to the lake edge from the north. "What the hell was that? I saw him try to cook Bev and then one of you grabbed him or something? What did I just see?"

"That…" Beverly says with suspense. "Was—"

I can't let her have it. Not when I've just figured it out.

"That was Abbadon." I tell the group.

Frank laughs. "Ha, not anymore."

"No," Beverly says. "The mighty hand. *That* was Abbadon."

"What?" Eddie says. "Who was that guy in overalls?"

"I believe," David says, as he walks toward us. His pickaxe rests on his shoulder and his eyes look worn and grim, "that used to be a friend of mine."

Chapter 22

WW

Closing Time

"Amusement park?" David asks. "Like Coney Island?"

"Yes," I shout. Now we're getting somewhere. The term "theme park" would be way ahead of his era, but the attractions they had at Coney around that time are close enough.

"And they turned this mountain into a, a what?"

"A rollercoaster," I answer. The term still perplexes him. "They added one to Coney a year after you, well, a year after the mine closed. Have you ever heard of a 'gravity railroad?' Or just a 'gravity road?' The Mauch Chunk, maybe?"

A lightbulb goes off in his head. "That contraption up in Pennsylvania?"

"Yes," I shout again. I knew I could explain it to him. I look to the rest of the ghosts in celebration of this personal triumph, but none of them are half as enthusiastic. "So, yeah, anyway, that's what this place turned into."

David looks at the carnage surrounding us. Port Juniper is still destroyed. Water still soaks the ground around the lake. "Floyd and I really made a mess of things, didn't we?"

"No," Frank says. "You did nothing wrong. You saved the lives of your crew."

Reagan nods. "It was Floyd that turned into a monster."

"Yeah about that," Rubén says. "How'd that work out? He was

working with Abbadon, or he was Abbadon, or what?"

Eddie gestures to David. "I think your friend gave you up. There was a cost for the powers he got and you were it."

David lets this thought settle into his mind. "He wanted to leave town so bad and I held him back. Then we got trapped. I guess that was his idea of revenge."

Reagan shakes her head. "That's a lousy thing to do to a friend."

"The rage I felt in those mines. It consumed me. It burned me up. But all I want to do now is forgive. Forgive Petersen. Forgive myself. All the mistakes we made."

Nuwa steps toward David. "Did Floyd tell you what he was going to do?"

David sighs. "He spoke so fast, I couldn't follow. When he left, it didn't feel like he was gone. It always felt like he was in those mines with me, all those years. And someone else, too. That voice that shook this place. That demon."

Nuwa turns back to me. "*Your power, your lands, your deal is forfeit.* That's what he said. Whatever power Petersen had, it went with him. I think we can leave now."

Reagan looks at the sky. "Yeah, I sense that too. It seems too good to be true."

"And what did that little goblin say?"

"Murl," I tell her.

"Yeah, him. *You forgot the balance.* Maybe Petersen didn't give us our powers. Maybe the things we can do were part of the reason we put up with being here so long. Maybe he was just supposed to keep us in line."

"He seemed to really want me to try and turn this place into what I wanted it to be. Like that would somehow make it easier to accept that I was stuck here."

David looks up. "Where are we supposed to go?"

Nuwa shrugs. "We all have to figure that out."

"Petersen always talked about going west."

Rubén chuckles. "I don't think you want to follow Petersen where he's going."

"Can we? Follow each other, I mean. I spent too long searching for fellas that were never there. Where'd they all go?"

Frank rubs his hands together. "I think you stumbled on a very important question. I don't think any of us can answer it for you."

David's eyes fill with wonder. "Maybe I don't have to look for anyone anymore."

"Yeah," Reagan says. "Take a break. You've earned it."

He looks at us, and we look at each other. I've spent forty hours in this place but, after all my trips over the years, and everything I know about these people, it feels like hundreds. We've fought so hard to escape, and now it's going to be hard to say goodbye.

Then, David begins to crumble. His skin turns to chunks of rock that slide off him, scraping up tiny dust clouds that float up through the air. I'm initially startled, but the scene feels so peaceful and purposeful. David looks like a majestic statue of a fallen hero as his spirit leaves this world. Without a word, the last of him drops to the ground then flies away in a swirl of ash, and he's gone.

Eddie looks down at where Mitchell stood. "I guess he had enough of us."

"So," Frank says, with a cough he saves for difficult questions. "Where are we going?"

"Wait, is this *goodbye?*" Blake asks. "I don't know if I'm ready for this."

Reagan raises her hands. "If we can, I'm leaving immediately. No offense. You all have been lovely, all things considered, but if I watch *Tomorrow's Promise* one more time…"

We all chuckle.

Reagan turns to Beverly. "I'm sorry I told you to 'can it' earlier. That wasn't nice, and you've always been nice to me."

Beverly smiles at Reagan. "Think nothing of it, dear."

I should apologize too. I look at Reagan. "And I'm sorry I got so worked up earlier."

Reagan shrugs. "Whatever. You can't help it. You're a nerd."

"Well, I'm sorry I'm a nerd then."

Reagan looks suddenly serious. "No. Don't do that. Never apologize for who you are."

I realize this is probably the largest group of friends I've ever had. And they're leaving me. I step forward. "Well, before you all go. I want to say thank you. We obviously couldn't have done this without working together."

Rubén laughs. "Don't get too choked up. We were following your plan. You know, annoy him until he does what we tell him to."

"I was making up for not having some sort of superpower."

Reagan looks confused. "What are you talking about?"

"All of your X-Men abilities. I never got one."

"You've had it this whole time, weirdo." The expressions on the rest of the ghosts indicate they're in agreement.

"What? What did *I* do?

"It's more like what you didn't do," Frank says. "You didn't buy into this place. Whatever Petersen was doing, you looked right through it. None of us could do that on our best days. You saw those symbols on the doors we couldn't get past. You didn't see faces on all those - extras - because they weren't real spirits. Not like the rest of us. Why do you think we've been stuck here for so long? We didn't know we were stuck. It felt all warm and fuzzy to buy into whatever Petersen was selling, but you shook all that off."

"Sure. If you say so." I still would have preferred some sort of action-focused ability like super strength or laser eyes, but I guess this will do for now.

"Well, I'm staying," Rubén says. "Now that I know we don't have to be here, it makes it even more special that I still get to do what

I do. As long as this park is still, you know, linked to the old park. However all that works."

"So you'll do a show tonight?"

"Yup, then we'll see about forever after that." Rubén bows to everyone. "It's been a long, strange trip. I wish you all luck. I have a feeling I'll see you again, later on." He turns back toward Gabbro Caverns and walks away.

Reagan waves goodbye and marches down Market Street. She takes off her tiny hat and spins it into the air like a Frisbee. It disappears over the rooftops.

"Where to?" I ask her.

"The beach," she replies, and does not look back.

"I am also not staying," Nuwa says to the group. "Who knows what waits for us out there? Perhaps one day I will find myself in your company again." She addresses me specifically. "Thank you for saying hello. I hope you find what you're looking for." She smiles and confidently raises her arms like she's conducting the spectacular finish to a symphony. Vines swarm around her. They curve up and dig back into the ground, and Nuwa's left us.

Frank waves. "I'll be in the mountain, if anyone needs me. Not forever, mind you, I just need to check on a few things before I jump ship. They say you can't take it with you, but I'm not so sure about that. I'm not about to just leave everything I've built here."

"Well," I say to him. "Thanks for everything."

"Never grow up, kid." Frank starts his hike.

Eddie looks worried. "I don't know what I'm supposed to do."

Beverly walks over and reaches out her hand to him.

Eddie takes it. "Do I stay here and wait? Will they find me?"

Beverly pats the back of his hand. "Do not be discouraged. The Lord will be with you wherever you go."

"I appreciate that. But I'm not looking for the Lord. I'm looking for my family. I don't want to just see them. I want to be with them."

"Then, whatever you do. Don't let go of that."

Eddie nods to Beverly, then back to me. His face is a stream of emotions, like he's trying on every feeling there is and seeing which one he wants to take with him.

Blake walks up to me. "Epic is not the word, dude. It'll have to do for now, but there's gotta be a better word for what just happened."

I have an idea. "A miracle?"

"What should I say to her? My mind is empty." He looks up.

I follow his eyes and see Josie dropping down through the sky. The sun is just about to hide behind the western mountains, and its yellow glow makes her look like an angel. She lands a few feet from Blake and kisses him, instantly. He takes her in his arms and the two hold there for a minute or two. I can't look away.

Their lips finally part and Josie looks to the rest of us. "The sky's opened up. I knew there was more out there and now I've seen it." She looks up and closes her eyes. "There are other people too. I didn't talk to any of them because I don't think they wanted to talk to me, but I felt them, and I heard them, and I saw them. They're up there. They're everywhere."

Blake touches her face. "Can I go with you?"

"We can't live underwater."

"We can't live in the clouds, either."

"Then where are we going to live?"

"You can fly," I remind her. "You can live wherever you want."

Josie smiles. "You can fly too, Jason. It's easy." She spreads her arms wide and does a few playful ballet kicks before floating upward and circling around Blake. On her third pass, she grabs Blake's hand and the two climb upwards until I can't see them anymore.

On the other side of the lake, Clarence pushes his ice cream cart. He waves at me like he did yesterday. Just a couple of old friends bumping into each other. The excited park patron and the dutiful employee. I watch him roll past Port Juniper and out of sight. I look around for Eddie but he's already left. I hope he can find the peace he so desperately deserves.

It's just me and Beverly. She holds out both hands. "There's something I want to show you before you leave."

I don't know. "Are you sure I want to see this?"

"I know someone that would want you to."

I know who she's talking about, but I guess I won't know if this memory is worth watching until I've already watched it. Before I take her hand, there's one thing that's still nagging at me. "Did you know all of this was going to happen? David? Petersen? Abbadon?"

"Sometimes, Jason, what you call 'knowledge,' I call 'faith.' I believed you were different from the others. And I believed that someday we'd find out what was beyond the gates. My patience and faith have been rewarded in life, and here. It sustains me."

I take Beverly's hands. In a second I'm back in the real Whirly World, not too far from where we're standing. Close to my favorite spot. This must be a few weeks into the future. Halloween decorations have been taken down and it's beginning to look like Christmas. April is wearing the purple coat she saves for the winter months. She's flipping a small piece of paper over and over in her hands. She wipes a few tears from her cheek.

This is probably the last time I'm ever going to see her. Even though we're standing near the same spot, it strikes me how far apart we really are. April Moore. The one and only. That redhead from down the hall who liked to go to the Ren Faire and taught me how to make the best scrambled eggs on the planet. I try to remember our final kiss, but the memory has escaped me. I want to hold her more than anything, but I just can't bring it into being. *I know I loved you, April, but I'll never know if I loved you enough.*

"I, well…" April says. "The note has it all. I just wanted to leave it here, in person. I don't know if you're still here, somewhere. It feels like you are. Even when I came here with my friends or family, without you, it was like you were standing on every corner, waiting to tell me why the ice cream vendors were dressed like they were, or what food stands had specials that week that weren't on the menu. I couldn't stand it before, but now, of course, I miss it."

April reaches into her mouth, and I notice she's been chewing gum. She stealthily puts the tiny piece underneath the back of the letter in her hand and smooshes the two against the metal railing that stands around Gizzard Lake. "I'm going to miss you, Jason. I hope you're having fun, wherever you are."

The note stays secured to the fence, with her written message turned upward.

Thanks for helping me not grow up too fast.
I will always love you. - April

I pull myself out of the dream, and there's Beverly. I bask in her warm, understanding smile. Behind her, a massive golden doorway has appeared. It is opened slightly, and glorious streaks of light shoot out of it, like a renaissance painting.

I nod to thank her. "Don't stop believin'."

She smiles and passes through the door like it's been there this whole time, ever since I arrived in Whirly World, just waiting to be unlocked. When it closes behind her, it fades away, leaving me and the entirety of this park I love so well.

If only we could tell the living. If only they knew that behind every nightly fireworks show, a spirit from another dimension gives each pop a bit more pizazz. Or that Clarence is searching for the next smile on the face of the next child, telling him that there are still good things in this world. Pure souls that search for joy, everywhere.

I look to my left and there's Nolan. He looks determined to have a good time.

"What are you thinking?" he asks.

I'm pondering so many realities at the moment, I don't know where to start. Then I realize he's not asking just any question. It's *the* question. What ride to do next? I think of everything I've seen since I've been here. There's only one glaring omission.

"Skid Greaser?"

Nolan clearly agrees because he grins and runs toward it, kicking up dirt as he speeds away. After walking through Buckthorn, I find him jumping up and down at the ride entrance.

The Skid Greaser is a horse coaster. A tribute to the equine attractions that took off in the first amusement parks of the twentieth century. There are four tracks, and one horse per track. A different horse "wins" each run, and the four finish in a different position, so you never know who you're going to get.

Morty, the green horse, has the best acceleration. Skinny, the black horse, has the biggest top speed on the straightaways. Soldier, the red horse, doesn't lose as much speed on the turns as the others. Finally, there's Stinky, the white horse, who's a psychopath. He wobbles back and forth, making you think he'll rattle off the track.

When we get to the loading platform, the horses aren't there. I wonder if I should have asked Reagan to turn all the coasters on before she left. I can sort-of-fly now, maybe I can figure out where all these power switches are hiding too. Nolan picks row one and I follow him in row two. Behind us, a quartet of noble beasts glides along the track, screeching to a halt at the edge of the wooden floor.

I get Soldier. Nolan, lucky kid, gets Stinky. Neither of us win, as Morty sneaks up at the last second. But Nolan crosses the finish line ahead of me and looks behind with a boastful smile. The ride is mostly as I remember it, but something feels different. It's more fulfilling. Profound, if that's a thing theme park rides can be. Having a kid with me elevates the entire experience across the board. It's like I took all of my nit-picky critiques, all of my uncertainty and insecurity, and just replaced it with Nolan's happiness. It is better than just seeing this world through his eyes. It's like reliving it.

"Favorite ride?" I ask him as we walk back to Gizzard Lake.

"Hooper Looper. The only one that goes upside down."

"Least favorite ride?"

"West Express. It doesn't go fast enough."

"Favorite food?"

"Barbeque ribs. Mmm-mmm."

We reach the corner of Port Juniper.

I point. "This is my favorite spot. What's yours?"

"Huh?"

"Your favorite place to be."

Nolan thinks for a second. "The top of the Iron Jaw. Before it drops. I like to see the whole park from up there."

"Yeah, that's great. This place is something else, huh?"

Nolan nods.

I shuffle my feet. It's time for me to go. "Hey, I think I'm going to take off for the day. Are you sticking around?"

"Where else would I be?"

"Well, I'm not sure, but I think you can go wherever you want."

He considers it. "Nah, maybe later."

I gently raise my fist between us, hoping he'll bump it. He does. He races to Sawmill Splash. In a blur he's all the way through the cue, on a flume, and through half the track. He slows down as he reaches the top of the fifty-foot drop and throws his hands up.

This park is a mess. Port Juniper is in pieces. Catlin Peak has a giant hole in it. Gabbro Caverns is just a pile of busted wood. This is not how I want to remember this place. I close my eyes and imagine it all reassembled. Untouched. I open them again and everything has returned to normal. It looks how it always looks from my favorite spot: "Natural."

The speakers around Gizzard Lake turn on, and Safety Dance by Men Without Hats begins. Rubén remembered. To the steady beat, fireworks light up the reds and blues in the sunset sky. It works. These two artistic mediums were destined to be together. One last show before I leave this place after a memorable two-day vacation. At this time of day, just before we lose the light of the sun, fireworks shouldn't show up against the sky. But these are different. You can't miss these.

I look down at my feet. *C'mon, Jason. This is what you wanted.* Nothing is holding me back now. I have to stop watching for what the world is going to do and start making waves. I don't know what's out there. No one really does.

Fall up, I tell myself. *Let go.*

My feet leave the ground. I still have a lot more work to do before I get used to propelling myself through the air. But I've got time. And who knows where I'll spend the next thirty years, or three hundred? There are more parks to see. More amusements to be had. I leave the fireworks behind and enter the clouds.

And just like that, I don't feel cold anymore.

Ladies and gentlemen, Whirly World is now closed. We hope you've enjoyed your day in the park and choose to spend another one with us real soon. Drive safe and good night.

Acknowledgments

First, I want to thank my wife, Amanda, for bearing not only the weight of this book, but my wish to become an author, and my dream to be a storyteller. Thanks to my 4-year-old, Milo, for keeping my narrating sharp, and my characters distinct.

Thank you to my novel-writing buddy, Jen, for showing me the ropes. And to her husband, Chris, for embracing my creative outbursts and passion for dramatic career changes.

This book would not exist without the copy-editing skills and theme park savvy of Eve Porinchak, the talent of artist Jeff Delgado (who has produced several lovely pieces for Knott's Berry Farm over the years) for the cover art and a theme park map that I will cherish forever, and the stylish eye of Mitch Baker, who gave not only this book, but the Whirly World park, its logo.

Hugs to Budde for taking my photo at a competitive price.

A hearty huzzah to Nerd Book Club, for helping me mold my understanding of good and bad narratives and letting me hang out countless times without reading the book.

Aatif Rashid and Radhika Sharma have my eternal gratitude, along with my fellow students from my Novel I and II classes at UCLA, for teaching me the basics and allowing me to spend time in their worlds. Special thanks to Elie, Lee Ann, Mary, and Sondra.

Lots and lots of love to my family: my parents, Ron and Karin, my brother, Chris, and my in-laws, Michael and Becky, for their support through a turbulent year of new beginnings.

And finally, to you, dear reader, thank you for your support. I hope you had a fun time in Whirly World, and I look forward to telling you another tall tale down the trail.